SWEET SEDUCTION

"Doesn't that feel just a little bit nice?" Tatiana asked, rubbing Erich's sore bicep.

"Too nice," he snapped, yanking his arm away. "Please, Tatiana. You don't know what you're doing to me."

"I think I do," she replied.

"No, you don't," he snapped again. "You mustn't touch me, and you shouldn't be standing around in that damn night-gown. You just don't know about . . . well, about these things."

"I know a little bit," Tatiana whispered. "I know enough to know that . . . well that I wouldn't mind if you . . ."

"You don't know what you're saying!"

"At least," she replied, snuggling closer, "I'd find out what all the fuss is about." Tatiana reached for his hand and forced it to her breast. "I want to," she said, her eyes wide. "I want to be your sweetheart."

Erich pushed her hand away. "You'll meet a nice man someday."

"No, I won't. I'm going to get shipped to Siberia, or worse. And I like you. I want to remember you. And I want to . . . do this."

Erich smiled. "Fine. Then take off that damn gown."

BOOK YOUR PLACE ON OUR WEBSITE AND MAKE THE READING CONNECTION!

We've created a customized website just for our very special readers, where you can get the inside scoop on everything that's going on with Zebra, Pinnacle and Kensington books.

When you come online, you'll have the exciting opportunity to:

- View covers of upcoming books
- Read sample chapters
- Learn about our future publishing schedule (listed by publication month *and author*)
- Find out when your favorite authors will be visiting a city near you
- Search for and order backlist books from our online catalog
- Check out author bios and background information
- Send e-mail to your favorite authors
- Meet the Kensington staff online
- Join us in weekly chats with authors, readers and other guests
- Get writing guidelines
- AND MUCH MORE!

**Visit our website at
http://www.zebrabooks.com**

NOW AND FOREVER

Elizabeth Doyle

Zebra Books
Kensington Publishing Corp.

http://www.zebrabooks.com

ZEBRA BOOKS are published by

Kensington Publishing Corp.
850 Third Avenue
New York, NY 10022

Zebra, the Z logo and Splendor Reg. U.S. Pat. & TM Off.

First Printing: March, 2000
10   9   8   7   6   5   4   3   2   1

Printed in the United States of America

Chapter 1

St. Petersburg—1880

Every lock was different, but they all had one thing in common. They could be picked. Every year, one locksmith or another claimed to have invented the "unpickable lock." And every year, Tatiana purchased it, took it apart, examined it, and discovered its secrets. She had never been defeated by a bolted door, and today would be no exception. The trick was never to feel nervous. Fear caused the hands to tremble ever so slightly, and that could be enough to make her picklock slip from the first pin while she searched for the second and third. Eventually, all pins would be brushed aside simultaneously, causing the lock to spring open, but valuable time would be lost. And in her line of work, speed was as crucial as a casual look on the face. She could not risk lingering long enough to be noticed.

The lock before her would be open in a matter of seconds. It was a simple gadget, suspiciously simple. A home this beautiful should have had tighter security. If she had not been watching the house for so long, she might have backed away right then. But she had been anticipating this break for far too long to be turned away by a mere suspicion. Behind the enormous door, painted in the brightest blue and trimmed in the most elegant of gold, lay riches. She was sure of it. And riches were something she needed desperately.

The Baltic wind slapped her face pleasantly, blessing her with droplets of water to cool her cheeks. The air smelled of fish and rain. The gray sky cast watery shadows on her chestnut hair, which gradually fell from her cap. She was just about to let go of her picklock to brush away a strand, when she heard something click. The heavy door popped open. She had done it. She smiled triumphantly, though her heart knew only fear. Her knees felt soft. This was it. Beyond the door lay either the riches she sought, or, if she weren't fast enough, her capture. She could hear her own terrified heartbeat.

A golden light shone warmly from the main entrance. Oddly, it almost seemed to be welcoming her. Looking up reverently, she stepped over the threshold. She could not believe how high the ceilings were. Five men could have stood on one another's shoulders and still not touched the top of the dome. Yet, with annoyance, she saw that there was no rug under her feet. The white marble was pretty, but it could not be stolen. With even more annoyance, she noticed that the walls were completely bare. There was not a single painting or mirror to adorn their plain white paint. "Am I too late?" she joked to herself. "Has somebody already robbed this man? Not surprising," she supposed with a smile, "even my grandmother could pick his front lock."

She decided to try her luck on the second floor and leapt the spiral staircase two steps at a time. When she reached the top, she found herself in total darkness. All the heavy curtains on this level had been drawn so tightly, she could no longer see the banister beneath her hand. With an arm stretched out before her, she felt for a wall. When she found one, it led her to a room whose curtains were just thin enough that she could make out the outlines of furniture. There was a bed in there. There was also a dresser and a night table, but that was all. There were no figurines, no goblets, nothing to steal as far as her eyes could see. She was just about to give up.

Then suddenly she lost her breath and her eyes flew open wide. She found her mouth held shut by an unyielding hand, and her whole body slammed against a hard masculine chest. She struggled in vain, only to find that her invisible captor had secured her in the most expert of grips, firm enough to prevent escape, steady enough to prevent injury. "Who sent you?" boomed a deep male voice very close to her ear.

The best answer she could give was "Mmmm-mmmm."

"I will remove my hand from your mouth," he informed her most officially. "You will have until my silent count of five to explain yourself." As promised, he freed her stinging mouth, allowing her to gasp deeply.

"I was just looking around," she began. His breath felt hot against her head and made the hair on the back of her neck stand upright. "I swear I've never done anything like this before. I just thought your house was so lovely, and the door was unlocked. . . ."

Her mouth was shut again by an even angrier hand. "I'll give you one more chance to tell the truth," he announced. "This time all I want is a name. The name of who sent you. If I don't get it, I break your neck."

His arms were like metal bars holding her expertly in place. She had no doubt that he could carry out his threat. "N-n-name?" she stammered. "What name?"

"You have three more seconds. Who sent you?" The arm around her neck tightened.

"I . . . no one sent me. I . . . "

"One more second!" he barked.

"Daveed Vinitsky."

He released her throat but held her firmly about the waist. Tatiana could feel his heartbeat at her back and did not like the feel of it. It was too steady. A man threatening to break someone's neck should be nervous, or at least angry. But he was calm, and as a criminal herself, she knew that the calm ones were the most dangerous. "Daveed Vinitsky?" he asked. "Who is that?"

Tatiana rolled her eyes, though her captor could not see this defiance. "Oh, I don't know. I suppose, if you insist, that he's the one who sent me."

"You're making him up," he observed.

"Well, of course I'm making him up! You threatened to break my neck!"

Her captor released her in full, allowing her to stumble forward from her own struggling effort. Tatiana could see him now and recognized him as being the resident of this house, whom she'd spied so many times before. As predictable as sunrise, he had left this house every morning at six A.M., and had not returned until dusk. Why today, of all days, had he suddenly changed his schedule? And why had she never noticed from afar how terribly handsome he was? He was fair, with flaxen hair that glistened in the low light. His face was a model of perfection, exhibiting strong cheekbones, a distinct jaw, and a straight nose that could have ornamented the finest of statues. His shoulders were massive, as was his chest, of which she could see a glimpse through his open silk shirt. But what startled her most of all were his eyes. They were an astounding color, a swirl of pale blues and greens all mixed together. She had never seen their like.

"Who are you really?" he asked, unrolling his sleeves and cuffing them. "I can see you are not what I presumed, so what are you doing here?" He didn't seem to be looking at her as he fussed with his shirt, but she felt him noting her every movement from the corner of his eye.

Tatiana looked helplessly around her for a chance to escape

but saw nothing. "I ... I swear I will never do anything like this again. If you let me go, I swear! I've learned my lesson."

He was amused by her answer and showed it with a curl of his mouth. "What is it that you will never do again?"

"Rob anyone!" she blurted out. "I'll never rob another soul if you let me go!"

Her captor let out a laugh. "So you're just a thief?" he asked, running a hand through his pale hair in relief. "You certainly picked the wrong house to rob."

"That's the truth," she muttered, glancing about at the spartan room covered in dust.

Her captor stopped chuckling. "Sit down," he ordered, sounding like someone who was very used to giving commands. "I'll have to decide what to do with you."

Tatiana flopped into the room's only chair, defeated and too scared to think. Nervously, she peeked through the heavy curtain beside her, thinking that this might be her last chance to see the sunshine before she was sent to perform hard labor. It was too frightening to think about. She could not bear to think that her life was in the hands of this stranger, but it was. And the more she stared at the pensive man standing by his dresser, trying to decide her fate, the more she feared the outcome. There was something about his eyes that was not quite right. They were beautiful, but they were expressionless. It was as though he were looking through a fuzzy glass, using his eyes as a barrier between himself and the things he saw. She wondered vaguely whether he was guarding himself from the world or the other way around. That strange ice in his eyes—was it a shield or a cage?

Her captor thought it was funny now that he had suspected this girl of being a spy. Her face splattered with dirt, her clothes better suited to a boy than a girl, she was clearly nothing but a street rat and posed no real threat to anyone. Increasingly, he felt genuine pity for the girl. It was a tragedy, he thought, the way these peasants lived. To think of a pretty young thing like this having to rob for a living! It was too dangerous a profession for a girl. Yet, what was her alternative? The frightened child would undoubtedly rather die than prostitute herself. He could just tell. The way she stuffed her chestnut hair into that boyish cap showed him that she was not interested in the attention of men. And while he suspected that those ample breasts would bring her enough customers, he could see in her warm, golden eyes that she would be devastated to discover what was required of her in a man's bedroom.

"Do you have a name?" he asked.

"What do you need to know my name for?"

His eyes narrowed. "Answer my question!" he ordered as well as any professional interrogator.

His startling voice made her wince. "Katja," she answered meekly.

"Your real name!"

"Oh, that would be Tatiana."

He became eerily polite in the wake of receiving an acceptable answer. "Very well, Tatiana. I have no wish to see you hungry. May I get you something to eat?"

"No, thank you," she pouted, absently kicking the nightstand.

"I see," he replied stiffly, "you're perfectly happy to steal from me, but you won't accept a gift. How typical." To Tatiana's horror, he whipped off his belt in one swift motion. At the sound of her gasp, he assured her, "I'm securing you to the chair only while I go to the kitchen. I can't have you running off."

He approached her with heavy steps, then knelt beside her while he worked. He showed no signs of noticing that he was touching the body of a woman but maintained his well-practiced, focused expression. Tatiana could feel his hands moving dangerously near her breasts but was relieved that he went out of his way to avoid touching them. "There," he said at last, tugging her bonds to make sure they would hold. "Is that too tight?"

"A little," she lied.

To her surprise, he cracked a smile. And for that moment, she thought she saw a strange glimpse of his true character, whatever that was. "I like you," he said. "You think fast."

She knew what he meant. If he had loosened those bonds even a quarter of an inch, she could have escaped. But he was too smart to fall for her ploy and left the room with a smile on his face. When he returned, Tatiana was positively red from struggling to free herself. He dropped a loaf of rye bread on the nightstand and said, "Oh, I'm sorry. I should have told you that it's impossible to get out of that. You didn't hurt yourself trying, did you?" With genuine concern, he whipped off the belt and with several quick squeezes checked her for torn muscles. "You're all right," he announced at last, patting her shoulder.

Tatiana scowled at him as he took a seat on the bed. "Why are you feeding me?" she asked. "So I'll be strong enough to perform hard labor in Siberia?" She'd had to put forth her fear. She couldn't just sit there and eat when her whole life was still in question.

He took a big bite of bread and studied her while he chewed. He liked her face. Her cheeks were round and expressive, crying out to be pinched. Her eyes were large and honest, the color of browning gold. Topaz, that's what they were. Two perfect topaz jewels set inside a face as warm as honey. Her body, from what he could see of it, was shapely and seductive despite her best efforts to hide it. Its roundness called out to be touched. Why had he always been so attracted to warm, soft women? Was it because he was so cool himself? Did his own cold skin long to rub against that of a rich buttery woman? Were his own cool aqua eyes drawn to the heat of golden ones?

So practiced was his personal restraint that he could think all of these arousing thoughts without once being tempted to act on them. He continued to eat as he announced casually, "I'll not have you sent to Siberia."

Tatiana met his eyes bravely. "Are you going to have me flogged?"

It so happened that in Russia, poor criminals could be whipped while wealthy ones could not. This was a practice that this particular gentleman found objectionable. With a firm shake of his head, he replied, "No."

Tatiana trembled her relief. "Then are you"—her voice shook—"are you going to let me go?"

"Wish I could," he replied, casually reaching for the jam, "but unfortunately, I was ordered not to let anyone inside my house."

Tatiana wrinkled her nose. "Ordered?"

"Mmm-hmm," he answered with a mouth full of bread. Once he'd swallowed, he tilted back his chair and met her eyes with those strange-colored jewels. "You see, the world is supposed to think I am wealthy. Now you've been here, and you know I'm not. And it's a bit of a problem."

"But I don't care!" Tatiana cried.

"No, of course you don't. But the problem is such. When you go back to the slums, you'll tell everyone about how you tried to rob my house. You'll tell them what you saw here, and word will get back to those who are interested in learning more about me. Any suspicions they harbor will have been validated in some small way, and, well, it's not fatal. But it's a problem." He bobbed his head, expecting her to understand.

"But I won't tell anyone!" she promised. "I swear! No one will ever know I was here!"

"I believe you mean that," he said with a tilt of his head. "However, I cannot help but notice that you are poor. And poor people can easily be bought."

Tatiana was infuriated by that statement. "If I swear not to tell, then it is the truth!"

He gazed upon her with pity, for he knew that she was in earnest. But he also knew that she must survive and that there were people who would pay a high price for any bit of information they could gather about him. "I'll tell you what," he said, "do you have any family?"

She shook her head miserably.

"Fine. Then no one would miss you if you left St. Petersburg?"

"What?" Her eyes grew perfectly round.

"Would anyone miss you?" he repeated.

She thought about Lev. "There is one person, a friend, but . . ."

"But she might assume you had been arrested?" he suggested. "Your friend knows your lifestyle? Might think you had merely been caught?"

Tatiana nodded solemnly. "Yes, he might."

"He?" Her captor lifted an eyebrow. "Interesting. You have a beau?"

Tatiana stiffened defensively. "I didn't say that. But why wouldn't I? Would that be so surprising?" A self-conscious hand rose to her tangled hair in a vain effort to fix it.

"No, it wouldn't be surprising." He shrugged. "I just asked. . . ."

"Maybe I do!" she snapped.

His brows lifted in confusion. "Fine. You have a beau. My only concern is that you are not with child. That would be problematic."

Her eyelids fluttered downward. "I don't think so."

"You don't think so?" he asked. "Or you are certain it isn't so."

She fidgeted nervously. "I . . . I don't know. I don't think so."

"Well," he asked as though he discussed such matters all the time, "have you been bedded since the last time you—"

"Of course not!" she interrupted. "I've never . . . I've never done . . . that."

He squinted his puzzlement. "Then obviously you're not with child if you've never . . . done that." he smiled, using her own charming term. "You do know that, don't you?"

"Of course," she lied.

He smiled at her innocence for a heavy moment. How long had it been since he'd met anyone who was innocent of anything? "Very well, then," he announced, rising to his feet. "Then I think I have a plan. Oh, blast it, that won't work," he realized. "Well, perhaps . . . oh, blast it, that won't work either. Oh, well," he said, resigned, "you'll just have to stay here until I can think of something. I'll have to keep you tied up while I'm at work, of course, but other than that, I promise you'll be treated well until we think of a more comfortable arrangement."

Tatiana couldn't stop blinking. "You . . . you're going to keep me captive?"

He shrugged. "Or I could just kill you." He actually said this with humor in his heart, for he saw no reason to harm the girl. But Tatiana had no way of knowing it was his idea of a dark joke.

"No!" she gasped.

"Then do as I say," he suggested, yanking open one of his stubborn drawers in search of a nightshirt. "We're hardly the same size," he muttered, "but one of these should cover you."

"But where will I sleep?" she asked frantically.

He bowed his head in thought. He knew where he wanted her to sleep. He couldn't help entertaining the shamefully pleasant thought of forcing her to sleep tied up beside him. He imagined how it would feel to hear a woman's breath in the darkness. To feel a round hip touch his own in the night. To feel a woman's warmth. Even if he didn't touch her, didn't reach out and fondle her helplessly bound figure. Just to feel her presence in the darkness, just to wake up to the sight of her warm face. How long had it been? He had to stop his thoughts. Of course, he would not sleep beside her. Of course he would behave professionally.

He turned toward her, prepared to announce his decision, but he was too late. Tatiana had pulled the sharpest picklock from her pocket, and was holding it forth as a threat. "If I put this in your neck, you die, bastard!" She had the look of a wild animal.

Her captor was unimpressed. He looked at the puny weapon, knowing that he could grab it from her without a thought. The trouble was deciding how to wrestle it from her hand without hurting her. He hated to twist and bruise her wrist. If she were a man, he might have used a quick slap to make the weapon drop. But he could not strike a woman, not even on the arm. So he was left in a bit of a quandary. "Please don't make me wrestle that from you," he implored formally. "It's better that you just put it down. I promise I'm not angry, and I won't retaliate."

But he had made a terrible miscalculation. To his shock, Tatiana smashed open the window beside her and leapt out, falling two stories to the cobblestones below. He rushed to the broken window, prepared to grab any limb he could still reach, but she was gone. Below, he saw her scramble to her feet and limp away at an unthinkable speed. "My God," he whispered in German. Within moments, she had disappeared into the maze of alleys that wound their way into the slums of St. Petersburg.

Late that night, her captor found himself alone, locked up inside his barren house, and feeling frozen. He stripped off his shirt and felt his muscles, testing their strength, for his job required him to stay fit. He went to the basin, splashed some cold water on his stubbled face, and reached for the shaving knife. When he caught a glimpse of himself in the looking glass, he noticed his eyes—colder and paler than they had ever been. Work was taking its toll. He studied his square jaw and his cheekbones, brushing back his blond hair with a stroke of the hand. Was he still handsome? Had he ever really been handsome? Oh, what did it matter? He wasn't here to go courting, he was here to work. Work. That's all it was. But that girl . . . something about her . . . he hoped she was all right. He still couldn't believe she'd jumped from the window. What courage! He couldn't help smiling. What an excellent spy she would have made.

He walked up the cold marble stairs to his sterile bedroom. With the curtains drawn, he could see nothing, but it didn't matter. He had made his peace with darkness long ago. Hands clasped behind his head, he stayed wide awake for hours, calculating, planning, but never resting. He estimated the chances that the girl would have told anyone anything by now and thought they were slim. He considered where he might be able to find her again. He recounted the functions and meetings he had to attend in the day to come and set his internal alarm clock to wake him in time. Then came the worst moment, the one he always dreaded. It was time to sleep. Thank goodness he rarely dreamed anymore. It was as though his mind could not replicate anything so horrific as the things he had seen in his waking hours, and so it did not try.

He sighed heavily, stretching out his neck. "Yes," he thought, glancing at the empty pillow beside him, "it would have been nice to have some company tonight." Something hot welled in his chest, something that burned and felt good at the same time. "God, yes," he went on to himself, imagining the scent of a woman's hair wafting toward him in the night.

Chapter 2

"Tasha!"

Lev was out of breath by the time he reached his friend. "Tasha! Are you all right? What's the matter with your leg?"

"Nothing," Tatiana moaned, "just twisted my knee."

"But you're bleeding." Lev pulled an old handkerchief from his pocket, offering to dab it on her cut face.

"It's not serious," she snapped, yanking the cloth from his hand. "Just some scrapes and scratches. Oww!" She found a shard of glass in her arm and pulled it out with a wince.

"What happened?"

Tatiana hobbled forward, motioning for her friend to follow. "Come on, let's go home before anyone sees us."

"What happened?" he repeated.

"Burglary didn't go so well," she groaned, flinching every time she put weight on her right leg.

"I can see that. But what happened?"

Tatiana didn't want to talk about it. She was not proud of her failure that afternoon and was still a little shaken from fear of that icy stranger. "House wasn't empty," she said. "I got caught and had to escape by jumping from a window."

"From what floor?"

"First," she lied. She didn't want to be scolded for her daring escape.

Lev's gray eyes were as knowledgeable as they were youthful. Out in the alleyways, wisdom didn't come with age. It came with experience. Lev knew better than to lecture her. A friend who gave unwanted advice to Tatiana would not remain a friend for long. "You sure you're all right?" was all he asked.

"Yes," she assured him, still struggling to limp along. "But I'll need some vodka to keep my cuts from infecting."

Lev was very possessive of his vodka. Nobody knew exactly how he came by his intoxicating loot or why he was able to sell it at such a low price. But everyone knew that if you were thirsty or cold and needed a good belt at a low price, there was only one man to seek. He was never difficult to find, with his startling shock of spiky brown hair that stood straight on end, and arms and legs that were much too long and lanky. "Will you need me to hold you down?" he asked Tatiana.

"I think I might," she admitted. "I've got cuts on my belly and legs too. Don't know whether I'll be able to stand the pain."

"When we get home, then." He slowed down his long strides so that his beloved friend, now feeling the burden of her injuries, could keep up with him. As always, his hands were shoved firmly in his coat pockets, absently checking on the merchandise within. Tatiana enjoyed the familiar sound of those bottles clanking together beneath his coat. Whenever she heard it, she knew Lev was near.

Their home was nothing more than an alley, but to them it was a very special place. It lay between two factories that had burned down long ago and were now entirely vacant. The alley's entrance was narrow, nestled snugly between the enormously high walls of these blackened buildings. But at the end of its tunnel, the path took a sharp left turn and came to a wide dead end. It was a hobo's dream home, for it provided absolute privacy. People on the sidewalk could not see around the corner to where Tatiana and Lev slept. And because the buildings surrounding them were abandoned, no one could peer out from the windows above and scoff. They had been very lucky to find this special spot five years earlier, and they made certain always to keep it a secret from their other friends, lest someone should try to intrude.

Tatiana was relieved when they slipped into the shadows of their secret hideaway. Far from the road and the crowds, no one would ever find them there. Lev pushed aside the blanket they'd hung around their bedding to make it feel more like a room. He made a comical gesture, as though holding a door open for a lady. "Please, after you," he said.

"Ha-ha," she replied dryly, for she was in a great deal of pain and not in the mood to joke about their living conditions. She stepped through a corner of the blanket and flopped down on the stack of moth-eaten quilts they called a bed. Lev hurriedly lit a candle. When the wind blew it out, he tried again, this time placing a broken bottle over it for protection. Tatiana groaned and stretched, looking up at the stars above. The high walls around her made for a long, gray tunnel to the sky. At its top there was a beautiful, sparkling display of light in black oil.

Lev gave her a few minutes to collect herself. He did not remove his long coat, for he never did, not even in his sleep. But he rubbed his spiky hair as though combing it and splashed some water on his face. When he could think of nothing else to do, he finally spoke. "Should we get this over with?" he asked.

Tatiana nodded miserably. "Yes. Have you got vodka?" It was a silly question, but she had nearly hoped he did not.

"Yes," he replied.

Tatiana let out a sound of discomfort as she wiggled to her side. She found the prospect of removing her shirt before Lev's boyish gaze a little humiliating, but there was no other way. If she wanted his help in cleaning her painful array of scrapes, she would simply have to throw aside her shame and expose her naked body. When she yanked off her shirt, the cold night air chilled her breasts. ''Please hurry,'' she begged, unable to look her friend in the eye.

Lev bit the inside of his cheek so hard, it bled. For despite what some men whispered about him, he was quite interested in women's breasts. In fact, he had often wondered how it was that women managed to go about living normal lives despite the temptation to stay in bed and marvel at their own magnificent bodies. When he asked Tatiana about it once, she seemed to think it was a ludicrous question and insisted that no such temptation existed. But he found it very hard to believe. For how could anyone resist something so plump and soft as a female breast? Something so . . .

He felt Tatiana peering at him and pretended to look away. ''This'll take only a moment,'' he assured her, unscrewing the top of a bottle.

She started to say something, but before she could, he had spilled the alcohol all over her arm, shoulder, and belly. There was a moment of dreadful anticipation when she could feel the wetness and knew that the burn was about to set in. Then it happened. Searing her like the most deadly of acids, the vodka disinfected her wounds in a brutal fashion. She writhed in pain, leaping to her feet as though by running she could escape it. Her face hot, her skin sweaty, she finally found that the burn was subsiding to a painful tingle. ''I don't know if I can let you do my leg, Lev.''

He shrugged. ''We have to. That's what's hurt the worst.''

She lay down once again but could not bear to expose her leg to the upcoming torture. ''I can't,'' she said desperately.

''I guess it's up to you.'' He waited patiently for a reply.

Finally, she nodded. "All right. Let's do it. But quickly."

She exposed her legs to the cold night air by yanking down her boys' breeches. She and Lev both gasped when they saw how bad her leg looked. Not only was the knee visibly swollen, the cut was dangerously deep. "I can't," she said in a panic, covering the torn flesh with her arm. "It's going to hurt like hell."

Lev chewed his lip, warily examining the task before him. "I'll do it fast," he promised.

"I can't . . . I can't move my arm away from the cut and let you do it," she blurted out. "I know I should, but I can't."

Lev saw her helpless round eyes and nodded curtly. He knew what she was nearly asking him to do. And as her friend, he did it. He forcibly pushed her arm aside, securing her in place with a movement so swift that she did not have time to resist. He dumped the entire remaining contents of his bottle onto her leg, bruising her in his attempt to hold her still to make sure the alcohol hit the entire length of the cut. Her shaking and screaming lasted a full minute. And it wasn't until it was over that Lev gave her a hug. It was an embrace of sympathy but also, perhaps, a plea for forgiveness.

Tatiana trembled in her friend's arms for a good long while, but she did not cry. "Thanks," she said, rubbing Lev's back. "Thanks for your help." She pulled away from him, eager to regain her dignity.

Lev retrieved yet another bottle of goods from his coat. "Let's try to remember what vodka is really for," he suggested.

Tatiana giggled while he poured her a shot glass. "I don't know. I think I may hate vodka for the rest of my life now."

"Blasphemy!" he jested, offering his own glass in toast. "Tasha, whatever you may do in life, do not ever hold a grudge against vodka."

She laughed and accepted his toast. "To decadence," she announced, clinking her cheap glass against his. They both finished their shots in one gulp and their next as well. But it was not long before Tatiana, as experienced a drinker as she was, found herself outmatched by Lev and had to go to sleep. "It's been a long day," she said shortly, tossing her long, rich brown hair over one shoulder. "And I for one am finished with it." She kicked off her dusty shoes and lay down on her side.

Lev knew that he mustn't keep the candle burning while she slept, so he too removed his heavy boots and lay down. But he did not fall asleep right away, as she did. He put his arm around her, squeezing her to his side for warmth. He gazed up through the tunnel of tall buildings to the sky beyond. He didn't know how he would be able to sleep if Tatiana ever went away. For six years he had drifted off to the feel of her soft, round body snuggled against his and awakened to the sight of chestnut hair touched by morning light. What would it be like to sleep alone? What would he have done if Tatiana had been sent to Siberia tonight?

Tatiana Siskova had shown up on the streets of St. Petersburg six years before, a twelve-year-old runaway. She didn't know anyone and was on the verge of falling prey to one of the men who thrived by offering employment to such desperate young women. But fortunately, some friends of Lev's had come across her first, drinking and mouthing off at a gambling hall. They liked her right away; she was tough. They took her into their club, taught her how to survive. They told her about the different "professions" she could take up that might keep her from starvation. Andrei was considered the best picklock back then, but after he spent a couple of hours teaching Tatiana the secrets of his trade, he announced that he'd met his match. The girl was truly gifted.

Lev had been smitten by her at first glance. She wasn't a beauty by most people's standards, but Lev was too young to know about most people's standards. All he knew was that he liked the way she looked. Those huge topaz eyes made him melt. And those rosy cheeks were adorable. Tatiana had been sleeping uncomfortably under a bridge ever since she'd arrived in the city. When Lev found this out, he decided it was time to exhibit his naturally generous disposition. He told her about his treasured secluded alley. "And it has a great view," he added, thinking about the stars.

Tatiana informed him in no uncertain terms that she was not looking for a beau. "That's all right," said Lev, scheming, "we can just be friends." *For now,* he thought. Then later, who knows?

Tatiana was skeptical. "You want me to sleep next to you every night, and you promise we'll just be friends?"

Lev nodded emphatically. "I promise."

And he kept his promise like the most gallant of knights. At least for about six hours. Then, when the sun went down, he made his move. It was the first time he'd ever made a move on a girl, and, he had to admit, it was not at all what he'd expected. He wasn't surprised when she pulled away and tried to wiggle out of his embrace. He'd heard that girls do that. But the punch in the eye really took him by surprise. His friends had told him that when a girl says no, he should just keep trying. It was all part of the game, they had explained. But he was stunned to learn how hard these games of courtship were on a fellow. In the course of their first embrace, just when he managed to grab hold of her round buttocks, which his friends had told him was one of his first goals, he found a knee lifted directly to his groin. He was fairly certain that it wasn't an accident. And after an elbow flew into his neck, he started to think that courtship just wasn't for him.

So Lev and Tatiana lived in that alley as friends for quite some time. Friendship, Lev concluded, was much less painful than romance. And Tatiana agreed to stay after Lev assured her that he had learned his lesson and sworn off women. Of course, Lev did eventually learn, thanks to an unforgettable night with a little blond bootlegger, that love didn't always have to be painful. But it was firmly planted in his mind that intimacy with Tatiana was not possible. Gallantry, he decided to call it. Whenever someone would ask why he and Tatiana did not engage in natural activities when they lay in bed, he would reply, "I'm much too gallant." He soon learned that this proclamation also worked well for explaining why he would occasionally come away from a dispute with Tatiana wearing bruises and scrapes. "I'm much too gallant to fight back," he would announce. Yes, Tatiana had taught him the virtue of being gallant. It kept one from having to face the humiliation of being rejected and brutally beaten by a woman.

Still, it was not until three years later that Lev fully dismissed his boyish infatuation with Tatiana Siskova. He remembered it all very clearly. He had been casually bedding a girl named Galina, a sweet girl with a mild face and a good heart. She was a prostitute but had stopped charging Lev for his visits. This made them lovers. It was not long before Lev looked forward to their meetings and could think of little else. He often made a point of picking a few scraggly flowers on his way to her apartment and offering them as a simple token of his affections. Their affair was no longer casual to him. He was quite in love with her. But one day she would no longer answer the door for him. "Galina!" he shouted, pounding on her window. "I know you're home! Answer me, damn you! Let me in!"

"I'm sorry," she said softly, at last opening the door. She held a silk robe tightly around her delicate form. She would not look at him. "I'm afraid you have misunderstood me. I like you, but . . ."

"I love you," Lev rasped, his gray eyes wild, nearly violent.

"I know." She smiled gently, apologetically. "That's why I'm sorry. Really."

Lev blocked the closing door with his arm. "Why?" he demanded. "What have I done?"

Her voice became a near whisper. "You fell in love with me," she replied strangely. "You want more from me than I can give."

The door was closed in his face.

It took him several hours that night to weave his way home to the alley. When he got there, he found Tatiana sound asleep. He flopped down beside her and stared for a good long while. It was strange. He found the sight of her comforting, like the sight of a warm fire on a cold night. But he felt nothing else. He did not look at her with lust or longing as he had ever since the first day he met her. Her soft brown hair was familiar and warm. Her breathing was peaceful and calming to him. But when he thought of love, he thought only of Galina.

In some ways, Lev aged many years on that night. He learned that one's first love was not always one's true love. He learned that even true love was not always reciprocated. And he learned that in the turbulent world of passion, there was nothing so valuable as a warm and familiar friend to come home to. From that day on, he and Tatiana were really and truly the closest of friends. Their friendship was no longer disturbed by Lev's periodic bouts of lusty frustration. They both knew what they were: mates of the heart and not of the body.

"Mmm, you're crushing my leg," Tatiana now groaned, wiggling beside him, trying to drag her leg out from under his.

"Sorry," he whispered, rubbing her shoulders. He planted an affectionate kiss on the top of her head.

"Stop that," she ordered, wiping her head as though to clean herself of the kiss.

Lev chuckled quietly, then waited for her to return to a deep sleep. "Don't you ever get arrested on me," he whispered once she could no longer hear. "Do you understand me, Tasha? You are my only family. You are my only home fire. Don't you ever leave me."

The two snuggled their way through the night, blessed by the cold Russian sky above.

Chapter 3

"Heard you were robbed."

Erich stiffened. "Robbed? How can I be robbed? I have nothing."

Senta, though petite, took impressively long strides so that her partner did not have to slow down to compensate. "Did the burglar see anything?" she asked, her lovely yellow curls blowing freely in the wind.

"Only that I am a poor man living in a rich man's house," Erich replied.

"Hold my hand," Senta ordered.

"What?"

"We should hold hands," she repeated. "It looks suspicious. A man and a woman out like this together and not even touching."

Erich's hands were planted firmly in his coat pockets. "I prefer not to," he stated stiffly.

"Then at least offer me your elbow."

Grudgingly, he obliged. Senta felt that his arm was so tight, it could have been made from marble. And he seemed so uncomfortable having her on his arm that the walk felt about as romantic as if she had indeed been strolling with a statue.

"The burglar?" she continued. "He got away?"

Erich swallowed. "She."

"She?" Senta was amused. "I've never heard of a woman burglar before."

"Why not? They have to eat too."

Senta never failed to be astounded by her partner's lack of humor. "Fine," she said dryly, "so it was a woman. You should find her and get rid of her somehow. We don't want any trouble."

"More like a girl," he said.

Senta shook her head to clear it. "What?"

"She was really a girl," he said, his face turned toward the wind. It was a lovely afternoon for strolling along the banks of the Baltic. The water smelled fresh and the wind was strong. The endless rows of connecting houses looked as though they had been there forever. "I don't think she was really a woman yet."

"Fine," Senta snarled, growing quite irritated. "Girl, woman, or sheep. It doesn't make any difference to me. But we can't have her running around loose now that she's been inside your house."

"I'm sure she's harmless," he lied.

"Well, let me assure you," Senta snapped, "that no one is harmless. Not when you're in our line of work."

Erich knew that this was true. But he also hated to go after the girl. If he were to find out that she'd caused trouble, if he were to discover that she'd been talking about what she saw . . . he knew what he'd have to do. "Fine, I'll find her," he said with a sigh.

Senta's dark green eyes spoke only of business. "Good. Find

her, find out who she's talked to, and then we'll decide what to do with her. Next." She glanced over her shoulder to make sure no one was behind them.

"Don't do that," Erich advised calmly. "You've got to learn to feel whether someone is behind you without looking. Nothing is more suspicious than what you just did."

"Sorry," Senta said, hating to apologize. "My mistake. Now, our next order of business. There's a ball coming up. It's a big occasion. A lot of important people will be there, people to whom we've never had access before. I've made certain that we will receive invitations, so we must go."

"Fine."

"But there's a catch," she continued. "We can't go together. It's too suspicious. We're the two blondest people in St. Petersburg. As long as we stay separate, it's not suspicious. But if we seem to be a couple, it will look a little bizarre. So I've arranged another escort for myself, and you must do the same."

"I doubt most gentlemen would fancy me."

Senta stopped walking. "Did you just make a joke? A real joke? That's wonderful. Before you know it, you'll be human. Now, listen. You know exactly what I mean. You need to find a lady to take to the ball."

"I don't know anyone," he said dryly.

"I know. And that's suspicious. What young bachelor wouldn't know even one single lady? You must find one and pretend you've known her for a good long time. Someone very Russian-looking preferably."

Erich grinned.

"What are you smiling about?"

He shook his head. "Nothing. I just thought of the perfect woman to ask."

"Who?"

He chuckled. "The burglar."

Senta was aghast. "What?"

"She's perfect," he continued mischievously. "I have to go find her anyway. She's desperate for money and would surely accept the task, no questions asked, for a price. Nobody in high society would know her. I could pretend she was my fiancée from Moscow. You can't imagine a more Russian-looking young woman. It's flawless."

Senta raised an eyebrow. "As long as she doesn't run away from you halfway through the night."

"I won't pay her till the job is done," he replied coolly.

"Will anyone believe it? Is she pretty?"

Erich shrugged. "It's hard to tell, but I think so. I'll need some funds to dress her up a bit."

"Consider it done." Senta let go of his arm. "Let us split here. Do you understand what you're to do next?"

Erich nodded.

"Kiss my hand," she said. "It doesn't look right for us to part without that. Someone is looking."

Erich rolled his eyes but did as he was told. Senta had a small and slender hand that rose easily to his firm mouth. "Farewell," he said stiffly, dropping it after the shortest of kisses.

Senta frowned, her heart sinking over the abrupt way he had let go of her gloved hand. It wasn't that she wanted her handsome partner to love her, exactly, but couldn't he at least like her? Wasn't it natural, after all they'd been through together, that he should feel an inkling of attraction for her? Surely, he found her pretty, didn't he? Everyone else did. His stiff back and cold gaze said no. Perhaps he had been a spy for too long, she thought mournfully. Perhaps his soul really was dead. "Farewell," she said meekly, turning away.

As he watched Senta fade into the distance, a slight smile curved Erich's lips. He had never thought himself so ingenious as he did just then. He was going to see that angelic Russian girl again. He was going to look into her honey-gold eyes again and maybe even offer her a bed for the night. But instead of having to antagonize her by kidnapping her or threatening her as he'd feared he must, he was going to feel like a real man again. He was going to ask her to dance. He was going to take her to a ball. Erich grinned all the way home.

Chapter 4

"Get your hands off of me."

Daveed Vinitsky was not, as Tatiana had once said, the man who sent her to Erich's house. But he was a real person. And at present, he was all over her.

"Do you speak Russian?" she asked. "I told you to get the hell off me." She gave him a none too friendly shove.

He was angered by the assault but not dissuaded. "Come on. Don't you want to have a little fun tonight? Why won't you at least talk to me?"

"I am talking to you," she reminded him. "I'm telling you to get lost. Now, go."

"Tasha," he warned, "I'm getting impatient. I've been trying to make friends with you for a long time, and I think you could be a little nicer. I—" He felt a sharp object at his groin. With both arms wrapped around his victim, he could not easily flick the object aside. At least, not before it sank into its mark.

"You have two choices," she informed him, her golden eyes locking casually with his blue ones. "You can get up and walk away, tell your comrades that you decided I wasn't your type after all. Call me all kinds of insulting names if you want. Or''—she lifted her eyebrows mockingly—''you can feel the worst pain you've ever felt, leave here bleeding, and have to tell everyone that you were assaulted by a girl.''

Daveed's hands shook as he lifted them to the air. ''Look. Fine. Just put that thing away,'' he stammered.

''You don't have to be nervous,'' she assured him. ''If you do what I say, you won't get hurt. I'm no liar.''

He was careful not to look at her as he rose to his feet. He wanted to pretend this had never happened, and he knew that the look on her face would be planted in his mind all night if he saw it. His only hope of forgetting this was to flee with haste. He did not say a word on his way out the door.

Tatiana was not elated by her victory. Though she was relieved to be alone once again, sitting in this heavenly establishment, nursing her glass of spirits in privacy, she was not at all happy about the confrontation she'd just had. Daveed Vinitsky was dangerous. She had won this round, but he would be back. She knew it. Oh, what bad luck that he had decided to fancy her! He could have set his sights on any woman in these slums. Why did it have to be her? He was handsome, of course. Tatiana may have been a tomboy, but she could scarcely help noticing what a nice tall, sleek, muscular build he had. And those narrow catlike eyes had driven more than a few girls around here wild. But Tatiana didn't care for him. He wasn't like herself and Lev. He wasn't a petty criminal just trying to survive. He was more serious than that. There was nothing he wouldn't do for money, even if it meant selling women. And he didn't do it to survive. He did it to feel important. She could just tell by the way he swaggered around, slicking back that dark, stringy hair. No, Tatiana wanted him as far away as she could keep him. She would never let him know it, but he scared her.

She tried to put Daveed out of her mind as she sank deeper and deeper into her vodka. She absolutely loved this place. It was so dusty that there were clouds of particles in the air, and it was so dirty that rats scurried about in the open, right in front of the customers. It was so noisy that one went home with a terrible buzzing in the ears, and so smoky that every time someone opened the door, a gust of cool, clean air blew in, and a cloud of smoke departed. But peasants were welcome here. The couple who ran the place didn't mind the homeless kids who came in to drink for hours and hours. Just so long as they paid for their drinks, the couple didn't ask how the money was acquired or put a time limit on their visit. So naturally, this place quickly changed from an establishment catering to hardworking factory employees to a nightly gathering for low-level criminals. The owners officially pretended not to notice. Yuravin's was still a family establishment, the elderly owners always insisted with a queer smile.

Tatiana felt a wonderful buzz every time she walked into this place. The smell of dust and cigars always lightened her spirits and made her feel she didn't need a drink in order to forget her troubles. But she usually ordered one anyway. She and Lev often came together but did not sit at the same table. They had sort of a friendly agreement that they spent quite enough of their lives in each other's company and didn't need to continue doing so at Yura's, as they called it. Tatiana was now watching a man at a nearby table try to win the attention of a very young woman. She smiled, always enjoying these dramas from afar. She made a bet with herself that the man would succeed and that the couple would leave together within the hour. If she was right, she'd buy herself another drink. She looked forward to going home tonight and sleeping under the stars beside Lev. It was not much of a life, she told herself, but she would enjoy it as much as she could.

Her heart suddenly stopped. This could not be happening. A tall blond man came in, a black coat flowing behind. It couldn't be. She had spied that coat from afar more times than she could count, as she had watched the house that would prove to be a most disastrous burglary. That was the coat, all right. The man turned, and she saw his eyes. Now there could be no mistaking it. Her heart pounded so hard, she feared it would be the death of her. Did she have time to race for the door? Could she . . .

"Hello."

Tatiana literally leapt from her seat.

Erich prevented her bolt with a firm hand to the shoulder. "Don't," he warned softly, "I'm armed." He nodded earnestly to confirm his threat. "Sit down."

Tatiana's large eyes were rounder than usual. Her full lips quivered as she obediently retreated to her seat. She could not believe her worst fear had arrived. It had happened so suddenly. The man she had fought so hard to escape was standing right in front of her. Her memory had not exaggerated the enchanting color of his pale aqua eyes. They were magnificent. And terrifying. He took the seat across from her. "I'm sorry to alarm you," he said, though she could tell this man was sorry for nothing. He slouched in his chair and played with a napkin as though he didn't have a care in the world. "I came here," he explained, "to make you an offer." He spoke softly enough that he could not be overheard even from the next table, yet loudly enough that no one would think he was telling secrets. Tatiana recognized this as a clever talent.

"You came all the way here to make me an offer?" she asked worriedly. What sort of offer could he possibly have in store? Surely, she had nothing he wanted.

"I need a dance partner."

Tatiana became speechless. Her face was frozen.

"You see," he explained with a half-smile, "I find myself in the rather awkward position of having to pretend I have a woman friend.'' He glanced up for her reaction. When he saw none, he continued. ''Truth be told, I don't know any women at all. Much less one who would be willing to put on such a charade strictly for my benefit.''

''Oh, now, wait a minute.'' Tatiana's eyes narrowed as courage strengthened her bones. ''I see what you're saying. Woman friend? Charade? For your benefit? Well, let me tell you something. I'd sooner go to Siberia than prostitute myself to the likes of you.''

Erich was amused by the misunderstanding but not by the scene she was making. ''Lower your voice,'' he ordered gently. ''Now, hear me out. I'm not asking you to prostitute yourself. Prostitution disgusts me.'' This was a true statement. ''All I'm asking you to do is come with me to a ball. You must not tell anyone of this, not even your closest friends. Not before you go, and not after you return. During the ball you must not let on anything about your true origins. We'll settle our story before we leave. And don't forget. I do have bargaining power with you.'' He gave her a look that was threatening in an oddly passionless way. ''So your silence will be your salvation.''

Tatiana's eyes were strangely distant. She did not speak for a long time, but when she finally did, Erich was surprised by her words. ''A . . . a ball?'' she asked meekly.

He nodded, meeting her eyes steadily.

She fidgeted with her oversized shirt.

''I'll provide you with a dress,'' he assured her, ''and dancing lessons if you need them. I—''

''I know how to dance,'' she gently interrupted.

He was surprised. ''You do?'' His eyes narrowed suspiciously. ''Do you know that Russian aristocratic manners are very strict? That even your gestures must be tight and your speech perfect?''

Tatiana nodded. ''I know.''

He tilted his head. ''Do you speak French?''

"That, I do not," she replied apologetically.

He nodded his assurance. "That's all right. Most aristocrats here prefer the sound of French, but I'll tell them it's just not spoken in Moscow. If they find out otherwise, they'll just assume I was misled by you. Here." He whipped a piece of paper from his pocket. "The address of the modiste. I've already spoken to her."

Tatiana looked timidly at the address. It was a very fancy street. She felt so confused. Did she actually want to go? Was she actually excited?

"And remember," he warned, "tell nobody. If you tell even one soul, I'll find out."

For some reason, she didn't doubt that. She watched dazedly as he rose to his feet, prepared to make a quick exit. "Wait!"

He turned around. "Yes?"

He was so tall and massive. All dressed in black, he looked like a phantom. Her question was frivolous, but she asked it anyway. "How . . . how did you find me here?"

He looked pointedly about him at the crowd of young criminals. It *was* a silly question. He turned away again.

"Wait!" she called out. "What . . . what is your name?"

"Markov," he replied stiffly, somehow wishing he could tell her the truth instead. "Markov Ladovich Evanov." He offered her a twisted smile. "And I trust you know where I live?"

She bowed her head. When she looked up, he was gone. Like a phantom. Like a strong, handsome statue of a phantom. Oh, stop that! She slapped herself on the wrist. "How can you even think such things, Tatiana Siskova! The man is blackmailing you. Blackmailing you!" She put a hand over her own heart. "Then why," she thought, "why do I feel like a schoolgirl who has just been kissed for the first time?" A ball. A gown.

Strangely, as she snuggled under the blankets with Lev that

night, she was not at all tempted to tell him where she would be going tomorrow. She didn't want him to know. She didn't want anyone to know. There was something about this that felt very private, like a birthday wish that would be denied if spoken. It took her a long while to fall asleep.

Chapter 5

Tatiana's thrill turned instantly to misery when she arrived at the dress shop. The people she knew didn't seem to notice her ragged boys' clothes, but the women in this shop certainly did. They tried to expel her from the establishment. "Get out!" cried a feeble old woman. "Customers only! Get out."

"But I'm supposed to be here," Tatiana protested. "Really!"

The old woman motioned for a man who must have been her son because he looked so much like her to help rid her fine dress shop of this street rat. "Come with me," the burly young man said, grabbing Tatiana roughly by the arm. "You can't beg here."

"I'm not!" Tatiana yelled as he dragged her toward the door.

He yanked her elbow with a jerk so rough that Tatiana instinctively kicked his kneecap. He leaned over to touch it, to make certain it wasn't broken. And it was clear that the moment he rose to his full height, he would attack the young vagrant with full force. But Tatiana stopped him with a few words. "Markov Ladovich Evanov sent me."

The elderly woman narrowed her eyes suspiciously and nearly didn't stop her son in time. But as the image stirred in her mind of that quiet, handsome man shoving money at her yesterday, she gradually stretched out her arm. "Stop it!" she called to her aggravated son. She peered at the ragged creature before her. "What is your name?"

"Tatiana," she panted. "Tatiana Siskova."

"Oh, dear." The woman touched her own throat. "Oh, dear," she repeated, scanning the young girl from head to toe. She turned once again to her red-faced son and said, "Yes, I believe she has an appointment after all." Then she cast him a look that plainly added "believe it or not" to her last statement. "Well, come in," she said to Tatiana, not quite meeting her eyes. "Let's see what we can do." She walked toward a dressing room, expecting Tatiana to follow.

It was not long before Tatiana began to see herself the way the old woman saw her. She felt embarrassed by the way the seamstress measured her. She did it loosely, as though she didn't want to have to touch Tatiana's skin. When she told Tatiana to let her hair down from under the cap, she stood back as if not wanting to get hit by the tangled mass. When she was picking out fabrics, she kept shaking her head as though she didn't imagine any of them would look good on this particular maiden. And when she asked Tatiana to try on a sample gown, the dress would not fit over Tatiana's robust hips no matter how hard the old woman tugged. It was mortifying.

Worst of all, perhaps, came when another customer arrived, a tall, pretty, well-bred girl speaking fluent French. Tatiana could not understand the girl's words and secretly imagined that a French person wouldn't be able to either, so Russian was the girl's accent. But when the girl looked at Tatiana and burst into a giggle, Tatiana imagined she knew exactly what was being said between the old woman and her new customer.

Tatiana watched miserably as the well-bred young woman slipped easily into the sample dress Tatiana had been unable to wear. She noticed the silky black hair that was twisted and tied up so neatly into a bun. Not a single hair was straying from its designated spot within that elaborate hairdo. Tatiana saw her own thick mass tangling past her shoulders and wanted to cry.

"All right, I think we're finished here," the old woman announced abruptly. "I'll have the dress ready for Mr. Evanov to pick up next week. Yes? Good-bye." She came as close to pushing Tatiana out the door as she could without touching her. Tatiana watched from the outside window as the dressmaker tended hurriedly to her more respectable customer. It wasn't until the two women started giggling and looking around to make certain they wouldn't be caught doing so that Tatiana turned around and fled. Ball gowns and dances. Who needed them? What had she been thinking? Why had she been so excited? Hadn't she known that everyone would laugh at her? A few tears raced down her cheeks as she picked up her pace toward home.

By the time she reached the alleyway, it had begun to rain heavily. Rain was always problematic in a home with no roof. Tatiana felt utter annoyance at returning to her haven only to find that all the blankets were soaking wet. It seemed the perfect closing to an awful afternoon. She huddled into a corner that was shielded from the rain by a small ledge far above. Ordinarily, she and Lev tried to shove all their blankets into this corner if the clouds overhead were threatening, but it was too late. It had rained while neither of them had been home. And their bed would be sloshy all night. Most likely, Tatiana mourned, she would awaken tomorrow with a horrible cold.

She sobbed into her hands. It wasn't the prospect of illness that caused her to do this. Nor was it the glum weather or the absence of Lev when she really needed him. It wasn't even her humiliation at the dress shop that caused her to break down so pitifully. But the combination of all three was more than she could bear. It made her remember the countryside.

Tatiana's parents had been serfs who spent their lives nurturing a small plot of land, praying that nothing would destroy their crops each year lest they receive a brutal whipping for their failure. Serfs could not be tossed from their land no matter how poorly they worked, but they could be flogged for their laziness. Tatiana's parents were not allowed to own their land, but their land seemed to own them. The law prohibited them from ever leaving it and required them to toil their entire lives, trying to make the best of their small crop. "The serfs are part of the land," it was often said.

By the time she was a young girl, serfdom had technically been abolished, but serfs could not leave their masters until they had finished paying their debts and the debts were endless. Every time a serf paid off a bill, a new one was thought up. It was clear the Siskov family would never be free to leave. But that didn't bother Tatiana at all, for she was truly a creature of the earth. Her bare feet were at ease only when they were sunk deep in mud. Her face felt fresh only when it was being beaten by the cold country wind. Her heart was full only when she was huddled by the fire in her one-room log cabin, listening to her father sing the children to sleep. Her belly was not truly full unless it was filled with her mother's rich country kasha, which may have looked like gruel but tasted both tangy and nutty.

Even as a six-year-old girl, Tatiana had to help her parents in the fields all day long. But she didn't know that it was work. She didn't know that she was supposed to dread it. She knew only that it was time she got to spend with her family, working while she chattered on and awaited her next scrumptious meal. She'd had three baby brothers, none of whom survived to be even one year old, but that did not discourage the Siskov family, who believed strongly that the boys were lucky to have gone so quickly to heaven. There had also been a tragedy before

Tatiana's birth, in which an older daughter had disappeared from the farm without a trace. Her parents had mentioned this to Tatiana once they'd felt she was old enough, but they would not go into detail. Tatiana always sensed that there were some important facts she was not being told. She often wondered what it would have been like if her sister had stayed home and lived with them in the cabin. She thought she would have liked that.

But as it was, Tatiana had only one sister, a younger one named Fania. Together, the two girls lived a mostly happy life with their peasant parents. The land was not rich, but it was spacious. No other cabin could be seen from theirs. In fact, one could walk for half an hour in any direction without finding another residence. The law might not have said so, but these were their fields of rye, their snow-covered trees, and their pale blue sky above. Reality hit them from time to time, of course, when the landlord would come for his pay. If anything had happened to the crops, and Tatiana's father could not pay his rent, she would have to watch him be whipped. Madame Siskova would cradle Fania, covering her face from the sight, but Tatiana would watch with wide eyes as her barebacked father bled and blinked sweat from his eyelids.

When it was over, he would wash up, put his shirt and hat on, and get back to work in the fields. At night, he would take Tatiana on his knee. "Why do you watch?" he asked once. "I hate for a little girl like you to see what we grown-ups go through."

"I watch," she replied earnestly, "because you never cry."

"Of course not," he said gruffly, "a man shouldn't cry."

"Why not?"

"Well." He scratched his beard over that one. "It's all right to cry, I suppose. But not in front of anyone. See, you get it all out when you're alone, and then you can be brave as a bear the minute anyone gets a look at you."

"Why?"

He kissed the top of her head and whispered, "Because you show your dignity in the little things you do, not the big ones." Then he lifted her up and carried her to a bed by the fire. Tatiana fell asleep to the crackling of logs and the rich smell of wood all around her.

That life would someday seem like a dream. For when Tatiana was only eight, her entire family died from fever. It was a slow process, an ugly death. Why Tatiana alone was spared, she would never understand. But she spent the last weeks of her parents' and Fania's life bringing them water for their terrible thirsts and wiping the sweat from their brows as they slowly and dreamily fell away from her. In her father's last hours of consciousness, he sent word to his sister that Tatiana would need a new home. His sister lived near St. Petersburg, where she worked as a house servant. Tatiana, he promised, would be a great deal of help if only the mistress of the house could be persuaded to find an extra bed for her.

This was Tatiana's fate. She would be moving to the city. No more summers when the winds were wild and the rye ripe for harvest. No more chilly autumns when hot breakfasts tasted so good and leaves crunched under her bare feet. No more icy winters when the world turned silver and the indoors were so snug. No more muddy springs when the breeze smelled like grass and the sun was so welcoming. Tatiana would be moving to the city, where the seasons had little impact on the sterile buildings. The earth was nothing more than a sturdy support for the man-made roads. And, as her father had once said, in the city, peasants have no souls. Out in the country, they have no money and no station. But in the city, they have no names either. And something terrible happens to their hearts.

Tatiana lived with her aunt for three and a half years but never felt wanted. Aunt Nadia resented having to ask her mistress for an extra bed. She felt she had risked her job for the sake of a little girl she did not know, and so she treated Tatiana with quiet disdain, as though the girl were interminably in her debt.

Tatiana tried hard to be helpful around the house. She dusted and swept and scrubbed. But it seemed that no matter how hard she tried, she kept making mistakes, and the master of the house would beat her for them. It was not long before she decided she would rather be dead than be beaten. And so she ran away. To her knowledge, Aunt Nadia had never come looking for her.

By the time Lev got home that evening, Tatiana was nearly finished with an entire bottle of vodka. That was unusual for her. "Hey, hey," he cried, yanking the bottle from her hands. "You know that stuff isn't free." He wiped the bottle with his shirt and kissed it. "My poor vodka. I left you alone for a few hours and look what happened to you." He examined the contents closely and was dismayed to find that there was no more than a splash left. "Oh, well." He chugged it down. "Nothing lasts forever."

"Do you have a cigar?" Tatiana asked this so desperately that Lev was genuinely concerned. Her eyes were red and swollen. Had she actually been crying? No, not Tatiana. It couldn't be.

"Sorry," he answered, patting his pockets, "I'm all out. Say, uh, is something wrong?"

Tatiana shook her head miserably. "No."

Lev kneeled down and patted the sopping-wet blankets. "Hmm. Looks like we'll have a nice cleansing sleep tonight. It stopped raining though. Should we wring them out?"

Tatiana's head was in her hands.

"Or maybe I'll just do it." He rose up and went to work.

Lev managed to get most of the water out of the bedding so that it was only damp. He had just put his arm around Tatiana and begun to drift off, when a small voice interrupted him. "Lev?"

He opened his eyes with a questioning expression. "Tatiana?'' The voice had been so meek, it hadn't sounded like her at all.

"Lev," she repeated. "Do you think I'm pretty?"

"How much vodka did you drink?" he asked, glancing around to make sure his other bottles were still in place.

She punched his side in a manner that was supposed to be playful.

"I'm serious, Lev. Am I pretty?" His silence made her heart sink. "Am I . . . am I ugly?" she asked pitifully.

Lev shook his head in the dark. "Tatiana . . . I . . . I don't know."

"What do you mean, you don't know?" she snapped miserably.

He sat up on one elbow and looked down at her weary face. A caring hand combed her tangled locks. "Tatiana, I've known you so long, I don't see you that way anymore."

"What way?" She just knew she was going to cry again.

"Like . . . like a stranger sees you," he stuttered, trying desperately to gather his thoughts. "I . . .I . . .''

"You think I'm ugly," she stated flatly.

"No." He took her hand firmly in his. When she looked into his eyes, she saw that he was being truly sincere. "Tatiana," he said, more like a man than the boy he was, "when I look at you, I see my friend Tasha. And to me that's a really pretty sight."

She blinked steadily several times, then said, "It still sounds like I'm ugly."

He shook his head with frustration. There was so much he wanted to say to her and so few words at his disposal. Finally, he burst out, "Tasha, I don't see you from a distance. I don't know anymore what you look like from there. But I know that from right here you look really good." He stroked her hand affectionately. "Hey, since when did you become a girl anyway?" he smirked. "I thought you just wanted to be treated like the rest of the boys. What's all this 'Am I pretty?' business?"

Tatiana pulled a damp blanket over her face. "I don't want to talk about it."

Lev raised an eyebrow. "Uh-oh."

She yanked the blanket back down. "What's that?"

"You must be in love," he replied, then ducked the oncoming blow.

"I am not!" she yelled, beating him with the pillow. "Take it back!" she insisted, swatting him again and again.

"I take it back!" he cried, laughing between gasps. "I take it back!"

"Good," she announced, placing the pillow properly under her head and lying proudly upon it with an expression of victory on her face. "Because we both know that the men around here are nothing but pigs, and I don't like any of them."

"True," Lev agreed. Then, after a long pause, he added, "Still, I don't think that Nordic bodybuilder you were talking to the other night was from around here. . . ."

Tatiana sat up, prepared to yell at him for spying on her, prepared to start beating him again. But Lev was ready this time and caught her arms. He pinned them to her sides with one hand so that he could use the other for tickling. They took turns laughing and besting each other in a long tickling fight until finally they were both too tired to go on. Tatiana fell asleep with a smile on her face after all. No longer embarrassed by the disaster that afternoon, no longer saddened by memories of home, she giggled herself to sleep from her play fight with Lev. She dreamed about turquoise eyes in a hard face, about strong arms trying to burst free from the sleeves of a tight coat, trying to grab her and drag her from this alley, which led nowhere. It was a pleasant though impossible dream.

Chapter 6

It was the day of the ball, and every belle in St. Petersburg woke up early to begin dressing for it. It would be the grandest event of the year. There was nothing as spectacular as a Russian ball, but this one, held in the Winter Palace, would be an extravaganza beyond all imagining. To be invited to enter the gates of the massive winter residence of the tsar was exciting enough, but to attend a dance there, at which every nobleman in St. Petersburg would be present, was the most thrilling event for any maiden. Many a young woman was forced to accept invitations from a gentleman she did not like simply because turning down such an opportunity was unthinkable. And, as well, many a neglected maiden was forced to watch an older or a younger sister spend her day swirling about in layers and layers of lace, preparing for an event more enviable than a wedding.

Even Senta, for whom this would be nothing more than a business meeting, could not help being a little excited. "Have you ever been to a ball?" she asked Erich as she spun around in his parlor, enjoying the feel of satin swishing around her legs.

Erich turned from the looking glass to give his partner a humorless glance. "Only in the line of duty."

"I'll bet the little girl you're taking is excited," she said brightly. "She's probably never been to anything like this before."

Erich grunted, still fussing with his shirt. "I doubt she's excited. After all, I did force her to come."

"Oh, I'd wager she's excited anyway."

Erich became so frustrated with lacing the intricate ruffles on his shirt that he whipped the whole thing off and started again. Senta nearly swooned at the sight of his bare chest. His arms looked as though they were lined with boulders. His shoulders were so broad. His chest was so—

"Erich," she snapped, "hasn't it occurred to you that I'm a woman, and you shouldn't be undressing before me." She crossed her arms uncomfortably.

He raised his eyebrows with surprise. "Oh, uh . . . I'm sorry. It was very unchivalrous of me." He pulled on his shirt and returned to working with the complicated buttons and laces.

As Senta watched, she felt a sudden loneliness. Why that feeling should arise at this moment she wasn't sure. But to distract herself, she mentioned, "Do you know who is taking me to the ball?"

"Yes," he replied disinterestedly, "you said it's that Muronov fellow. What is his name? Tomasz?"

"Yes. Tomasz Muronov. He's one of the only men close to the tsar who believes firmly that the tsar's life is in danger. If I can get him to talk to me, to tell me more about the threats against Alexander . . . well, I don't need to tell you what that could lead to."

Erich rubbed his face thoughtfully, then returned to dressing.

Senta's squint held suspicion. "Erich? Do you still have doubts?"

He stopped dressing to think a moment, then replied, "It isn't my place to doubt my orders."

"But do you doubt them anyway?"

He let a booted foot drop heavily on the marble floor. The bang was enough to make Senta flinch. "It is my opinion," he said flatly yet menacingly, looking directly into his partner's frightened eyes, "that Russia would make an excellent ally for Prussia, that the Russian love of France is nothing more than a fascination with the French styles and language, and that this country could be persuaded to side with us instead. But don't ever accuse me of questioning my orders." He took a thundering step closer to Senta, towering over her yet remaining strangely stiff. "I have given my life to my country! I have been beaten, I have been tortured, I spent six months in prison, charged with spying, awaiting my death. But no matter what was done to me, no matter how I was whipped or stung or burned, I told nothing to my interrogators. Nothing!" His eyes gradually cooled to their usual ice, but they held no apology for his outburst. "So don't accuse me of questioning my duty," he finished dryly.

Senta swallowed hard. It was so rare that she saw him lose control of his temper. The rage had been so tangible for a moment, and then, just like that, it was gone. She felt positively eerie in its wake. "I'm . . . I'm sorry," she stammered.

A knock at the front door prevented his reply.

Outside, Tatiana was shifting nervously. She had passed so many open windows through which she glimpsed beautiful young girls wearing marvelous costumes, having their hair done by their mothers. She could hardly believe she would be going to the same ball they were. If they had seen her in her boy's cap and trousers, sauntering past their homes with long, unladylike strides, they surely would not have believed it either. Tatiana didn't know whether to be excited or petrified. But she made one solemn vow to herself. Somehow, she was going to make certain that no one got the best of her tonight. She would not be humiliated again.

Erich answered the door wearing a magnificent cream-colored uniform. It was called a uniform because nearly every nobleman had one just like it. But it certainly didn't look commonplace on Erich. The slim-fitting pants were embroidered with gold braids like a stripe along each leg. The shirt was more like a coat, coming down to mid-thigh. It was of matching cream silk, but there were golden leaves embroidered in a thick line down the front and around each cuff. The sword at his side she knew was ornamental only, but it certainly added something. It made him look like a knight. His yellow hair was neatly combed, and his blue-green eyes were dazzling in contrast to all the pale colors around him. When he saw her, he smiled slightly, drawing her attention to his magnificently carved face. "Please come in." He held the door wide.

Tatiana stomped in with arms crossed. She felt so ashamed of her appearance. And when she saw a beautiful blonde swirling about in Erich's parlor, she felt even worse. The petite woman was wearing a baby-blue dress comprised of so many lacy layers that she took on the shape of a wide bell. The sleeves were long and wide, like lace curtains whispering against her slender arms. And the high neck was sealed with a beautiful cameo. When the pink-cheeked woman rustled toward Tatiana, her heavy gown made lots of beautiful musical noises.

"Tatiana"—Erich bowed courteously—"may I introduce Irina." This was Senta's cover name. "She will help you with your gown, as I am a just a man and know nothing of such things."

The women smiled at each other. But for Tatiana, this was a very odd moment. Why did this Irina woman look as though everything were so normal? Didn't it strike her as strange that a girl dressed as a beggar or thief was going to a ball with Markov? Perhaps the two of them were involved in some sort of a criminal organization. Something very odd was indeed going on here, and Tatiana wasn't certain she wanted to be mixed up in it. Nonetheless, she did not resist as Senta urged her toward a private room. And when Tatiana saw what lay inside that room, she stopped thinking of anything else. For hanging on a peg was her very own ball gown.

It was magnificent, even more so than Senta's. It was made of plain satin with no lacy trim. The color was sparkling gold. How anyone got satin to glitter with gold was beyond Tatiana's imagination, but she did not care. The gown did not cover the shoulders but was cut in a straight line from arm to arm. The sleeves were long and sleek. A heavy train of the same magical satin dragged behind the wearer. And the skirt was rather straight. But interwoven into the rich, shiny fabric were red roses hung from silver vines. The rose vines twisted and entwined all over the front of the skirt, along the trim, then continued their glorious cascade to the end of the train. Tatiana thought she must be dreaming.

"The dressmaker didn't want too much lace or bustle," Senta said apologetically. "She said it was better to let your figure speak for itself."

"She . . . she said that?" Tatiana stammered.

"Uh-huh." Senta opened a large trunk filled with hair-brushes, pins, and more. "She said you had such a lovely figure that it was better not to make a distracting dress."

Tatiana was stunned. The dressmaker had thought she was pretty? But she had acted so disdainful. Was it possible that she had been dissatisfied with the dress and not with its wearer? Was it possible that the mean old woman had thought her beautiful? No, it couldn't be.

"I . . . I hope you don't mind its simplicity," a worried Senta offered.

Tatiana shook her head with wide eyes. "Oh, no! It's . . . It's beautiful! The roses . . . the satin!"

Senta relaxed into a smile. "Good. I hate to think you are

disappointed. Now, sit down." She waved a hairbrush threateningly. "We have a lot of work to do."

Erich felt he could have read a great deal of Tolstoy while
waiting for the women to return from dressing. In fact, by the
time they emerged, he noticed he had developed a distinct ache
in his back from sitting so long. But whatever pain he felt was
instantly diminished by the sight before him. Senta rustled out
of the spare room, beaming with pride over her accomplishment.
She then gestured toward the open door as though announcing
the entrance of a queen. And shyly, hesitantly, a blushing Tatiana emerged. If that gown shone gold, Erich thought, it was
paled by the golden aura that seemed to surround this startling
girl. Her ivory skin glowed as if it had been touched by heaven.
And so much skin was showing! He could see the warm flesh
of her naked shoulders, her soft neck, her angelic face. Her
large eyes beamed full of light and youth. Yet, there was comfort
in their warm cinnamon color.

Her ample bosom seemed nearly to spill from the top of that
dress, offering him a peek at what those lovely mounds would
look like. A slight incline at the waist, then another deep curve
at the hips, made for a perfect hourglass shape. Her lips had
been pinched into a deep scarlet to match the roses on her
gown. Her bright hair had been brushed until it positively
gleamed. Piles of it had been pinned to the back of her head
with a red, flowery clip. If there had ever been any doubt in
his mind before, there was none now. Tatiana Siskova was a
beauty. "Do I look all right?" she asked timidly.

"Irina, go home."

Senta was startled. "What?"

"That is"—he cleared his throat—"I'm sure your escort
will be coming for you soon, and Tatiana and I have some
matters we must discuss."

"Do I look all right?" Tatiana repeated.

"Yes," he croaked, clutching the hilt of his sword so hard, he thought it might break. He couldn't steer his eyes from her breasts, though he knew that he must. If he didn't move his gaze soon, the girl would catch him staring.

"I have to admit," she said blushing, "I've never worn anything like this before."

"Well, you should," Senta said warmly. "You look wonderful."

"Why are you still here?" Erich looked at his partner in the way a man might look at another in the presence of a long-sought feminine prize. It was a look of annoyance but also a look that conveyed the expectation of understanding.

Senta was not amused. Didn't he realize she was not a man? Didn't he know she would not be sympathetic to his yearnings for another woman? It wasn't that she loved him, of course, but . . . Well, maybe she had done too good a job fixing up the street rat. She fetched her cloak with a hint of silent despair. Something was terribly wrong with her today. Some old pain was catching up to her. "I'll leave you be," she whispered shakily. Then, realizing she was being unpleasant, she offered Tatiana one last reassuring smile. "You look beautiful," she said. "I'll see you two there."

"I'm confused," Tatiana said, developing a new fear, a fear that this ball would never happen, a fear that this was somehow all a trick. She didn't know why that had never occurred to her before, but it was definitely entering her thoughts now. This was all just a bit too strange. "I thought you said you didn't know any other women. I thought that's why you were taking me."

"I told you not to ask questions," he replied curtly.

"No, you didn't," Tatiana said as she fidgeted with her dress. "I'm quite sure that you never said that."

"Yes, I did."

"No, I'm sure you didn't."

"Well, I'm saying it now!" he announced more loudly than

he'd intended. Wanting to make up for the startling volume of his voice, he lifted Tatiana's soft hand to his lips and kissed it. "In any case," he said gently, "Irina is only a friend. And she is going to the ball with someone else."

"Oh," Tatiana said, completely misunderstanding him. Her eyelashes fluttered in thought. "I'm sorry. I'm sure she would've gone with you if she knew how you feel about her." Tatiana, of course, did not know this at all. But she thought it was a kind thing to say.

Erich shook his head with annoyance. "I don't feel anything for her," he said. "Now, listen. We must get our story straight before we go." He began to pace with authority. "You are my fiancée from Moscow. We met, oh, say, two years ago. Our meeting was arranged by our parents, who thought we would be well matched. We do not yet have a firm wedding date because your mother is ill, and we must be certain she is healthy before we hold the festivities. I won't give you a false name because I can't trust you to remember it."

"I'll remember it," she objected.

"No, no"—he shook his head—"remembering a false name is very tricky business. You'd have to train yourself not only to respond instantly to the new name but also to refrain from responding to your real name. You'd have to learn that if someone even says the first syllable of your false name, you have to appear confused for a moment, as though expecting him to address you. It's not as easy it sounds. We'll use your real name. Nobody will have heard it before. Now, you say you know how to dance?"

"Yes." Tatiana nodded demurely. "I used to be a servant in a wealthy family. They had a daughter who took dancing lessons, and I got to watch."

"But did you ever try it?" he asked anxiously.

"Well, with myself in front of the looking glass, I did."

"That's not the same," he announced with worry. "Here, we should practice."

He grabbed her before she could make a sound, pulling her to within inches of his enormous chest. As he began to move, she was very aware of his strong hand on her back. She could feel his arms encompassing her, urging her so gently despite their strength. She tried to dance with him, clumsy and self-conscious at first. She offered him several apologetic looks as she stumbled about, but he would not receive them. The look in his eyes held complete confidence in her. He encouraged her with every nod of his head until at last she was dancing smoothly, remembering all she had once learned. She felt such a tenderness in his arms, it was uncanny. How could someone so staunch and secretive as this man suddenly be so warm? She could smell him, and it was a wonderful manly scent.

"Look up at my eyes," he whispered gently. When she did so, he nodded his approval. "That's right."

Looking at his magically colored eyes was very hard for Tatiana. She felt she could see all the colors of the ocean in them, ominous yet beautiful. But she could see nothing of the man behind them. The couple's motions became increasingly graceful as they grew used to each other. Tatiana felt as though she knew what move he would make next and could prepare her response in advance. The dimming sunlight beamed through a crack in the heavy parlor curtains. Tatiana wasn't sure she cared whether they ever made it to the ball. She was content right where she was. "Hold on to my waist," he whispered.

"Wh-what?"

"For the next move, put your hand here." He placed her palm firmly on his side. "Like that. Good." He lifted her in a circular motion and made her dress cascade in a swirl before placing her gently on her feet again.

"Oh," she said, startled, trying to regain her balance. "I certainly never practiced that by myself."

He smiled, then continued to dance with her slowly and intimately. This lesson, he knew, could have ended several minutes earlier. She had the hang of it now. But he didn't want to stop. He had never felt so close to a woman in his life. Her skin was softer than the satin of her dress. Her breath was steady against his chest. Her eyes . . . those golden jewels . . . they were as welcoming as a fire on a snowy day. And such honesty in her face! Honesty. When was the last time he had met anyone honest? She would probably be a terrible actress tonight. He would have to cover for her heavily. But he didn't care. He didn't want her to be a good actress like Senta or like himself. He wanted her to be exactly what she was. She was so beautiful, he thought. Her lips so rosy, her hair so bright. And yet *beautiful* didn't describe it. Beauty was so cold. And Tatiana was so warm. He wanted to hold her all night. He wanted to do some other things as well, but he would settle for holding her. For what he was feeling now had little to do with his masculine needs. It had everything to do with wanting a safe haven, a place to call home.

"I'm . . . I'm surprised," Tatiana stammered after he finally released her, "that . . . well, that you couldn't find another girl to take. I mean, I'm not the prettiest girl around, and . . . well, I'm just surprised that you don't know anyone else who would go."

Erich stretched out his back. He hated it when she started chattering like that, because it was too much like asking questions. Questions that he couldn't answer.

"I mean, I'm surprised that you don't have a sweetheart or something," she said. She was talking more than usual because she felt an awkwardness about the dance being over. She felt that something might have happened between them, something she should be ashamed of.

"A sweetheart?" He grinned, reaching for his coat.

"Well, yes. You know, like someone you go to dances with, and . . . well, kiss and everything."

He thought he would die of laughter if he let out even a chuckle. So he did not. "I have no one like that," he announced. He held out a cloak for her. It was Senta's and wouldn't fit well, but it would provide some protection for her dress during the carriage ride.

"Well, why not?" she asked. "I mean, I thought everyone did except me. And the only reason I don't is because I dress like a boy all the time. Well, that and the fact that all the men I know are creeps. And, well, I don't know. I guess I don't really like the idea of lovemaking. It sounds sort of uncomfortable, if you know what I mean. It—"

Erich stopped her with a sharp look. "A girl your age shouldn't even know what that word means," he announced angrily.

Tatiana felt ashamed for a moment, but it didn't last. "Well, I do live on the streets, you know. And I can't help knowing what I know."

Erich gathered control of himself. His outburst had been ridiculous, and he knew it. Of course the girl knew about intimacy. Of course she had seen more than most girls her age. He hadn't meant to say something so senseless. But the thought of Tatiana lying in the arms of another man had suddenly popped into his head. The thought of her learning about lovemaking from a drunken stranger, lying vulnerable beneath his touch, had occurred to him for the first time. For while they were dancing, he had imagined her a pure angel of a girl. And when she'd made such a crass statement about lovemaking, he was shaken into the reality that she lived in a very harsh world. He hoped desperately that she was telling the truth about never having tried it because it sounded "uncomfortable." If not, he thought he might just have to go find the bastard who ruined her and perform his first unauthorized execution.

"Well, don't use such language when we get to the Winter Palace," he said at last.

"All right. I promise." Tatiana did a double take. "Wait a minute. Did you say Winter Palace? You didn't tell me we were going to the Winter Palace! You're joking, right? No. No, this is impossible. Winter Palace?"

It was true. A hired buggy was waiting outside to drive the couple to none other than the majestic Winter Palace. Being a foreigner, Erich could have had no notion of what this meant to the anxious woman beside him. The Winter Palace was the crowning glory of St. Petersburg and completely off limits to anyone of Tatiana's humble station. Its heavily guarded gates were as menacing as its glorious towering beauty was enchanting. Seeing the inside of the Winter Palace was as distant a dream to Tatiana and her friends as fame and fortune itself. It was something one should simply never hope for. Within those gates lay a world that was forbidden to them. Yet, in one instant, Tatiana had learned that this impossible dream was going to become real in a matter of minutes. She could scarcely sit still in the back of the buggy. She kept looking around her at the other carriages, sometimes kneeling to get a better peek out the window. Were all of those carriages going to the palace? *We* are going to the palace, she thought excitedly, bouncing up and down in her seat. We are all going. A little noise peeped from her throat.

Erich was enjoying her anticipation too much to ask her to alter her reaction. He would have to remind her at the ball that she mustn't act so astounded by everything she saw. But what difference did it make if the buggy driver saw her peculiar behavior? Erich loved watching her eyes widen as she viewed the streets of St. Petersburg. He loved feeling her bounce on the seat beside him. He even had the pleasure of receiving a pinch on the arm from time to time when she couldn't contain her excitement. She kept rubbing the maroon velvet on the seat, as though savoring every precious detail of her excursion. He couldn't help suspecting that all of this joy could only bode well for his chances of getting a kiss at the end of the night.

Erich suddenly caught himself. He stopped his thoughts in mid-track. What was he thinking? He couldn't kiss this girl. She was there to enhance his alibi for one evening and one evening only. Afterward, he would return her home and never again endanger her by making contact. A kiss was out of the question.

But Tatiana was still squirming and bouncing beside him. Her wonder and joy was quite catching, actually, and Erich found shortly that an amazing thing had happened. He was feeling excited about the palace ball. It had never occurred to him to anticipate it before. In fact, it had been many years since he'd looked forward to anything. He cast a glance at his topaz-eyed companion. She was truly a remarkable young woman to have such an impact on a tired soldier like himself.

When at last the buggy pulled up to the Winter Palace, Erich allowed the driver to open his door so that he might in turn swing about and open Tatiana's. His manners were so rigid as he offered his hand that Tatiana felt like a clumsy fool, trying to move her golden skirt out of the way before tripping out of the coach. What she saw as she stepped down from the buggy was a sight she had beheld many times before. A dusky blue palace laced with white stretched not only high above her but so far to either side of her that she could not see an end. The tall, narrow windows could not have been entered except sideways by even the skinniest of thieves. (She could hardly help noticing such a thing, being in the line of work she was in.) There were no domes on top of this mansion as there might have been in Moscow. But instead, there were silvery statues on the roof, impressing St. Petersburg with their loftiness and intimidating any who would think of entering the tsar's securely locked iron gates. Tatiana had seen this palace many times in her life, but in the light of the sunset this evening, it sported a distinctive new feature for her. The gates were wide open.

When Tatiana stepped inside she saw, in her mind's eye, the faces of her parents. Could it be, as the Orthodox priests would say, that her parents were in heaven right now, witnessing their daughter's entrance into the tsar's own home? Could they believe their eyes? Were they proud?

Looking up at the ceiling, she saw oil paintings of angels.

Beneath her feet was velvety red carpet. In each enormous room, flowers and vines were carved into the white walls, and shiny vases and trinkets adorned even the shelves twenty feet in the air. One could get lost in this palace, yet there was a quietness about this place. Even the crowd of people coming for the ball could not make one of these massive rooms seem full. There was a holy silence that broke with every footstep of every guest. And if one were to wander off, it seemed one might eventually reach a place where no one had ever been before and sound had never disturbed the stillness.

Tatiana felt a surge of panic when she reached the ballroom. She saw the crowd, the musicians, the massive room, and knew that she did not belong there. "Markov," she pleaded, gripping his arm with a tight fist. "No, stop. I can't go in."

"Why not?"

"They'll . . . they'll know. They'll just know."

"Know what?" he snapped.

"They'll know that I'm . . . I'm not supposed to be here." There was genuine panic in her eyes. As she clutched Erich's sleeve, he saw that she was quivering heavily from fear.

One might have expected Erich to ignore her protests and force her into the ballroom. He had, after all, gone through a great deal of effort to make certain that this evening went smoothly. To be stopped now, at the last second, by Tatiana's irrationality would have frustrated anyone. But Erich was much more sympathetic than that. For as a spy, he knew exactly what Tatiana was suffering from. He was all too familiar with what insiders called the fear of discovery. He took her hand with understanding and led her away from the crowd. "Shoosh," he said soothingly, settling her down on a carved white bench. "I know what you're feeling. I really do."

She was shaking her head wildly. "I—I'm so sorry," she panted. "I just can't go in there. I'll think of some way to make it up to you, I swear. But I just can't face those people in this disguise. They're going to know. I just know they will.

Look at them talking! They all know one another. They'll stare at me the minute I walk in. And then they'll whisper about me, and they'll all know. I could be arrested!''

Erich let her emotions run their course before trying to speak to her better judgment. He held her shaking hand and whispered ''shhh'' from time to time until he felt her trembling subside. Once he felt that the initial panic had partially worn off, he spoke gently and calmly. ''You know what's odd?'' he asked, causing Tatiana to look at him with curiosity. ''It's odd the way people perceive reality,'' he answered himself. He let his strange comment settle into her mind until she had completely turned her thoughts to it. ''For example,'' he continued, ''what color is the sea?''

''Blue.'' She shrugged. ''Or sometimes gray.''

''Hmm.'' He took a dramatic pause, then said, ''I would tend to agree with you. However, some would argue that it has no color at all. That is the sky that makes it appear blue or green or gray.''

Tatiana squinted her frustration. ''So?''

He shrugged again. ''Exactly. What is the difference between appearing blue and being blue. Right? For what is it to be blue except to look blue.''

Tatiana was puzzled and slightly annoyed by the change of subject. ''So why do you bring it up?''

''I don't know,'' he lied, ''I'm just considering the subtle difference between truth and ficton.'' He gave her a pointed look.

''Oh, I see,'' she said, ''you're saying that pretending to be your fiancée from Moscow is the same thing as being that lady.''

''Not the same,'' he conceded, ''not the same to you and me anyway. But is it so different to everyone else here?'' He gestured toward the growing crowd in the ballroom. ''If you look like my fiancée, and you act like my fiancée, isn't it a trivial matter for them to know that if they should drive out to

Moscow next week, they'd find no trace of you? Insofar as it affects their lives, aren't you truly my fiancée from Moscow tonight?''

Tatiana was still thinking, but while she did so, she muttered, ''You certainly have a creative way of looking at things.''

It's my job, he thought. But, of course, he did not say a word.

''Well,'' she consented, realizing she had recovered from her initial panic, ''I suppose I can pretend.''

''Don't pretend,'' he advised calmly. ''That's what I'm trying to tell you. You're not trying to fool anyone. If you think that way, you'll slip up. Instead, just consider that you're showing them one possible reality. That it isn't reality that came to pass is nothing more than a detail.'' He rose to his feet and offered her a solid hand. ''Come.''

She let him help her to her feet. ''Tonight you're my fiancée. And I will believe it if you will.''

''I can't help thinking,'' she ventured, ''that there must be a lot of ax-wielding lunatics who agree wholeheartedly with your philosophy.''

''Could be. Now, come.'' He led her once again to the ballroom entrance where she first had become paralyzed with fear. He stood behind her and held her waist, whispering in her ear. ''Look at it through the eyes of Tatiana from Moscow, betrothed to Markov Ladovich Evanov. What do you see?''

Tatiana tried to use her imaginaton. ''I—I guess I would . . . I would be comparing how this ball looks to the ones in Moscow.''

''Excellent. What else?''

''I—I would be wondering which of these people were friends of yours?''

''That's a calculated answer. Don't think. Feel what Tatiana from Moscow feels.''

Tatiana closed her eyes, letting the character engulf her. When she opened them, she announced, ''I would be homesick.''

"Good."

"I would hope that you think I'm as pretty as I was the last time you saw me."

"Perfect. And those women who are talking? The ones whose judgment you so feared?"

"I would be wanting very much to make it clear to them that you are taken, lest they set their sights on you in my absence."

Erich stepped away and offered her a bow. "My lady, shall we enter?"

She smiled brightly. "I suppose I'll give you the honor." She giggled, taking his hand and walking fearlessly into the crowd.

The ball began with a promenade, a simple stroll about the room. It was led by Alexander III, the tsar's son, who stood in place of Alexander II during the summer months. He was not a handsome man, his beard was so puffy, and his head so long, but his clothes were embedded with the finest diamonds, and he wore them as though he fancied himself to be quite deserving of them. He and his exuberantly proud lady led the promenade, while all the other couples locked arms and followed behind in a straight line. The line twisted and turned at the corners of the rooms, moving like a snake as all the privileged guests marched forward with pride. The ladies' gowns sparkled under the light of the heavy chandeliers, as did the gold and silver embroidery of the men's costumes. Swords shone gallantly at the men's sides. Lace swept the floor clean beneath the ladies' feet. It was a sight to behold even for a jaded Prussian spy.

Tatiana felt quite relaxed now. As she pranced forward in line, she felt that she was borrowing strength from the arm she held. Erich's confidence seemed to protect her from doubt. His impressive stature made her feel insulated from the crowd. The more she walked and encircled this heavily windowed ballroom, the more she forgot that she wasn't supposed to be there, and the more she remembered what a beautiful dress she was wearing. Indeed, it was as Erich had said. No one seemed to be staring at her one bit. She looked like one of them, so for all it concerned them, she was one of them. She compared her dress to the many she saw around her. She loved all the variety of colors. It was good, she decided, that some gowns shouted "I'm red!" or "I'm black!" while others whispered songs of spring in their soft pink, lavender, or yellow. Some gowns invoked the sea with their greens or blues or aquas, while some sang of heaven in silver and gold. She was thankful for the variety, for it made looking around so much more interesting than if all the women had all decided the same dress was the best and worn it. Likewise, she thought it interesting to examine the women beneath the gowns. Some were so tall and slim, like ballerinas. Others were small and stout like the most hard-working of peasants. But most were in between, each blessed with a unique combinaton of curves and straight lines. It was wonderful to look at them in all their glorious variety.

When the promenade stopped and the dancing began, Erich led Tatiana to the edge of the room. She knew that the introductions were about to begin, and this is what she had feared most of all. Yet, somehow she felt so cheered by the gaiety of the night that she had little anxiety when Erich brought her to the first of his comrades. "Mr. Kreivakov"—he gave a stiff bow—"this is my fiancée, Tatiana Janinevna Siskova."

The man who kissed her was elderly but not gruff. "Ah," he said, holding her face in both hands, "she is a rose. How do you like St. Petersburg? I hear you are from Moscow."

"Well, naturally I am homesick," she said nervously, "but, well, I like this city . . . that is, your city, very much. Because it is very nice, and . . . I've never been here before, so . . ."

Erich would have fired her if she had been working for him. All his talking may have helped her nerves, but apparently it had no effect on her presentation. "Will there be a meeting tomorrow?'' he asked his comrade, feeling that a change of topic was just the thing this awkward greeting needed.

"Why, yes. Yes. Ten o'clock sharp."

"I'll look foward to it," Erich replied. "I feel there are many important matters we might resolve."

"Indeed." The man played with his gray triangle of a beard.

"Until then," Erich excused himself. As the couple approached their next target, Erich gave Tatiana a none too tender squeeze. "Don't say so much this time," he warned her. "Just answer yes or no or whatever other word seems appropriate. But try to keep it to one short word."

"All right," she consented, unaware that she had done a poor job of lying. "But it seems that if I were really your fiancée, I wouldn't be so quiet as that. After all, usually one member of a couple is talkative and the other is quiet, and, well, you're not exactly a chatterbox. . . .''

"Silence," he ordered through clenched teeth. "From now on, just one word." Tatiana was taken aback by the way he said that. It had come out with such roughness, it reminded her she had once been afraid of him. And why.

For the next several introductions, Tatiana held her tongue. "And how do you like our fair city?" one lady asked.

"Mmmmm," she said, tilting her head back and forth as though thinking.

"She loves it," Erich said with annoyance.

"Oh!" the woman replied, delighted. "And what do you love best about it?"

"I don't know. Why don't you ask Markov? Ouch! I mean, the, uh, the scenery."

"The scenery?" The woman touched a brilliant emerald at her throat. "Which aspect of it?"

"I'm not sure there's any way to answer that in only one word. Ouch! Buildings."

"Oh, yes," the woman gasped proudly. "We borrowed our architecture from other parts of Europe, you know. I'm glad you appreciate it, though it must be strange coming from Moscow, where the buildings are so traditional.''

''Yes.'' She received no pinch this time.

''Well, you two certainly make a lovely couple. Do you have plans yet for the wedding?''

''No,'' Erich replied. ''I'm afraid Madame Siskova is not well and must recover before we can continue with our plans.''

''Oh, how unfortunate!'' She touched the jewel again. Tatiana was starting to wonder whether this was really an expressive gesture or she was trying to draw attention to the expensive piece. ''Oh, her illness isn't serious, I hope.''

Tatiana shook her head. ''No.''

''Madame Siskova is a strong woman,'' Erich finished for her.

''Well, do send my regards.''

''My mother doesn't even know who you are. How weird would it be if I—ouch!''

''We will be certain to do that.'' Bowing as he backed away, Erich led Tatiana roughly by the arm. ''Fine,'' he muttered, ''I understand your point. You don't like to be told to be quiet, so let's just dance.''

Without waiting for her reply, he took her to the center of the dance floor. Tatiana had hoped they might hide near one of the pretty candelabras on the wall, but she had no such luck. They were in the middle of all the dancing couples and many eyes fell upon them. The setting sun's orange glow had by then stopped streaming through the windows. Now there was only blackness outside. And the windows were transformed into mirrors, reflecting the candlelight and the sparkle of colorful costumes. Once again Tatiana felt awkward when she and Erich first started moving to the music. She was intensely aware of the other dancers around her, moving with such expertise. She could also feel the casual eyes of those leaning against the walls, chatting and gazing at the dance floor as though the couples were performing a ballet for them.

"Look at my eyes," Erich said. And just as easily as that, she forgot all about the stares. She remembered him saying those very words when they were alone in his parlor. And she remembered the warmth that had existed between them. When she saw his dazzling aqua eyes, even more magnificent than usual in the dim light, she could tell that he was not angry about their little spats during the introductions. She could tell that between them there was an automatic forgiveness, an under- standing that took precedence over any spat. They had known each other for such a short time, did not even truly know each other yet, but already there existed a treaty between them, a promise.

Tatiana smiled shyly at Erich. She felt a blush run over her face as the hand on her back began to caress her in a way that was not essential to the dance. The two of them moved as though they had been dancing together since childhood. They were graceful and fluid, bold and athletic, and no one watching could ever doubted that they were madly in love and engaged to be married. Tatiana felt so warm when she was so close to him, so delicate, and yet in such safe hands. She looked at his strong features and thought she would trust him with absolutely anything. She had complete confidence in this stranger, this statue, this man. She caught a glimpse of herself dancing in the shiny window. Her dress was so beautiful! It might not have been the most elaborate of the gowns here, but it had to be the most exquisite! The roses cascading down her skirt floated around every time she spun. And the gold satin absolutely sparkled in the candlelight. She felt pretty in this dress with her hair all pinned up. She caught one last glimpse of herself before the music ended and thought with a startled grin, *Well, what do you know? I might just be beautiful after all!*

Erich led her from the dance floor with a proud expression. He too felt that his partner was a rose among tulips. He thought he would like to take her for a walk by the water in the moonlight. But Senta stopped him on his way out the door. "Mr.

Evanov," she greeted him, curtsying as though they barely knew each other. "This is Tomasz Muronov."

Erich found himself greeting a rather handsome young man. This Muronov fellow was tall and slender, sporting a black uniform trimmed in gold. His eyes were dark and narrow but conveyed character rather than menace. His brown hair was long and wavy. Senta must have been pleased to meet him, Erich thought. But then he looked at his small, fair companion with curiosity. Did it matter to her? Had she been happy to learn that her next assigned seduction was a dashing young man, or was it all the same to her? For the life of him, Erich had never been able to imagine how Senta was able to do what she had to do for her country. It was admirable and yet unthinkable. He would have liked to know what went on in her mind sometimes. He would have liked to know how she felt when she lay beneath these men, priming them to reveal information she was after.

"It is such a strange coincidence!" Senta cried gracelessly. Her bubbly "Irina" act always startled Erich. "Tomasz is a domestic affairs adviser to the tsar, and Markov here is in foreign policy! It's almost like you two do the same thing!"

Erich felt his stomach turn. "Well, either the same or the opposite, depending on how you look at it." He couldn't stand to see such a bright woman acting so stupid. "This is my fiancée, Tatiana," he announced curtly.

"Charmed." Erich gritted his teeth as the handsome Russian kissed Tatiana's cheek. Did she find him handsome? Of course she must, he thought. Anyone would. Why did it bother him so much to think that she might be admiring Senta's escort? He must not let it bother him. Tatiana was not his, he reminded himself; she could never be his. If she fancied another gentleman, that was her right. But he could not convince himself to feel unthreatened. He had hardened himself to withstand torture during so many unbearable hours, but he could not harden

himself to accept that he could never have Tatiana Siskova.
Why did it hurt him so?

"Come," he said, lifting Tatiana's hand gently into his. "Let
us explore the outdoors."

Tatiana was delighted. It seemed this glorious evening would
just go on and on. "Pleased to meet you." She beamed at
Tomasz before Erich whisked her off. "Markov?" she asked
as they made their way toward a wide, winding marble staircase.
"I know I'm not supposed to ask questions, but shouldn't we
have been a little friendlier to Irina and her escort? It seemed
they wanted to talk. You acted as though you hardly knew
her."

"Sometimes I'm not sure I do," he muttered.

"What do you mean by that?"

"Nothing," he replied. Once again, he knew he was being
irrational. How could a spy fault another spy for being phony?
Yet, as much as he admired Senta von Sundt for her talents
and for her service to her country, he knew that he could never
love her, or even be attracted to her. It was just as well, he
supposed, since it was strictly forbidden to bed her while they
were working together. Such a distraction could easily destroy
their mission. But he did feel a bit guilty over his lack of
attraction to her. He knew it was wrong to fault her for the
very same talents that served their country so well.

Tatiana enjoyed the privacy on the stairwell. Stepping away
from the crowd was like leaving a wedding for the honeymoon.
Their footsteps made clicking sounds on the white marble stairs.
Tatiana made a point of letting her hand glide along the golden
banister as she descended, racing a bit to exaggerate the flow
of her dress behind her. When she saw the stars twinkling
through the narrow windows on each landing, she had the urge
to imagine that she lived here and was trotting downstairs for
a late-night cup of tea. Imagine, she thought, getting to dress
up like this every day! And getting to live in a palace! She
knew she should be happy that she got to live like this even

for one night. And indeed, she was. But she couldn't help imagining how it would feel to live like this forever.

When they stepped outside, Tatiana was surprised by the chill. Her dress was long-sleeved, but her shoulders were quite bare. When Erich saw her cross her arms and bounce, he excused himself to fetch her wrap. "Is it too cold for a walk?" he asked her, arranging the cloak around her shoulders. He wanted desperately to let his fingers linger on the soft skin of her neck and shoulders, but settled for a quick brush in passing as he pretended to make certain the cloak was held secure.

"I don't think so," she lied. She would rather catch a cold and die than let one precious opportunity pass her on this night.

"All right, then." He led her toward the nearby sound of water bumping gently against the shore. He used the cool air as an excuse to keep his arm around her. It was something etiquette forbade him from doing, but he suspected Tatiana would be ignorant of that rule. And so he let himself squeeze her ever so gently as they strode forth in the darkness.

"Was I a very bad actress?" Tatiana asked, breaking the crisp silence.

Erich's smile was mild. The quiet night was so intoxicating, as was the splashing water of the Neva River. "No, you were fine." *I don't want you to be a good actress,* he thought. *I never want you to learn.*

They stopped for a romantic pause when they reached the wide river. The lights of the Winter Palace reflected in its dark water. They were so near the gaiety of the ball and yet so very alone. Tatiana wondered whether this would be a good time to bring something up, something she had been thinking about all evening. But when Erich saw the moonlight casting its white glow on Tatiana's tender, angelic face, he interrupted her thoughts by reaching out to her. His hand caressed her shimmering brown hair, treasuring its softness without disturbing its complicated design. *What am I doing?* he thought. *What am I doing?*

"May I kiss you?"

Tatiana's eyes flung wide open. Her heartbeat quickened and she had to swallow several times. No one had ever asked her that before. What was she supposed to say? What ... what would kissing be like if she weren't kicking and punching, trying to get the bastard off her? She had never even thought of inviting someone to kiss her.

Her time to answer had expired, and she was now being pulled into a rough embrace. Erich locked her into a hug that she could not have escaped even if she were trying her hardest, intentionally trapping her between his massive arms and his rock-hard chest. Every muscle in his body was telling her that she could not leave until this kiss was over. Meanwhile, his lips rubbed smoothly over hers, brushing them with expertise unbecoming a man who had never been in love. He used every inch of his lip to snuggle with every inch of hers. It was in that way a soft kiss, yet the grip he held on her was so fierce that it was clear his mouth was holding back.

He wanted to let his lips fall lower. He wanted to use their flesh to snuggle with her neck, her collarbone, her shoulder, her— He couldn't resist looking down at those scrumptious breasts. They were so big, he wondered how much of them he could hold in his mouth. He was desperate to find out. He couldn't control himself. When he withdrew from the kiss, he came up breathless, squeezing her tender arms to her sides. He looked down at her hourglass figure and wanted to throw it to the ground, make it shake, kiss every last inch of it. With a painful wince, he looked away. *This is why,* he thought. *This is why I have to keep control. I'm dangerous. I'm dangerous. I was trained to be.*

"Why don't I take you home," he said miserably, not daring to look at the woman who could turn him to a wild animal just by standing in the moonlight.

Tatiana had a silly grin on her face, left over from the kiss.

"Why?" she asked. "It's not as though I have work in the morning."

He looked at her sharply. "Well, I do. Come." He hesistated even to take her by the hand after what had just happened between them. But grace required him to do so. And so he led her briskly to their waiting carriage.

It was fortunate that Tatiana did not notice Erich's abrupt behavior. She was still grinning dizzily from that kiss, wandering dreamily at her own pace no matter how urgently Erich pulled her ahead. She had never known kissing could be so exciting. She hoped they would do it again soon. As their carriage pulled away from the Winter Palace, Tatiana found herself actually waving good-bye to the brightly lit building. She had never known such a night as this one. She would eagerly have traded a thousand of her nights at Yura's, drinking vodka and dreaming, for one such magical evening as this one. She was still smiling as she watched the blue palace grow smaller and the crowds of brilliantly dressed people disappear into their carriages. It was not until she noticed her old clothes, stuffed in a sack beneath the bench, that her heart felt troubled.

The carriage would be taking her directly home. The evening that she'd hoped would never end was coming to a very abrupt close right now. Had she hoped that she could linger for a while at Erich's house? Drink some wine? Talk and laugh? Had she hoped to spend the night? She wasn't sure what she hoped. But she had not envisioned it all ending like this. Reality hit her heavily. She would never again go to a ball. This seemed an excellent time to bring up her thoughts to the quiet man beside her. "Markov?"

"Mmm-hmm?" he grunted, looking out the window, away from her.

"I—I was wondering something. I—" She twisted her gown with a tight fist. The answer to her question meant so much to her. She thought she might die if he said no. "I know I'm not supposed to ask questions," she continued bravely, "but—but, well, I can't help thinking." She punched her leg a couple of times. "I can't help thinking that you and Irina . . . well, you must be sort of, well, thieves or something. And I promise I won't tell anyone! I swear! But I was just thinking that . . . well, you know I'm a very good picklock. And I'm pretty good at sneaking around. I can keep a secret really well, and . . . and I'll work for a very small percentage. Honestly! I don't need much."

Erich's reply was quiet. "We're not thieves, and we don't need help."

Tatiana's heart sank. "Do you . . . do you not trust me?"

"No, it's not that at all," he sighed, reaching for her hand. "You've been a big help already. I do thank you for coming with me tonight. As for the rest of it, it's best if you forget it all. Forget Irina, forget me. Hold your silence, as I told you." He knew he should follow that up with a threat but couldn't do it. It would sound so phony. Surely, she knew by then that he would never hurt her. "Just . . . just hold your tongue when you get home, like we agreed." He turned his head to receive her nod. "Now, I need to speak to the driver. Where exactly do you live?"

Tatiana did not want him to know. She didn't want to show him the alley she called home. "Just drop me off at Yura's," she replied miserably.

"What's that?"

"The bar," she sniffed, "the bar where you asked me to the dance."

Erich shouted his instruction to the driver. In truth, he was not feeling any better about this than she was. He too had become intoxicated by the ball. Ordinarily, he would never have enjoyed such an event. It was just business, just showing his face in the proper place at the proper time so that no one would doubt his identity. There was nothing fun about it. But Tatiana had been so excited all night that he had become enchanted by the splendor also. He had seen the colorful ball through her eyes, had felt the joy of it just like an ordinary man. And what's more, he now knew beyond all doubt that he had intense romantic feelings for the lady beside him. It had been a pleasure pretending for one night that he might actually have a—what was the word she had used?—a sweetheart. A smile curled his mouth. What a perfect word to describe Tatiana.

Now he was heading to that empty, echoing dungeon he called home. He would draw all the curtains. He would lie on his back and try to sleep. For hours he would lie there, trying to force slumber. Then he would slip into a world of nightmares, memories of capture and prison. He would wake to the sight of no one. He would eat breakfast alone. He would go to that boring meeting. And he would try to convince Russia to destroy itself. Why? Because it was his job. His job had become naught but a chore. A dangerous, deceptive, life-threatening chore. But tonight . . . oh, God . . . tonight he had known music and color and moonlight.

"How . . . how shall I return the dress?" Tatiana asked pitifully. She would not cry in front of Erich, but she showed visible signs of wanting to do so.

Erich chuckled softly despite his foul mood. "What am I going to do with it?" he asked. "It's not even my size." He nodded his head in earnest. "It's yours."

"I'm afraid," she choked out, fingering the crisp fabric, "that I'll have just as little use for it as you would."

Erich thought his heart might shatter into a thousand pieces. He hated to think that Tatiana would never get to go to a ball again. But he knew that it was so. He swallowed hard, as though his emotions were stuck in his throat. "Still, you should keep it," he said. "Sell it if you can't wear it. It should be worth a good price."

Tatiana did not want to sell it. She wanted to treasure it forever and look at it whenever she felt sad. But she knew that her need for money was stronger than her sentimental yearnings and that she would probably sell it after all. But not for at least a few days, she promised herself. She just wanted to look at it for a few more days. "Might I visit you sometime?" she asked, not knowing that a proper lady would never make such a suggestion. Hope filled her eyes while she awaited his answer.

The shake of his head was devastating. "No, you're supposed to be in Moscow, remember? We can't have people spotting you. In fact, I was going to ask you to avoid the society section of St. Petersburg for a good while, if you don't mind."

Tatiana was breathless as the buggy pulled up to Yura's. "Then . . . then, will I never see you again?" she asked weakly.

Erich couldn't go that far. It was one thing to discourage her, one thing to set her free, but he could not nail the windows shut. He was certain he could put a bullet through his own head if his country required it of him, but he could not say good-bye forever to Tatiana. "I'll come to the bar some night," he promised hurriedly. "I'll visit you. We'll have a drink."

Tatiana smiled, though she did not know what "some night" meant and suspected it meant never. As she stepped onto the filthy cobblestone road, Erich said, "Wait! Shouldn't you change first?"

"I'll change," she promised. "And trust me, no one will recognize me until I do." They shared a brief smile before the carriage took off.

After a few turns of the wagon wheels, the carriage driver cleared his throat. "Pardon me, sir."

Erich was annoyed. "Yes?" he responded stiffly, feeling quite certain that a carriage driver in Prussia would not take such liberties.

"I couldn't help wondering," the driver began nervously, "whether this is such a good place to drop off a lady. Streets are dangerous around here, you know."

Erich was silent.

After letting the silence be for quite some time, the driver asked again, "Sir? Sir, are you just going to leave her here?"

Erich remained stoic, eyes narrow, lips perched in thought. When he finally spoke, it was in a whisper to himself. "I don't know." He looked behind him at the empty sidewalk, where Tatiana had stood moments before. "I just don't know."

Chapter 7

When Tatiana arrived at Yura's, her gown was in the satchel and she was wearing her comfortable old rags. Her hair was still pinned up in a pretty style, but her hat covered the last suspicious trace of her forbidden escapade. For the first time in her life, she found Yura's to be depressing. The smoke stung her eyes and the noise was annoying. She ordered herself a hefty shot of vodka and swallowed it down in one gulp. The second one she savored. She hated the feel of her old clothes. She'd never noticed before how filthy they were. She wanted to sit alone for a while, just to readjust to her real life, but a conversation caught her ear.

"The only reason he abolished serfdom was because he knew that if he didn't, there would be revolution."

"How do you know?"

"Oh, what do you think? He's some kind of a saint? The tsar is just like everyone else: He's interested in himself and himself only. Why else would he do it?"

The conversation was taking place among a crowd of boys

gathered around a circular table. Tatiana caught sight of Lev. He was saying nothing but listening intently, sitting right in the center of the commotion.

"Alexander II is the best tsar we have had—probably ever!" one of the boys shouted.

"Yes, but why? Why is he helping the peasants? It's because he fears for his life, and he should!"

"Watch what you say. The tsar is holy in the eyes of God."

"There is no God!" Some boys gasped, others listened more intently. "What better way to keep us from revolting than to tell us that God wants us to obey? The Orthodox Church is in on this too."

"You lie!"

"No, I agree with him!"

"So do I. We may not be serfs anymore, but we certainly aren't free. You call working at the factory all day long freedom?"

"That's right! You can't be poor and free. It's one or the other!"

"If Tsar Alexander wants to help us so much, why doesn't he give us some of his money?" There was laughter.

"Yeah, it's pretty easy for him to sign a piece of paper saying we're free, or sign a piece of paper saying the zemstvos have legislative power, but what has he ever given us that mattered to him?"

"He's no better than any of the other tsars. He gives us what he thinks he has to, to keep us quiet. Well, I say we don't take it anymore! He wants to know what he can give us? He can give us his riches! He can give us his palaces!"

"He can give us his life!"

Much later, when the commotion began to settle, Lev rose cheerfully to his feet. As though he didn't have a care in the world, he strode over to Tatiana. "Hi, Tasha! I didn't see you come in."

Her eyes were narrow and warning. "What do you think you're doing?" she spat out.

Lev was genuinely surprised. He looked over each shoulder as though making certain she was speaking to him, then asked, "Me? I, uh, I don't know. I was just listening to those university students who came in here. That, and having a drink." He gestured for the owner to bring him another.

"Stay away from those people, Lev." Tatiana's warning was bitter and passionate.

"Who?" He looked around him innocently.

"Dammit!" she shouted, hitting the table. "You know who! Those Decembrists, or whatever they're called."

"They're not Decembrists," he groaned. "That's an old-fashioned term."

"Well, whatever they are, stop talking to them."

"Tasha," he said, slouching into a chair, "I think they have some good arguments."

"I'm not worried about their arguments," Tatiana replied. "I'm worried about their murders and their terrorism and their—"

"Oh, come now," he moaned. "They're not all like that."

"It doesn't matter whether they're really like that or not," she said plainly. "The point is, the law thinks they are. And if you're caught with them, you'll be killed. It's as simple as that, Lev."

"Oh, since when have you been afraid of the law?"

"It's different!" she snapped. "Lev, what we do . . . we'll get in trouble only if we get caught. Nobody looks for people like you and me. They don't worry about us unless they see us. But people like that"—she jerked a thumb toward the few who were still straggling around the table—"the law has entire committees sent out just to find out who those people are. We don't need that kind of trouble, Lev."

Lev thanked the owner for bringing him a drink, then swished it around his glass a bit. His silence meant nothing, Tatiana knew. It did not mean he agreed with her or even was listening. "Lev"—she pulled at his shirtsleeve—"do you promise you won't talk to them anymore?"

"I don't promise anything," he snapped, then stopped teasing his glass. He chugged the healthy helping of vodka down in one gulp. "Let's just not talk about this, all right? It's getting late."

Tatiana had to run to catch up with him as he took long, angry strides out the door. "What is wrong with you?" she asked as the black wind smacked her in the face.

"What's wrong with me?" he asked. "Me? I've never told you what to do, Tasha. I might ask what's wrong with you!"

Their pace did not slow down but in fact quickened. Even though it was only autumn, traces of their breath could be seen in the air. "I just don't want you to get killed. Is that so wrong?"

He stopped walking. "Well, maybe some things are worth risking your life for, Tasha. Has that ever occurred to you? Do you want to spend the rest of your life living like a criminal when it's they who are criminals?"

"Who?"

"The . . . the rich people!" He stuffed his hands in his pockets and started walking again, frustrated at how poorly he was explaining himself. "Look, maybe you can't understand, and that's fine. But leave me alone."

"What can't I understand? Why not?"

"Because you had a family," he accused her. "You grew up in the country; you lived where peasants had a place."

"So?"

"So I didn't!" He gritted his teeth in a way that was so unlike the Lev she knew that she was more worried now than ever. "I grew up on these streets, Tasha. I don't even know who my parents are! I was raised by the bums."

"So?"

"So I never had a chance, Tasha! I never—" He swallowed back what might have been tears. "I spent my whole life thinking I'm nothing but street trash. Someday, I'll either be dead in one of these alleys, getting eaten by the rats"—he swallowed hard—"or I'll be arrested. And I've been doing a lot of thinking, Tasha. A lot of thinking. If I'm going to prison one day, I want it to be for something that matters. I don't want them to be able to say, 'Oh, look. We got another filthy bootlegger off the streets.' I want them to know that I'm not the criminal."

"Killing the tsar won't convince them of that."

"I didn't say anything about killing the tsar," he objected. "I just want to stand up for something."

"But, Lev." Tatiana's face held more understanding now. "You know that they, those people—whatever you call them . . ."

"The Will of the People."

"Fine. The Will of the People. You know, don't you, that they want to do more than make a statement. They want to cause riots, they want to blow up buildings, and, yes, they want to kill Tsar Alexander. You know that, don't you?"

Lev looked at the ground. When he lifted his face again, he seemed more mild. "Look. I'm just thinking about it. That's all."

Tatiana nodded and let him wrap his arm around her shoulders. She settled her head on him, leaning on him for balance the rest of the way home. They both thought of all they had been through together and wondered where the years had gone. It seemed they still thought of themselves as children playing mischief on the dangerous streets. But they were both their full heights now. And their game was becoming less fun. Why did they never see silver-haired peasants running amok as they did? Because no street rat ever lived that long. Theirs would be short, dangerous lives.

When they got home, Lev straightened the blankets. They were both so tired, they literally fell into their little bed. They did not even stay up for a drink, a smoke, or even a short conversation, as they usually did. In fact, they were within seconds of falling asleep, when Lev suddenly asked, "Hey, Tasha?"

She grunted in reply.

"Say, where were you tonight? I was looking for you earlier."

Tatiana breathed heavily for several moments, then she replied, "I don't know. I don't remember."

Chapter 8

"You want me to kill her? Are you insane?"

Senta's face said business as usual. Her green eyes held neither guilt nor doubt. "Erich, I know you like the girl, but be reasonable. If she's seen anywhere by anyone, your cover will be blown."

"Who the hell saw her last night that's going to go wandering down to the slums?"

"Erich!" she shouted, feeling cornered by a good argument. "She is a liability, and you know it! The girl has no family, no one to report her missing. . . ."

"I can't believe what I'm hearing." Erich rubbed his face hard, as though trying to wake up from a dream. "Why didn't you mention this earlier?"

Senta bent her head apologetically. "Frankly, Erich, I hadn't thought of it. I know that sounds odd, but I had my own concerns, my own problems to worry about. I'm sorry I didn't consider your own situation sooner, but frankly, it should have occurred to you."

Erich shook his head. "Senta, I'm not killing anyone. I think maybe you should take a holiday."

"I don't think I'm the one shirking my duties!" she shouted, rising to her feet. "I didn't want to say it, Erich Reitz. I did not want to say this. But now you leave me no choice." She straightened her back, lifting her short body as high as she could. "You have developed an inappropriate attachment to that girl, and it is interfering with your ability to serve this mission."

"This has nothing to do with personal attachment," he growled. "I wouldn't kill an innocent girl, even if—"

"You've killed lots of people!" she shouted.

She'd expected this to silence him, but she was very wrong. Erich did not flinch but only countered, "Politicians! Soldiers!" The sound of his voice made the lanterns shake overhead. Even Senta found herself hunching her shoulders in a nervous retreat. "Never in my life have I been ordered, or even had cause, to murder an innocent civilian."

"But you've never displayed one publicly before, never gotten one involved in our schemes before."

"That was your doing," he reminded her harshly. "You're the one who told me to bring someone to the ball. If it had been up to me, I'd have gone with you."

"There's no sense in placing blame," she said, her voice more timid now. "I should have had more foresight, it's true. But then, so should you have. The question is what to do now."

"I've already answered that," he replied steadily. "We do nothing. We leave her be."

"And I," Senta retorted, as she lifted her chin, "have already answered that. I told you that isn't acceptable. And if you thought about it, you'd realize I'm right. Listen to what I'm saying, Erich." She tried a new, pleading tone of voice. "We are at war. It's an unofficial war, true. But, nonetheless, it is a war. And nothing matters except winning it."

Erich scowled as though he seriously doubted that, but Senta continued more forcefully.

"Listen, Erich! As long as there's even the smallest chance that the girl could be spotted, that is reason enough to dispose of her! It is simple math. The danger of leaving her alive is somewhat, and the danger of seeing her dead is nothing. The girl is completely insignificant and disposable. No one will ever miss a street rat like her!"

Erich grabbed his partner with a movement so swift, anyone watching would have recognized his years of extensive training. Senta found her back slammed brutally against the parlor wall and her arms pinned helplessly to her sides. When she opened her eyes, Erich was looking down at her from what seemed like far, far above, his eyes frozen solid. "The girl is not disposable," he whispered the way a phantom whispers a curse.

Senta wanted to tell him to unhand her. She wanted to remind him of the consequences for such an action, remind him that such violence was strictly against all regulations. But she was too frightened.

When he let her go, Erich made a point of letting her see the loaded pistol he slipped into his trousers. "I trust that you understand," he said, his eyes still completely unfeeling, "that should you take this matter into your own hands, I would take it as a personal assault against me. And I would retaliate."

Senta found herself nearly unable to speak.

"If I find that the girl is missing or has met some unfortunate accident, I will hold you solely responsible, whether you are the cause or not. So I suggest you devote your life, if necessary, to making sure that Tatiana Siskova remains safe."

Senta found herself able to make a few small sounds. "Erich, please. I'm concerned only about us."

"We'll talk later," he announced, pulling on his overcoat, "after I've cooled off."

Senta nodded.

"But in the meantime," he added coldly, "if you'll excuse me, I have a country to destroy." He made his abrupt exit.

The slam of the door made Senta jump. Her head fell into her hands. What was happening? What had she done wrong? She collapsed into a chair and played with a torn piece of fabric. Fingering it, tearing it further, she thought hard. And as always happened when she found herself alone and defeated, her thoughts turned to her father.

Senta had once been a cheerful and privileged little girl. She had grown up on her father's estate, its massive gardens and balconies overlooking more than a hundred acres of well-tended rolling hills and land. She had been blessed not only with wealth but with enviable golden curls, bright emerald eyes, and a "perfectly Prussian" face, complete with a splattering of pink over each firm cheekbone. As a child living in a world of elegant adults, she had been gleeful, her mother's "little actress," always entertaining the grown-ups with her antics and impressions.

But Senta, like everyone else, had more than one obstacle on her road to lasting happiness. In her case, the worst of them was her father, Wolfgang von Sundt. He was a man who wanted only three things from life. He wanted enough food to feed his family, he wanted a strong son, and he wanted to see Prussia take over the world. That was all. He was even willing to negotiate the first item. But to be denied a son was unbearable. And Senta, though she could be many different things, actress as she was, she could not be a son.

Nature sometimes compels people to dwell on those who hate them rather than on those who admire them. Such was the case with Senta, for she would not be content until her father, the one person who did not notice her beauty or laugh at her childish antics, would gaze upon her with affection. She grew, in fact, to be a rather stern child, changing from the delightful little girl she had been into a studious and uncompromising young woman. It was a shame that Wolfgang von Sundt was too blind to see, as everyone else did, that his child had grown to be a near perfect reflection of himself.

Senta's eyes were no longer like the forest in rain but were a deep jade, as cold and firm as the stone itself. Though her face may have resembled that of her weak and unassuming mother, her expressions were so much more fierce that one would hardly have thought the two had sprung from the same bloodline. Senta never fell in love, nor did she so much as have a fleeting whimsy over a boy. She sought the attention of only one man, and if she could not have his love, she did not crave the love of any other. She studied hard and excelled in schoolwork. She was clean and exhibited excellent manners, never giving her father any excuse to scold her. She did not chatter in the way he hated so much but spoke only when she had something important to say. She walked as though always having somewhere important to go. But still, her father did not notice her.

It was, she thought, a brilliant idea she had one evening as she overheard her father lecturing a guest in the study. Wolfgang was more of a militant than a gentleman and did not mind assaulting guests with his fervent political dogmas. She remembered the conversation quite clearly. Her father said, "You see? That is the problem with young people today. They see themselves as Germans and not as Prussians. They don't remember that without von Bismarck, there would be no Germany. Without Prussia, the rest of Germany would fall prey to the Russians, or, God forbid, the French. We are Germany, but the rest of Germany is not us." And that is when it occurred to her. Her father did love something. He loved his country. If she were to serve his country, he might just love her too. She fell asleep that night with her ear against the study wall. Cigar smoke and laughter soothed her into sweet dreams. And when she awoke, it was with an excited knock in her heart. She knew exactly what she was going to do with the rest of her life.

As it turned out, her natural dramatic ability was helpful in her new career, for a spy, she learned, must be three things: infinitely courageous, unquestioningly patriotic, and a very good liar. And what was acting if not lying? St. Petersburg would mark Senta's first mission. She had undergone torturous training and knew that this mission was her only chance for glory. If it succeeded, she would forever be an asset to her country. If it failed, she would have to return to her father with her head bowed. And that she could not do.

She had no doubts regarding her newfound destiny, not even standing naked before a committee of calculating bureaucrats. "She's too small," one said, tapping the ashes of his cigar. They stared at her as though she were not a woman but a fine piece of military equipment. "Not enough bosom. She won't be able to seduce them."

"I disagree," another said. "Her face. It's extraordinary. Perfectly German."

The cynic raised an eyebrow. "Too German?"

"Not at all. Some Russians fancy they look like us. She'll be fine."

The cynic shook his head. "I don't know. Not enough flesh, not enough figure."

"I beg your pardon." They were all stunned when Senta spoke. Perhaps they had forgotten that she was able to do so. "I beg your pardon," she repeated, "but I would like to say a few words."

She took their silence as an invitation to continue.

"First of all, I am not German. I am Prussian."

They all winced at this tender topic but did not argue.

"Secondly," she continued, holding her angular chin up high, looking more like her father than she could have realized, "I believe it is my talent you should be judging and not my figure."

Some of the men snickered.

"Do you doubt it?" she asked. "Would you judge a male

spy according to how thin he was? Or how dark? Well, why not? Surely, a thin man could better sneak and hide than a fat one. And surely a dark man is better concealed in shadows. But you don't choose spies that way, do you? No. You choose the most talented man because you know that what he does with his body is more important than how it is shaped. I would argue the same holds for me.''

The men laughed uproariously. And Senta was pleased, for they immediately gave her the mission. In fact, in her joy she found herself laughing right along with them. It was not until much later, after she first wound up in bed with a groping Russian politician, that she wondered whether those men might have been laughing at her rather than with her.

Chapter 9

Erich leaned back in his chair. As usual, he was the first to arrive in court. He was the only councilman who seemed to understand that ten o'clock meant ten o'clock and no later. He used his spare time to proofread his reports. His Russian was excellent, but it never hurt to double-check. Then, at last, the Russians staggered in. A brief, annoying period of gossip and greeting ensued, but at last, the councilmen seemed to remember why they had congregated.

"Mr. Alexeivich!" The chairman of the Municipal Council paced excitedly before his colleagues. "Peasant riots, as we all know, have increased dramatically in the past year, and it is Mr. Alexeivich's pleasure to update us on the situation of getting them under control. Mr. Alexeivich?"

Erich waited breathlessly as the young speaker fumbled with some papers.

"We have located the source of the terrorism that threatens our domestic security," he began nervously. "It is a small

organization composed of rebellious university students—
nihilists, who do not believe in God, and also gullible urban
peasants who lack the mental faculties to question the extrem-
ist fanaticism of the organization. It is called the Will of the
People. But I think you will find that it represents the will of
no one except a few power-hungry intellectuals and their
followers. The organization seeks to drive Russia into a state
of anarchy by destroying buildings with dynamite and causing
general panic. In addition, they have targeted the very life of
Tsar Alexander II, thinking that his death will further confuse
the people of Russia. From this state of anarchy, they reason,
will arise a new way of life in Russia, led, of course, by
them.'' He shrugged, apparently finished and ready to take
questions.

Igor Vastavol, Senta's least favorite conquest, was there. It
had been her job to seduce him when she first arrived in St.
Petersburg. But after several miserable encounters, she determined, to her relief, that he had no valuable information and
there would be no need to continue relations. Today he was
the first to speak. ''I think this is all a bunch of nonsense,'' he
said gruffly, his bulbous cheeks growing hot. ''This is what
happens when you're kind to peasants. They never behaved
this way when they had a stern tsar. No, it's only now that
they have a gentle tsar that they're complaining.''

''That is rather off the point,'' another councilman objected.
''Mr. Alexeivich, what level of threat do you believe this organization poses?''

''Well,'' he stuttered, ''umm . . . well.'' He hated answering questions. It was so much easier to read from a prepared
speech. ''Well, their numbers are small,'' he said at last. ''Well,
at least we think they are. It's really hard to tell how many
members they have, since not everyone will admit their sym-
pathies.''

''Should we run some interrogations?'' another councilman
asked. ''Should we comb the ghettos a bit? See who's involved?''

"Yes," another said, "perhaps a few public executions will warn other members to silence themselves."

The meeting's head looked at Erich. Erich had been deceptively quiet and seemingly disinterested until then. "Mr. Evanov?" the speaker asked him. "You're on the committee for national security. What do you think of all this?"

Erich was careful with his words. What he said right then was so important to the future of his mission that he didn't want to make even the slightest mistake. "Well," he began casually, "I think that there will always be peasants who are discontent, but that's no cause for alarm. In fact"—he stretched his arms overhead, trying to appear relaxed or even bored—"I would tend to say that drawing too much attention to this could give the impression to other nations that we have civil unrest here. It might make us look weak. And that certainly would be a shame, since it seems fair to say that there are no true threats to this government."

"I agree!" Igor chimed in. "Enough of this nonsense! So they say they want to kill the tsar? Do you have any reason to think they can do it?"

"Well, no," Alexeivich admitted.

"Well, then," Igor cried, patting his belly, "what more is there to say? Forget the peasants! We waste too much valuable time discussing them as it is."

"I hate to say it," a gray-haired man joined in. "But on this occasion I must agree with Igor. We can't make a fuss every time we hear about unhappy peasants shouting murder, can we?"

And so the meeting continued. Erich tried to keep a triumphant smile from curling his lips. He had done it. He had turned the conversation and in some small way had helped mold the official stance regarding peasant unrest. It hadn't been difficult, of course. These noblemen were eager to believe that nothing was wrong and that nothing truly threatened their stations. The way they were all shouting in agreement now told him that.

But he had no complaints about a job being easy just so long as it was done. There would be work ahead, of course. The subject would be raised again the next time a building exploded. But if he could help it, he would be there again, assuring them all that there was no need to worry.

Chapter 10

"Get your stinking hands off me!"

Daveed Vinitsky was at it again. Only this time he was angrier and more frightening. "Hey, hey, hey," he urged her, pulling her against him as though for a hug. "Come on now, I'm not playing around."

Tatiana didn't like his odor. He smelled like sweat. But even more, she didn't like the way he was squeezing her, not like a man embraces a woman, but like a cobra strangles its prey. His eyes were so small and biting that she didn't know how women ever found him handsome. His strong arms, which so many girls praised for their sleek, muscular contours, felt like wire cutting into her flesh as she tried to escape his tireless advances. He had cornered her on her way to Yura's. He'd cut into her path and made her nearly bump into him. Before she could even see who had approached her, he had pulled her into the darkness. There was no one to help her. Tatiana, as usual, was on her own.

"Hey, hey!" he shouted when her fierce struggles succeeded

in aggravating him. "None of that," he warned, giving her a stern look of disapproval. "Now, just hush."

He bent forward with his eyes closed for a kiss. He looked as though he believed they were in love, as though he had not sprung from an alley and wrestled her into the darkness. It made Tatiana want to laugh. But instead, she stepped on his foot. "Ouch!" he yelled, accidentally releasing her. Tatiana gave him a good hard kick in the knee. "Dammit!" Instinctively, he pulled back his fist and planted it in her eye.

Many women would have been felled by much less, but Tatiana was an experienced fighter and did not even stumble. Instead, with one hand covering the throbbing, stinging left eye, she used the right one to aim her mark. Her own fist landed on Daveed's unsuspecting nose. It was, perhaps, the shock of realizing how hard this sweet little girl could punch that stunned him even more than hearing his nose snap. The pause that followed gave Tatiana ample time in which to knee him in the groin and then run off, out of the alley and into the safety of the well-lit street. But when she reached the street, she did not stop running. She kept flying down the road, holding on to her cap, looking like a runaway schoolboy in her breeches and shirt. She did not dare to look behind her to see whether Daveed had followed. For the slightest glance behind, she knew, would slow her down. Every thief knew that. And besides, a crook should never give the police an extra glimpse at her face. So, instinctively, she ran all the way to Yura's, not even slowing when she yanked open the front door with a bang.

It was not until she came to a jolting halt inside the jolly, smoky bar that she realized how out of breath she had become. Fortunately, no one really noticed. Anyone who did just assumed that she was running from the police—again. That didn't matter, since most of them had done the same at one time or another this week. Tatiana took a deep breath. That had been a close one. She desperately needed a drink and was pleased when the owner brought her one before she even asked.

"Thanks." She winked, lifting the gold shot glass to her lips. After she swallowed the vodka, she realized she was sweating from that little jog she had taken. She used a handkerchief to wipe her forehead and cheeks, then asked for a glass of water.

Settling herself in a chair, she leaned back, stretching and groaning, bending her neck from side to side to relieve the tension. She thanked the owner for the cool glass of water and held it up to her warm cheek before drinking it. This place was already working its magic on her. The laughter was making her smile; the yellow lanterns were making her feel at home. The sight of all her outlaw friends, so at ease in the calm of night, was making her joyful. Her eye hurt, of course, but this was not the first black eye she'd received in her life. She knew that as long as she kept it closed, the stinging would stop.

Tatiana looked around her. She would not walk home alone tonight, that was for certain. Daveed was still out there, probably angrier than ever. Lev wasn't much of a fighter, but at least he would be a witness. Maybe a witness would be enough to steer Daveed away for the time being. She gazed around at the tables, hoping to see the face of her friendly companion, and hoping she wouldn't find him talking about revolution with those suicidal atheists. But she had not looked around for long at all, when she spotted something much more startling than Lev or his assassination-crazed friends. She spotted a black coat.

Tatiana's heart sped up. Her hands moved instinctively to her hair, trying to untangle it, trying to neaten it. When that did not work, she stuffed it more tightly under her cap, so as to hide it at least. She couldn't believe it. She had never dreamed he would come here. Not after so many nights had passed! The evening she had spent with him seemed like a distant fantasy now. The ball, the gown, the castle, the man . . . She had not been able to conjure his face. She would get the eyes right, but then something would be wrong with the image of his chin or his nose. The memories had turned to clouds. And now, here he was in the flesh, more handsome than she remembered. His yellow hair so striking, his fine cheekbones so perfect, his nose so aristocratic, his shoulders so broad. How could she have forgotten? And how, she thought, looking over each shoulder, could she have missed him walking in?

Gathering her courage, she bounced toward the figure in black. He was sitting in the corner of the room with his back against the wall. It could not be said that this man was "lounging," for there was always an alertness about him, a straightness in the back, a suspicion in the eyes. But he did, at least, appear relaxed as he drank from his water glass and read some papers. "Hello," Tatiana greeted him, hiding all signs of nervousness from her voice.

He lifted his gaze as though he'd known for hours that she was there. It was his job never to be startled. But when he saw her, he found himself raising his voice. "What the hell happened to your face?"

Tatiana was wounded. Her face? He didn't like her face? Then, with a little relief, she remembered that he must be referring to her bruise. "Oh! I . . . I just got in a little fight."

Erich was already shaking his head, disappointed with himself. He should never raise his voice in public, the spy in him scolded. He should never draw such attention to himself, but even more important, said the gentleman in him, he should never cause a lady to look as ashamed as Tatiana did just then. The poor girl was bowing her head with embarrassment, trying in vain to hide her tender eyelid. "Never mind it," he said softly. "Please . . . sit down." He motioned to the empty chair before him. The more he thought about it, the more he felt sorry for the girl Tatiana had been fighting. She could probably be a tough opponent when she needed to be. He noted that her fist also bore a dried streak of blood. *That's my girl,* he thought with amusement.

"I—I'm surprised to see you," Tatiana nearly whispered as she flopped into the chair. Her posture was all wrong for a lady. One foot was tucked under her while the other kicked the table leg.

Erich took no note of her casual manners. He was glad to see her, even fresh from a fight, and showed his appreciation with the gentlest of smiles. "I said I would come, didn't I?" he asked in a low voice.

"Yes," she replied frankly, her good eye opened wide, looking plainly into his. "But I didn't think you really would."

"Why not?"

"Because I'd served my purpose, and I doubted you had any more need for a dirty peasant girl." The words had come out before she'd monitored them. She couldn't believe she had spoken so bluntly. She wished she could take them back.

Though wounded, Erich carefully held his anger at bay. He had never thought of Tatiana as a dirty peasant girl. In fact, *dirty* was the last word he would use to describe the girl who warmed his heart so. It was her clarity, her purity, that drew him. "You seem angry with me," he observed casually.

"Not really," she lied, but she was very angry. Angry that he had shown her such a dream as that night at the Winter Palace and then let it disappear without a trace.

He nodded. "Well, I'm glad to hear that, because I enjoyed your company very much, and I wanted to thank you again for allowing me to escort you to the ball."

Tatiana's face lit up. "Do you think we might go again sometime?" It was a hope she had dared not entertain.

He cocked his head in thought, pondering whether another such event might require him to display his fiancée again. He too had never dared to entertain such a fancy. But at last, he shook his head in defeat. "I'm sorry. I don't believe there will be another ball before I leave."

"Before you . . . you leave?" Tatiana's heart sank, and she could feel her face blanch.

"Afraid so," he replied gravely. "I'll not be in St. Petersburg for more than a few more months."

"Where—where are you going?" She tried to seem eager for the reply, but she really didn't care. He was leaving, and she would never again see him. Strangely and suddenly, that was all that mattered.

"I can't tell you that," he replied, swishing his water around in its glass as though it were a fine wine. "I've told you not to ask questions, and I tire of repeating myself."

Tatiana forced herself to offer him a repentant look, but it was only pretend. "Sorry," she said.

She was so bad at phony apologies that Erich couldn't help laughing. "You are not," he chuckled brightly.

Tatiana joined in the laughter. "All right, I'm not."

Tatiana suddenly felt a pleasant thickness in the air. There was a dam that crumbled only when two people whose souls were so well matched shared a drink in the wee hours of the morning. "Don't you want a real drink?" she suggested.

"I had one earlier, and that was enough. I don't like to lose my senses."

"Why not?" she teased, planting her elbows on the table and leaning forward. "I think I'd like to see you without your senses."

He chuckled again, for he had not been teased in a very long time. Her soft round face was irresistible when it was full of mischief and laughter. "A lot of people would, I'm sure," he replied more honestly than he'd planned. "Which is all the more reason to keep my sobriety."

"What do you do?" she asked bluntly. "Come on." She reached across the table to nudge his shoulder. "Tell me. I promise I won't let anyone know. Do you embezzle from the government? Are you a thief? Or a spy?"

Erich was so well practiced that he did not react when she gave the correct answer. The closest examiner could not have detected even a sideways eye movement. "I'll tell you what I am," he said, putting down his glass with a little bang. "I'm

very hungry. Would you like to join me for something to eat?"
He was already putting on his coat.

"I'd love to!" she cried. "But, uh . . . but, uh . . ."

"I'm paying," he assured her.

He let her walk in front of him, then mentioned casually,
"No restaurants are open at this time of night, I assume. So if
it suits you, let's take our fare to your apartment."

Tatiana froze. "My . . . my apartment?"

"Yes, is that all right?"

"Uh . . . uh . . . well"—she swallowed—"maybe, umm . . .
how about at the park? We can sit in the park and eat under
the stars."

"A bit chilly for that, isn't it?"

"No."

Erich shrugged. "If you wish. Can you show me a good
place to buy bread and caviar?"

"Madame Yuravina is a great cook," she offered, relieved
that the subject had changed. "You won't find much caviar
around here, but her bread is great, and so are her cabbage
pies."

Erich had grown accustomed enough to the Russian food
that he did not recoil at the sound of cabbage pie, as he would
have at one time. "Very well," he agreed, "let's see if we can
fetch her."

Madame Yuravina was more than pleased to prepare the
requested fare. She was, as Tatiana had promised, an excellent
cook. Originally, she had intended to help her husband run good
old Yura's, combining his bartending skills with her baking. But
it was not long before it became clear that none of their customers had any interest in spending their money on food. Given a
choice between a glass of vodka and a bowl of soup, these
miserable children of peasants did not hesitate to buy the liquor.
Food, after all, could only sustain life, and their lives were
barely worth sustaining, but vodka promoted cheer, and that
was something they would pay any price to attain. So Madame

Yuravina had resigned herself to sweeping floors and wiping glasses. But when Erich requested that she prepare and pack up all her finest dishes, her face positively beamed. She regretted only that she would not be there to see the couple's faces when they ate the delicious feast.

Tatiana was so looking forward to eating as she inhaled the delicious smells rising from the basket under Erich's arm. It had been a long time since she'd had a full meal. "It smells good, doesn't it?" she asked him as they stepped out into the clean night air.

"Yes," he replied, looking worriedly at the sky above.

Tatiana knew what he was thinking. She could sense rain in the air.

"We'd better not eat in the park," he said, confirming her worst fear. "It looks as though it may rain. Still, I'd like to get away from the crowd." He looked at her squarely. "Is your apartment far?"

Tatiana stammered, "My . . . my apartment?"

"Yes. Is it far?"

"I . . . I don't think we want to go there." Her eyes did not meet his.

"Oh." He thought he understood, but he didn't. "I see. Well, you know, there's no need for you to be ashamed of having humble accommodations. That doesn't matter to me. It doesn't matter at all." He lifted her chin with a finger. "All right?" he asked again, his eyes sparkling down at her with kindness.

Tatiana felt positively trapped. She was ashamed, more ashamed than Erich could imagine. But with a heavy sigh she said quietly, "All right. I'll take you to my home." And she began walking ahead of him.

Erich was bewildered by her demeanor. Her head was bent, her face was blank, and her steps were sluggish. He decided he would pretend to be impressed by her home no matter what, for he could not bear to see her so ashamed and forlorn. He hoped the hot meal would lift her spirits. But what Erich had not counted on was Tatiana's stopping at the end of an alley and saying, "All right, we're here."

Erich looked around. "We're where?"

She pushed aside a filthy cloth and showed him the pile of blankets that lay beyond. Now he understood. He saw a score of candles, some wooden matches, some empty bottles of vodka, and the bag that held her golden dress. He looked up as though hoping miraculously to see a roof overhead. Of course there was none. Only a brilliantly starred sky. As he stood breathlessly in the "doorway," Tatiana went to work lighting candles so they could see each other more clearly. She flopped down on the blankets, sat cross-legged, and stared into a little flame. She did not look at Erich. Pouting like a little girl, a fist holding up her cheek, she raced her finger back and forth through the fire, testing herself to see how long she could hold it inside the head before there was pain.

Erich was overcome by pity. He knew that most people in Russia were peasants and that many of them lived like this. But knowing it and seeing it were two different things. How could anyone live this way and still smile like Tatiana? Then he felt guilt. He had taken her to a ball. He looked at the dress, all folded up in that bag, and thought for the briefest of instants that he might weep. He had shown her the life that others enjoyed, and then he had tossed her back into this hole. No wonder she had wanted to see him again. No wonder she had wanted to join his "diamond robbery" operation. She had just wanted out of this place, any way she could go. And he had denied her even the smallest of hopes. He had forbidden her to visit him, told her the job was over and she could not help him again. My God, he hadn't even let her spend the night indoors. To think that on the very night of the ball she had come home and slept here. A rat crawled across his foot, squeaking loudly. It was unbearable.

"Why didn't you tell me you were homeless?" he asked sternly.

"I'm not homeless," she sulked. "This is my home."

"I thought you were a thief," he demanded. "What do you do with all the money you steal?"

Tatiana shrugged defeatedly. "It's not often that I score. When I do, I spend it on food and drink."

"You mean you buy vodka before you get yourself a place to live?" he snapped.

"The two are hardly the same price," she reasoned. "And besides"—she lifted her golden eyes to his icy ones—"what would I have if I didn't have Yura's to go to every night?"

Erich didn't know the answer to that. A brief silence fell between them before he decided to let this matter rest. Casually, he removed his coat and sat on it like a mat. He opened the satchel Madame Yuravina had provided and began unloading sweet-smelling pies, soft hot bread, and bowls of only slightly cooled soup. "You'll return these dishes to her tomorrow?" he asked sternly.

Tatiana nodded, eager to receive her fare. "Yes, of course." She scooted closer so as to get a better look at the treats to come.

"Now, I want you to take as much as you want," he ordered. "Don't eat delicately just because you're in the company of a man."

"Don't worry"—she shrugged—"I wouldn't have even thought of that."

He smiled. Of course not, he thought. Of course not. He carefully divided the food unevenly so as to give Tatiana the larger helpings. Ordinarily, she might have tried to protest, but she was so hungry, she was only too thankful to receive the heaping portions he set before her. "Thanks for buying all this food," she said with her mouth full. "I think you really made Madame Yuravina happy too. She loves to cook."

He did not reply. He had never had a talent for small talk and couldn't think of anything to say.

Tatiana was not bothered by his silence. Her father had long ago told her that when a guest won't talk, simply ask him more questions. People can't help talking if you just keep asking them questions. She knew she mustn't ask him about his life or his past, since that seemed to upset him, so she thought of something creative to ask him. "Do you have a favorite color?"

He waited until his mouth was no longer full, then replied, "Blue," and continued eating.

"Blue?" she asked, bobbing her head with interest. "Why is that?"

"I don't know," he answered briskly, then returned to his plate.

"Do you know what my favorite color is?" she asked. She was so warmed by the meal that she was now fully recovered from the initial awkwardness of showing Erich her home.

He gave her a cool stare. "Of course not. How would I know what your favorite color is?"

"Good point," she agreed. "Well, it's yellow. Do you know why?"

He shook his head.

"Because it's the color of my mother's dress. She had only one, you know."

What had begun as a tediously trivial conversation suddenly became interesting to Erich. "Your mother is still alive?" he asked.

"Oh, no." She shook her head. "She's dead, and so is my father. So is my sister. In fact, just about everyone in my family is dead except for me, and . . . well, my older sister might be alive. I don't know. She ran away when I was a baby. And then there's my aunt. She's alive too, but I kind of wish she weren't."

Some might have scolded Tatiana for saying such an irreverent thing about her own relative. But Erich was not one of them. He understood hate very well and saw nothing distasteful in it. "Why?" he asked casually. "What did she do?"

Tatiana fell onto her back with her arms stretched high above her head. "She was awful," she moaned.

Erich was not comfortable with the view he now had. If Tatiana had been wearing a skirt, he would be looking under it. Even though she was wearing a man's breeches, the creases in the pants, combined with his imagination, showed him more than he ought to know of her thighs and what lay between them.

"I tried to help out around the house," she continued, rolling to her side, propping her head on one elbow. Her legs were closed now, and Erich was relieved. "My parents sent me there right before they died. Well, actually I went there after they died, but they arranged for it before they died. Well, now, wait a minute. You can't send somebody anywhere after you're dead. Oh, never mind. The point is, I had to go there. And I was expecting her to be really happy to see her long-lost niece. But instead, she treated me as though I were imposing on her. She wouldn't talk to me, she never smiled. And when the master of the house would whip me, she wouldn't do a thing!"

Erich looked up. "You were whipped?"

"Well, yes," she replied. Hadn't she just said that? "So anyway, my point being—"

Erich was filled with a rage so intense that it even managed to show through his steely eyes. He gritted his teeth while his eyes flickered angrily with sparks of blue and green. Someone had taken a whip to his Tatiana. Someone had marred her soft skin with callous blow after callous blow. He had suffered under the whip himself and knew the pain of it. It was not an ordeal that any woman should see much less feel. Especially not this one. He wanted to protect her somehow, to console her. The only way he knew to do this was to quietly move closer to her, and gently, slowly, wrap his arm around her shoulders.

Tatiana giggled nervously. "Umm, is my story boring you?"

"Not at all," he replied, pushing a wisp of her hair carefully from her face. "Go on."

Tatiana didn't know how she could do that with him sitting so close that she could feel his warmth. She felt shy beneath his tightly wrapped arm. He smelled so clean. She wanted to bury her face in his silk shirt just so she could smell it, just so she could hear his strong heartbeat. "Well . . . I," she tried to continue, "I, uh, well, next I met Lev and . . ." She looked up at his face. His eyes were so startling, the way they sparkled. How could they be so caring and so cold at the same time?

Erich couldn't look at her face any longer. He would either have to turn away or kiss her. And so he kissed her. He pulled her so close to him that she was nearly sitting in his lap. His arms held her up, squeezed her, pulled her ample breasts tightly against his hard, thumping chest. He noticed this more than anything else as he touched her lips with his, parted her teeth with his tongue, forced her mouth to open wider and wider. All the while, he remained keenly aware of her breasts pushing against him like pillows. When the kiss was over, Tatiana rubbed her cheek against his, enjoying the slight roughness she found there. She wrapped her arms around his huge shoulders and there found a resting place for her head. She couldn't get enough of the smell of him, so crisp. The shirt under her hands was soft. She dared to lift her fingers to the short golden hair on his head and found it to be thick and silky. He stiffened, as though he did not quite like being touched, but he did not move her hand. So she continued to stroke his smooth hair.

At last, he whispered, "Let me hold you in my lap. Come up all the way." And without waiting for her reply, he lifted her hips and settled them on his thighs.

"Oh, aren't I too heavy?" Tatiana asked nervously. "I don't want to crush your legs."

He silenced her by pushing aside her hair and sucking fiercely on an earlobe. He sucked so hard, she thought he would devour it. And then it happened. Inch by inch, ever so gradually, she felt her old shirt being lifted. Still sucking her ear, Erich was feeling his way from her soft waist upward. At first, Tatiana thought he would stop before he reached her breast. Surely, he wouldn't . . . would he? His strong hands continued their journey until at last, with a little jump, she felt a finger on the very crest of her bosom. Then, before she knew what was happening, Erich's entire hand had encompassed her bare breast. Tatiana was startled. No one had ever touched her there. Instinctively, she pulled away from his kiss.

"Do you want me to stop?" he whispered in the ear he'd been nibbling.

"I . . . no . . . no . . . but, do you think I might get pregnant?"

"From this?" he asked, giving her another squeeze.

She nodded.

"No," he assured her in a whisper, "it takes more than that."

"I—I—" Tatiana was gradually regaining her senses. "But . . . but you're leaving, aren't you? Didn't you say you're leaving?"

Erich promptly removed his hand from her breast. Gracefully, he lowered her shirt and patted it firmly closed. With a gentle kiss on her head, he whispered, "Come. Let's just look up at the stars, all right?"

Tatiana felt ashamed. "You're not angry, are you?"

He gave her a reassuring smile, which showed clearly that he was not upset. "No, sweetheart. Just lie down here on the blanket with me." He stretched out on his back with a little groan. He felt it was important to spend some more time close to her, showing her that he was not disappointed with her. After all, she was right. And he had been very wrong.

"Did you just call me sweetheart?" Tatiana asked with a little smile.

He reached for her and pulled her until she was lying down. Once he had her, he drew her to his chest, kissed her on the crown of the head, and caressed her back with firm strokes.

The stars above were magnificent. They shone more brightly than all the diamonds in the Winter Palace. "I learned it from you," he said in answer to her question. "You asked me once whether I had a sweetheart. I liked the word and thought it suited you."

Tatiana was grinning, in part because she was pleased to have taught someone a new word but mainly because it seemed that this man liked her. "Markov?" she asked.

Erich was quite absorbed with the starry scenery above and answered with a certain fogginess. "Hmm?"

"Do you think you'll ever get married?"

He stiffened a bit and had to adjust Tatiana to compensate. "I . . . uh," he said, wincing, "I doubt it."

"Me neither," she replied, to his surprise. "I used to want to get married," she began dreamily, rubbing his powerful chest. "But honestly, who would I marry? I mean, look around. I don't even know a man who has a place to live! Well"— she shrugged—"not a place with a roof anyway." There was a long pause. Tatiana's head rose and fell a bit every time Erich breathed. She could hear his heart beating, and it was a comforting sound. "You're really strong," she observed, pinching one of his bulging arms. Erich could not believe her gall but did not stop her. "I'd bet you could beat up just about every man I know," she mused. "Even Daveed Vinitsky, and he thinks he's pretty tough."

"Who's that?" he asked disinterestedly.

"The guy who did this." She pointed to her eye. "But don't worry, I got the best of him. I think his nose is broken!" She giggled triumphantly.

Erich stopped gazing at the stars and turned directly to his newfound angel. A trembling hand reached toward her swollen eye and touched it so gently, one would have thought it was his own soreness he wished not to aggravate. "A man did this to you?" he asked, swallowing violently.

"Sure." She shrugged. "Didn't I already tell you that?"

He shook his head, his magnificent eyes piercing her like shards of ice. "You told me you were in a fight. I'd assumed it was between women."

Tatiana chuckled. "Not likely. How many women do you know who get in fistfights when they're mad?"

He closed his eyes, trying to contain his swelling emotions. "Why . . . why did this"—he gritted his teeth while he spoke the name—"Daveed Vinitsky hit you?"

"Oh, you know. He's one of those thugs who thinks a man should get to choose whatever mate he wants. Sort of like the cave men did, I guess."

Erich didn't follow. "What . . . what are you saying?"

"He likes me, but I don't like him," she explained cheerfully. "And instead of getting mad at God for it, he gets mad at me. As if I can help who I like!"

Erich was very confused. "He hit you because you don't like him?"

"No. He hit me because I wouldn't let him take off my clothes."

That was the last straw. First the pile of blankets which she called home. Then the obvious hunger. Then the whippings she suffered under her master's hands. And now this. "He tried to . . . touch you?" he spat out.

Tatiana was too scared to answer. Erich looked even more frightening now.

After observing her silence for some time, Erich rose angrily to his feet. Tatiana wasn't overly alarmed by this until he reached for his coat. "Hey, wait," she called. "Wait, don't go. What did I say? Are you angry?"

"I'll see you tomorrow," he grumbled, then stomped through the curtain, down the alley, and toward the street. Tatiana was left in a bit of a stupor in the wake of his abrupt exit. What could she have possibly said? Why was he leaving in such a huff? Oh, this was perfectly awful. It was the first time she'd ever let a man touch her, and now he was storming away. Then suddenly her face relaxed. Her arms unraveled, and her eyes widened. Then ever so gradually, a smile crossed her lips. He had said "See you tomorrow." He was coming back! She would see him tomorrow! Oh! She fell backward onto the blankets with a sigh. She would be looking forward to it all day long.

Erich had left without speaking further about Tatiana's eye for one reason. He was a man who believed he had only a limited number of words allotted to him during his lifetime. And he wished to waste none of them. He would save each precious sound for the moment when it would truly matter. And this was one of those moments. When Senta answered the pounding on her door, she found herself facing a worn and distraught man. "I want to let her in," Erich announced, panting from his long jog. "The girl, Tatiana. I want to let her in . . . on everything."

"Who . . . what?'

"Everything," he repeated.

Chapter 11

"I believe you have completely lost your wits."

Erich had been reluctantly invited into the living room despite Senta's late-night state of undress. She held her satin robe tightly around her while Erich paced. "Hear me out," he ordered in a tone that left no room for compromise. "You said it yourself, Senta. It isn't safe to leave her wandering around. She could be seen; we could be discovered."

Senta started to object, but Erich did not allow it.

"You were perfectly happy to kill her!" he recalled. "Why should you be any less excited about my new, more humane solution to our problem?"

"How does telling her that we are spies solve our problem?"

"Senta," he scolded in a low, disappointed voice. "Surely you understand my plan better than that. We've given her a part. Now let's let her play it. She will be my wife. Let's say we, uh . . . we were forced to marry a bit sooner than expected."

"Why?"

He offered her a sinister smirk. "Why are couples normally forced to marry with speed?"

"Oh, please," she begged sarcastically to the heavens, "please tell me that this is only an act and that you have not really impregnated the girl."

He gave her a sharp look of scorn.

"Oh, silly me," she mocked. "I should have known better. How could a man of steel possibly give in to his disgusting primal urges. Naturally, you've not touched her."

"Naturally," he agreed. "Now, publicly, we will announce that our decision to marry quickly was based on a mere whim. No one will believe that, so, of course, they will gossip about us and declare her with child. There is nothing quite like a minor scandal to detract from a major one. The more they talk about my rushed marriage, the less they'll talk about my politics."

"This is ridiculous," Senta exclaimed, hands on hips. "The girl is no spy. She can't be trusted with all of this, Erich! My word! From what I saw at the Winter Palace, she can't even play a role well! She's a terrible actress."

"She'll do fine," he grumbled. "She'll rarely need to make public appearances, and when she does, I'll make sure to cover for her."

"And if she decides to tell our little secret?"

"There's less danger of that when she's here," he pointed out, "than when she's running loose on the streets. As long as she lives here with me, both of us can keep a close eye on her. We'll have to worry about her much less than we do now."

"And if she doesn't agree to this?" Senta asked, her eyes now showing the weariness of interrupted sleep. "If she doesn't want to play the part of your wife?"

Erich looked surprised. "Oh, there's no question of that," he replied as though Senta should have guessed. "I don't intend to give her a choice."

Senta was relieved to see that he had maintained some rationality. To tell the girl that they were spies and then let her run off was unthinkable. She was glad that Erich had not lost sight of that despite his obvious infatuation with this girl. Yes, Senta could see it. Erich was talking patriotically about ensuring the success of the mission, but Senta was no fool. She could see what was going on here. Erich was looking forward to having that honey-eyed peasant in his bed. He was excited about this plan for reasons that had nothing to do with saving the mission. "It's dangerous," Senta announced at last, but her words were, in fact, a form of consent.

"I don't think so," he assured her. "I think it will be safer this way."

"And if one of us isn't around to keep an eye on her?"

Erich shrugged. "I'll tie her to the bed."

Senta shook her head in disbelief. Yes, Erich was going to enjoy this all right. Man of steel, huh? She knew it was an act. She'd always known it was an act.

Chapter 12

Tatiana took her time getting to Yura's the following night. She was afraid she had made a poor impression on Markov. She had babbled too much, a sign that she was nervous and eager to please. She had accepted every suggestion he made, a sign that she was desperate. She had even let him touch her. This she tried not to think about. It had been exciting, like flinging open the door of a locked estate. He had made her skin feel all tingly. No, it wasn't that she wished he hadn't touched her. She just hoped she hadn't seemed overly eager.

It was probably for this reason that Tatiana decided to go home before heading to Yura's, even though it was already very late. In the back of her mind, she feared he might not wait this long for her. But in the front of her mind, she was determined to take her time. Needless to say, she was startled when she found Markov in the alley, beside her bed, waiting for her. When she saw the black-clad figure, his coat blowing behind him in the breeze, she gave a little start. "What—what are you doing here?" She just couldn't help being glad to see him.

"I'm sorry," he said stiffly. "When you weren't at Yura's, I came directly here. I didn't have time to wait for you."

Something in his expression was so serious, Tatiana felt uneasy. He was always stiff, but he was more than that today. He was cold. His pale eyes were not blinking. His mouth was set in a mild frown. His hands were stuffed rigidly in the pockets of his black coat. "Well, uh, that's all right," Tatiana began. "I—"

"It's important," he interrupted. "We have to go to my house. Bring anything you care about, and come."

Tatiana was baffled. "What? Your house? I thought you didn't want me to go to—"

"Quickly!" he ordered. He reached for the bag that held her golden gown, then dropped a pair of boots on top of it, as though helping her pack.

"No, not those," she objected, snatching the boots. "Those are Lev's."

Erich scowled. He did not know she had a living mate and was disturbed, to say the least, that a boy was in the habit of leaving his boots here. But there was no time for that now.

"Is this your way of saying you want me to spend the night?" Tatiana asked, stuffing a satchel with the seven or eight items she owned and was not wearing.

"I'll explain later," he replied stiffly. "Be sure to take any meaningful items, gifts from your parents, that sort of thing. You may not be back for a while."

"I don't have anything like that. I . . . what?"

Erich explained. "Look. You said you wanted in on the deal. Well, you're in."

Tatiana needed no further push. She hiked the satchel over her shoulder.

Erich relieved her of her satchel, insisting that he carry it for her. Tatiana objected to this at first, not because she didn't appreciate good manners, but because living on the streets, she had developed a suspicion of people trying to relieve her of her belongings. Instinctively, she thought he was trying to steal them. Even after they had walked some way, she kept an eye on him to make sure he didn't bolt with her satchel in hand. It wasn't until they arrived safely at his front door that she relaxed. Markov fumbled for his key.

"Oh, don't worry about that." Tatiana grinned, retrieving her picklock from a pocket. With a mischievous light in her eye, she sprung the lock in just a few easy seconds.

Erich's face, though lacking a smile, held a certain expression of humor. "You're really a showoff," he teased, marching through the open door. Tatiana held it open for him with a silly bow.

"You should tighten up your security," she announced playfully.

"I plan to," he replied with a strange darkness crossing his face. Tatiana was startled by a sudden frost that seemed to harden his features. He did not look angry. Not angry at all. He looked incapable of emotion, incapable of any emotion. His calm but powerful arm slammed the door shut behind her. He motioned toward the parlor and offered a shallow, polite bow. "Please."

Tatiana entered the parlor with a trembling in her stomach. Something was wrong, she just knew it. This was no ordinary crime ring he was involved in. This was serious. She held a vague worry that it might be a trap. "Yes?" she asked meekly, settling into the chair and looking up at him with wide eyes.

Erich drew the curtains, then turned to face the frightened girl. His eyes were distant. Hers were anxious. "My name is Erich Reitz. I am a servant of von Bismarck's, and a retired soldier in the Prussian Army." With hands clasped firmly behind his back, he waited for this first dose of information to sink in. When he saw that Tatiana's eyes were quite frozen and that she was not likely to speak, he continued. "Some of my Prussian brothers were sent ahead of me to determine the viability of a 'Russian threat' to our empire. Russia was kind enough to remain neutral during my countrymen's spat with France, but there is some fear that should it happen again, Russia would side with our enemy. Since in all likelihood we will find ourselves at war with France again, we thought it necessary to determine once and for all what we could expect in terms of a Russian reaction. My 'brothers' returned with the unfortunate news that Russians were experiencing a cultural love affair with France and were not likely to remain neutral the next time we find ourselves at odds with our western neighbors. Naturally, a two-front war would be disastrous for my country. Therefore, it is in our best interest to improve relations with this powerful eastern neighbor. But at the same time we mustn't sit still and let Russia's strength increase, knowing as we do that we are destined to find ourselves at odds one day.''

Now Tatiana just looked confused.

''That's where I came in,'' he explained. ''We were sent to analyze and exploit Russia's weaknesses from the inside, so that we could wage war without losing any soldiers and without giving them cause to cross our borders in anger. Do you understand?''

Tatiana blinked rapidly. ''You mean you're not Russian?''

Erich's head fell into his hands. Had she understood one word that he'd said? Could she really be this ignorant? ''Right,'' he said at last, looking up from his palms as though he might either laugh or scream.

''But you speak Russian so well!''

A smile now crossed his lips. ''Thank you.'' A few bobs of his head later, he added, ''Do you understand what I've just told you?''

''I . . . I'm not sure,'' she hedged, biting and playing with her lip. ''How . . . how do you speak Russian so well if you're not really from here?''

Erich groaned. ''Do you think they would have sent me here if I couldn't overcome my German accent?'' He shook his head, letting his frustration scatter to the wind. ''I'm sorry,

Tatiana," he said, a flicker of humanity shining through his chiseled face. "I'm sure this is all very confusing to you. Why don't you just go ahead and ask me your questions. I promise to be patient."

"Where is Prussia?"

That almost made him break his promise. He gave her one pleading look, as though praying her question had been only in jest. But when he saw that she was genuinely curious, he swallowed his pain and answered. "We're the country just west of you."

"Oh." She pondered this for a moment. "I thought that was Germany."

"Excellent!" he exclaimed, eyes filling with hope. "You've heard of Germany? That's good. That's a very good start. All right, then. Well, Prussia is ... well, to make things simple ... let's say it's"—he recoiled—"part of Germany."

"Then you're German?"

"Prussian!" he scolded. Then, clearing his throat, he added with regained formality, "Technically, as you say, all Germans are united under the kaiser. But Prussia is by far the most important state in the *Reich*. And without us the other Germans would be little more than helpless deer waiting to be hunted by their neighbors."

"Well, if you're German, then how come you don't speak German?" she asked.

"I do speak German!" he cried. "Will you please ask about something else! For God's sake, woman, I just told you I'm trying to destroy your country! Doesn't that draw any response from you?"

Tatiana wasn't sure why he was so angry. But he wanted another question, so she asked the first one that came to mind. "What's Germany like?"

"Prussia!" he shouted. "Prussia!"

"All right, don't get so angry," she said, pulling her knees to her chest. "What's Prussia like, then?"

He rubbed his tired eyes and moaned. "It's ... it's filled with sensible people who are concerned when their country is being infiltrated by spies. I don't know." He dropped his hand. "It's nice," he said, "it's a nice country. I'll tell you all about it sometime. But first we have something more important to discuss. Much more important." His demeanor was no longer suitable for a interrogator, or even a man who was preparing to threaten a young girl into silence. He looked tired and frustrated, but he had to regain his composure. "The issue at hand is this," he explained. "You are a liability to us as long as you are wandering freely on the streets, telling people tales about how I took you to a ball."

"I never told!" she shouted, rising to her feet. She was mortally insulted by the implication that she would ever break a promise.

"I trust that," he said, placing a hand between himself and her. "But the point is, my partner doesn't. Sit back down." His expression was so firm that no one would have considered disobeying. Tatiana was no exception. "Now," he continued, "there is a solution. There is a way for you not only to cease being a liability, but in fact to aid our cause in some small way."

Tatiana's face showed a distinct willingness to listen. This was the good part, she knew. This was the job.

"You will play the role of my wife," he announced, causing Tatiana to freeze in her anticipation. "You will live here, and you will do as I say. Should anyone ask, we will explain our hurried wedding by saying that your mother's failing health had gotten worse, and we feared she would not be alive to attend the ceremony if we didn't rush."

Tatiana was still waiting for him to finish. There was a long, awkward pause before she spoke up. "Well, all right. That's my cover story. So what's my job?"

"That is your job," he replied dryly. "To stay where we can keep an eye on you."

Tatiana frowned. "Well, that doesn't sound like a very exciting job."

Erich shrugged. "I didn't promise it would be exciting."

"Well . . ." she stumbled. "Well . . . well . . . can't I at least break a safe open for you or something?"

"We have no need for that," he replied. "But if it makes you feel more useful, let me assure you that having you around will significantly enhance my alibi."

Tatiana shook her head with disgust. "Well, all of that sounds fine, I suppose. But how much will you pay me?"

"Nothing," he answered, "except, of course, you'll be housed, clothed, and fed."

Tatiana looked at him as though he must be mad. "Hey, when I said I'd work for a small percentage, I didn't mean zero! You've got to do better than that."

"Feeding you and clothing you will cut a bit into my earnings," he assured her. "That's sort of like getting a percentage."

"I suppose it would be," she agreed, rising to her feet, "except for one little problem. I'm not planning to live here!"

"You must," he replied calmly. "There's no other option. I can't have my 'wife' seen sleeping somewhere else."

"Yes, there is another option," she argued. "I can turn down your stupid deal! And that's exactly what I'm going to do. You know, you have a lot of nerve, dragging me down here to convince me to take a job that pays nothing. I mean, did you really think I was just going to leave all my friends behind, leave my whole life, and move in with you—for nothing?"

"I'm afraid you don't fully understand," he said, his voice touched by regret.

"Oh, yes, I do," she objected, moving toward the door. "I understand perfectly. You want me to help you out but you don't want to pay me for it. Believe me, I know all about lousy deals."

"What do you know about threats?" he asked, stuffing his hand pointedly in his coat pocket.

Tatiana's eyes flung wide. She looked at his pocket and knew he had a gun. Then she looked at his stony face and knew that he might use the weapon.

"Move away from the door," he said casually, almost as though he regretted having to say it. "Come on"—he nodded—"I said move away."

Tatiana had a moment of doubt. She glanced at the door, realizing this would be her last chance to make a run for it. Then she looked back at him, worrying that she might get shot before she reached the handle.

"Don't do that," he said, observing her quandary. "I don't like to bluff, Tatiana. So I'll tell you outright that I have no intention of killing you." He bit his lower lip as he forced out his next words. "But I have sacrificed most of my humanity for the sake of my country." His steady gaze held no sign of the deep regret he felt about finishing this speech. "I would certainly be willing to sacrifice your leg." With frighteningly glassy eyes, he lowered his aim.

Tatiana lifted her chin. She was caught. Erich was a killer, she was certain of it. He would pull that trigger in an instant. She could see it in his fixed features, in his stony cheekbones, in his stiff chin and his regal nose. He had done this before. Tatiana's parents had not raised a fool. And so she moved away from the door and toward Erich. Anger made her face hot and flushed. Fear made her tremble. "Last night I thought we were . . . friends," she dared to say.

"We are," he replied.

She shook her head slowly and bitterly. "And just like that," she asked, "just like that you can pull a gun on a friend?"

"If duty requires it . . ."

"Just like that?" she repeated.

His final nod was a stiff one. "Yes. Just like that," he replied, his eyes filled with pride over his own callousness. "Now get upstairs,'' he ordered angrily. His anger was at himself. ''I'm too tired to argue with you. Someday you'll see I've done you a favor.''

''Nothing is worse than someone who would betray a friend! Nothing!'' she accused.

Erich felt no love for Tatiana at that moment. She was not his soft angel or his tender little girl. She was a demon, a creature sent from the netherworld to taunt him for what he had become. What he had been forced to become. ''Except a man who would betray his country,'' he corrected her in a menacing whisper. ''Now get upstairs.''

One glimpse at Erich's callous face, hardened into ice except where anger sparked and melted it, told Tatiana that he was on the verge of hitting her. She knew that look. And so she stormed upstairs to his bedroom.

Chapter 13

"I hope you know," Tatiana announced, crossing her arms firmly, "that I'm not going to let you touch me again. Not ever again! Not now that I know you're a liar and a traitor to your friends!"

Erich was shaving at the basin, trying not to cut himself. "Has it occurred to you," he asked with controlled annoyance, "that you're not in a position to deny me anything?" He continued about the task of shaving while keeping a close eye on his prisoner. He remembered with unease how she had once leapt from a second-story window. He would not allow such a thing to happen again.

"Why not?" she demanded. She was sitting on the edge of his bed, fully prepared to sleep beside him. After years of lying next to Lev at night, she saw nothing in the least bit strange about a man and a woman sharing bed space. In fact, she wasn't sure she could sleep at all if she were alone. That Erich might believe lying beside him was a sign of willingness to make love did not occur to her. "I'll have you know," she threatened, "that I'm a pretty good fighter. And I know exactly where to hit a man to make it hurt. So if I were you, I'd keep my hands to myself."

Erich rolled his eyes. It was an expression uncharacteristic of him, but he was not feeling like himself tonight. "I have no intention of bedding you," he announced, wiping his freshly shaven face with a towel. "Our arrangement is strictly business." He couldn't possibly justify touching an innocent girl as being part of his patriotic duty, could he? He thought about it for a moment. No, no chance of that. "Very well, then," he said resignedly, turning to his captive. "Did you bring clothes for sleeping? You may change privately in the closet, where there are no windows for you to break." This last part he added with a goading look.

Tatiana frowned. "I can't afford to have just-for-sleeping clothes, you know. Anything I have, I wear all day."

Erich looked puzzled. He should have thought of that, of course. But he was such a clean man, it was hard for him to imagine sleeping in clothes that had been exposed to the elements all day long. "Hmm." he frowned. "We'll have to take care of that tomorrow. But tonight you can wear one of my shirts. It should cover you well enough."

"I'm comfortable like this," Tatiana insisted, flopping backward to test the mattress. She had never in her entire life slept on a real mattress. She didn't know whether it would be comfortable or not, but she thought it was fun, the way it bounced.

"You can't sleep like that," he replied dryly, "not on my bed. And take your boots off. I'll get a clean shirt."

"I don't want one of your shirts," she argued hotly. "I like sleeping in my clothes."

"It won't be indecent," he promised her, yanking open a stiff drawer.

"I don't care about that," she retorted. "I just don't want to wear anything that belongs to you!"

Erich found his heart aching in a most peculiar way. He hadn't known that a woman's scorn would affect him after all these years of isolation. But it truly did. He was sorry that she hated him so. It even, he admitted, hurt a little bit to hear her spit out her anger. But naturally, he did not let this affect his professionalism. "Here is a shirt," he said, tossing it to her with forced gentleness. He swung open a closet door. "And here is your opportunity for privacy. Please use it." Then he turned away from her and saw to the task of removing his own clothes. After he'd unfastened all his shirt buttons and sensed that Tatiana had not yet moved, he stated, "You're not sleeping in my bed with filthy clothes on. Change them or I'll change them for you."

It was then that he heard her move toward the closet. After the door shut, he paused a moment with his own undressing. He had to consider something very odd. How much clothing should he remove? Normally, he would have removed all of it, or all save his leggings, depending on the weather. But what should he do with Tatiana sleeping in the room? If she were there as his lover, he would remove everything. If she were there as a guest, he would sleep elsewhere. But how does one undress before a political captive? The term made him smile. Imagine hotheaded, sweet-hearted Tatiana as a political captive. The image was impossible. No. She was merely a new partner. An unwilling partner at this moment, yes. But still, he decided, he should consider her a partner. Like Senta, only . . . only she was Tatiana.

He threw off his shirt and shoes and left the rest on. In a moment he heard a timid voice calling, "Markov? Or . . . Erich? Whoever you are? Will you come here for a second?"

Trying to erase the smile from his lips, Erich moved toward the closet door. "Yes?" he asked sternly.

"This shirt," she said softly, "this shirt doesn't cover me." She opened the door a crack so he could see the problem but left it closed enough that he couldn't see it well.

Erich was not the sort for playing games. If he were going to observe a problem, he wanted a full view of it. So he forced the door farther ajar and then immediately spied the dilemma. He had thought the shirt would be long enough for her, since his torso was a good bit lengthier than hers, but he had not taken into consideration the extent to which her breasts would hike it up. Poor Tatiana was pulling the shirt taut against her chest, trying to hide what otherwise would have been in Erich's plain view. "I see what you mean," he observed stiffly, then allowed Tatiana to close the door. "I'll get you something else to wear." He searched his drawer for a pair of clean leggings.

It was much better this way, he thought anxiously. For he had just gotten a glimpse at her full, shapely legs and did not want to be tortured by their naked presence all night long. Leggings would be just the thing. Unfortunately, he had not anticipated how adorable a young woman could look in a man's clothes. Tatiana emerged from the closet, clad in his silk shirt, ballooning around her, and his skin-tight leggings. She looked round and playful and, strangely, more feminine than if she'd been wearing a gown. "Fine," he choked out, "let's sleep." Then, as quickly as he could, he extinguished the lanterns.

Tatiana was feeling a bit out of sorts herself. Erich had worried about his state of undress because he feared that a woman would be intimidated by a half-naked man. Intimidated in the sense of feeling threatened or insulted. But it had never occurred to him that Tatiana would feel lustful at the sight of his bare skin. Erich had forgotten that he was a handsome man. In fact, he had secretly suspected that hardship and imprisonment had robbed him of his looks. But he was very wrong. Tatiana was invigorated by the sight of his bare upper body. She had known he was huge but had never suspected his mass would be so well defined. Every muscle on his arms was distinct and round. His chest and stomach were rippled with tight lines and brushed with just enough hair. His leggings did a lot to flatter his strong, round buttocks. And from what she could see of his thickly corded legs . . . this would certainly be nothing like sleeping beside Lev.

"I'm sorry to do this," he muttered, moving toward her with a rope. He gently pushed her into a full recline, sliding pillows under her head. "But I'm too sound a sleeper to trust that I would wake if you ran off." He held her hand as a doctor might a patient's. His eyes were warm and sympathetic. "I don't mean to cause you discomfort," he assured her, "but I'm afraid it's necessary." He dangled the ropes for her to see.

Tatiana swallowed hard. "I—I won't run off."

"I'm sorry," he repeated quietly. Then he pulled her wrists together and secured them with an expert knot. He was very careful with his work, making certain that while firm, the ropes would not cut into her skin. Tatiana was almost inspired by the careful way in which he worked. She couldn't help wondering about all the dangerous spying missions he'd been on. Of course, she wasn't exactly sure what spies did, but she now imagined it must be very exciting.

For a moment, he considered tying the freshly secured wrists to a bedpost. But the more he pondered it, the more he felt that was too suggestive a pose to leave her in. He didn't want her to feel he was taking advantage of the situation. And so he secured her wrists to her waist instead, wrapping them tightly against her pelvis. He bound her ankles in a similar fashion, then concluded that though it was still possible for her to hop away from the bed, she would be unlikely to do so without bouncing a great deal and making enough noise to wake him. "Do you think you'll be able to sleep?" he asked, genuinely concerned.

"No," she replied stubbornly, "but it has nothing to do with the ropes. I just want to go home."

"You didn't have a home," he reminded her.

"Yes, I did," she insisted through clenched teeth. "You just don't understand."

He sighed deeply, then planted a tender kiss on her forehead. "If you get thirsty, or need to relieve yourself, wake me up."

Tatiana turned her head away from him in protest of the kiss. So he climbed in bed beside her without another word. He lay as far from her as he could manage and clasped his hands behind his head. Sleep never came easily to him, not since prison. And tonight, it would be even worse, for he was not accustomed to having a bed partner. Why it didn't bother Tatiana more was a mystery to him. He almost wanted to ask what made her so at ease but decided it was best not to say another word to her until morning. Perhaps by then she would have forgiven him and realized that her life would be better now.

Erich had lain awake for a good long while, staring at the ceiling, when, to his surprise, Tatiana spoke. "Erich?"

"Hmm?"

"Aren't you going to open the curtains?"

He looked at the thick blue wool that covered the windows. Only the faintest light of the moon made it past them into the dusty room. "Mmm, I don't know," he grumbled drowsily. "Why?"

Tatiana's voice was also a bit sleepy. "I can't sleep without looking at the stars," she said meekly.

Something about that touched Erich, and he found himself rising to his feet. He pulled back the curtains, only to be startled by the bright moonlight beyond. It was as though someone had lit a lantern. "Is that better?" He squinted.

"Uh-huh." She enjoyed the view of Erich's unclad body glowing like an illuminated statue in the moonlight. She was disappointed when he climbed back to bed. They both breathed heavily for several minutes. Then, "Erich?"

"Yes?" he answered a bit more expectantly this time.

"I can't smell any fresh air in here."

"What? Are you joking?" He scowled. "There's no fresh

air anywhere in St. Petersburg with all these factories. The air
is probably cleaner in here than out there.''

He turned his head and saw Tatiana's golden face shining
in the moonlight. She looked like a cherub, so wide-eyed and
soft. ''All right,'' he grumbled, rising once again to his feet.
Grudgingly, he pushed open the window, letting a burst of
freezing air blow right into his naked chest. ''Oh, that's wonderful,'' he moaned, crossing his arms. He hurried back to bed
and pulled the blankets up to his neck.

''Erich?'' he heard after another moment.

''What?'' he nearly shouted.

Tatiana blinked her long black lashes adorably. ''Thank you
for opening the window.''

Erich relaxed, then felt the overwhelming urge to put his
arm around the girl. But he did not. Her wrists and ankles were
bound. With her in such a helpless state, it would be wrong to
touch her even so much as that. He had learned to tie knots so
he could keep witnesses from escaping, after all, not so he
could prevent pretty girls from resisting his advances. He kept
his sturdy hands to himself.

Strangely, the cool night air did not keep him awake as he
had feared. Instead, it had the unexpected effect of calming
him, as did the bright glow of the moon. Erich fell asleep faster
that night than he had in a very long time. It was Tatiana who
could not sleep. She kept wondering about Lev, what he must
be thinking. He would certainly be worried when she hadn't
come home by morning. Would he go looking for her? She
wished she could tell him she was all right. But even more,
she wished she could go home and stay there. But she knew
that even if she could somehow get out of this house, she could
not go home. Erich knew where she lived and knew where she
drank. This was a terrible fix. Her only hope was to convince
him to let her go, and he did not seem the sort who could be
easily convinced of anything.

She turned her head from the moonlight and saw Erich sleeping soundly beside her. He was wonderfully handsome, she decided. If God had used cotton to make her own soft face, then He surely had used ice or stone to make Erich's. Every line was carefully sculpted, creating cheekbones that were high and hard, creating a strong chin that was carefully indented at the cleft, creating a nose that was sturdy and straight. Tatiana looked enviously at his silvery-blond hair. Why should a man get to have such silky yellow hair when she, who needed it more, was given only tangled brown locks. His eyes were closed, but she could remember the magnificent color that lay beneath his lids. It was as though he weren't human. He was like a creature chiseled from a perfect block of ice, then brought to life by otherworldly lights that shone through his strange eyes.

She couldn't help wondering at the strength of the body she had observed before the blankets had so cruelly concealed it. How much would it hurt if he punched someone? A lot, she decided. She would really like to see that someday. Not that she wished anyone harm, but she was devilishly curious to see such a strong man fight. She remembered his sturdy legs. Then she began to wonder about something else, something she felt she wasn't supposed to wonder at. But she couldn't help it. She had never seen a fully naked man before. And seeing Erich tonight had surely aroused her curiosity. What exactly would she see if Erich were to take off those leggings? She had a vague notion but could not quite conjure a picture.

"Why are you staring at me?" Erich asked, eyes still closed. He had awakened several minutes before to the feeling of being watched.

"I'm not staring," she protested.

"Yes, you were," he chuckled. "What were you staring at?"

Tatiana thought fast. "I . . . I was staring to see what sort of man would hold a friend hostage!"

"I don't believe you," he said. But he took careful note of the fact that she had said friend. He rather liked that.

"I don't care whether you believe me," she exclaimed.

Erich moaned. "Look. I have work to do in the morning, so if you don't mind, I'd like to get some sleep."

Tatiana looked puzzled. "And what am I supposed to do while you're at work?"

"Senta will look after you."

"Who is Senta?"

"Irina."

Tatiana pouted mightily, though with her back turned to him, Erich could not see it. "I want a code name too," she announced.

"What?" he asked with no small degree of exasperation. "What are you babbling about?"

"I'm not babbling," she insisted. "If I'm going to be a spy with you, then I want a code name."

"Why?"

"Because everyone else gets one!"

Erich rubbed his forehead. "Can we talk about this tomorrow?" he asked, flustered.

"Of course," she replied haughtily. "I'm not the one who **told** you to wake up. Go back to sleep."

Erich felt more tired now than he had the last time he fell asleep. The girl was exhausting. The good news, he thought, yawning heavily, was that with his days filled by Tatiana, he was likely to welcome sleep each night. And he might even be too tired to have dreams. "Sleep well," he said courteously before shutting his eyes.

"I will as long as you don't snore," she informed him. "And if you do, I'll kick you."

"Very well," he groaned, feeling confident that it wouldn't be a problem. "Good night."

There was a long pause, and then, "Erich?"

"Please go to sleep."

"Erich?"

"I'm begging you. In the name of whatever is holy, will you go to sleep?"

"Then I guess you don't want to know that your house is on fire?"

"What?!" He sat up straight.

"Just kidding," she giggled. "I only wanted a drink of water."

Erich was ready to bang his head against a wall. Or at least put a gag in the girl's mouth. "I thought you were the captive," he grumbled, rising to do her bidding.

"Well, if you would untie me, I wouldn't have to wake you," she reminded him.

Erich ignored that remark. "Is there anything else you'll need while I'm up?" he asked. "Make up your mind now."

"No, that's all," she replied casually, enjoying the sight of his scarcely covered body stomping around the room. When he returned with her water, she thanked him, then tried to annoy him with loud, slurping sips. Erich would not take the bait. He forced himself at least to appear to be sleeping soundly, faced entirely away from her. He let the slurps and "ahhs" go unnoticed. But when at last she said "Erich?" he nearly exploded.

"What?" he shouted loudly enough to make her want to cover her ears.

"Nothing important," she assured him meekly, pretending to cower from his temper. "I just wondered what I should do with the glass now that I'm finished with it."

"I don't know," he growled. "Why don't you tap on it all night!"

"I'm sensing anger," she said coyly. "Have I done something to upset you?"

He scowled down at her, having no doubt now that she was doing this on purpose. If he didn't put a stop to it right then, she would continue all night, and all the following night as well. He had no wish to harm her, but he knew that if he did not establish his dominance, he would never get another peaceful night's rest. "Listen," he said sternly, moving his face uncomfortably close to hers. "If you keep me awake any longer, I'm going to assume you're wanting me to bed you." At her gasp, he replied, "Why else would you be so determined to keep me awake? Now go to sleep before I oblige you." When he saw her shock, he fell onto his side, determined, at last, to find sleep.

It had been an ugly threat and one he had not wanted to make. But it worked. The girl did not say another word. And wasn't that what his job was all about? Using any means at his disposal to achieve the best results? *God,* he thought, just before losing consciousness, *I really do hate myself.*

Chapter 14

When Erich awoke, he had the pleasant sensation that there was something to look forward to. It had been a long time since he'd felt that. The sunlight shining brightly in his eyes seemed to welcome him to the day. Why had he never opened those curtains before? It was so nice to wake up encompassed in particles of sunlight. He turned his head to see a comfortably sleeping Tatiana. He wanted to brush the hair from her eyes so he could see her whole face. She looked so pretty in the morning light, all curled up like a kitten in his oversized clothes. He would like to have kissed her good morning. But he knew that he could not. Still, he felt invigorated just knowing that she was there. Just knowing that she would still be there when he got home. There was something to fill his life besides work. "Wake up," he whispered, daring only to brush her cheek with the back of his hand. "Wake up," he repeated, giving her a gentle shake.

This time she groaned. Squinting, and raising a hand to keep the sun from her eyes, she said, "Oh, no, it's you. I was hoping it had only been a dream.'' With a moan, she closed her eyes again.

"You have to get dressed," he informed her. "I have to leave for work, and Senta will be here soon to watch you.''

"I don't need a nursemaid," she grunted.

"No, but you need a guard. So, come on. Get up." He rose to his feet and rolled his shoulders a couple of times. They were always so tight. "Get up," he repeated. "You'll have to wear your old clothes today, but I'll bring home some dresses. And a nightgown," he added after a moment's thought. He stretched his neck with a little wince.

Tatiana grudgingly stumbled from the bed. She had not enjoyed sleeping on the mattress. She wasn't used to it, and it seemed to make her back hurt. She hunched toward her clothes, not even looking up at Erich. She hated mornings. It always took her at least an hour of shuffling around before she was willing to speak with anyone. Lev was the same way, so it had never bothered him. "Hurry," Erich urged her, strapping on his belt.

"I could probably go faster," she sulked, "if my ankles hadn't been tied together all night. I don't think they have any blood in them.''

"Yes, they do," he replied sternly. "I checked your circulation when I tied them. You should have no trouble walking.''

"Thank you for informing me that I'm not in pain," she said, sliding her breeches over Erich's underwear. "I guess if you say it doesn't hurt, it must not.''

"That's right," Erich agreed cheerfully. "Now, finish up. I can't leave without breakfast. I have a big appetite in the morning.''

"Do I get to eat too?" she asked, tiredly lacing up her boots. "Or do captives get only gruel?''

"That depends on how well they behave," he answered flippantly. "An obedient captive might get as many as . . . three meals a day.'' With a hand on her elbow, he led her toward the stairway.

"What's for breakfast?'' she asked, trotting behind him down the stairs.

"I think it's potato pancakes,'' he replied with some regret. "I don't think I have the fixings for anything else today.''

"Why don't you have any servants?'' she asked, peering into the gloomy, windowless kitchen.

"Can't afford them,'' he answered matter-of-factly. He scooted by her into the kitchen and fumbled for the necessary cooking utensils. For some reason, Tatiana preferred to linger in the doorway. Something about that kitchen made her uneasy.

"Why don't you just move into a smaller house so you can afford a servant?''

"Can't,'' he said, reaching for a knife. "I have to look as though I've no shortage of money. It would be strange for me to live in a small house, but as long as I don't invite anyone inside, they don't need to know about the servants. Hand me that spoon?''

Tatiana did so, but with a thousand questions rattling her mind. "Are you poor? I mean, in Prussia, were you poor?''

"I wouldn't say that,'' he answered brightly, "I was about average.''

"What did your father do?''

Erich's neck stiffened and his eyes closed. When he opened them, he set himself firmly on the task of making breakfast. "I don't see that as any of your concern,'' he answered bitterly.

"Why not? I thought all the secrecy was over now.''

"You may ask anything you wish about my job!'' he belted out. "But that's all.''

Tatiana widened her eyes in an almost comical expression. "Could you put the knife down when you shout at me?'' she asked.

He hadn't realized he was holding it but now looked at his hand. He returned to the task of chopping onions. Sensing that she would be ignored, Tatiana stomped into the parlor. "That's far enough," he called calmly without lifting his head. "Stay where I can see you."

Tatiana gave him a phony salute, then flopped into a chair. She wondered what she would do all day. She wondered whether Irina, or Senta as she was now called, would be friendly. Surely, her company would be livelier than Erich's. Erich emerged from the kitchen with a rag and hurriedly wiped off the coffee table in front of Tatiana. Tatiana smiled at his meticulous nature. She had always been more of a casual sort herself. "You know," Erich grumbled, planting a glass of water before her, "it does seem a little strange for me to be cooking, when there's a perfectly competent woman in the house."

"I'm a thief." Tatiana shrugged. "If you want a loaf of bread, I'll steal one for you. But don't ask me how to bake one."

Erich frowned but did not argue. "It seems you ought to be able to cook Russian food better than a German can," was all he muttered.

"I thought you were Prussian?" she said, pointing a playfully accusing finger in his direction. "I thought you didn't like being called German."

"For God's sake," he moaned, "I'll be gone to work in a few minutes. Can't I have peace until then?" He shuffled back into the kitchen to retrieve their pancakes.

"You know what I think?" she called in between sips of water. "I think you're just so used to living alone that you think it's strange to hear someone talk!"

Erich returned with two plates of food and placed them on the only table in the house, the coffee table. "Could you sit on the floor?" he asked Tatiana. "I prefer to sit on the chair while I eat. My legs don't bend as easily as a woman's."

"I prefer sitting in a chair too," she announced, tearing off a giant piece of pancake with her fingers.

"Yes, but it's my house."

"Not anymore," she taunted him, licking her fingers. "You said I have to live here with you. I said no, but you said I had to. So now it's our house." Despite his earlier comments, Erich's cooking was delicious. The pancakes were fluffy and sweet, and the potatoes within had just the right grainy texture.

"I suppose it would be useless," he scowled, finally taking his seat, "to ask you to use utensils." He observed in disgust the ways she picked at her food with bare fingers.

Suddenly, there was a knock on the door. "Thank God," he announced, rising to his feet, "you're Senta's problem now."

Tatiana stuck out her tongue at his turned back. "I saw that," he stated to her surprise. Then he opened the door. "I'm very glad to see you," he greeted the little blonde before him.

"So am I!" Tatiana yelled. "More glad than he is!"

Senta raised an eyebrow at her partner. He shook his head in reply, as though it were too painful to discuss. But Senta was not blind to the extra glow in his face this morning. He looked as though he had actually gotten a good night's rest. "It's nice to see you again, Tatiana," she said as Erich removed her coat.

Erich felt a little pang at hearing her say that. Only a few days ago, she had wanted to kill Tatiana. Now she was offering the girl a false show of friendship. "I hope Erich's planning to get you some nicer clothes." She grinned with a wink. Erich's expression was grave. His face said plainly that he resented Senta's good cheer. He thought just a little less of her than he had before. Senta's heart sank when she noticed his thoughts, but she did not let that stop her performance. "How are you, Tatiana?"

"Terrible!" the girl cried, causing Erich to roll his eyes. "He even tried to suffocate me!"

Erich gave her a look of annoyed puzzlement. "Wait a minute. I never did that."

"Erich!" Senta couldn't believe this even of her mentally anguished partner.

"That's right!" Tatiana cried. "Protect me from him! Please!"

Erich grabbed his coat.

"But wait, I . . ."

Erich closed the door firmly behind him. He could hear Tatiana's wailing cease the moment he was gone.

"Don't you have work too?" Tatiana asked Senta. "I thought you were both spies."

"We are," Senta replied cynically. "You could say I take the night shift."

Tatiana, of course, had no idea what that meant. "I see," she said. "Then shouldn't you be sleeping during the day?"

Senta stretched out across Erich's couch. "That's what I intend to do," she announced, "just as soon as Erich comes home."

"I guess he told you not to let me get away, huh?"

"Yes." Senta sighed and let her eyes close a little. She desperately wanted sleep. Last night had been a perfect nightmare.

For weeks, she had been pursuing Tomasz Muronov. It had been a complex seduction, but finally she had made her way into his trust. She hadn't expected last night to be any different from the other nights she'd spent with him, but it was. Since his stay in St. Petersburg was a short one, he had rented a room. Senta had gone to see him, as always, and was just removing her stockings, when he said something remarkable. "Irina?" he asked. "Would you have any means of leaving Russia if you had to?"

Senta was more than a little surprised. Her eyes opened wide, and one stocking still clinging to her leg, she answered, "I don't think so. Why on earth do you ask?"

He was pacing pensively, as though something horrible had just happened and he was debating whether to tell her. "It's just this," he said, "I believe the tsar's life is in danger, and"—he swallowed hard, looking uncomfortable, almost pained—"and his son will be the next tsar, Alexander III."

Senta tried to look calm, though she was positively drooling for information. She gave him a bubbling shrug and said, "So?"

"Irina," he said, grabbing her by the shoulders. "I just don't want you to get hurt."

"You silly!" she laughed, pinching his belly. "Why would I get hurt?"

"This is very hard to say," he told her in earnest, the weight of his message showing painfully on his face. "I—I'm afraid that we will soon have a new tsar, and—"

"And what, silly?"

"And . . . and he's a madman."

"What?" Senta cried that out with more urgency than she'd intended.

"I know it's frightening," he continued, "but I am afraid I've had the misfortune of speaking at some length with the man. He's . . . he's hungry for power. He wants to undo all the good his father has done. He wants to put the peasants 'back in their place.' He . . . he will refuel the fires of the revolutionaries. There will be nothing but more trouble and more division when he comes to power. I don't want you to get caught in it."

"But the tsar's not going to die," she said stupidly, a dumb grin on her face.

Tomasz bowed his head gravely. "I hope you are right, of course. But I fear you are wrong. The Will of the People is not a joke, and it will not go away."

"Who's that?" she asked falsely.

"I can't go into it," he said, to her disappointment. "The tsar doesn't take them seriously anyhow. I'm the only one of his advisers who has told him to tighten security. The others just scoff and call the Will of the People 'those thankless peasants.' If I can't get him to listen to me, I—'' He lifted a hand to her face and looked deeply into her eyes. "Irina," he whispered hoarsely, "I swear ... whatever else happens, I swear, I will get you out of here."

"Out of here?" She tried to laugh. There was something about the way he was looking at her that made Senta very uncomfortable.

"Yes," he assured her. "I know you love your country. We all do. But if anything happens, well, it just won't be safe here anymore."

Senta backed toward the bed, dragging him with her by the hand. "You sure are talking gloomy," she said. "Why don't you just let me loosen you up a little."

He was a man, so naturally he accepted her invitation. He watched as she stood on the bed, stripping down to complete nudity. Every time she pulled off a piece of clothing, she wiggled whatever was freshly revealed, trying cheerfully to distract him from his worries. A silly smile warped her intelligent face. "Come on," she teased once she had nothing left to remove, "it's no fun dancing alone."

Tomasz fell on her like a brick. He squeezed her breasts with enthusiasm, kissed her mouth and ears with impatience, then wiggled his way inside her. Senta was still playing her part, letting out little oh's and ah's, to give the impression that he was surprising her with his virility. She was letting him bounce her up and down, giggling from time to time at the incessant movement. Then he lifted his head and said, "I love you, Irina. I will rescue you, I will take you away from here."

Irina's face turned into Senta's. There was no silliness on those lips now, no bubbles in the eyes. "Don't," she whispered in her true voice, "don't say that. Don't say you love me."

"But I do," he insisted. "I see the real you, Irina."

"That's ... that's impossible," she whispered in return, placing her hands on his shoulders as though to push him away.

"No." He shook his head passionately. His brown eyes were

filled with warmth and appreciation. "I see the real you. Not 'Irina the lover,' who tries to please me, but 'Irina the woman,' who lies deep within. I see her."

"No, you don't." She was shaking her head wildly.

"Yes." He kissed her gently. "Yes, I do. I love you, Irina. And that cannot be undone. It is forever so."

Senta shut her eyes tightly, trying to regain control of herself, trying to remember her part. At last, she said in Irina's voice, "I'm sure someday you'll meet a girl who's right for you, Tomasz. You know you can't marry a lady like me, for goodness' sake, huh?" She slapped his back as though it were all a big joke.

"I can do whatever I want," he said, smiling, "and from now on, I shall hire you every night so that you will never sleep in the arms of another."

This was good for the mission, she told herself all night long. She needed to spend lots of time with this man. He was important. This was an excellent turn of events . . . for the mission. She was doing the right thing, accepting his business night after night. This was her job. But she did not sleep a wink. And now she was having to keep her tired eyes fixed on the brat her partner had captured. Her partner. Sometimes she could swear that it was she who did all the truly hard work while he just put on a uniform and went to meetings. It didn't seem fair. If she had been a man, she could have done the same work that Erich did. She could be the one sweet-talking councilmen while they still had their clothes on. She could be the one who served her country without being called a harlot for it. She could have made her father proud. . . .

"Why don't you and Erich get married?" Tatiana asked. "You spend so much time together anyway. And you're so pretty."

"Thank you," Senta replied dryly, "but Erich and I are not in love. He prefers curvier women, and I prefer . . . humans."

Tatiana giggled. "Erich's not human?"

"I doubt it." Senta scowled. "But I think they're still running tests."

Tatiana decided she liked Senta. She had a sharpness about her. She wasn't the sort of fluffy, airheaded woman Tatiana had always disliked. No, she was a hardheaded sort—and a real spy at that! "Well, I think he might just be shy," Tatiana admitted, surprised to find herself defending Erich. "I bet he'd talk a lot more if you really got to know him." She looked at Senta questioningly. "Haven't you ever even thought of marrying him?"

"Never even thought of it," Senta lied casually. She did not want to tell the girl how handsome she'd found Erich the first time she met him. She didn't want to discuss how hurt she'd felt when as weeks and then months passed in St. Petersburg, Erich had still shown absolutely no signs of attraction to her. He·didn't even want to be her friend. He saw her only as a coworker, a business associate. He would not stay up at night, talking to her. And he would not come to her place for a drink. He was an ice man. It wasn't that Senta was in love with him. If they'd been living in Prussia, she never would have given him a second thought. But he was her only friend in Russia. They were on this adventure together, and she had hoped they would grow close. How could they not? What was so wrong with her that when she was the only woman in this stranger's life he would not even glance her way? It seemed that had they been trapped on a deserted island together, Erich would have put up his own separate hut. It was insulting. But more than that, it just hurt. "What about you?" she asked coldly. "Don't you have a man in your life?"

Tatiana blushed, ashamed of her complete lack of romantic history. "I've never had a sweetheart," she confessed, "not even once."

Senta felt compelled to say something reassuring. "Well, I'm sure that once you get some nice clothes, that will all change." Her yawn demonstrated her complete lack of interest in their little chat.

"You look worn out," Tatiana observed. "Would you like a drink or something?"

"I'd love a nice hard belt of vodka," Senta groaned. "But Erich doesn't drink much, and what he's got he keeps locked up."

Tatiana shrugged. "So?"

"So, I don't have a key."

Tatiana laughed. "So?" she repeated.

Senta looked at the girl as though she were daft. "So," she said, "obviously, I can't get a drink."

Tatiana rose to her feet. "Leave that to me," she promised. "Where does he keep it?"

Senta grudgingly rose to her feet. She was in no mood to be upright, but she couldn't help being a bit curious as to what the girl was up to. "It's over here," she instructed, leading her toward the tiny kitchen. She opened a lower cabinet and pointed to a lock. "See this wine?" she asked, lifting a bottle of yellowish liquid. "This is Prussian wine. We make some of the worst wine in the world, but Erich patriotically insists it's the best." With disgust she examined the label. "I wouldn't offer it to a drunken beggar. It's horrible." Then she pointed again to the lock. "But in there is where Erich keeps his real wine collection. The one he doesn't want anyone to know about—it's French."

Tatiana knelt beside the lock. Within seconds it had sprung. "Is this it?" she asked boastfully, lifting a slender bottle of ruby-red wine.

Senta put a hand over her mouth when she read the label. "My God, I didn't know it would be this good," she gasped.

"There's more," Tatiana said, retrieving four more bottles.

"We'd better take only one," Senta said. "He'll kill us."

"I'm not afraid of him," Tatiana insisted, pouting. "This is my house too now. If I want a drink, why can't I have one?"

Senta's lips twisted with amusement. But then her eyes narrowed. "How did you do that?" she asked in a low voice.

"Do what?"

Senta jerked her head toward the lock. "That. How did you open the lock?"

"Didn't you know?" Tatiana asked proudly. "I'm a burglar and a picklock." She said this as though she were quite proud of her vocation.

"But how?" Senta persisted. "How exactly?"

Tatiana fluttered her eyelids. "Don't you know?"

"No."

A little disappointment wrinkled Tatiana's brow. "Well, how did you get through spy school without learning to pick locks?"

Senta's lips curled upward again. "Spy school?" she asked.

"Yes. What did they teach you there anyhow?"

"Not this," Senta snickered. "But really, can you show me how?"

Tatiana felt very proud that a real spy would want a lesson from her. She was eager to oblige. "Sure! Let's go in the other room." She marched ahead of Senta, two bottles of wine in tow.

"We need an opener," Senta said, looking at the deeply set corks.

Tatiana whipped out her picklock and stabbed the corks, yanking them out with a fist. "I swear, I don't know how rich people get by," she muttered. "Without their fancy gadgets, they couldn't even open a bottle." Then she poured herself and Senta each a glass.

Senta moved the thick red ambrosia around and around in her cup. She sniffed it, finding the bouquet to be of a lovely smoke and licorice. The first taste hit her palate like rose petals falling on her tongue. She let it linger in her mouth as she moved the velvety gulp from one side of her jaw to the other.

Soft cherry undertones began to pucker her tongue. And when she swallowed, the oak taste lingered in her throat. She paused for a long time before beginning the journey again with a second sip. "No wonder we want to conquer France," she whispered, closing her eyes in ecstasy.

Tatiana crossed her arms with impatience. "I thought I was going to teach you how to pick locks!" she pouted. "Now, are you going to pay attention?" She had gulped down her first glass of wine and had just poured a second. It was all right, she thought. But it wasn't getting her drunk as quickly as vodka would, so she determined the stuff was a waste of money and badly overpriced.

"Yes, yes," Senta replied, awakening to her senses. "I'm listening, I promise." She sat up straight and tried to focus her eyes on her teacher's hands.

Tatiana wasn't fully convinced. "Are you sure you want me to teach you?" she asked sadly. "Because if you don't, then I won't." Her drooping eyes told Senta that she would be heartbroken if her pupil had changed her mind.

"Yes, I'm certain," Senta assured her. "Please, show me."

"We'll need a lock," Tatiana said. "Do you have anything with a lock?"

Senta reached over the back of the couch to retrieve her purse. "Here, this is locked," she said.

Tatiana took the purse with some trepidation. The lock was so simple, she had really wished to show off her skills with something more challenging. But she sighed, "Well, this will do for the first lesson, I suppose." She held the lock so that it was at Senta's eye level. "Now, the first step is to stare it down."

Senta's expression was patronizing. "What?"

"Stare it down," Tatiana repeated. "You see, the most important trick to opening a lock is knowing that you can do it. That's what keeps most burglars away—not the lock itself, but the fact that you have a lock."

Senta shook her head. "That makes no sense."

"Sure it does." Tatiana shifted so that she was sitting on her knees. "You see, a lock is designed to look as though it can't be opened. When you see a lock, what do you think? You think, 'Oh, no, there's a lock. I can't go in there.' Do you even try to fiddle with it? No. You just assume that if there's a lock, there's no way in."

Senta shrugged. "Yes? And?"

"And I want you to change the way you think," Tatiana explained. "Look at this lock again. But this time, instead of seeing it as a barrier, see it as a task."

"Well, that would be easier if you showed me how to complete the task," Senta argued dryly.

Tatiana frowned. "The mind is just as important as the hand," she declared. "If you don't believe you can open the lock, you won't be able to."

Senta was growing impatient. "Fine. So, what's next?"

"Next, you'll need a pick," she replied, "and you'll need to use one that's the right size for the lock. Me, I carry an assortment—one for every occasion." She emptied her pockets in demonstration.

Senta was impressed by the collection of long silver pins. "What if you don't have them with you?"

Tatiana shrugged. "That makes it a lot harder, but if you can find something that's about the same size and shape, you can use that instead. Even the hair on your head, if you moisten it enough, can be used for very light locks."

Senta was astonished. "So, what's next?" she asked impatiently.

"Next," Tatiana continued, lifting a pin to the lock, "you insert your pick and gently, very gently, push each inner bar to the side until . . ." They both heard a click. Tatiana grinned as she opened the purse wide.

"That is amazing," Senta said in complete earnest. She was

not the sort to give compliments easily. Tatiana's skill had genuinely impressed her. "Can you open any lock?"

"With practice, yes. But if it's a kind of lock I've never seen before, I would have to get a copy of it and practice at home before I could pick the real one."

"But most locks?" Senta pressed. "Do you know most locks?"

"I try to stay current," Tatiana stated proudly. She refilled both of their glasses with the wine. "So do you think I'll make a good spy?" she asked brightly.

"You just might," Senta replied, toasting the girl's glass. "You just might."

Chapter 15

Erich's day had been rather flustering. Shopping for pre-made dresses had proven to be no easy task. He'd had trouble judging which gowns would fit Tatiana. He'd stare at one for several minutes, tugging at the fabric, trying to see how wide it would be if it were three-dimensional instead of hanging flat. He hated to spend money on something he wasn't sure would fit, but there had been no choice. He could not bring Tatiana to town in her rags. Ironically, he would have to dress her up even before bringing her shopping. All things considered, he'd been tempted to buy the cheapest gowns. After all, there was a good chance that whatever he bought would be the wrong size and would wind up in the garbage. But when the moment came to make his purchase, he could not bring himself to buy something substandard. Whether it was his own pride that drove him, or his secret yearning to win favor with Tatiana, he wasn't sure. But he bought some of the prettiest dresses in the shop.

Walking home along the Baltic Sea, Erich felt a bit annoyed with himself. These gowns he was carrying had likely been a waste of money, and their cost would prevent him from affording any clothes for himself for months to come. But he resolved not to let Tatiana know that. After all, she had not asked him to buy them. He moved silently along the cobblestone road, noticing the people around him more than he ever had before. The Russians were a stout lot, a robust and handsome group of people. Generally, Erich's own people considered themselves to be the best-looking in all of Europe. They had such clear, unblemished faces. Their features were carved with such precision, and they tended to achieve such impressive stature. But Erich wasn't at all certain that Prussians were more attractive than Russians. The more he saw of them, the more he rather liked the bright color of the Russian face, the fierce rosiness. Russian people had big eyes, and a round sturdiness in the shoulders. They were so strong and stout, their hands so short and callused, it looked as though they could survive storms and calamities that would topple their European neighbors.

Of course, Prussians and other Germans had been coming to Russia for ages. Even the legendary Catherine the Great had been of German descent. So some of the Russians in St. Petersburg looked rather fair and "well cut," like Erich. But he was not interested in them. Today he noticed only the truest Russians, only those who reminded him of Tatiana. Old women were wrapped in layers of black wool, though the weather was not yet freezing. Their huge, bright eyes peered out at a never-gentle world, as if to say, "Just try to knock over this heavy body." Young men paced quickly with hands in their pockets and quiet mischief in their eyes. They were not vain men, these young Russians. Few of them fancied themselves handsome or wealthy. But they were intelligent, and they knew it. They seemed to saunter with a strange combination of dangerous volatility and infinite patience. They made eye contact only with lazy disdain, as though to say, "I could kill you, but instead I'll wait for you to die naturally and call that my revenge." They were a slow but unbreakable people, these Russians.

Erich felt a growing chill in these late afternoon walks home. Autumn was growing older, and winter would be here soon. He did not look forward to that. Russian winters were famous for their severity. They had killed Napoleon and his entire army! Erich chuckled at the thought. It was difficult to dislike the Russian winter when it had accomplished something so noble as that. The sky was darkening to a deep navy, and the smell of saltwater was in the air. St. Petersburg was beautiful, he thought. What care had been placed into the construction of each ornate building! At night, when lanterns were lit, St. Petersburg looked like a city of castles. A city of nothing but bright, tall palaces stretching along the seacoast. The cold wind gave him a shiver. He would always remember the beauty of this walk home. Why tonight's walk home, and not another, he wasn't sure. But he knew that his heart had marked this place and time, and that he could return to it whenever he liked.

He was delighted to hear Tatiana's giggle ringing from the parlor, but when he stepped from the darkening sky into his high-ceilinged entryway, he was greeted by a most disturbing sight. Senta and Tatiana were on the floor, laughing and speaking senselessly in a way that could be construed only as drunken. On the table before them was not one but two empty wine bottles. And not just any wine. It was the wine he had locked away, his private collection. It was the wine he treasured for its quality even as much as he shrunk from the shame of owning it. French wine. The only thing those French people knew how to do was make wine, and so he had entitled himself to a few precious bottles. He didn't know which made him angrier, that the wine was gone or that it had been discovered.

"Are you enjoying yourselves, ladies?" The question was asked stiffly, eerily.

Tatiana jumped, spilling a little wine on herself. "Oh, he scared me!" she announced overly loud. Then she nudged Senta, as though her fright had been a big joke.

Senta was a bit more cautious. She knew her partner better

than Tatiana did and could tell by his face that he was deeply offended. She'd known he would be annoyed but had thought his annoyance would not measure up to her need for a drink. She now realized she'd been wrong.

Erich's footsteps were heavy and brief as he entered the parlor. "Thank you for looking after our charge, Senta," he said in a dry voice that surpassed sarcasm.

Senta found herself feeling rather flustered. She was quite tipsy from the wine but wanted to regain her senses enough to straighten this all out before she left. She did not want Tatiana to take the blame. For whatever else could be said about Senta, she was not a traitor, and she was not a coward. "Erich," she began, "this really was my doing. I wanted a drink, and I—"

"And you picked the lock?" he asked Senta, his focus fixed completely on the other woman.

Senta's eyes grew wide as she glanced toward Tatiana. She was genuinely afraid for the silly girl. Erich wouldn't dare make a scene with his own partner—he was far too professional for that. But what protection was there for Tatiana? "Look, Erich," she said, rising to her feet, "it really was my fault. I didn't know you would mind as much as this. I—"

"Go home, Senta."

Senta shook her head. She didn't like the way Erich was eyeing Tatiana, as though he planned to kill her the moment he lacked a witness. "Erich," she pleaded gently, "we were just having fun. Don't be like this."

Erich looked for the first time at his partner. "Just go home," he said. And this time Senta thought she would. She could see his eyes in full view now and realized she had misinterpreted his intent. He would not harm Tatiana. No. His anger was shallow while his adoration was deep. Besides, Senta had never seen Erich raise his hand against a woman, and she could see plainly that he had no intention of hitting this lady. He wanted only to scare the daylights out of her.

"I'll see you tomorrow," Senta announced, grabbing her purse.

"Oh, sure," Tatiana laughed, "leave me with this madman. Are you coming back tomorrow?"

"We'll see," Senta called over her shoulder. "Good-bye."

When the door slammed shut, Tatiana reached for her glass once more. Erich snatched it from her hand. "Hey, that's mine," she declared, looking up at his black-clad form standing so menacingly over her, the glass of wine in his fist.

Erich lifted the corner of his mouth in a fashion that conveyed anything but humor. "What an interesting objection," he observed. "You could have said many things. But 'that's mine' is the one protest not at your disposal." He carried the glass to the ledge of an empty fireplace and let it be. "But, then again," he mused, "I must remember that I'm speaking to a thief. I should have guessed that you have an interesting concept regarding what constitutes being yours."

Tatiana scowled but did not rise. "I know," she suggested brightly. "Why don't you sit down and have a drink with me? We can open another bottle!"

Erich lifted one of those bottles and tossed it against the wall with a quick movement. The crash made Tatiana cover her head with both arms. "Why do you test me?" he shouted with a calmness unusual for someone so angry. "Do you think that if you aggravate me, I'll let you go?"

Tatiana did not answer but remained half curled into a ball.

"Well, you should know that's impossible," he answered himself, leaning toward her cowering form. "You should have made the calculations yourself by now and realized that I could not release you even if I wanted to."

"Why not?" she asked meekly for the sake of stalling. In fact, she knew quite well why not.

"Because your confinement is a matter of national security!" he shouted, enraged that she would try to play stupid. "For God's sake, I could shoot you for knowing what you know!"

"That's not my fault," she remarked with indignant, wide eyes. "You're the one who decided to tell me everything."

Erich placed his hands on the coffee table, bending toward her so she could not escape his terrifying glare. "You told me you wanted in. You told me you wanted to be a part of whatever Senta and I were doing. And worse yet, you showed me how you lived. You couldn't have possibly expected any civilized man to leave you out there." He paused but did not allow her to interrupt. "Silence," he ordered when she started to speak. "I've done you a favor. A favor for which I expect no thanks, but a favor nonetheless. And I'll not let you make my life hell."

Before Tatiana could argue, she found herself being lifted over Erich's shoulder. "What are you doing?" She kicked and punched. "Put me down!"

Erich rose to his full height and carried her writhing body up the stairs, clinging only to her legs. "Here," he announced, tossing her to the bed, "if I can't trust you, then you'll just have to stay put."

"What do you mean?" Tatiana asked, struggling to sit up.

Erich prevented her efforts. For the first time, Tatiana really felt his strength as he held her in place with one hand and yanked each arm over her head with the other. He even managed to secure the knots around her wrists with only one hand. Once both of her arms were tied to the bedpost, he released her to work on the ankles. She kicked and squirmed, trying desperately to prevent this final phase of confinement. But with a cold glare, he grabbed a kicking ankle and easily secured it to the lower bedpost. The second ankle was an even easier capture. Tatiana was unnerved by the ease at which he had conquered her. She had seen his strong body but had not quite been able to grasp what he could do with such muscle until then. She was almost as impressed as she was angry.

"You can't leave me like this!" she cried desperately, testing all her bonds and finding them secure.

Erich ignored her and merely removed his coat, which had remained on until then.

"I can't stay like this!" she pleaded, feeling a distinct pull in one of her shoulder muscles. "My hands are up too far! It hurts!"

This comment concerned Erich for an instant. He turned toward her, a blank expression on his face, and kneeled by the side of the bed. A careful examination of the bonds and the extent to which they were stretching her convinced him that she was not merely griping. Without saying a word, he released her wrists one at a time, then rebound them, this time leaving extra rope so her arms could bend slightly. He got up and left her again. To Tatiana's horror, she saw that he was actually making his way toward the staircase. "You're leaving?!" she cried. "You're going downstairs?"

"Why not?" he asked flatly. "It's too early for sleep."

"Let me come too!" she begged.

He turned from her and strutted down the stairs.

"No!" she cried, tugging uselessly at her bonds. "I'll scream!" she promised, anger replacing terror. "I'll scream until it awakens all the neighbors! I'll burst your eardrums!"

"Do it and I'll gag you," he called up the stairway. His words silenced her completely. She thought she would die if she were gagged as well as bound. And she knew Erich would do it too.

The minutes passed very slowly. To be forced to lie still without anyone to talk to or anything to look at is a desperately frustrating thing. Truth be told, as the next two hours passed, Tatiana began to weep in her misery. What if Erich never let her up? What if he left her like that for all time? If she'd been thinking clearly, she may have realized that the chances of this were slim. But at the moment, the possibility filled her with absolute terror. It seemed very real to her that she might be left to suffer like this forever. And she didn't think she could bear it. To be paralyzed, to have no freedom of movement. To be left alone in the darkness with her own thoughts—it was horrific. She sobbed genuinely. Her pride did not let Erich hear her weeping. But she could not keep him from seeing her sopping wet face when, at last, he came upstairs for the night.

Erich's face underwent a drastic transformation when he saw Tatiana in tears. He had come upstairs fully prepared to untie her, expecting that she would be fuming at her humiliating treatment but hoping that she'd learned a lesson about who was in control. When he saw a face that was red not from fury but from agony, his rigid expression turned to one of remorse. "What is it?" he asked stupidly, then wanted to hit himself. "Or, rather"—he stumbled to his knees—"What . . . why are you crying?" He tried to tear open the ropes at her hands but found he couldn't quite do it. They were too tight, so he nervously fumbled for a knife.

"Because you were going to leave me here forever!" she wept, the panicked sobs returning to her.

Erich shook his head vehemently, knife now in hand. "No, I swear I wasn't," he assured her in a hoarse whisper. He tried to cut the ropes, but his hands were trembling. He was afraid he might slice her skin by accident if he didn't calm down. So he stopped and took a few deep breaths, his head bent low. Then, with a swallow, he freed Tatiana's wrists. Before he could get to work on her ankles, however, she threw her arms around his neck and wept on his shoulder.

"I couldn't move," she sobbed into his ear, "I thought you might never come back for me."

Erich hardly knew what to do with a whimpering young woman. Especially one who was attached to his neck. But after only a moment's pause, he realized that the only thing to do was return her hug. With knife still in hand, he wrapped his strong arms around her and whispered, "Shhh, it's all right." This felt awkward to him at first. His hug was stiff, and he wore an expression of bewilderment. But Tatiana kept weeping, moistening his shirt, making pathetic little noises in his ear.

He could feel her heart beating, and he could feel her warmth. Within moments, he completely melted into the embrace. "I'm sorry," he whispered in genuine repentance. He squeezed her firmly, knowing that he did not have to fear the breaking of her strong back. He let his head hang and breathed down her neck. He let his hands gently stroke her. "I'm so sorry," he whispered again. "I wanted to teach you a lesson. I didn't know it would scare you so much. I—I never would have done it."

"Well, have you ever been tied to a bed?" she asked. "So tight that you couldn't move?"

She could feel him shake his head.

"Well, then, how would you know whether it's scary?"

"I'm sorry," he repeated, rubbing her back in deep circles.

The couple hugged for many minutes more. How long is difficult to say, for they both lost track. Erich spent this time coping with the realization that he could never, ever bear to see Tatiana cry. When he had come up the stairs and seen her all red-faced, he had known that he must do whatever it took to make her happy again. To let her weep was unthinkable. His body had reacted to her suffering with a trembling he had not experienced since prison. Since prison . . . while he waited to be tortured. Yes, that was it. Despite his efforts to inflict a "humane" punishment on Tatiana, she had experienced torture just now. And seeing it happen to her made him feel as though it were happening again to himself. *She is my heart,* he thought. *I wondered where I had put that.*

"Do you feel better?" he asked solemnly.

"No, not really." She tried to flop her head back on his shoulder, but he held her at arm's length.

He brushed her cheek with his thumb. "I don't think I can stand to see you cry," he admitted, a little trembling smile crossing his face.

Tatiana thought he had a very attractive smile. "Well," she replied, thinking that she should return the compliment, "I don't think I'd like seeing you cry either. Of course," she added warily, "it's a little hard to imagine you crying."

Erich stroked the face before him, treasuring its softness beneath his fingers. He loved every inch of it: the full cheeks, the ample lips, the shiny, round eyes. It seemed to him that he had known this face all his life. He could not remember a day when this girl had been a stranger to him. "What are we going to do?" he whispered to himself more than to Tatiana.

She obviously didn't understand the question and wasn't meant to. Her lips parted slightly as she shrugged. Erich shook his head in awe. The smallest trace of a smile lingered on his face. How could such a girl, so hardened against the world in so many ways, be so ignorant of a man's feelings, be so vulnerable to love? He could see plainly that she did not realize what had happened. She did not know that he had seen himself in her eyes. She did not know that she was in danger of being ravaged. And she did not consider that he was worried over their future. It was as though she lived day by day, enjoying an embrace but never wondering what it would lead to. Enjoying a little tenderness but never worrying that she had found it in the arms of a man who could not marry her.

"Let's go to sleep," he suggested, rising silently to his feet.

Tatiana followed him with her wide, golden eyes. "Are you going to tie me up again?"

He caught his forehead in the palm of his own hand. He had forgotten about that. He couldn't trust her not to run off if he left her untied, but how could he do it now? With eyes shut in utter turmoil, he paused before his dresser. Then he made a decision that was utterly impractical, thoroughly unprofessional, and completely irresponsible. "Tatiana," he said through clenched teeth, "do you swear to me that if I leave you unbridled, you will not run off?"

Tatiana didn't hesitate. This was her only chance at avoiding the ropes for this night, and possibly, all future ones. "Sure I do."

"Swear on something that matters to you," he ordered. "Swear by something you would not betray."

"All right." She paused for a long time while she thought. Finally she said, "I swear by my father's grave." She'd had a lot of graves to choose from.

"Fine," he said brashly. "Now say the whole thing. Go on." He rotated his wrist as encouragement. "Start from the beginning. I swear that . . . go ahead."

"I swear," Tatiana said, "on the grave of my father that I will not try to run away tonight, even if you don't tie me."

Erich noticed she had left a window open for herself by saying "tonight," but he decided to let it pass. He would make her swear again tomorrow night. "All right," he agreed, though he was still extremely nervous about this arrangement. "Then, uh . . . then go ahead and get ready for sleep. I . . . uh, I bought you . . . something . . . to wear." He nodded toward a satchel and said, "Choose whichever sleeping gown you like best. I— I hope they all fit."

Tatiana sensed his anxiety about her looking in the bag, but she had no idea why he would be nervous. "Thanks," she said cheerfully, peeking inside to see what gifts he'd brought. "Oh, this is pretty!" she exclaimed, lifting a long, dark brown sleeping gown from the bag. There was a lot of lace at the bosom and on the cuffs. The chocolate color would go splendidly with her hair. "I like it," she assured him with a grin.

Erich was relieved. He didn't know why he was feeling so shy about the purchases he had made that afternoon. But he felt vulnerable about it, as though the gifts might reveal something of his feelings for Tatiana. If she hated the gifts, he would fear that she hated him too. He watched with a schoolboy's anticipation as she reached for the second nightgown. "Oh," Tatiana said hesitantly. This one was a bright lavender and irresistibly shiny. But it did not have long sleeves like the brown one. It had only the narrowest strings over the shoulders to hold it on. And the bustline was shamefully low. "I . . . I'm not sure this would fit,'' she noted diplomatically. She saw his eyes droop a little, and added, "But it's absolutely beautiful! I'll be sure to give it a try." *When I'm good and alone,* she added to herself.

The final gown was the most shocking of all. At first, Tatiana gasped with delight to see its silvery satin completely covered by a layer of the most elegant matching lace. Unlike the other gowns, this one would cling to her, squeezing against her figure to emphasize her curves. She had never worn anything silver before, but she suspected it would look lovely against her skin. The gown did not appear to be too scantily cut, and the sleeves were appropriately long. But when Tatiana put her hand beneath it, she found that she could still see her hand, every last detail of it, and its true color. The gown was perfectly transparent! "Erich," she said crossly, holding up the gown with her hand still showing through. "This nightgown is obscene."

Erich was mortified. He had not noticed that in the shop. He had chosen it only for its beauty and the excellent quality of the lace. But he knew that no lady in her right mind would believe his innocence. "I . . . I had no idea," he stammered weakly. "I didn't notice, honestly. I—"

Tatiana giggled. "Yes, I didn't notice at first either. Oh, how funny. Isn't it a good thing I didn't put it on before we both noticed?" She laughed gaily.

Erich was warmed and relieved. Tatiana was an unusual woman, that was for certain. "Well, wear whichever one you like," he instructed cheerfully. "I'll change out here while you change in there." He nodded toward the closet. "And I'll try to have the covers over me before you come out." Why this simple courtesy had not occurred to him last night, he wasn't sure. Perhaps it was because he'd been so angry.

Tatiana grabbed the brown nightgown and went to the task of dressing. The nightgown fit well, much to her relief. She would have been embarrassed if it had been too small, for she did sometimes feel that she was rounder than a woman ought to be. But Erich had taken no chances with failing to cover her lusciously full figure. If anything, the gown was a bit loose. She emerged from the closet looking positively ravishing. The gown was the exact color as her rich brown hair. And it made her eyes look darker and less gold than usual. Furthermore, the lacy top was snug against her impressive bust, and the shiny satin held her tightly about her circular hips.

Erich had left the lantern lit on his night table. He had done this to help Tatiana find her way to bed, but now he wished he had not. He wished he had never gotten a glimpse of her in that, the most conservative of the evening gowns he had purchased. At least, at the shop it had looked conservative. On Tatiana it looked positively enticing. "I need to brush my hair," she said, pulling a ragged six-bristled brush from her night bag. "I'll try to be fast."

"You need the light for that?" he asked, hoping he wouldn't be forced to watch the arousing act of this woman brushing her hair.

"It helps," she said, jumping on the bed. She made the mattress bounce several times. "I'll never get used to that," she remarked cheerfully. She glanced at Erich and found him far less amused than she. "Well, anyway." She retreated, pulling her long hair to one side. "I don't brush my hair too often, but every now and then I have to get out the knots." She slapped her hair with the bristles several times in an attempt to undo one such tangle. "I hate my hair," she murmured.

Erich had been carefully looking the other way but now offered his attention. "Why?" he asked, genuinely puzzled by the remark.

"It always gets tangled," she complained. "And besides that, it's ugly. Brown," she said bitterly. "Brown. Who wants brown hair? Blond is the best color, then black, then maybe red. But brown? It's so ordinary."

Erich spoke impulsively. "Well, your hair's brown," he observed thoughtfully. "I can't argue with that. But I'd say there's nothing ordinary about it.'' When she looked at him inquisitively, he continued. ''On the contrary, I find it to be an unusually striking shade. Very bright. It reminds me of well-polished oak.''

Tatiana felt tingles in her stomach. She loved getting compliments. And her appearance was the last thing about which she expected any flattery. She wanted to say thank you but felt too happy to get the words out. She just finished brushing her hair, and then, with a grin she tried to suppress, announced, ''All right, you can turn out the light.'' Once the lantern was safely put out, she broke into a big, bright smile. She had pretty hair! Or, at least, Erich thought so. Maybe she should wear it down more instead of tucking it into her hat. No. Then creeps like Daveed Vinitsky would never leave her alone. That's the problem with wearing attractive clothes, she'd decided long ago. Not only are they uncomfortable, but you never know who you're going to attract. It never seems to be the right people.

She glanced at Erich, who was pretending to sleep. He made her feel so soft inside, so weak. But it was a good feeling. She even loved arguing with him, she realized. She wondered what everyone at Yura's would say if they knew she had befriended a real spy!

''Erich?''

''We're not going to do this again, are we?'' he asked miserably. ''If you're thirsty, you can get water yourself tonight.''

''No, no,'' she objected, ''it's nothing like that. I wanted only to ask you a question.''

''Yes?'' His question was impatient.

''I was just wondering . . . when are you and Senta going back to Germa—Prussia?''

''We don't know,'' he muttered, ''but I imagine it will be within the year.''

''Oh.'' She bit her lip nervously. ''And what will you do with me then?''

''Let you go,'' he replied with less impatience in his voice now that he knew she wasn't just trying to annoy him. "It doesn't matter what you tell people once Senta and I are gone."

"Oh." She was very relieved to hear this, naturally.

"But don't worry," he continued. "I'll not drop you off on the streets. I have every intention of finding you someplace suitable to go before I leave."

Tatiana rolled her eyes. "No, thank you."

He only grunted in reply. This was not the time, he knew, to have this discussion.

"Erich?"

"Yes?"

Tatiana blushed, but Erich, of course, could not see this. "Do you," she began slowly, "do you remember the ball?" She paused. "When . . . when you kissed me?"

Erich's eyes flung wide open. "Yes?" he answered into his pillow.

She bit her lip, then told him, "I . . . I liked that."

"Good," he replied gruffly.

"And do you remember at my place? You know, in the alley after we went to Yura's?" She paused again. "Do you remember how we . . . well . . . when we were kind of snuggling?"

Erich's jaw tightened, as did most of the rest of his body. "Yes," he whispered hoarsely.

"Well, that was pretty good too," she admitted, "except the kiss was better, of course, because it was in front of a palace."

Erich thought he might laugh out loud, but he managed to muffle the sound with his pillow.

"Anyway," she continued nervously, "I just wanted to tell you, because I didn't know how you would know unless I tell you—whether I liked it, I mean."

Erich managed to get out, without even the slightest laughter, "Thank you for your consideration."

"You're welcome," she replied earnestly. "I mean, the only

reason I made you stop that night in the alley is just that, well, because you're leaving and all."

"I know," he assured her.

"Because otherwise I probably wouldn't have even stopped you, and that's saying a lot! Because I've given boys black eyes for doing a lot less than what you did. So, I mean, it's a compliment that you're walking around without even a limp or anything. I mean, you shouldn't feel rejected or anything. You should feel good."

Erich was silent.

"So, what I'm trying to say, I guess," she continued bravely, "is that if you, I don't know, if you wanted to, maybe do that again sometime, I . . . I wouldn't mind."

"I had already deduced that from your chattering," he said dryly.

"Oh." She wrung her hands together anxiously. Had she just made a fool of herself? She could think of nothing to say now, nothing to remedy the awkwardness she had created.

Erich swallowed hard, then rolled to face her. He tried to appear understanding as he gently brushed her cheek with his knuckles. "I think it's best we just go to sleep now," he said softly.

He had no idea how much his words hurt her. "I see," she replied, then rolled stubbornly to face the opposite direction.

"Tatiana," he whispered.

"Good night," she replied stiffly.

"Tatiana," he repeated.

"I hope you have horrible dreams," she pouted. "Now stop bothering me and let me sleep."

Erich was too frazzled to point out that he had done nothing to prevent her from sleeping. He merely rolled to his back and tried to concentrate on lessening his arousal. It would not do for him to fall asleep like this. He closed his eyes and tried as hard as he could to soften. This was all becoming far too complicated. Tatiana had practically offered herself to him, and yet she really hadn't. She had no idea what she was offering. He had noted, on the few occasions when the topic had arisen, that Tatiana had very little understanding of the facts of life. She seemed to have only the vaguest notion of what went on between men and women behind closed doors. She had offered something to him, yes. A kiss? A peak at her breast? But surely, he reasoned, surely she had no idea what would follow. And when someday she learned, he thought, it should be in the arms of someone less jaded than he. It should be in the arms of someone patient and gentle. If he got one bite of her, he would tear her apart, and he knew it. And yet things were even more complicated than this. For Erich was no longer certain he could leave her behind when he left Russia. He was no longer certain he could leave her behind ever. He was no longer certain that God Himself would allow them to be separated. For surely, the two of them had first met in heaven. He didn't know what to do, but he knew he would get no sleep if he kept thinking about it.

The breeze blew through the open window and soothed him to sleep.

Chapter 16

Senta arrived early the next morning, for she had an important matter to discuss with Erich. Erich told her she must wait while he prepared breakfast, for he was not a man who liked adjusting his schedule for interruptions. This aggravated Senta, but he paid it no mind. He had purchased groceries and wanted to present Tatiana with a truly edible meal that morning. He prepared what might have been called a Russian feast, complete with a bowl of mixed berries and nuts, individual spice cakes with strawberry jam, and, of course, rye bread. Tatiana was so pleased with the feast that she decided not to tell Erich that some of these were not breakfast foods.

"Thank you!" she said as he spread the platters before her. "Are you going to eat both of your spice cakes, or can I have one?"

He narrowed his eyes. "You have two of your own."

"I know, but I thought three would be even nicer."

He sighed with more amusement than genuine frustration. "Go ahead, take it."

She sank her teeth into one of the fluffy, spongy cakes just as he went to fetch their water. "Mmmmm." She closed her eyes in ecstasy. "These are wonderful!" She could not believe what a remarkable cook Erich was. And to think he wasn't even Russian! "Oh, Erich!" she called. "We're going to need some more strawberry jam!"

"What happened to what I put out there?" he asked from the kitchen.

"I don't know! I guess it wasn't enough!"

Erich groaned. Secretly, he was a bit flattered by her obvious adoration of his culinary skills, but he would never have told her so. He returned to the parlor, where Tatiana was happily seated on the chair, and plunked a pitcher of water and two glasses before her. "I'm going to talk to Senta now," he informed her. "Try to leave some breakfast for me."

"What about the strawberry jam?" she asked, licking her fingers.

"You can get it yourself," he answered calmly, "and if you finish and get bored, you can go in the kitchen and practice making me something for supper. It's ridiculous, a man waiting on a woman like this."

"Maybe Senta will make you something," she suggested. In reply to his scowl, she added, "I know. You'd probably be too scared to ask Senta to do something like that, huh? She'd probably shoot you. Does Senta carry a gun?"

"Eat," he ordered, marching from the room. "And you'd better not be in my seat when I get back!"

"What is it?" Erich marched into the vestibule, wiping his hands with a wet cloth.

Senta's arms were crossed, her expression unpleasant. "You've no right to keep me waiting," she snapped. "When I tell you I've something important to discuss, I expect your breakfast can wait."

"My breakfast did wait," he replied, tossing the soiled towel into a bucket. "I was just feeding Tatiana. What is it?"

Senta shook her head irritably at the thought of him making his partner wait just so he could please his mistress—if that was, as she suspected, what Tatiana had become. "Fine," she snapped, "let's get down to business. I've been spending a great deal of time with Tomasz Muronov. He's been very helpful."

Erich offered Senta a chair, then leaned against a wall. His expression showed her that she had his full attention. "He knows Alexander III," Senta continued, her eyes alight with the thrill of sharing a discovery with her partner. This was one of the moments she had longed for when she had decided to become a spy. The feeling of accomplishment, the delight of finally reaching a jewel after all her tiresome digging. "He's met the tsar's son on a number of occasions, and he had very exciting news for us. Are you ready?"

Erich nodded, but there was no excitement in his eyes. A ray of sunlight caught his sternly chiseled face at a moment of absolute blankness.

"Alexander III is a monster," Senta announced with a thrill. "He will destroy Russia. He will make the peasants so angry that they are certain to rebel."

Erich's nod held more satisfaction this time. "Excellent," he congratulated her. "Are you sure your source is trustworthy? This is, after all, the opinion of only one man."

"I intend to check his story," she assured him. "I'll do whatever it takes to meet more men who know the tsar's son. But I feel confident that Tomasz is right. He's a smart man, and he was speaking from his heart."

Erich tried not to wince at that. He didn't like to imagine the details of Senta's interrogations. He hated to think what had caused poor Muronov to spill his heart. "Well done," he congratulated her.

"But there's more," she went on excitedly. "You didn't tell me that little brat in there could pick locks!"

Erich's voice was loud with authority. "You'll not insult her!"

"Sorry," Senta said, having forgotten she was most likely speaking of Erich's new mistress. "But what I meant is that she—Ta—what is it?"

"Tatiana!" he barked.

"Tatiana," she repeated. "Well, she was showing me yesterday how to pick locks, and she's really quite remarkable!"

"I'm glad you brought that up," he scowled. "Speaking of yesterday, let me be the first to congratulate you for a job thoroughly screwed up."

"What do you mean?" Senta asked indignantly. "I kept perfect watch over the girl."

"You drank!" he spat out. "If you'd had a few more, she could've gotten away without bothering to disarm you."

"That's ridiculous. I wouldn't have drunk that much."

"You finished two bottles!" he scowled indignantly.

"She had most of it," Senta argued. "The girl must've been weaned on vodka. You wouldn't believe her speed!"

Erich waved his hand in dismissal. "Never mind. Just be more careful next time. Tatiana's smart."

Senta held her ground. "I was careful," she sneered. "But if we could change the subject, I wanted to discuss something else with you, something related to your beloved Tatiana."

She'd used the word *beloved* to bait him. But he did not react. He was perfectly content with the phrase.

"It just so happens," Senta said, "that Tomasz keeps a safe in his rented room. I don't know for certain what's in there, but I suspect it may contain some of his correspondence with other officials."

"It might just be money," Erich pointed out.

"Perhaps," Senta agreed, "but what if it's not? Imagine what might be in there, how useful it would be!"

Erich met her expectant eyes with frigid ones. He chewed warily on his lip while Senta waited for the answer to her unasked question. There was a long pause. Erich's thoughts were moving rapidly, just as Senta's patience was coming to an end. Finally, Erich stopped biting his lip and announced, "It's out of the question."

"Why?" Senta would not let this go so easily.

"I won't have her do anything dangerous," he swore. "I won't allow it."

"It won't be dangerous!" Senta promised, spinning around to watch him pace to the window. "There's nothing dangerous about it! I'm not suggesting she break in!"

"Then, what?" he demanded.

"She can come with me," Senta suggested, "tonight! I can tell him we're working together, or—"

Erich's mouth flung open as he prepared to use language he reserved for only the most horrific of occasions.

Senta was prepared for this, and quickly offered her second suggestion before he could get out a single word. "Or," she interrupted, putting up a hand, "or she could just pretend to be my younger sister. I could tell Tomasz that she doesn't have anywhere to sleep tonight and ask him to let her stay. Then, when he falls asleep, she can open the safe, read the documents, and put them back. It will be perfectly safe."

"What makes you think Tatiana can read?" he asked, stalling.

"Fine," Senta admitted, "you might be right. So then I'll slip out of bed and read them, then put them back."

Erich's expression was so dark, he wore almost a look of disgust. "And what is she supposed to do while you're"—he swallowed—"working?"

"Whatever she wants!" Senta cried in exasperation. "What is going on here, Erich? This is for the sake of the *Reich*. It is for the sake of the kaiser. Erich"—she moved toward him imploringly—"it is for your hero, von Bismarck. My God, it could help ensure *Weltmacht.*'' Senta allowed a long silence. *"Weltmacht,"* she repeated. "Germany will be the greatest power in all of Europe someday, Erich. And it is people like you and me who will make it happen. *Weltmacht.* We will rule Europe.'' She allowed for another long pause, then added, "But we can't do it if Russia decides it doesn't like us and is strong enough to do something about it.''

Erich scratched his head as though trying to tear his hair from its roots. "Tatiana,'' he began weakly. Senta rolled her eyes. Not this again, she thought. "Tatiana ... I don't want her to watch you ...'' He did not finish. And he didn't need to. Senta knew exactly where this was going. She knew only too well.

"You think I'm trash, don't you?'' she asked sternly. Her eyes were distant. Her face conveyed something between deep hurt and surging anger.

Erich looked at her with surprise. "No,'' he protested instinctively, "no, not at all.'' But he sounded insincere. He could even hear it himself.

Senta looked at him as though she were three times his age. Her expression held both wisdom and disdain. "I see,'' she said in a low, possessed voice. "I see perfectly what's going on here.'' She stepped closer to Erich slowly, as though she were in a trance. "I disgust you,'' she announced mildly. "When you serve your country, it's noble. But when I do it, I'm cheapening myself.''

Erich shook his head but could not bring himself to look her in the eye.

"Don't lie to me,'' she said menacingly. "You're not the only one who feels that way. Even the men who sent me were laughing at me. Not in front of my face, of course. But I could hear their chuckles behind closed doors.''

Erich's guilt overwhelmed him, and he had to lean against a windowsill to stay upright.

"Do you know what the worst part is?'' she laughed bitterly.

"The worst part is that I couldn't tell my father what I would be doing on this mission. Oh, Erich, you should have seen him. He was so proud!" She blinked rapidly, as though she might cry. "His useless daughter—that was me—his useless daughter was actually going to do something worthwhile. She was going to work for Prussia—in foreign espionage no less! Imagine a useless, weak girl child whom nobody wanted being able to do something like that." She smiled miserably at the memory. "How could I tell him what I would really be doing?" She chuckled tearfully. "He thinks I'm posing as a cleaning woman! Isn't that funny? As though anyone tells secrets to his cleaning woman." She looked sharply at Erich's turned head. "Did you know they tested me before they sent me to Russia?" she asked. Erich only shook his head in shame. "Of course they did," she snapped. "They wouldn't send you here without quizzing you on Russian politics, would they? They had to make sure I was good." She raised a trembling fist to her face. "Can you imagine how I felt?"

Erich closed his eyes. "I'm sorry, Senta. I didn't know."

"You didn't think about it!" she snapped. "You've never thought about me." She took several heavy paces toward the wall. She stared at the silvery-blue paper for some time before finishing. "I know you don't want Tatiana to go with me tonight. I know you think she's too good for it." Her voice became steadier, her green eyes calm. "But, you know, she's not the Virgin Mary." She turned to face him once more. "She's flesh and blood like everyone else. She's had evil thoughts, erotic dreams, probably done some terrible things in her life that would really repulse you if you knew about them. Just like everyone else. And you know what?" She nodded proudly. "I'm not Jezebel either. I can cry—like everyone else. And there are nights I just want to be held. It's easy to label people, Erich, but it's very hard to accept them in all of their complexity."

Erich frowned. "I know I haven't been a very good friend to you, Senta."

"You haven't been a friend at all!" she corrected him. "You won't even speak to me unless it's about the blasted mission!" She covered her face with a shaking hand. But when she looked up, her eyes were dry. "But I understand," she conceded, "I understand that. I can live with that—I know you have your own problems. But the reason I put up with it, the reason I put up with everything, is that I care about this mission. It's my first one, Erich, and I want it to be a success. I want to tell my father that I did it. That I really did it." She looked away. "That safe could contain information about the Will of the People—*Narodnaia volia*. And you know they are the key to our mission!"

"Are you talking about *Narodnaia volia?*" Tatiana asked, appearing suddenly in the doorway.

Erich and Senta felt terror for a moment, until they remembered that Tatiana could not have possibly understood their conversation. They had been speaking German. "You look lovely today," Senta cried. She was much better at putting on a show than Erich was. Looking at her sweet smile, one would never have guessed that she had been so upset only moments earlier. "Is that a new dress?"

Tatiana did, in fact, look lovely in her new white gown. It had long, puffed sleeves, a full skirt, and a high, impressively embroidered neck. She looked clean and fresh, her figure complemented by the tight lace sash and the puffiness above. The crisp white emphasized her own bright coloring. "Yes, Erich got it for me," she replied, spinning around to show off how the skirt flared. "The only problem is it's too big. Erich thinks I'm fat and got me dresses that are big enough for three people."

Senta repressed a laugh. The dress appeared to be a bit roomy, but it fit better than Tatiana described.

"I just didn't want it to be too small," Erich broke in defensively. "I thought it was safer to get one a little too large than—"

Senta interrupted him with an upraised hand and a look that said perfectly, *Don't take her bait, Erich. She's trying to upset you.*

"Well, it looks lovely," Senta said graciously.

"Thank you." The second compliment in less than two days! Tatiana was ecstatic.

"Hey, what are you doing in here?" Erich suddenly remembered to ask. "I didn't tell you it was all right to interrupt."

"I heard my name." She shrugged. "What was I supposed to do?"

"You were supposed to do what you were told!" he growled.

"Do you see how mean he is?" Tatiana asked Senta. "Do you know what he said earlier? He said that you should make his supper, like a good woman would."

"I did not!" he shouted. "I said that *you* should!" He glanced at Senta apologetically. "I didn't say that. I swear it."

"You'd better not have," she grumbled.

"I didn't," he promised. "Tatiana, go!" He pointed forcefully at the doorway.

"Fine," she retreated, throwing up her hands. "I just wanted to hear what you were saying about the Will of the People."

"It's none of your concern," he assured her harshly.

"It is my concern," she protested, hands on hips. "My very best friend in the world is thinking about joining them. I would say that makes it my concern."

Erich and Senta exchanged frozen looks. Senta was the first to speak. "What?" she asked timidly. "What do you know about them?"

Tatiana frowned. "Pretty much everything, I guess. I can hardly avoid them nowadays. Seems like they're everywhere."

Senta's face was as suspicious as it was hungry. "How can

that be?'' she asked briskly. "Erich and I have been searching for them ever since we first heard about them, and we can't find anyone who'll admit to being a member.''

"Well, of course not,'' Tatiana scoffed. "You're traveling in the wrong circles. These people don't exactly spend their days dancing around in court. They're peasants like me.''

"But I thought they were secretive,'' Senta objected. "I thought they would never admit to being a part of the movement.''

"Well, they wouldn't admit it to you,'' Tatiana assured her. "They hate aristocrats. They'd take one look at you and think you were going to call the police.''

"How can we find them?'' Erich spoke up. "Can you take us to them?''

Tatiana eyed her two companions with doubt. "Not dressed like that,'' she told them. "They'll never trust you.''

"What if we changed?''

Tatiana shook her head. "Everyone at Yura's has already seen you, Erich. They'll recognize you, and they'll know you're doing it purposely.''

"But they don't know who I am,'' he pointed out. "If you told them I'm your friend—gave me a cover story—they might listen.''

"I suppose so.''

Senta broke in. "Maybe I should go instead.''

"Don't you have work tonight?'' Erich asked as gently as he could.

Senta nodded. "Do we have to do this at night?'' she asked Tatiana.

"Yes. That's when they come around.''

"Then it's settled,'' Erich said "You'll take me tonight to meet them.''

"Well, now, I don't know,'' Tatiana answered as she stumbled backward a step. "My friend might be more involved than ever by now. I mean, I don't like the Will of the People any better than you do, but I don't want them to get hurt. Not when Lev might be involved."

Senta grinned mischievously. "I can see you don't understand," she said, wrapping a friendly arm about Tatiana's shoulders. "We have no intention of hurting them, you see. We want to help them."

Tatiana looked worriedly at Erich. He nodded. "It's true," he assured her.

"All right, then, we'll go tonight. But only on one condition!"

Erich scowled. "What's that?"

"You have to let me speak to my best friend. I just want him to know I'm all right—I won't tell him anything!"

Erich and Senta exchanged looks. "All right," Erich said at last. "But you won't be alone. I'll supervise the visit. And if I see one hint . . . one signal . . . the visit is over."

Senta squeezed Tatiana with affection. "See, Erich? I knew she would turn out to be useful."

Tatiana snuggled against Senta's shoulder. "Erich thinks women are useful only if they cook."

"That's not true," he groaned.

"Yes, it is. He told me so. I just hope I can finish washing the breakfast dishes in time to go undercover tonight."

Erich helped Senta with her coat. "How big is your apartment, Senta? Are you sure you don't have a little extra room?"

"He's trying to get rid of me because I don't cook," Tatiana explained. "If I were a boy, he'd probably thank me for helping him with the mission."

"If you were a boy," he scowled, "I'd take you upstairs and whip you."

"Protect me, Senta! He's threatening me again."

Senta broke into a genuine smile. "Somehow," she said,

patting Tatiana's hand, "I suspect that you don't need much protection. Seems to me you have everything under control." The way she looked at Erich told him that he was the "everything."

Chapter 17

Lev had been searching frantically for his lost companion. He was not usually the worrying type. On the first night of her disappearance, he had not been concerned at all. The bed was a bit lonely, and the air felt cold without the warmth of a second body, but he had assumed she would return in the morning. When a second night passed without any sign of her, he panicked. He questioned every thug he knew, everyone from the wealthiest loan shark to the poorest pickpocket. His early interrogations were casual. He took "I haven't seen her" with a nod and a thanks. But as he moved on, cornering the last group of his acquaintances, he became impatient. If one of them hadn't see her, he wouldn't know what to do. "Come on," he demanded, "you had to have seen her! How could she just disappear from the face of the earth without one of you morons seeing it?"

"What do you think?" a cigar-smoking bookie sneered. "We're lying?"

"Wouldn't doubt it," Lev spat out, then stormed off to find another potential witness.

"What's with him?" someone asked.

"Lost his sister."

"Is Tasha his sister?"

"I think so. Oh, no, wait a minute. I think they're just friends."

"Well, if he wants to find her, he should ask Daveed Vinitsky. I hear the man's got it out for her."

Lev was getting ready to do just that. All the while he had searched for Tatiana, there had been two horrible possibilities he had not wanted to face. One, that she had been arrested. And the other, that Vinitsky had killed her. "All right, Daveed. Where the hell is Tatiana?"

Daveed turned slowly from the bar. His eyes were narrow, and his nose had not healed well. Its new, crooked shape made him look meaner than ever. "How should I know?" he asked bitterly.

Lev did not usually talk to the likes of this man. Daveed was sleazy, the lowest form of life—a seller of human flesh. He treated his women like animals. But worse than that, he was known to be a good fighter and one who would resort to cheating. He didn't mind stabbing his opponent with a pocket knife just after the fight was pronounced over. Lev, who had neither an impressive stature nor a great deal of combative skill, tried to avoid men with reputations like Daveed's. In fact, he tried to avoid fighting altogether. But just then he was scared enough to put his life on the line. If Tatiana were dead, he didn't care about living. "Come on," he said, lifting his chin with bravery, "you're the only one who hates Tatiana, and she's been missing for two days. Just tell me where she is!"

"I don't know where she is!" he shouted. "I know where I hope she is—in hell! But I don't know where she is, and I don't care."

Lev shrunk back. "All right, if you put it like that." He started to turn away.

"Hey, kid." Daveed stopped him.

Lev faced him with arms crossed.

"I'm having a little party tomorrow night. We could use some good bootleg. Want to come?"

Lev's gray eyes were spiteful. "Get lost, Vinitsky."

"You sure?" The invitation was sincere. "Might be your best chance at getting lucky."

"For your information," Lev smirked, "I can have any prostitute in this city . . . provided I pay in cash, of course."

It was meant as a joke, but Daveed did not get it. "Yes, but it'll be free tomorrow night."

"Thanks anyway." Lev stormed off, his heavy black boots shaking Yura's floorboards. He had to find Tatiana. Wait a minute. Had he just turned down a free night with a hundred loose women? What was he thinking? Oh, well. It wouldn't have been worth it anyway, having to spend the whole night with the likes of Daveed Vinitsky. He ordered a drink.

"Not unless you have money this time, son." Mr. Yuravin was apologetically stern.

"I have it, I have it," Lev groaned, reaching deeply into his coat pocket. "Here you go."

"Thank you," the kind old man said. "I don't ask where it comes from, just so long as it comes."

"I'll drink to that." Lev lifted his shot glass. "Hey, Mr. Yuravin?"

"Yes?"

"You haven't seen my chum Tatiana, have you?"

Yuravin scratched his bald head. "The doe-eyed girl who dresses like a boy?"

"Yeah, that's Tasha. Have you seen her lately?"

"I'm looking at her right now."

"What?"

Lev spun around to the beautiful sight of none other than

Tatiana Siskova bouncing into the pub. "Tasha!" he cried, leaping from his seat and running into her open arms. "Tasha, where have you been?" He held her as though he were afraid she would slip away again. "Don't do that to me." He sighed, snuggling into her hair.

Erich cleared his throat. When Lev looked up, he saw what he had previously been blind to. The sight of Tatiana, in her old familiar clothes, beaming like an angel, had overwhelmed him. He had not even noticed the sturdy black-clad form of her companion. "Oh," Lev said, lifting his head from Tatiana's shoulder. He squinted for a moment in thought. "Oh," he repeated. "Oh, that's where you've been! Oh, Tasha!" He returned to their embrace, rocking her back and forth. "I thought you were dead or in Siberia. And all you were doing was getting lucky. Thank God!"

"Getting what?" she laughed, slapping the side of his head.

"Ouch." Lev looked sympathetically at Erich. "She doesn't know how hard she hits, does she? You must've had a hell of a couple of nights. No wonder you're returning her."

Tatiana slapped him again. "Shut up, you," she teased. "And give me another hug. I missed you too, Lev! It just isn't the same, sleeping without you."

"What?" This time it was Erich's exclamation.

Lev winked cautiously at Tatiana's new beau. "Don't worry, comrade. We're just roommates. I wouldn't touch her with a ten-foot pole."

Tatiana socked him again. "Take that back!"

"Ouch!" Lev extended his hand to Erich. "I'm sorry, comrade. I don't believe we've met. I'm Lev—no last name. Just Lev."

Erich's jaw was stiff. He was not at all happy with what he'd just seen. There was, of course, the matter of their previous sleeping arrangements. He didn't know what to make of that. But just as bad, there seemed to be a rapport between them, a bond that Erich felt he could never break. "Markov Ladovich

Evanov,'' he responded coldly. When Lev kissed his cheek, he flinched. He really hated that.

"Markov wants to meet Pyotr Nezhdanov,'' Tatiana explained. "He wants to join the Will of the People.''

Lev received this news with shy uncertainty. He did not want to say outright that Tatiana's new friend was too suspicious a character to be introduced to the movement. But looking over the man, Lev could not believe that this stiff bureaucrat was really interested in peasants' rights. Could this handsome stranger have seduced Tatiana just to expose the Will of the People? Lev wanted to speak privately with his friend. "Umm.'' He hesitantly made eye contact with Erich. "What . . . what would interest you in an organization like that?''

"I won't discuss it,'' Erich replied just as a real revolutionary would.

Lev nodded his satisfaction. He was still not convinced, naturally, but he was at least appreciative of the answer to his question. "Well, Pyotr's over there,'' Lev said, jerking his thumb. "I'll introduce you, but I don't know you well enough to vouch for you.''

Erich thrust some money into Lev's hand.

"Or,'' he conceded, "I could at least tell them that you're a good friend of Tasha's.''

Erich gave him another fistful.

"Welcome to the Will of the People, comrade.'' Lev wrapped his arm about Erich's wide shoulder. "Come on.''

Tatiana watched as Lev led Erich to the discussion table. The rebels now practically had a nightly reservation at that center table. Their numbers were growing, and the Yuravins appreciated the business. Lev returned to her with a casual stride. "So,'' he announced cheerfully, "looks like I'll be eating well for a while.''

Tatiana squinted into the distance, watching how Erich was handling himself in the discussion. She was too far away to hear anything. "Don't lie," she teased Lev, "you'll spend it all on liquor and women."

"That's not true," he insisted, "I plan to buy cigars too."

Tatiana socked him. "Shut up and buy me a drink, you miscreant."

Lev obliged with a grin, but as they waited for her drink to arrive, his expression mellowed. "Strange lover you've found there," he couldn't help mentioning.

Tatiana's reply was little more than a whisper. "I know."

He looked at her, hoping to get a glimpse at her feelings. "Do you like him a lot?" he asked.

"Pretty well." Her shy, lowered gaze told him that she liked "Markov" a good deal more than she was letting on. "But he's not my lover," she objected fiercely. "He's just a friend."

Lev lifted an eyebrow. "You've spent two nights with a man who looks like that, and you're still just friends? Tasha, you've got to work faster than that." He managed to suppress a laugh by sipping from his drink.

"Very funny." Tatiana scowled. "But as it so happens, I'm sleeping at his house only because it's warm. There is nothing going on between us." Erich had agreed to this simple explanation.

Lev was startled. "You mean you're not coming back?" The thought hadn't occurred to him. "You mean you're . . . you're just here for a visit? And then you're going back with him?"

Tatiana felt weak. "Yes."

Lev's lips parted, but no sound emerged. With a swelling in his throat, he turned the other way. It was unthinkable. She was leaving him for good. The alley would be only his now.

"I'll be back someday though," Tatiana promised him. "In a few months, when Eri—Markov leaves."

"He's leaving?" Lev tried to hide his relief with this simple question.

"Yes," she replied soberly. "He'll be going to . . . Moscow in six months or so."

"And you . . ." Lev swallowed. "And you're going to stay with him that whole time?"

Tatiana nodded. Oh, how she wanted to come home! Oh, how she wanted to spend the rest of the night here at Yura's and then go to sleep just before sunrise, snuggled under her torn old blankets with Lev's arm wrapped around her. She felt so desperately homesick. But she was a captive. And she could not tell Lev about her true feelings, else she would put him in the same danger she found herself in. "The time will fly by," she promised.

Lev looked warily at Erich, who was sitting so suavely at the discussion table, his cheek resting on a fist. "Why does he want to join the Will of the People?" he asked point-blank. "What's the real reason?"

Tatiana was cautious. Erich was watching her from the corner of his eye. Nobody else would have noticed it. He truly looked as though his head were turned from her and he could not see. But Tatiana knew he had the gift of circular vision. She had to appear calm. "He just wants to help," she replied softly. "He doesn't like . . . Russia."

"Are you sure he's not a spy?"

Tatiana nearly leapt from her seat. "What?"

"Are you sure he's not a spy," Lev repeated, "sent by the police to stop the uprising."

Tatiana relaxed. "Ohhh," she sighed. "No, no. He's not that," she assured him. "Believe me. He is definitely not trying to help the government."

Chapter 18

Tatiana was relieved when they finally left Yura's. She felt a terrible burden had been lifted from her now that Lev knew she was safe. She had worried terribly about what he might be thinking, what he might be doing to try to find her. But tonight she had played her part well. She had no doubt that Lev was convinced she was safe and happy—even if he did have the annoying notion that she and Erich were lovers.

"Did you find out what you wanted?" Tatiana asked Erich, bouncing beside him with her arms crossed tightly to fend off the cold air.

Erich nodded. "Yes, it was very helpful. Thank you." To Tatiana's delight, he wrapped an arm around her to lend protection from the cold.

"What did you talk about?" she asked, wondering whether he'd mind if she snuggled her head against him.

"Oh, I mostly just listened," he said. "They ranted on about Karl Marx—a German of whom they understand very little. And then they complained about Alexander for a while."

"You mean the tsar?"

"Yes."

Tatiana frowned mightily. "I think they're all a bunch of know-nothings," she pouted. "Alexander is the best tsar we've ever had except for Peter. Killing him would just be stupid!"

"Not for them," Erich explained, rubbing her back for added warmth. "If they kill Alexander, they'll get a crueler tsar to replace him. A crueler tsar will make more peasants angry and bring the Will of the People more followers."

Tatiana scowled. "Hmmm. They're a tricky bunch, aren't they?"

Erich said nothing. It was very late at night, and he had a lady on his arm. He had to keep a very careful watch on the streets for any sign of danger.

"I hate them for all sorts of reasons," Tatiana continued after more thought. "For one thing, they don't believe in God!"

"They're nihilists," Erich explained. "They don't believe in anything."

"Yes, they do," she chuckled. "They believe in nihilism, don't they? That's something!"

Erich couldn't argue. A slight smile traced his lips.

"In any case," she continued, "can you imagine anyone not believing in God?" When she received no reply, she asked cautiously, "You are a Christian, aren't you, Erich?"

He glanced her way. "Yes," he assured her, "I'm a Protestant though."

"What's that?"

He cocked his head thoughtfully. "Mmmm, it's just another kind of Christian. We don't have an Orthodox Church in Prussia."

"Oh." She hoped she hadn't offended him. "Do Protestants believe in God?"

"Yes." He smiled, pulling her more tightly against him. "Yes, we do."

She looked at him wonderingly. "Then, what's the difference between Protestants and regular Christians?"

Erich sighed. "I don't know," he said on the out breath. "We had a thirty-year war to try and figure that out."

"So it doesn't bother you that I'm a different kind of Christian?"

"Not at all."

"I guess German people must be pretty open-minded about religion," Tatiana concluded with a satisfied nod.

Erich scrunched up his face. "Well . . ." he hedged, "that might be a bit of an overstatement, but . . . that's really another story."

Tatiana dared to snuggle against his chest. To do this, she had to hold on to his waist. She felt him stiffen when she did that, but he did not push her away. They walked for many long blocks toward home. Most of this time they spent in silence, but Tatiana didn't mind. She had gotten used to Erich's silences. From someone else she might have mistaken a stilled tongue for hostility or unease. But Erich, she knew, was just being Erich. And she rather liked to accept people the way they were. "Aren't you even going to question me about Lev?" she asked at last.

"I'm afraid to." His reply was swift and only half serious.

"Why?" she asked. "He's my best friend."

"I think he's been sharing your bed," he replied blandly. "And I'm not sure I want to know why."

"Because we're friends," Tatiana explained. "What's so strange about that? I share a bed with you, don't I?"

"Yes," he replied, fumbling through his pocket for the house key. "But I have inhuman levels of self-control. I don't expect that from another man."

"Self-control from what?" she asked sincerely. "I already told you you could kiss me. But you didn't want to!" The memory of it made her angry.

Erich thought it best to leave this subject untouched. He

found his key but discovered with alarm that there was no need for it. The door was unlocked. He couldn't have forgotten to lock it, could he? "Well, I just hope that Lev character hasn't been taking advantage of you without your knowing it," Erich stated simply. "If he hadn't done anything yet, he was sure to start soon."

"We are just friends," she insisted.

Erich's mind was on something else. Not only had the door been unlocked, but there was a lantern lit in the parlor. "Stay back," he mouthed to Tatiana, emphasizing his words with an outstretched arm, like a barrier between her and the house. He drew his gun. Slowly and noiselessly he moved toward the parlor, pausing only when he'd reached the very edge of its entrance. He listened and heard a strange sound. It was a woman's sobbing. With an expression of bewilderment, he lowered his weapon. Could that really be Senta? He peered around the corner and saw none other.

"Senta." He greeted her uneasily, motioning for Tatiana to come in. "What are you doing here? What's the matter?"

There was panic in her eyes. Her face was the brightest shade of pink. She shook her head frantically at her partner, shame and fear making alternate appearances in her jungle-green eyes. "He knows," she cried, "Igor knows!"

Erich narrowed his eyes. "Who's Igor?"

"The man . . . the man I was seducing before Tomasz," she sniffed. "He's on the council with you."

Erich nodded his recognition.

"Oh, God, Erich." She sounded desperate, terror-stricken. Her frail palm covered her open mouth. She breathed heavily, raggedly, for several gasps.

Erich was so startled by her demeanor, so shaken by her transformation, he found himself at a complete loss for words.

Senta calmed down enough to blurt out her story. But she told it quickly, as though she feared she must tell it before the sobs returned to her. "He stopped me on my way to Tomasz's.

He wanted to know why I never came to see him anymore. He was angry." She swallowed and struggled to catch her breath. "We got into an argument. He wouldn't let me pass by. I should have drawn my gun, but . . . but I didn't think things were that bad. He started to wrestle with me, and my purse dropped. I didn't have my weapon anymore." She stopped, her eyes wider than Erich had ever seen them. For a moment, her face was frozen, her mouth hanging open. Then she broke the silence. "I lost control of myself," she said as though she could not believe her own words. "I panicked. I started screaming at him . . . in German."

"What?" Erich's shout was murderous.

"I wasn't thinking!" she pleaded. "He was going to rape me! I was just trying to scream, trying to get away—I didn't think about what I was saying!"

Erich gritted his teeth so hard, they might have cracked. "What did he do then?" he asked, his voice loud and deep.

"He . . . he stepped away from me, and he said, 'Who are you?' And then I saw it . . . I saw it in his eyes. He realized what I was. And he ran away . . . he ran away like he was going to tell someone. Oh, God, Erich! He is going to tell everyone tomorrow to look out for Prussians spying in St. Petersburg. Oh, God!"

Erich was too alarmed to show sympathy. "Why didn't you kill him?" he demanded. "Why are you here? Why didn't you follow him?"

"I tried," she gasped. "Oh, God, I tried, Erich. I found my purse, and I pulled out my gun while he was still running. But—" Her mouth opened wide for several seconds before the words came out. "I couldn't."

Erich's eyes seemed suddenly to be the color of steel and as sharp as blades. "You had a clean shot?" he asked slowly, breathily. "And you didn't take it?"

Horror covered Senta's face. "I . . . I couldn't," she sobbed.

"I . . . I always thought I could. I always thought that when the time came, I could. I—"

Erich's shout made her shake. "Silence!" he yelled, storming deeper into the room. "You're a spy, woman! What are you doing, weeping like a helpless girl? Get yourself together!"

Tears forced Senta's eyes to close. "I . . . I know," she whimpered. "I know."

"Good," he growled, checking her gun to make sure it was loaded properly. "Now, we can't afford to dodge an internal investigation just yet. Our mission isn't complete, and we have to remain in the government's trust for some time longer. We don't want panic to spread, and we don't want to be searched. So make it look like a suicide if you can. If not, that's all right. They'll just blame it on the Will of the People." He slapped the gun into her hand. "Now, go."

Senta was weak from too much crying. Her eyes were limp, and her voice was soft. "I can't," she whispered hoarsely.

Erich's expression was nothing short of appalled.

"I can't," she repeated. "Don't you see? I . . . I can't."

"Dammit, woman! You were trained to fire a weapon!"

Senta nodded miserably. "At a target, yes. But never . . . never at a human." She reached imploringly for Erich's hand. She found it cold and unreceptive. "Please," she whispered pitifully, "please, please."

She didn't have to say anything more. Erich knew what she wanted. "Senta," he said softly but darkly. "You can't possibly hand me this burden."

She clutched his huge hand with all her might. "Please," she begged, "oh, please. We can't let him get away, we just can't!"

Erich looked down at her with eyes that stung. He was furious. His lips were parched from being squeezed together, his jaw hard as stone. But he said nothing for a long time.

"Oh, God, Erich," Senta continued her pleading. "I'm . . . I'm so sorry. I . . . I know it's all my fault. But please don't make me go! Please!'' She looked up at his fierce turquoise eyes, then bowed her head in shame. "Oh, God, they'll never send me on another mission, will they?" she moaned. "I'm a failure. I'm a failure. My father . . .''

Erich lifted Senta's gun from her hand. Quietly but firmly, he placed it on the coffee table. "Watch Tatiana," he ordered, spinning on his heel. "We'll never speak of this again."

Senta collapsed on the chair, crumpling in relief. She would have said something, but she could think of nothing to convey her gratitude. She felt too ashamed to look at Erich as he walked out the door, hands in his coat pockets. She only jumped when the door slammed. Tatiana bit her lip curiously. "So, uh, I don't understand German. Did I miss something?"

Senta and Tatiana waited for hours. Tatiana tried to cheer her friend by offering her more wine from Erich's hidden liquor cabinet, but Senta thought that wouldn't be a good idea. It seemed that all Senta wanted to do was sit there in a daze. Tatiana was afraid she might be ill. She looked feverish, and her eyes were half closed. "Can I get you a blanket?" Tatiana asked.

Senta wearily shook her head. "No, thank you. I don't deserve one."

Tatiana fetched her one anyhow. She wrapped it tightly around Senta, all the way up to her neck. "Would you like some coffee or something else hot?"

Senta shook her head. "Please, just leave me alone."

Tatiana did. She sat cross-legged in the corner, hoping that Erich was all right. The night seemed very lonely in this dusty, empty house, all closed in with heavy curtains. The longer Tatiana sat in that corner, the more she missed Erich, the more she wondered whether something terrible had happened. The more she wondered what it would be like the day he said good-bye forever. Would it be just like this? Would she be left in a dusty corner, always wondering what had become of him? She suddenly felt very lonely. She suddenly felt that if something happened to Erich, and he did not return tonight, a piece of her life would end. She hadn't realized she'd grown so attached to him.

When the front door was flung open, both women rose to their feet. Erich's footsteps were slow and heavy. His face was expressionless. He didn't immediately acknowledge the women in his parlor, but instead went to work lighting a log in the fireplace. Once he'd gotten it going, he tore off his leather gloves with his teeth and tossed them into the flames. Senta was the first to speak. "Is he . . . is he dead?" she asked fearfully.

Erich gave her a look that made it clear how stupid he found her question. Then he returned to his kindling.

Senta swallowed, still holding Tatiana's blanket tightly around her. "Will it . . . will it look like a suicide?"

Erich chewed on his cheek for a minute, then looked at her again. "It should. As long as the investigation's brief." He fixed his gaze on Tatiana. "What are you doing awake?" he asked sternly. "There's no reason for you to be up. Go to bed."

Tatiana crossed her arms. "I wanted to make sure you were all right," she explained timidly.

"Well, since I obviously am, you can go to bed now. It's hard enough waking you up in the mornings when you've had enough sleep. The least you can do is retire at a seemly hour." He knelt to rub his hands together over the fire for a moment, then rose to his feet. Seeing Tatiana still standing stubbornly before him, he pointed to the stairs and shouted, "Go!" Even the chandeliers shook. And Tatiana found herself scurrying upstairs as though she were on fire and her bed were a pond.

Erich sighed heavily, then stomped toward the kitchen basin. Senta followed him, watching as he splashed cold water on his face. "I was worried," she said hoarsely. "It took so long."

Erich reached for a towel. "He has a wife." He rubbed his

hands and arms rigorously. "I didn't want to leave the body where she would find it. It'll be hard enough on her just hearing about it."

"She's better off," Senta assured him. "I was only one of the thousands of women he slept with. Who knows how many he's raped?"

Erich looked at her coldly while he dried his neck. "Is that supposed to make me feel better?"

Senta bowed her head in shame. "I'm so sorry, Erich."

He tossed the wet towel in such a way as to make it hit the hamper with violence. Then he stormed from the kitchen.

"Erich." Senta followed him imploringly. "Erich, I . . ."

He stopped walking and faced her. His eyes were deadly, but his voice was warm. "I can't forgive you tonight, Senta." He spoke from his heart. "And I probably won't forgive you tomorrow either. But I've done this before, and I'll recover." He nodded as though to ask her if she understood. "All right? So go home and don't worry about it. I won't put this in my report."

"Really?"

"Yes. Now get out of here quickly. I mean it."

Senta wanted to kiss him, but of course she did not. Instead, she grabbed her cloak and ran from his house, taking his warning in complete earnest. She thought for a moment she might sob in relief. But she found, instead, that she was back to her old self, and she would sob no more.

When Erich went upstairs, he found Tatiana in her nightgown but wide awake. The lantern was still lit. "I thought I told you to go to sleep," he scowled, yanking off his belt.

"I can't sleep when you're so upset," Tatiana explained. "I'm worried."

"Well, don't be. I'm fine." He did not look at her, but instead faced the open window while he undressed.

Tatiana, who had learned to anticipate this moment, rose to

her feet instead of enjoying the sight. "Why don't you talk to me?" she asked. "I can tell you're not really all right."

"Sit down!" he barked. "I don't want to be bothered. Just let me sleep."

"Do you really think you'll sleep?" she asked, her golden eyes shining in the dim light.

He grumbled something incomprehensible, then tossed his shirt to the floor.

"Well, I think I'll stay up with you," she announced, leaning on the edge of the bed. "It's so lonely, staying up all by yourself, I know."

He muttered something again.

"What?"

He cast her a look of annoyance. "Nothing, I just . . ." He sighed with exasperation. "I don't get lonely."

Tatiana laughed. "I don't believe that. I think you're very lonely. After all, you don't even have any friends here in St. Petersburg, do you?"

"I don't have any friends anywhere," he informed her curtly. "I've never had one."

Tatiana was startled, but she tended to believe him. She was able to picture it, just as he said. He'd been like this his whole life. Imprisoned in his own quiet pain. "You must have had a strict father," she said thoughtfully. "He must have taught you to be so staunch."

Ordinarily, Erich would have avoided the question. But tonight he felt direct and raw, as a killer should. "I don't know my father," he replied, looking at her squarely, almost challengingly.

Tatiana's lashes flung high. "You don't? Are you an orphan like me?"

"No," he grumbled, sitting beside her so he could pull off his boots. "My mother just didn't know who my father was."

"What? How could that be?"

Erich met her eyes sternly for a moment but refused to

explain it to her. Then he returned to the task of removing his boots.

"Wasn't your mother . . . married?" she asked.

"No, she wasn't," he replied dryly. "She was a prostitute."

Tatiana couldn't believe it. "How . . ." she asked. "How did you become a big fancy spy if your mother was . . . well, poor?"

"She wasn't all that poor," he replied mildly. "She did well for herself. And this job isn't fancy, Tatiana. It's just a job." His eyes showed a flicker of sadness for the first time.

"Well, your mother must be proud of you," she offered encouragingly.

"She's dead," he said flatly. "Died of syphilis some years back. But, yes," he added, "she was proud of me before she died."

Tatiana was truly sorry for him. "Were you . . . were you young when she died?"

A corner of his mouth lifted despite himself. "Are you saying I'm not anymore?" He didn't let her answer. He added quickly, "Yes, I was fairly young. But I was already in the army."

"Did you fight in a war?" Tatiana was most curious about such things as armies and wars.

"A short one," he replied. "A quick battle with the French."

"Did you win?"

He let out a dark half-laugh. "Well, my country won. I, however, was taken as one of the few Prussian prisoners of war."

"You were in prison?" Tatiana was impressed by anyone who could go to prison and then talk about it so calmly. Her friends who had been in prison couldn't even speak about what had happened to them there, it was so terrible.

"I was a prisoner of war," he corrected her. "It's a little different." He scratched his chin. "They tortured us more than regular prisoners, but then again, they were more careful to feed us."

Tatiana gasped. "You . . . you were tortured?" she asked.

Erich looked away. He couldn't talk about that. The only way he'd held his sanity was to promise himself he would never return to that torture cell, even with his mind. If so much as a dream brought him back there, he would lose his wits completely. He changed the subject by saying, "But it wasn't all bad. The other officers were impressed by how I handled myself under torture. They recommended me for espionage work."

"And you like this better than being in the army, I'll bet."

"Less killing," he replied with a funny blank stare in his eyes. "But then, a soldier never has to be introduced to his enemy."

Tatiana wanted to console him so much, she touched his arm. It was such a beautiful arm, so strong and virile. He shook her off cruelly and rose to his feet. "Don't touch me," he ordered.

"Why not?" she asked.

"Just not tonight," he said more gently. "I'm out of sorts tonight. I just"—he glanced warily at her soft body hugged by brown silk—"I just need some time alone."

"You've had your whole life to be alone," she objected. "I think you need some time with company for a change."

He shook his head exhaustedly. "Don't . . . don't bother me, Tatiana. Just go to sleep."

"I won't," she insisted, rising to her feet. "I won't go to sleep, and I won't let you be alone." She stroked his arm again. When he flinched, she caught up with him and continued her massage. "Doesn't that feel just a little nice?" she asked him, rubbing the bicep again.

"Too nice," he snapped, yanking his arm away.

Tatiana's face suddenly took on an unusual maturity. She did not approach him this time as a well-meaning girl but as a persuasive woman. "You know, we're not so different from each other, Erich."

He was startled by her change in tone. "What?"

"You heard me," she replied calmly. "You and me. We're both orphans—at least, we are now. We're both outlaws of a sort. We both know what it means to be battered."

Erich groaned. "Please, Tatiana. You must go to sleep. You don't know what you're doing to me."

"I think I do," she replied. Her round eyes were clear and bright.

"No, you don't," he snapped. "You mustn't touch me, and you shouldn't even be standing around in that damned nightgown."

"Why not?"

"Because I'll hurt you!" he yelled, facing her.

Tatiana shook her head. Her face and hair were alight with gold. "I'm not afraid of you," she said softly, "not anymore." She blinked innocently, sweetly, and with warmth. Her eyes looked a bit confused yet strong. "You're my friend now," she said gently. "I don't think you'll hurt me."

"I will," he snarled. "You just don't know about . . . well, about these things."

Tatiana's face was soft, its roundness like a reflection of the full moon itself. "I know a little," she offered. "I know enough to know that . . . well, that I wouldn't mind." She lowered her gaze to hide her embarrassment.

Erich's eyes were still hard, but they took on a new longing. He desperately wanted what she was offering, but he couldn't let himself have it. "You just don't know," he insisted, "you don't know what you're saying. Dammit, woman! I would tear you apart!"

Tatiana shrugged. "Oh, well. At least I'd find out what all the fuss is about."

Erich was trembling. This was all too much. First he'd killed a man. And now he was coming home to this. What more could happen before he laid his head upon the pillow?

Tatiana reached for his strong hand and forced it onto her

breast. "I want to," she said, her wide eyes fluttering, "I want to be your sweetheart."

Erich let go of her breast. "You'll meet a nice man someday," he told her abruptly.

"No, I won't," she laughed. "I'm going to live a few more years, and then I'm going to get shipped to Siberia or worse. That's the way it is with peasants like me." She smiled at herself, then added, "But I like you. And I want to remember you. And I want to do this."

Erich's eyes were hard, almost menacing. His jaw trembled, and then something inside him said "Fine. Then take off that damn gown."

Chapter 19

Tatiana flung her nightgown aside in a swift motion, challenging him. Erich came to her without mercy. He wanted to show her that he'd been right in not wanting this. He wanted to punish her for unleashing what should always have remained under close guard. But most of all, he wanted relief. Relief from the heavy waters that had lapped at his ever-thickening wall of control. He tested the length of her entire naked body with hungry caresses. Her smooth shoulders, her ripe breasts, her soft waist, her firm hips, her voluptuous thighs.

He held her to the bed, her back flat, her legs dangling from the edge. He began to feast. He sucked the flesh of her thighs, nibbling at them, opening his mouth wide to devour what he could. Without gentleness he parted her legs, then lowered his head. "What are you doing?" she giggled, putting up the first signs of a struggle.

"Be quiet," he commanded. While Tatiana's eyes fluttered wide in amazement, Erich drank of her moistness and flicked his tongue against her most tender secrets. Next, he turned his attention to what he had anticipated most of all. Her heavy breasts looked even more delicious in their nudity. They were so full, he hardly knew how to begin their ravaging. But he was enthusiastic about the challenge. He gripped both of them at once, kneading them fiercely, hardly caring whether he caused her pain.

"Ouch," she said, recoiling.

Erich met her eyes with iciness, what could almost have been described as anger. He looked drunk or mad as he whispered, "Do you still want it?"

Tatiana knew this was her final chance for escape. She could sense that he was losing all control. But she liked it. She liked seeing Erich with his calculating mind turned off. She wanted to face the beast within him and make peace with it. If she could befriend the violent, wounded monster Erich himself feared, then she knew they would forever be bonded. "Yes," she said bravely, anticipation lighting up her face. "I'm not afraid."

With the strength of a giant, Erich lifted her and tossed her to the center of the bed. He kneeled between her open legs and lowered his breeches. What Tatiana saw then was enough to make her gasp. She had never seen a naked man before, and somehow this was not what she'd expected. How could something so prominent, so long, be hidden so well in a man's breeches? And what exactly was he going to do with it?

Erich picked up a knife. It was the one he had used to cut her bonds in the early morning. "Do you believe," he asked darkly, "that we must suffer for what we love?"

Tatiana was nervous about answering that. She held her silence.

He fell forward, catching himself with his hands. He kissed her like an animal bites its mate. When he looked up, his eyes were fierce, their blue-green circles moving like the ocean. "Would you bleed for me?" he asked with a stiff jaw.

Tatiana was paralyzed with fear but only for a moment.

Would she bleed for a friend? Yes, she would. Bravely, she nodded.

"I would bleed for you too," he replied, sitting upright. He took the sharpest edge of the knife and held it to his forearm. Then, unbelievably, he cut himself.

Tatiana gasped but reached up and touched the wounded arm. He looked at her coldly, expecting her to be repulsed by his madness, but saw that her eyes were strong and faithful. He smiled his approval. "All right, then," he whispered hoarsely. "Now it's your turn."

He tossed the knife aside, letting it hit the floor with a clank. He fell on her, kissed her fiercely, and roughly held her still. Tatiana was not sure what would come next. She felt his member press against her but did not know exactly what to expect. When she felt the first stretch of penetration, she cried out, "What . . . ?"

Erich bit her lip to silence her. He bit it hard. Hard enough to make it pink and swollen but not hard enough to draw blood. Then he thrust into her with a heavy, violent push. He felt her fingers scratch the skin of his back, making it raw as she tried desperately not to yell in pain. He loved those scratches. He wanted her to tear into him, to rip him apart as he was doing her. He thrust deep inside her over and over, shoving through the entrance, enjoying the challenge of the tight squeeze. He struggled to get hold of one of her luscious breasts, which bounced beneath him. "Tear at me harder," he whispered in Tatiana's ear. "Scratch me to shreds. Kill me if you can."

Tatiana was positively dizzy. She felt a horrible pain where Erich had broken her open. Now each of his thrusts was making her more and more sore. Yet somehow she felt excited by the muscles in his back flexing and releasing under her hands. She felt chills every time he stopped kissing her bruised lips and looked straight into her eyes. He looked at her as though he adored her just as much as he wanted to destroy her. His yellow hair was not neatly brushed tonight. It was wild and free, hanging moistly over his forehead. He had never looked so handsome as he did then—he was so raw. She had no trouble digging her nails deeper into his back. In fact, she loved the way it made him tremble ever so slightly as he struggled to withstand the pain. When she realized that her own thighs were trembling in just the same way, she suddenly understood. "I am your sacrifice tonight, aren't I, Erich? And you're mine?"

He nodded, his face drenched with moisture, the ocean within him spilling forth. A few more merciless thrusts and the ritual would be complete. "No mercy," he whispered fiercely, his breath searing her cheek. "I'll show you no mercy. Tender or no, you'll take my full burden."

"I want it," she whispered, squeezing his buttocks with all her might.

"Open your mouth wide."

She did so, and when her lips parted, he spilled into her other sacred opening, filling her with the heat that had plagued him for so long. The heat he'd had to combat with so much bitter ice. Within her, his silky juices felt warm and comforting. As soon as he would let her, she closed her thighs, trying to keep his offering from spilling out. It tickled and delighted her. "I like it," she said soberly. "What's a burden to you is a blessing to me."

Erich was already sitting upright on the edge of the bed, turned away from her. No more hungry words, no more violent offerings. He felt humbled, naked in the truest sense. He rose to his feet and fetched a towel, keeping his eyes lowered against Tatiana's wide gaze. Swallowing nervously, he proceeded to wipe her thighs clean. He seemed cautious about touching her, as though they had not just made love. "I'm . . . I'm sorry," he murmured, "about the . . . the blood." The full impact of what he had just done was now hitting him. A nervous smile crossed his lips. "Funny, it doesn't seem like the first time tonight I've found myself wiping up blood." It was a dark joke, but he'd hoped it would break some of the tension. To his relief, Tatiana smiled.

He tossed the towel to the floor, then dropped his head in his hands for a moment. He was not crying, he was just thinking. "Is something wrong?" Tatiana asked.

"No, no," he replied, looking at her face for just an instant before lowering his gaze once more. "No, I'm just . . . tired." He offered her a false smile.

"Well, then, maybe you should come to bed," she suggested, covering herself with blankets.

Erich swallowed hard and nodded. "Yes. Yes, I guess it must be getting late." He found his leggings crumpled on the floor and pulled them on. Then without further ado, he crawled under the blankets. There was some silence as both of them lay stiffly, several inches apart from each other. All four eyes glowed brightly in the dark. At last, Erich decided, he really should put his arm around the girl. He felt certain she hated him now, certain he could never look her steadily in the eye after this. But it wasn't her fault, it was his. He was a monster, a killer, and a violent lover. Putting his arm around her would be the right thing to do, he reasoned. A girl should have some comfort after her first time. She might hate him, but a comforting arm was still a comforting arm, wasn't it? Anyway, she could push him away if she pleased. He would understand.

Hesitantly, like a young boy with his first love, Erich slid his arm under Tatiana's shoulders. She did not flinch but only smiled. She curled herself against his chest, letting his arm be her pillow and his legs a prop for her feet. Erich widened his eyes with bewilderment. When she smiled up at him adoringly, he smiled back with cold courtesy. "Guess what." Tatiana grinned.

"Uh . . . what," he replied according to protocol.

She tapped the tip of his noble, straight nose. "I still like you."

He lowered his eyes to hers for a moment, stiffening and scrunching up his eyebrows. He gave no reply.

"In fact," she continued, snuggling deeper into his hard but comfortable chest, "I like you even better now."

Erich ground his teeth for a few moments, not knowing what to think.

"I bet you thought I wouldn't." She smiled, playing with his soft chest hair. "I bet you thought that if I really got to know you, I wouldn't like you anymore."

He felt a crick in his neck and wanted to roll it. But he couldn't get up with Tatiana weighing him down. "No, uh . . . I didn't think that," he replied, scratching his head frantically.

"That's good. Because, you know what?" She rolled on top of him, forcing him to take her full weight. She placed an elbow on either side of his neck. "I think I'm going to like being your sweetheart."

It was not until Erich saw her rich, dark eyes smiling down at him, melting him with their trust and truthfulness, that he fully believed Tatiana's words. He felt a very sudden and painful relief as he stretched up his arms and took her into a hug. "Do you mean that, my little angel?" he asked, rocking her and planting kisses on top of her head.

"Yes," she whispered, "I really do."

He suddenly pushed her away, his arm muscles shaking as he held her above him. "Are you all right?" he asked, genuine concern in his eyes. "Did I hurt you too much? Did I—" He looked as though his earlier behavior was about to return to his memory and crush him.

"No," Tatiana assured him, touching his lip. "I'm a tough girl. You didn't hurt me."

He looked at her bruised lips. They were usually nice and full, but right now they were positively swollen. "I hurt your mouth here, didn't I?" he asked, touching his own.

She shook her head. "It doesn't hurt."

"What about"—he glanced downward but saw nothing because of the blankets—"what about your . . . your . . ."

His rapid swallowing told Tatiana what he meant. "It's a little sore," she confessed, greatly understating the matter.

He rolled her to her side and gently lowered the covers. "Shhh," he said, touching her bruised mouth, "don't be afraid, I'm just going to see if I can do something for the pain." He touched her gently, gingerly, as though he had never touched her before. Tatiana was a bit red-faced with shame, for he was closely examining a place she normally thought private. He moved the brown curls aside and checked for signs of remaining blood. Then he touched the very pinkest part of her to see where the soreness lay. Tatiana thought she would die from embarrassment by the time he rose to his feet. "Sorry," he consoled her, kissing her lips as a gentleman would kiss his bride. "I didn't mean to embarrass you." He carefully rewrapped her in the blankets. "I'll be right back."

He returned with a cloth and a bucket of warm water. "I think this will make it better," he told her, wringing out the cloth. He reached under the blanket and felt for his destination, his eyes fixed all the while on her eyes. He pressed the cloth against her firmly and in just the right place. "Does that feel better?" he asked.

"Yes, but only for so long as you hold it there. Then the pain returns."

He thought about this for a moment, then finally yanked down the covers. Carefully, he resoaked the cloth and tied it around her hip, making sure it held firmly in place and provided just the right pressure. "That was creative," Tatiana noted.

"It's my job." He smiled mischievously. "Well"—he cocked his head—"not this, exactly, but . . . well, tying knots and such." He started to put the bucket away, but Tatiana gasped.

"Your arm!"

He looked down and saw that it was still bleeding where

he'd slashed it. "Squeamish?" he asked devilishly, clearly oblivious of his own wound.

Tatiana grew defensive. "No!" she snapped. "I was just concerned."

He smiled at her, then found something to use as a bandage.

"You should clean it," she suggested when he started to wrap it.

He ignored her, though she was sure he had heard.

"If you don't clean it," she repeated, "it will scar!"

He finished wrapping the cut, then sauntered toward her. "I want it to scar," he said calmly, then gave her another kiss and went to bed.

Tatiana snuggled against him once again. There was something very special about being allowed to snuggle with someone who hated to be touched. It made her feel privileged; it made her feel special. It made her feel butterflies in her stomach. "Oh, can't we stay up talking?" she asked when she saw him close his eyes. "I'm too excited for sleep."

Erich was fondling her hair, trying to stroke it to the rhythm of his breath. "I hate talking," he grumbled. "I've always hated talking. Why can't everyone just be quiet for a change?"

Tatiana laughed with him. "I'll bet that's not true though," she remarked. "I'll bet you talk more than you let on, if not to other people, then at least inside your head."

Erich did not deny this, but he didn't confirm it either. "Well, what do you want to talk about?" he relented.

"Oh, I don't know," she sighed, "I'm just wondering . . . oh, how you're feeling, I guess."

"I feel wonderful," he said, to her surprise. "I feel like a man again." He gave her a strong squeeze.

"Thanks," she giggled. At least, she was pretty sure that was a compliment. "But I just meant, you know . . . about . . . earlier tonight."

"Oh, that," he replied dryly.

"Yes, that. I mean . . . I just wondered what you're thinking.

I mean, now that we're sweethearts, we should tell each other everything. Don't you think? Of course you do. So I just wondered, well ... are you dreading tomorrow? When you face all those men, and they tell you that Igor is dead, and you'll have to act as though you don't know about it? Won't you be horribly nervous?'' She clutched her throat, imagining how she would feel.

Erich sighed. After a moment's thought, he said, ''Yes. I'll be nervous.'' He paused again and rolled to his side. He looked his lover in the eye and reached out to stroke her face. ''I'll be afraid of being found out,'' he confirmed. ''It'll give my heart a little startle the first time someone brings up the topic.'' His face was stronger than his words. He didn't look like a man who could ever be scared. ''But I'll get through it,'' he promised her. ''And do you know why?'' He waited for her to shake her head. ''Because I know,'' he said passionately, ''that when I get home, you'll be here, waiting for me. You know, I've survived a dozen mornings just as awkward as tomorrow, even though I had no real reason to survive them. So, now that I have a reason to come home, just imagine how well I'll get through.''

Tatiana smiled her delight. No one had ever said something so sweet to her before. ''Do you really like seeing me?'' she asked. ''Do you really look forward to it?''

''Yes.'' He nodded happily. ''I don't think I knew how lonely I was before you came.''

Tatiana thought about that. ''Mmmm, no, I'll bet you knew that you were lonely already.''

Erich kissed her forehead with a little chuckle. ''Good night, Tatiana.''

''My friends call me Tasha,'' she informed him.

''I don't like that,'' he replied. ''You're much too lovely to have such a casual name. I like Tatiana.''

She could hardly argue with that line of reasoning. ''But, Erich?''

"Yes," he grumbled, though a smile still lit his face. "And please make it brief. I do need to sleep."

"I just wanted to remind you," she whispered, "that you forgot to make me promise I won't run away tonight. But just to be nice, I'll stay anyway. Just this once."

"That's kind of you. Now, sleep well."

His breathing grew heavier. His face relaxed into the expressionlessness assumed by those in the world of dreams. He was almost there, in a quiet and distant place. "Erich?"

"No, no. What is it?" he asked.

"You forgot to open the window."

"You can do it yourself," he moaned. "You're not tied to the bed."

"But you're lying on my hair!"

He looked to his left and saw that this was true. Exhaustedly, he lifted his shoulder. "There. Now, good night."

"Erich?"

"Good night, I said."

"Fine," Tatiana pouted, rolling away from him. "Then I just won't tell you what I was going to say."

He didn't push his luck by speaking. He pretended that was the end of the conversation.

"I guess you'll never know," she continued, "I guess I'll never tell you that . . . that . . . I think I love you," she whispered into the pillow.

Erich's voice was gentle when he replied. "Good."

Tatiana wrinkled her nose. "What's good? That I might love you or that I'll not disturb your precious sleep by telling you?"

"Both."

"Well, aren't you supposed to say something now?" she snapped, turning toward him.

"What?" he laughed. "You didn't say anything. You said you *might* love me. *Might*. What's that?"

"It's more than what you deserve, that's what." She pouted. "Now, you'd better say it too or I'll be really mad."

"Will you let me sleep if I say it?"

"Yes."

"Very well, then." He sat up and took her face in both of his hands. "Tatiana, I have never loved a woman before. Not ever. But you . . . you are my missing half. And I don't think I could live without you." At Tatiana's glare, he finished with the assigned words. "I love you."

"Well, I guess that's good enough." She shrugged, settling back into bed. "For now."

"Good, then maybe you'll let me get some sleep," he muttered.

"What?"

"I said good night. Good night, my love."

"Hmmph."

Chapter 20

When Tatiana awoke from a most pleasant slumber, she had a marvelous idea. Erich was still asleep. Wouldn't he be delighted if she were to go downstairs and make breakfast? The excitement of having such a brilliant plan enabled her to spring to her feet with little in the way of yawning. Oh, how surprised he would be! She clasped her hands together in anticipation of the expression he would wear when he smelled delicious smoke rising from the kitchen. She could hardly bear to get dressed first, for she feared her motion would wake him and spoil the surprise. But she snatched one of her pretty new gowns and crept downstairs with it, deciding it would be quieter to change in the parlor.

There was really only one flaw in her plan. And this did not occur to her until she was fully encased in her spring-green gown, so striking beside her warm skin, and she had crept into the dank little kitchen to begin her wondrous scheme. She didn't know how to cook. How deeply this glitch would pierce an otherwise spotless plan, she wasn't certain. Surely, she thought, looking at the pots and pans with puzzlement, it couldn't be all that difficult a skill to master in the course of one morning. Could it? She rummaged the cupboards for signs of tasty-looking ingredients and with a bounce of delight began her experiment.

Erich awoke to a rather strange odor. At first, he thought the house might be on fire, but then he decided it smelled more like a pigeon had gotten stuck in the chimney. He opened his eyes and saw that Tatiana was missing. This gave him a jolt, and he sprung to his feet in a flash.

"Don't come down here!" Tatiana cried when she heard his footsteps on the stairs. "I'm . . . I'm having a bit of a problem. Go back to bed!"

Firmly disregarding her warning, Erich continued his trek downstairs and burst into the smoking kitchen.

"Oh, Erich!" Tatiana nearly sobbed. "You're ruining my surprise!" She pushed at his chest with both hands in an effort to remove him from the kitchen. But shoving Erich was a little like trying to tip over a huge rock. He barely noticed her efforts.

"What's the surprise?" he asked, marveling at her sweat-streaked face framed by long, limp strands of hair. "Are you going to burn down my kitchen?"

"No," she cried, plummeting his chest with a series of hard punches. "I'm fixing your breakfast. Can't you see that?"

Erich, who had not taken much note of her efforts to shove him, did feel the sting of her pounding fists, at least enough to still them with gentle hands. He looked over her shoulder at all the filthy dishes blackened by burning sauces. He saw vegetables that had fallen on the floor and not been picked up. He saw failed concoctions thrown sloppily into a wastebasket. "Look at that," he said, smiling. "You are making breakfast, aren't you?"

"Yes!" she exclaimed, "Now, please, go out there so I can bring it to you! You're ruining everything."

Erich was so touched that he didn't mind the mess. And this

was saying a great deal, given his meticulous nature. "All right," he agreed, repressing a very powerful temptation to burst into a chuckle. "But might I just give you one suggestion?"

"What's that?" she asked, wiping some of the raw dough from her hands onto her apron.

He approached the topic gently, not wanting to seem over-critical. "Sometimes," he began, "sometimes, things cook better when you heat them slowly."

Tatiana looked shocked. "They do?"

He nodded, biting his lips to keep from smiling.

"But what's the difference?" she asked. "Won't it cook faster if it's right up next to the fire?"

"Possibly," he reasoned diplomatically, "but, for example, a loaf of bread"—he picked up a hard, flat, blackened failed experiment from the wastebasket—"needs time to rise before you hold it over the fire with a . . . with a stick." He found the charred stick to which it had been attached. "Pans can be useful, as well."

"Wow, I never knew cooking could be so complicated." Tatiana tilted her head thoughtfully before proceeding to shove him out. "Now, go! Oh, what's the use? You're not even going to be surprised!"

"I will be if you want."

"Oh, it doesn't work that way! Now, get out!"

This time, he turned on his heel and left, a broad grin on his face. Tatiana was such a darling. He flopped down on the chair and glanced uncomfortably at his watch. It would be such a shame if he had to leave before Tatiana finished making his breakfast. He hoped she would hurry. On second thought, he rose from the chair and settled himself, instead, on the floor. He hated sitting on hard wood. It made his back hurt. But if Tatiana could compromise, as she was doing so touchingly this morning, then he could too.

He was just returning to his worry that he would have to leave, when Tatiana appeared, carrying platters of steaming something or other. "Here it is!" she announced proudly. She dropped a plate under his nose, and another one at her own place. "Do you see?" she asked excitedly. "I did make your breakfast!"

Erich was not certain what had been served. It looked as though it had started off as pancakes of some sort but had fallen apart and been reworked into gruel. He smiled. "Thank you." And then, as only the bravest of men could do in such a situation, he lifted his fork.

Tatiana happily plopped down on the couch. "Ha!" she said. "You didn't move fast enough, and I got the chair!"

Erich smiled again, then returned to studying his plate. No good, he decided on second thought. Contemplating the dreaded act ahead of him only made it harder to perform. This was the sort of task that was better dived into headfirst. He began eating.

"Do you like it?" Tatiana asked before he'd even had a chance to swallow. She was having no trouble cleaning her own plate, for she was quite accustomed to bad food.

Erich nodded diplomatically, his mouth still full. He took a hearty gulp of water. "It's . . . good," he said. "It's . . . well spiced."

"Spiced?" Tatiana's eyes widened in horror. "You mean you have spices?"

Erich repressed a laugh as he nodded. "Yes, in the third cupboard from the left."

"Darn it!" Tatiana hit her own forehead. "Imagine how much better it would taste if I'd used spices!"

Erich calmly and bravely finished every last bite of food on his plate. He did not once grimace, and he did not slow down toward the end. He behaved in every way as one who was enjoying a respectable meal. "Thank you," he said at last, wiping his lips with a napkin. "I genuinely appreciate your . . . your noble effort."

"I'll make supper tonight," she promised, "just like you said you wished I would. Remember? Remember when you said a woman should make supper for a man after he's been at work all day, and—"

"No! Or, rather"—he cleared his throat—"perhaps I have been unfair. Perhaps there is no reason that a man shouldn't be the one to cook."

"But I don't mind," Tatiana insisted. "I think I'm getting the hang of it."

"No, I . . . I think it's important for us to set an example to others that, uh . . . that a woman's role in society should be . . . versatile. Oh, look. It's time for me to go."

Tatiana sprung to her feet and followed him anxiously to the front door. She helped him with his coat. "Well, what should I do while you're gone?" she asked frantically. "Where's Senta?"

Erich fit an arm into his second sleeve, then turned reticently toward his lover. He held her cheek in his large hand. "Senta isn't coming today," he informed her gently. "We've had a disagreement, and I'll not see her until tomorrow."

"Is it because of the . . . the . . ."

"That's not your concern," he said, stroking her chin with his thumb. "All that concerns you is that I am trusting you today. I am trusting you, period." His aqua eyes were sober and sincere. "I cannot hold you hostage anymore. What happened between us . . ." He bowed his head briefly, then met her eyes again. "I feel I must trust you now. I know you're smart enough to realize that your running away would put me in a terrible position. I hope you won't do that. But"—he shrugged stiffly—"this is my first try at love, and . . . and I feel I should start it on honest footing. So you're free"—he nodded—"but I'm asking you to stay put."

Tatiana loved being trusted. Keeping promises gave her the feeling of personal dignity that her father had spoken of so many years before. "I'll stay here," she said to him, eyes bright with joy, "so long as you keep your promise to let me go in a few months, when''—she lowered her eyes—''when you go home.''

"You have my word." He kissed her solemnly, as though to seal the promise. His lips felt soft and warm, making Tatiana feel tender.

"Are you scared?" she asked when their mouths parted. "Are you scared about going to town today?"

Erich shook his head. "No," he whispered, "I feel reasonably calm."

Tatiana gave him a squeeze on his bulky arm. "I'll be waiting right here, thinking about you."

He kissed her again and then departed. He had to keep his mind on business today more than ever. And one more kiss would have done him in.

The worst moment for him came when he first entered the court, where all of the councilmen gathered for discussion. He felt just as Tatiana had before entering the ballroom at the Winter Palace. He instinctively credited all the court's inhabitants with the supernatural ability to guess that he had committed murder last night. He felt certain that despite the improbability, all the councilmen had been discussing nothing except the disappearance of Igor until his own arrival. He had to calm himself. He had to remember what he had told Tatiana. The truth. The truth was only a reflection of one's beliefs. And one could adjust one's beliefs. If he believed that he had done nothing wrong, then there would be a certain truth in it. With that in mind, he sauntered into the courthouse with the gait and expression of an innocent man. And within the first five seconds of his arrival, everyone judged him to be just that.

"Have you heard Igor is dead?" A face approached Erich, grinning with the excitement of freshly released gossip.

Erich was not surprised that the body had been discovered so quickly. He had not tried to hide it, only to make certain that the lady of the house would not be the first to reach it. He reacted as he would have if he had truly known nothing of the event. He stopped walking and faced the young man with skepticism. "What are you saying?"

"He's dead! Shot himself, they say. Can you believe it?"

"No," Erich said, "I can't. You must be mistaken. He was the last person who would take his own life." Be the first to say it, he told himself. Be remembered as the first to mention that.

"That's true," the lad speculated. "He was so full of himself, I'd think he would want to stay alive forever, just to enjoy his own company." The boy chuckled. "Don't think anyone will miss him, in truth. If he'd had his way, Russia'd be set back a thousand years, what with all of his antipeasant policies."

Erich continued to walk stiffly toward the meeting hall, pretending to be deep in thought over the matter of Igor's death.

"I'll bet his wife's happy," the youth said, jogging along beside Erich. "I think the only people who'll actually miss the man are the local trollops. And they, only for the lost business."

Erich stopped dead in his tracks. His eyes were hard. "I prefer not to be subjected to such vulgarity," he scolded. "I disapprove of prostitution and refuse to consider its role in the lives of respectable men."

"You consider Igor respectable?" the youth scoffed. "Nobody else does. The man never helped a soul, not once in his whole life. He would've killed his own brother for one shiny ruble."

"That's no way to speak of the dead."

"Well, if it were anyone else, I'd agree. But you have to admit, the man was nobody's friend. He stole from the taxpayers, wanted to send peasants back to serfdom. If he'd had his way, execution would be the punishment for every crime. Except his own crimes, of course."

"That doesn't mean he deserved to die!" Erich's voice had been too loud, his eyes too heartfelt. He had nearly lost control.

"I see you're really torn up about it, aren't you?" the lad

observed. "Since you're the only one who is, maybe you should write his eulogy."

"Oh, that would be something," Erich muttered.

Despite a rough start, Erich's day continued with reasonable ease. He handled himself like a pro, even at the most awkward moments of gossip. No one would have suspected him to be Igor's murderer, or even to have known about the death before that morning. Someone who had witnessed the murder might even have doubted their memory as they watched Erich's cool performance. Indeed, near the end of his day, Erich felt certain that he had succeeded in ensuring that he would hear no more about the disappearance of Igor. It was a wonderful relief. He could now relax his mind and let it wander to more pleasant topics. Like coming home to Tatiana.

He could feel her warm eyes in the distance, watching, and waiting for him to arrive home. He could imagine the comforting smile she would offer him when he stepped through the front door. He could remember the feel of her, lying so soft and cushiony beneath him the night before. Her little gasps as he pushed deep inside her and then pulled out—all in his own time. How he'd been able to control her panting by changing his speed. How she had clung to him, as though she would fall from some great height if she released his anchor. He thought about those breasts, naked and fleshy, their tips aiming for him, beckoning him. With tremendous agitation he glanced at an ornate grandfather clock. When would this day be over? When could he get home and ravage Tatiana?

The time did arrive, eventually. Erich, who prided himself on his ability to focus, had found his mind wandering frequently throughout the day. Even something so innocent as a table would make him think of the color of Tatiana's hair. And that, in turn, would make him think of the hair only he was allowed to see. And that would make him enflamed, leaving him in a potentially embarrassing condition until he forced his thoughts to return to the mundane world around him. But at last, his day was over, and he could rush home. He stepped into the chilly late-afternoon air with glee. But he had not walked far, when he suddenly had the distinct sensation of being followed. Instinctively, he shoved one hand in his pocket, but he did not draw. He waited for the stalker to make his move.

"Excuse me, sir."

Erich turned abruptly about, only to find himself cornered by a woman. He relaxed and withdrew his hand from his pocket, using it, instead, to remove his fur hat. "Madam," he greeted her. He did not know this woman, but something about her was strangely familiar. Yellow eyes peered at him from under a heavy wool scarf.

"I'm sorry to trouble you," she began. "I'm afraid we've not been formally introduced, though I saw you at the Winter Palace."

"Indeed?" he asked with a courteous bow. "Well, I fear our neglected introduction was my own loss."

She thanked him for the compliment with a smile. "You're very kind. And I hear a congratulations is in order."

"How so?"

The woman tightened her lips in a most mysterious manner. Her words came out pointedly, as though she were gently accusing him of some unforgivable sin. "I hear you are recently wed."

"Ah, yes," Erich replied. "Yes, I am. But how were you informed?"

"That is what I wish to discuss." She straightened her back. "I saw your betrothed at the Winter Palace. That is the lady you married, is it not?"

"Yes." Erich's reply was smooth, but he was deeply puzzled. He had told only a very small number of people that he and Tatiana were wed. He did this so as to have an alibi in case she were ever witnessed coming and going from his home. But he professed to have married quietly and did not think that he had yet become the subject of gossip. Who was this woman, and why was she so concerned with his personal life?

"I saw her at the ball," the woman continued, "a very pretty girl. From Moscow, I hear?"

Erich nodded. "Yes, that's right."

"And you hurried the wedding because of her mother's failing health?"

Erich was becoming distinctly nervous. "May I ask how this concerns you, madam?"

"I will need to speak to you privately. Might you have a few minutes for a cup of mors? I don't live far."

"I'm afraid I don't have time."

"Well, then, perhaps you should make time."

Erich was astounded by her gall. "I beg your pardon?" he asked in disbelief.

The woman's slightly wrinkled face was stern. "You heard me, Mr. Evanov. I don't know who you are or what you're hiding, but you are lying about that girl. You are lying about where you found her, you are lying about her family, and you may even be lying about the marriage. I don't care why. I don't care what you're up to or what your story is. But if you don't come with me and tell me where you really found that girl, then I'll start putting my nose in places you really don't want it."

Erich would not be baited. "What on earth makes you think I'm lying about Tatiana?" he asked as though insulted.

"Oh, believe me, young man. I know."

"How?"

The golden-eyed woman lifted her long chin. "Because I am her mother."

Chapter 21

In very little time, Erich found himself in this woman's parlor, graciously accepting a glass of sweet berry juice called mors. The woman's name, he had learned, was Anna Kratchaya, and she appeared to be of respectable means. Her parlor was decorated in the most fashionable style of the aristocratic Russians: crowded. There was so much furniture in every room that a path had to made, else no one could pass. Ornate table was slammed against ornate desk, rendering all furnishings completely useless. Each shining wooden piece, so elaborately decorated with carvings of vines, flowers, and cascading waves, would have been a masterpiece if left to stand for itself, but crammed against so many other antiques, the beauty of each piece was lost. There was nothing but clutter and utter gaudiness. Even the walls were plastered with clashing picture frames and clocks to the point that it was impossible to determine the walls' original color. Erich much preferred the straightforward simplicity of German decor. He could not even see through the windows of this otherwise lovely home. Too many grandfather clocks blocked the way.

Madame Kratchaya wore a black, high-necked gown with a sheer cape flowing behind. The dress was full, the skirt layered like the tiers of a wedding cake. After she had removed her heavy woolen wrappings, Erich saw that she was a fine figure of a woman. She was not terribly tall; surely, she was shorter than Tatiana. But she carried herself well, with good posture and head held high. Her graying blond hair had been braided and then coiled into a very wide bun at the back of her head. Her skin was paler than Tatiana's. In fact, she was extremely white. But that may just as easily have been caused by lack of sunlight as by nature. Her large eyes were round like Tatiana's but paler. They seemed to swallow up her entire face like ever-spreading pools of honey.

"My husband is a general in the army," she explained proudly, touching the lace at her throat as though she were having trouble breathing evenly. "We try to make it to all the balls and court dances. Oh, I don't enjoy them as much as I did when I was younger, but we feel we should make an appearance." She smiled nervously, only to find that Erich's face was completely stern. She thought she had best get to the point. "I knew it when I saw her at the Winter Palace," she sighed, "I knew she was my daughter. I could see myself in her, of course. But even more, I could see"—she bowed her head—"her father. That chestnut hair, you know."

Erich was silent. One elbow was propped on the arm of his green velvet chair. He frowned and bounced his leg impatiently. He did not like being held hostage.

"I asked about her," Madame Kratchaya continued. "I was told that she was your fiancée and that you'd brought her from Moscow just for the ball. When I heard this, I thought I had been mistaken, that perhaps she was not my daughter after all. But then I asked her name." She lifted her soft eyes boldly to Erich's callous ones. "Tatiana Janinevna Siskova, I was told.

Tatiana Siskova.'' She rose to her feet and moved toward the open window. She could not stand directly before it, of course, because of all the clutter. But she got near enough to feel some cool breeze on her face.

"I was sixteen,'' she began distantly. "Sixteen when I gave birth to her. I was not married, and my parents disapproved of my beau. He was on his way to becoming a professor, not an admirable profession for the husband of an aristocrat. My parents forbade the courtship. But I was in love, so I met him privately. As soon as our meetings became covert, they became dangerous. If we'd been allowed to court properly,'' she spat out bitterly, "it never would have happened! But we had to meet in dark places, we had to sneak around. We lost all respect for decency. And ... well''—she blinked rapidly, shamefully—"I don't need to tell you what happened.'' She bent her head in dramatic pause before returning to her story.

"My parents sent me away, far into the countryside to have my baby. They didn't want anyone to know about it. But, of course, everyone did. Everyone knew my shame. They snickered at me as my carriage rolled out of town.''

"Where was the father?'' Erich interrupted for the first time.

She looked at him as though startled to hear his voice. "Nikolai? Oh, he ... he professed his continuing love at first. He told me he'd marry me and take care of the child. But my parents would rather have seen me tormented by my own shame than married to him. Especially after what he'd done. They forbade the marriage. And though I expected Nikolai to persist, he''—she crinkled her mouth as though about to weep—"he took another bride within the month. I guess it's silly of me to be angry about that. After all, I did reject him.''

"Not when you should have,'' Erich pointed out callously.

A trace of annoyance crossed Anna's face. "I loved him,'' she announced defensively.

"Not enough to defy your parents?'' Erich glanced impatiently at the clock. "Never mind. Just go on.''

Angrily, she turned away from him and continued her story. "In any case, I gave the baby away as soon as she was born." Her neck stiffened visibly. "My parents told me in no uncertain terms that I could not return to St. Petersburg with that baby in my arms. But she was so adorable! Oh, she was so precious. I couldn't bear to leave her. And there was no one would take her. So I brought her to some peasants who were working in a field nearby, and I offered them money in exchange for raising the child." She smiled. "They were a funny family. They were so poor, I thought their roof was going to fall on them. But they wouldn't accept my money. They said they'd be happy to take the child if I stayed long enough to finish nursing. And that's what I did. I named her Tatiana, and I visited the Siskov family every day for a year, checking on my daughter, giving her what only a mother can give. I'm sure she was in good hands," she sighed.

"But, oh, how I missed the glamour of St. Petersburg! I was still so young, I had my whole life ahead of me. I wanted to be courted again, I wanted to wear pretty dresses again." She stopped, as though it were too painful to discuss. Then, at last, she said plainly, "So, anyway, the Siskov family told me that they would raise my little girl, and if she ever had any memories of me, they would tell her I was her older sister who had run away from home. I returned to St. Petersburg, married Boris, the general," she reminded him, as though she couldn't say it often enough, "and never saw my little girl again until that night at the Winter Palace."

There was a long, thick silence. Erich was still shaking his leg impatiently, waiting for her to speak again. When she did not, he finally broke in. "So, what do you want from me?" he asked coldly.

Anna's eyes flung wide. "Why, I want you to reunite us, of course. I want you to tell her about me, to convince her to meet with me."

"Why don't you talk to her yourself?"

Anna shook her head passionately. "No, I couldn't do that. I couldn't! She doesn't even know me. I wouldn't know what to say!"

Erich frowned. "Fine, I'll tell her about you. Is that all?"

"Well, you have to do more than just tell her," Anna objected. "You have to convince her! You have to convince her to . . . to see me, to talk to me, to . . . to come live here with me if possible. Don't you see, Mr. Evanov? I want my daughter back."

Erich took a long, deep breath and stretched his arms over head. At the end of the stretch, he rubbed his face wearily. "I have no quarrel with relaying our conversation to Tatiana. But I cannot promise a favorable reply."

Anna's eyes filled with rage. "You bring me my daughter, Mr. Evanov!" she cried. "Or I'll tell this whole city about the deceit you have lain upon them. I don't know why you've done it, and I don't care, but I'm sure you would find it most humiliating to be unveiled."

Erich was not a man who coddled threats. He rose abruptly to his feet and reached for his hat and coat. "I doubt you'll do that," he replied mildly, "for that would require your public admission that you'd allowed your child to be raised by peasants."

His words were true, and, thus, silenced Anna.

"It has been a pleasure to make your acquaintance." Erich bowed stiffly and falsely. "I shall deliver your message, and for your sake, I hope it is well received. For Tatiana's sake"— he paused—"I don't know what I hope. Good day."

Chapter 22

Erich had complete confidence that Tatiana would be home when he arrived. He had come to trust in her absolutely, so he was startled to find the house completely dark. Not one lantern illuminated the majestic windows of his house. "Tatiana?" he called with concern, as he creaked open the front door. "Tatiana?" A horrific thought occurred to him. What if she had been harmed, or fallen prey to a burglar, or . . . or worse? He would not be able to bear it. Anger clenched his jaw as he ventured farther into the hallway. "Tatiana!" he shouted, touching the hilt of his gun.

He heard a giggle. "Erich?"

He was overcome by relief at the sound of that sweet voice. "Tatiana, where are—"

"Don't look," she laughed, peering around the corner with only her head. "I have another surprise for you."

Erich hoped she had not fixed dinner, for he did not think he could get through another one of her meals. "What is it?" he asked gruffly. "Why are the lights out?"

Tatiana stepped in front of him. She was wearing the night-gown of sheer lace, the one he could see through. Her long hair, brushed out and thrown over one shoulder, covered what would otherwise have been a highly visible bare breast. Her eyes were luscious in the dim light, specked with shards of gold. Her ivory skin glowed like the moon itself. Her hair had never been so beautiful, so shiny, thick, and long as it was that night. And the gown—it provided only the slightest camouflage for her otherwise deliciously naked figure. Erich could not see the breast that was hidden by her hair, but the other was in plain sight. Firm despite its magnificent size, the soft mound was held by lace, as though captured by a net. Erich's eyes wandered downward. Her midriff was not bony, but lush. It swooped inward, like a wave, and then out again just as dramatically. The lace was pulled tight about her hips, then flowed freely to the floor, exposing but not gripping her long, shapely legs. His eyes returned to her hips. He could see her womanhood like a dark promise held forbidden only by one lacy flower.

"For me?" he asked, raising an eyebrow with delight.

Tatiana nodded, blushing fiercely, and trying to repress her giggling. "I thought you'd like it."

Erich was gritting his teeth so hard that he could not speak.

Worriedly, Tatiana crossed her arms, suddenly wanting to hide her nudity. "You . . . you don't like it?" she asked painfully.

Erich dropped to his knees. He wrapped his arms around her legs and kissed her womanhood through the lace. "I love it," he replied. He hurriedly yanked off his coat and threw it to the floor.

"What are you doing?" she giggled, struggling to pull away.

"Stay still," he ordered, holding her legs tight. He lifted the gown until it was high above her waist and kept from dropping by the breadth of her hips. He touched her soft hair. His thumb combed it while his eyes examined the swelling beyond the darkness. "Do you like this?" he asked. "Or do you prefer this?" He licked her quickly with his moistened tongue.

"I prefer," she exclaimed red-faced, "doing this on a bed! So stop it!" She whacked him on the shoulder.

Erich was quick to oblige. He grabbed her legs once again, but this time he stood up. By the time he reached his full height, Tatiana was bent over his shoulder. "Don't drop me!" she cried frantically. "If you drop me, I will kill you! Do you understand? Kill you!"

Erich was smiling as he climbed the stairs. But he believed that Tatiana must be afraid of heights, so he lowered her to the bed gradually, with a gentleness that was beyond what was necessary. He kissed her full, quivering lips. Then he worked on the clasp of his breeches. Tatiana gasped nervously. He stopped. "Are you scared?" he asked, touching her blushing cheek.

She shook her head bravely, but Erich knew she was lying. He could see the fear in her moist palms and her lowered gaze. "It won't hurt this time," he told her with a kiss.

"Really?" She looked up at him sheepishly.

His nod was solemn. "I swear it."

Tatiana felt a nervous smile lifting the corners of her mouth. "I . . . I feel so shy all of a sudden."

Erich kissed her smile. "That's because you're thinking too much," he whispered. "Don't think." He lowered the straps from her shoulders, kissing her collarbone, her neck, her shoulder.

"Take . . . take this off?" she asked meekly, tugging on his silk shirt.

He tore it off and threw it to the floor. He grabbed her hand and placed it on his bicep, a mysterious curve on his lips. "Go ahead," he whispered close to her ear. "It's all right to be curious."

Tatiana stroked his arms as though exploring a newly discovered mountain range. At his nod of consent, she let her fingers drizzle along his stony chest, catching silken hairs on their way down. She touched his belly button and was surprised this didn't make him laugh. She should have known he was not ticklish. She did not allow her hands to travel any farther. "You can if you want to," he assured her, noticing the question in her eyes. Tatiana bit her lips pensively, then shook her head. Erich was relieved, for he was not a man who liked to be touched. But he was also glad he had offered her that intimacy. It was good for his conscience that he had denied nothing to his love.

Tatiana batted her eyelids, only an inch away from his. She could feel his breath, so heavy against her face. She could hardly bear to look into his eyes when they were so close to her. Their color was so frightening, so cold. But once she got the courage to stare into them, she could not look away. They were like skating ponds at sunset.

He hoisted her up and rolled to his back. She did not know how to position herself, so he did it for her, spreading her knees and straightening her back. "There you go," he said softly. "Now . . . no, hold on," he interrupted when she began to move. "We're not quite ready yet. I need a little more incentive." He reached up for her breasts. "Here, give me these." She bent forward so that he could reach the tips with his mouth. She giggled and sucked her finger while he began to play. His tongue stroked her, then half of her breast got swallowed. She was beginning to feel strange. She became increasingly aware of her naked womanhood sitting so blatantly on his belly. She felt it moisten and grow tingly. The harder he sucked her breast, the more she longed to rub herself hard against his flat stomach.

He lifted her hips high in the air, held her up with one hand while he struggled to lower his pants, then gently guided her to the mark. "There you go," he advised, settling her down. "When you're ready."

"All . . . all the way?" she asked.

"All the way," he answered firmly. He gave an encouraging nod. "You can do it."

She started with shyness, not at all certain that she wanted this to work. She bounced a little on his hardened tip but did not let the penetration occur. "Do it," he ordered, rapidly growing frustrated. "Do it or I'll flip you over and do it myself."

He had not meant to be cruel. He'd not been able to stop the agitated words before they left him. When Tatiana responded by lowering herself with force, he took her in his arms, trying to show his repentance. "Is it all right?" he whispered, grabbing hold of her buttocks.

Tatiana nodded against his shoulder. "It feels . . . funny. Not the same as yesterday."

He lifted her by the loins, drawing her up, then lowering her again. Over and over, he taught her how to move in this way. Tatiana became slick with excitement. She did not know what was happening to her. Her eyes closed erotically as she became engrossed in her own rhythm. Up and down she moved, grace-fully, like a dancer. Her arms overhead, making motions of swimming or flying. She did not look down at Erich but let him be the music that guided her movements. His stiffness was a welcome intrusion into her soft body. She let it rise deep inside her, supporting her like a post supporting a flag.

Then her ethereal expression changed. She was feeling some-thing new. A hunger. She flung her eyes open wide and looked down at Erich, who had been enjoying the dance. "Erich," she whimpered, "I . . . I feel funny."

"Keep moving," he urged her, slapping her bare hip.

"But . . ." Her eyes were round with confusion as she found herself quickening her pace. Wildly, she was moving up and down. She was hungry, desperate. She felt as though she had some terrible itch from which Erich must relieve her before he departed. Frantically, she gripped his shoulders, as though he might fly away if she did not. "Erich!" she screeched. "I—" She yelled loudly enough to awaken all the neighbors. Her cry sounded like begging; it sounded like an urgent question or a plea. And then, finally, it softened into the sighs and moans of a woman who had no more wants. She collapsed against Erich's supportive chest, kissing it in thanks and awe.

He graciously returned her kiss, squeezing her reassuringly. But only for a moment. Then he said, "Tatiana?" He waited. "Tatiana?" he repeated.

"Hmm?" Tatiana's smile was huge. Her eyes were closed and restful.

"Tatiana." He scowled. "You're not finished yet."

She yawned pleasurably. "Yes, I am."

"No, you're not," he growled, then pushed her up none too gently. "Finish," he ordered. When she did not, he rolled her over.

He finally exploded into his own calm haven, shaking her wildly as he did so. "Now you can relax," he said, rolling to his back and pulling her naked body against his chest. He kissed her head affectionately. She was so warm. He wanted to wrap her all around him, let her golden light insulate him from the world.

"That was fun," she whispered against his chest, breathing in his wonderfully clean scent. "I wish we could just stay in this room all the time and never have to get up." She felt its blue light all around her; moonlight filtered through heavy blue curtains into the barren, dusty room, which nonetheless felt luxurious. "No wonder my parents never wanted to tell me about this," she sighed. "If I'd known what fun it was, I would have tried it right away."

Erich winced.

"What is it?" she asked, feeling his muscles stiffen beneath her cheek.

"Uh," he stalled guiltily. "Oh, Jesus."

"What is it?" she asked more urgently. "Is something wrong?"

He rubbed his face agonizingly. "There was something I

was supposed to tell you," he muttered miserably. "I don't know how I got distracted."

"What is it?!" she demanded, rising to her elbows. "Tell me right now!"

He met her eyes waveringly. "Well, uh," he sighed, "it's about . . . it's about your mother."

"What about her?" Tatiana asked indignantly.

"Apparently, she's alive."

Tatiana's face froze. "That's not funny," she said blankly.

Erich swallowed and reached toward her, trying to let his compassion overcome the guilt of forgetting to tell her sooner. "I wouldn't joke," he assured her. "I—I spoke with her today. Not Madame Siskova, you understand. This is another woman, a woman you may have come to know as your older sister. The one who disappeared."

Tatiana could not move or even blink. "What are you talking about?" she rasped. "Stop it, Erich! This is cruel!"

"I'm sorry," he said, reaching for her imploringly. "I'm—I'm not good at this sort of thing. I—I know this must be hard for you to hear. But she cornered me today—Anna Kratchaya was her name. And she told me a long story about how she gave you to the Siskov family to be raised, but she's your real mother. Look, I don't know what to make of it, Tatiana."

"I don't believe it," she said distantly, her face clouded.

"And I'm not saying you should," he urged. "Look, she could have been anyone. I don't know. All I know is what she told me. Now, I've written down her address. It's in my coat pocket if you want to pay her a visit and straighten this out."

"Oh, I'll pay her a visit, all right," Tatiana spat out angrily. "I'll pay her a visit like she's never had before! I am going to make that woman, whoever she is, wish she had never been born! Imagine telling such lies! That my mother isn't my real mother. I can hardly wait to tear this woman to shreds."

"Oh." Erich shrugged. "Well, I'm glad to see you're taking it so well."

Tatiana put up her hand when he tried to kiss her. "Not tonight. I need my sleep. I've got a job to do tomorrow, and I mean to do it well."

Tatiana had trouble willing her eyes to close. She was angry that some woman was talking about her, telling Erich that the Siskovs had not been her real parents. If the woman were lying, how cruel she was! But what troubled her even more was the alternative. Suppose she was telling the truth? Suppose everything Tatiana knew about herself was a lie? She would not rest well until she had settled this matter. It couldn't be true. It just couldn't.

Chapter 23

Tatiana dressed in the morning as one who had an audience to impress and intimidate. She wore the most conservative day dress Erich had bought her. It was pinstriped in blue and white, puffed mightily at the bust and sleeves, and held securely in back by a very large bustle. Tatiana pinned her hair to the top of her head, not prettily, but very neatly. She secured a small, flat, flowered hat to the crown of her head to complete the businesslike effect. She intended to carry a parasol. Not one of those heavily ruffled, frivolous ones, but a chic, practical parasol in pinstriped blue, to match her gown. "How do I look?" she asked Erich.

"Like a woman on a mission," he replied, setting a plate of pancakes before her.

"Oh, no!" she cried. "I can't eat! What if I stain my dress? I've always been such a messy eater."

"That's what napkins are for," he informed her.

"Napkins? Oh, that's right. I keep forgetting all the nifty tools you rich people keep around the house."

"Utensils were a classy discovery as well," he mocked, thrusting a fork into her fist.

"They're too much work." She dropped it and tore off a piece of pancake with her fingers.

Erich retrieved the abandoned utensil. "Use it," he insisted, his eyes narrow and stern. "That's an order."

"You know, I'm not in the army," she said, "and if I were, I'd be in the Russian army, not the Prussian one. So you'd still have no business telling me what to do!"

"After we'd crushed your troops and taken you all prisoner, I would. So use the fork."

His mischievous smile was uncharacteristic of him. Tatiana liked it so well that she felt compelled to smile back. "Just this once," she relented, diving into her scrumptious fare, fork held cheerfully in hand. Tatiana was glad that Erich was the official chef now, and she had promised never again to gripe about it. His cooking was so marvelous, she didn't know how she'd ever done without it. But what had changed his mind and convinced him to cook without complaining, she really didn't know. All she knew was, she was glad of it.

When she finished eating, she rose to her feet. "Well, I'm off to do battle."

Tatiana walked determinedly toward the address Erich had given her. Her head was held high, her jaw was clenched, and she was quite determined to get to the bottom of this upsetting matter. That deep inside her chest her heart was beating rapidly with both fear and, oddly, hope, she would not acknowledge. Anger was the most comfortable thing to feel at this awkward moment. She stood in front of a bright yellow house attached on both sides to other houses. Its windows were long, and some were of stained glass. It towered more than four stories high and would seem to have a beautiful view of the sea. She double-checked the address. Yes, this was the right place. Perhaps Madame Kratchaya was a housekeeper here.

Tatiana knocked loudly, as though she were a landlord collecting overdue rent. When she received no reply, she knocked even harder and did not stop pounding until the door was opened. "Tatiana!" the small woman on the other side of the door gasped. "Oh, it's really you!" She clasped a hand to her mouth as tears fell fiercely from her eyes.

Tatiana was a bit taken aback for a moment. She had not expected the woman to greet her with tears. And she had not expected the woman to have round eyes just like her own. But when the woman tried to embrace her, she pulled back. "Madam," she said stiffly, imitating the most snobby aristocrat she had ever met, "I do not believe we are yet on hugging terms. In fact, I don't believe I know you."

Anna wanted to laugh at her daughter's false pride. She looked so funny with her nose stuck up in the air like that, her words so haughty yet her accent so terribly boorish. But wisely, she did not snicker. Rather, she opened the door a bit wider and invited the girl inside.

Tatiana was astounded by the clutter of antiques in this home. Her own tastes were not developed enough to be aware of the clashing of patterns and the insufferable impracticality of the decor. She was of a mind to think that the more beautiful things could be crammed into a room, the better. The Asian rugs under her feet changed from red to blue to green as she followed Anna into the parlor. Their path through the clutter was narrow. But when Tatiana was urged to take her place on a wide, intricately carved chair cushioned in white satin, she thought surely, she had never seen a home as lovely as this one. "I apologize," Anna said, fetching a pot of tea, "that my husband is not here to meet you. I'm afraid he works long hours."

Tatiana's eyes flung wide. "You mean, you ... you live here? This is your house?"

"Why, yes, of course," Anna answered in surprise. "What did you think?"

"Nothing," Tatiana lied, then thanked her hostess for the tea.

"Oh, dear," Anna sighed sympathetically as she settled herself into a love seat of dark red velvet. "This all must be a terrible shock to you."

Tatiana scowled, examining the tea as though it might be poisoned. "Yes, it is!" she announced angrily. "To be honest, madam, I don't know why you would spread such lies about me! What have I ever done to you?"

Anna shook her head in sorrow. "Oh, Tatiana, don't you see that it's not a lie? Can't you see it in my eyes that I am your mother?"

"The Siskovs were my parents!" Tatiana insisted bitterly. "They loved me and raised me—and died in my arms! How dare you speak ill of them!"

Anna placed a hand on her heart. "Oh, my!" she gasped. "My darling, I never meant to speak ill of them. Oh, no. On the contrary, they saved both of us! They were wonderful people. Is that what you thought? That I meant to disgrace them?"

Tatiana became more hesitant now. Her scowl became more withdrawn as she answered, "Well, I guess."

"Oh, no," Anna assured her. "I have nothing but thankfulness in my heart for that family."

That helped. Tatiana felt much better knowing that this strange woman did not mean to dishonor her real family.

"But I implore you," Anna continued. "You must accept that what I say is true. I am your real mother. I gave you to the Siskov family in your infancy because I . . . I could not raise you. Don't you see that this is a blessing?" She smiled warmly. "Your other family is gone now. But you are not alone. You will have me from now on."

Tatiana worked hard at harnessing her anger. "How do I know you're not lying?" she demanded.

"Just look at my face," Anna replied, leaning forward. "Can't you see the resemblance?"

Of course Tatiana could. But she would not give in so easily. "Well, why should I forgive you for abandoning me?" she asked. "Why should I accept you, when you rejected me?"

"I never rejected you," Anna begged. "Oh, please, don't think that. I loved you desperately. But I was too young. Do you understand that? I was too young to take care of a baby— by myself anyway."

"But I thought you were married," Tatiana pointed out skeptically.

"I am now," Anna said proudly, "but not to your father. He . . . he and I went our separate ways."

Tatiana let all of this sink in while she stared at her teacup. She did not like this. She did not want to know about this even if it was true. "Well, I think you have a lot of nerve," she snapped, "just marching into my life, and—say, is this real china?" She lifted her shiny white teacup inquisitively.

Anna nodded.

"Lovely! Anyway"—she blinked rapidly—"you might be my mother by birth—might be, I repeat. But you certainly haven't been a good mother, and I—are those real diamonds?"

Anna touched her prized brooch. "Yes," she whispered warmly.

"They really do sparkle." She shook her head. "Anyway, I don't know what you want from me, but I am not such a fool as you think. If you want me back, you're going to have to prove yourself to me." She crossed her arms, pouting.

Anna's face was reflective. "You look just like your grandmother, may she rest in peace." She shook her head in amazement. "That look on your face . . . the way you cross your arms. Everything. You're so beautiful."

Tatiana's face perked up. "You really think so?" she asked.

"Oh, yes," Anna replied. "You're a very traditional Russian beauty."

Tatiana smiled broadly. "Well, this isn't really my best angle," she confessed. "I think I look better from this side. What do you think?" She turned her head to the left.

Anna wanted to chuckle, but instead she agreed. "Oh, my. From that angle, you're an absolute princess."

"Really?"

"Oh, yes. Of course, that's only natural, since you are related, very distantly mind you, to the Romanovs."

"You're joking!"

"Oh, no, I'm quite serious," Anna assured her. "Our family has frequently intertwined with that of the royals. Unfortunately, all we have to show for it is a great deal of money."

"A great deal?"

"Oh, my, yes. How often my husband and I have thought it a pity that we've never had children. It's simply impossible for us to spend our fortune with only the two of us here. How he would love to have a precious girl to dress up in gowns and jewels."

"He . . . he would?"

"Oh, yes, naturally. He is a general, you know. Every general wants at least one daughter so he can show off her beauty and then deny his subordinates the pleasure of her company." She chuckled gaily.

"A general?" Tatiana's eyebrows rose high. "Does he . . . does he go to all of the balls, then?"

"Ugh! Don't even mention balls. I grow so weary of them!"

Tatiana swallowed hard. "Well . . . well, I guess," she stuttered, "that . . . well, that just because the Siskovs weren't my real parents doesn't mean I can't still love them."

"Absolutely not!" Anna cried excitedly. "Oh, now, wait a minute. Wait a minute. Stop." She placed a hand over her breast. "Oh, my, you're doing it again. You've got that royal look in you."

Tatiana froze, trying desperately to maintain the "royal look," whatever that was. "Am I doing it now?" she asked.

"Oh, yes," Anna assured her. "You really don't even have

to try. It just comes so naturally to you. Oh, my. Would you like to see a picture of your grandmother? It's in the spare bedroom.''

She shrugged, rising timidly to her feet. ''Why not?''

''Just watch your step as we go upstairs,'' Anna warned. ''The housekeeper is always forgetting to pick up the crystal trinkets my husband brings home as gifts.''

Tatiana came bounding home late in the evening. ''Erich!'' she cried, finding him in the front room with Senta. The two of them had obviously overcome their spat. ''Erich!'' she repeated. ''You'll never believe it!''

''What?'' he asked, rising to his feet. ''I was worried about you.''

Tatiana worked hard to catch her breath. ''I . . . I had the most incredible meeting today with Madame Kratchaya, that is, with my mother. Oh, Erich! It's really true. She is my mother! And do you know what? I'm possibly distantly related to the Romanovs! Can you believe it? The Romanovs! And she says I look just like them. She says that I'm beautiful in a very aristocratic sort of a way. Do you think I'm beautiful? I never thought I was. But maybe, when I turn my head a certain way. Do you think? Oh, Erich! I just can't believe it! All my life I thought I was nobody. But I'm really blue blood all the way! I knew I should've been drinking from crystal and eating from china. I just knew it. There was always something about those things that really appealed to me, and now I know why! It was in my blood. Oh, I just can't wait to go back there tomorrow! Did you know she has real carpets from Asia? I didn't believe it myself at first, but then I looked at them very closely, and sure enough, they're the real thing. I learned how to tell so I'd be a better burglar, of course. But I haven't told my mother about that yet. Somehow, I doubt it's fitting for a highborn lady to rob houses. Do you think? I guess I'd better keep that a secret for now.''

Erich could hardly believe she'd stopped chattering. He hadn't expected to get a word in edgewise for at least another twenty minutes. But miraculously, he managed to break in with ''Well, that's wonderful.'' He didn't mean it, and Senta knew he didn't mean it. Tatiana would have known it too if she hadn't been so self-absorbed at the moment.

''Oh!'' she cried, jumping up and down. ''I must tell Lev all about it! You don't mind if I go see him now that I'm not a prisoner, do you? I haven't seen him in a long time, and I know he'll want to hear the good news!''

''Ummm, yes,'' Erich murmured. ''Yes, of course. Go right on. But don't you want to eat first?''

''I'm too excited to eat!'' she cried. ''I'm too excited to do anything!'' She threw her parasol and hat to the floor and fled the house as quickly as she had entered it.

A long silence lingered in her wake. Erich was staring uncomfortably at the floor. And Senta was staring intently at her partner. ''Something wrong?'' she asked at long last.

''No,'' he lied, pacing to the window so he could watch Tatiana disappear down the street.

''I know better than that,'' Senta said.

Strangely, Erich felt the urge to confide. He wasn't sure why, but he suspected he would feel better if he put forth his feelings for someone else to examine. Perhaps it was part of this ''being in love'' business. ''I suppose,'' he said lifelessly, ''that it's easier to be attractive to a woman who has nothing than to a woman who has everything.''

Not realizing how cruel she was being, Senta laughed. ''Well, of course, Erich. I'm sure a peasant girl will fall into bed with any man who can house her and feed her. What did you think? That she was in love with you?''

Erich spun around and gave her a look that surely could have killed.

Chapter 24

Lev, while he could be flighty when it came to matters of personal responsibility, was quite hardheaded when it came to matters of uncontrollable circumstance. He had made his peace long ago with the seemingly random world of fate. And so, while lonely, he was not at all angry or disillusioned by the realization that Tatiana would never come home. He knew it was so. She was gone from the streets forever. What reason would she have for returning? She had met a handsome man, she was living in a nice house, she didn't have to risk her life by burglarizing anymore. She would have to be a fool to return. And Tatiana, he knew, was no fool. So he had resigned himself to his newly reacquired orphan status. He hoped she would stop by sometime, and he hoped that man of hers was treating her well. But he held no grudge.

As luck would have it, Lev had just come to accept Tatiana's permanent absence, when he found a ''roommate.'' It was one of his new friends from the Will of the People, a boy about his own age named Mikhail. Lev had been spending more and more time sitting around Yura's, talking to the revolutionaries. The other members had proven to be pretty good customers for him, so he was losing no money by loitering in their company. And more important, he was beginning to feel as though he really belonged to something. Lev had never belonged to a family. He had never belonged to a village out in the country. He didn't belong to a church. And he most certainly did not belong to Russia. Or, if he did, his country had not claimed him but left him on the streets to die.

The Will of the People told him things that made sense to him. They told him that the tsar really didn't care about him, which he was certain must be true. They told him the aristocracy didn't care about him. Again, he couldn't argue. And when he said, "But wait a minute. I don't care about them either," they said, "Oh? Then why do you let them live in the lap of luxury while you suffer?" When he suggested he didn't have a choice, they insisted that he did. He could join. He could become part of the family and help to make Russia "his" country instead of "theirs." Lev worried over the words Tatiana had spoken so long ago. Was joining these men really like jumping off a cliff? Was it really that dangerous to be seen with them? He worried about it. But when it came time to join, the Will of the People had been there, and Tatiana had not. He did not regret his decision.

Now that he was part of a family, of course, it seemed only right that he should take in one of his brothers. So when Mikhail had announced that he had only recently run away from home, where his parents had abused him, Lev thought he should offer the kid Tatiana's half of the bed. At first, he'd regretted that invitation. Mikhail snored. Not softly from time to time, like Tatiana. But all night, long and loudly. And he smelled worse than Lev did himself. Worst of all, Lev had accidentally put his arm around the boy one night in his sleep. When he woke up to find that he was snuggling not with Tatiana but with a redhead of his own physiological persuasion, he literally shouted. "Ahh! What are you doing here? Get out of my bed!" The next morning had been rather awkward. But now Lev was getting used to the lad. It wasn't like sleeping with his oldest and dearest friend, but it was better than being alone. At least, he had someone with whom to gulp shots of vodka before bed.

Lev was slouching out of the alleyway when he spotted a young middle-class lady in blue pinstripes. He thought about begging her for change just because he knew that young ladies walking alone in bad neighborhoods were usually eager to pay him for his absence. He wouldn't threaten her, of course. He was no animal. But there was a good chance that his grubby appearance would be enough to make her fork up the dough. Then he caught a glimpse at her face. "Tasha!" He ran to her, his thin legs lending him great speed.

"Oh, there you are!" she cried gleefully, putting one hand on her hat to keep it from flying off as she jogged.

The old friends embraced just as the warm night air caught their hair and made it entwine. "It's great to see you!" Lev grinned, looking her over with enthusiasm. "My, you look great in a dress."

Tatiana laughed, her cheeks rosy from excitement. "I guess this is the first time you've ever seen me in one, isn't it?"

"Yes," he marveled, then added teasingly, "and what I have been missing!"

They both laughed again. "This isn't even my best dress," Tatiana boasted. "You should see the white one! Oh, but the best one is gold with red roses. But that's only for special occasions."

Lev nodded his approval. "Sounds like Markov is taking good care of you. By the way, did you know he's come down here a couple of times without you?"

"Really?"

"Yes. He's been giving money to Pyotr for the . . . you know"—he shrugged, knowing how Tatiana felt about the Will of the People—"for the cause."

"Oh, I see," Tatiana replied uneasily. "Well, I'm glad he's such an asset."

"Yes, he sure is," Lev agreed. "But I'm kind of surprised it doesn't bother you. You nearly had a fit when I thought about joining. How come it's all right for him?"

"Because he'll not get arrested as easily as you," she replied with a certain amount of honesty. After all, she had no doubt that Erich would be harder to arrest than Lev.

Lev scowled a little at the implication that Markov was smarter than he. But then he decided to assume she had meant only that rich people had more protection. "Well, in any case, I'm glad he's buying you nice things."

That reminded Tatiana of what she really wanted to discuss. She started bending her knees anxiously, over and over, as though preparing to jump. "Oh, Lev!" she cried. "I won't need to rely on anyone's charity anymore!"

"I didn't know you ever did," he remarked.

"What do you call what I have with Eri—Markov?"

"An arrangement?" he suggested.

"That's not an arrangement!" she scolded. "When he buys me things and I give nothing in return, that's just charity, and I won't have it anymore!"

Lev lifted an eyebrow. "You call that 'nothing in return'?" He laughed. "I wish the women I lusted after thought it was 'nothing.' Then, when I bought them drinks and they asked me 'What's the catch?' I could say 'nothing,' and it would be the truth."

"Lev!" She socked him hard on the arm, which had finally healed from all his previous bruises. "What makes you think that I . . . that I do . . . that," she spat out, "with him?"

"Oh, I don't know," he drawled. "It's just an outrageous guess."

"Well, in any case," she said, slamming her fists to her hips. "Even if I did do that, it wouldn't be like some kind of a payment."

Lev shrugged. "He probably doesn't think that taking you in is some kind of payment either," he reasoned. "He probably likes having you there."

Tatiana sighed with exasperation. "Can I just tell you my exciting news?" she asked impatiently.

"Sure."

"I found my real mother!" she screamed, bouncing up and down. "I mean, I'd thought that I knew who my real mother was. But I was wrong! Oh, Lev, she's a real classy lady! Not like the Siskovs."

"Hey," Lev interrupted despite his bewilderment. "The Siskov family raised you, Tasha. I thought you loved them."

"Oh, I do," she said reluctantly. "But this lady has a beautiful house and Asian rugs! And crystal and diamonds! Oh, and, Lev, she goes to balls, and she's married to a general! Can you believe it?"

Lev could not. "What makes you think she's your real mother?" he asked, a suspicious scowl creeping over his face.

"She said so! And why would she lie? It was a real tragic tale, you see. She was forbidden to marry my father—he was a professor, you know, which explains why I'm so smart."

Lev rolled his eyes despite himself.

"And so she gave me away to the Siskovs to be raised, but then she saw me at a ball and she asked my name. When she heard it was Siskova, she knew it was me, and she told me today that she wants me back! Can you believe it, Lev? I'm related to real aristocrats, which explains why I've always liked pretty things so much, and good food too."

"Tasha, everyone likes pretty things and good food."

"Well, not as much as I do!" she insisted, pouting. "But I guess I shouldn't expect you to understand. You'd have to be an aristocrat to really know what it means to crave the finer things in life."

Lev wanted to start laughing and almost did. "Tasha," he

implored her, "you became an aristocrat only a few hours ago! It's a little soon to be looking down your nose at people."

"I'm not looking down my nose! I am just . . . just explaining to you what it's like to have such blue blood. Anyway, can't you be happy for me?"

Lev swallowed, trying to collect himself. "I—" he sighed. "I am happy that you're happy. But isn't this all happening a little fast?"

"Oh, Lev," she pleaded, "can't you understand? All my life I thought I was nobody, like a . . . like a—"

"Like me?" he suggested coldly.

She shook her head. "No, Lev. You, at least, are a boy." A long silence fell between them. Tatiana's face grew morbid. "Don't you see, Lev? Out here, girls are nothing but weaker versions of men. And worse yet, they have the inconvenient habit of making babies no one can afford to keep. But up there it's different. In their world there are gowns and jewels and dances and courtship. They can afford to have two sexes. They even enjoy it. I'll be worth something. For the first time in my life, I'll be worth something."

Lev groaned a bit, tilting his head from side to side. He'd always known that Tatiana hated being a girl. And it was true what she was saying, that poor people had less use for girls than rich people did. He imagined that made her feel pretty worthless. He ought to be happy for her, he told himself. He ought to congratulate her. But there was something wrong about this. "What . . . well, what about Markov?" he stumbled. "I thought you liked him. Are you just going to up and leave? Move in with your new 'family'?"

"Wouldn't you?" she asked.

"No," he said stubbornly. "No, I wouldn't. Not if I had someone."

"Well, it's not as though I won't see him anymore," she insisted. "I'll just see him in a more . . . proper setting. You know, real courtship and all of that. It wouldn't be right for a lady of my standing to live in sin.''

"Never bothered you before.''

"That was before!'' she cried indignantly. "It was before I knew who I really am!''

"I think you already knew who you were,'' he challenged. "I think you're forgetting it now.''

"You just don't understand!''

"Does Markov understand?''

Her lips quivered for a moment, then she lowered her eyes. "I haven't told him yet. Well, not the part about moving out anyway.''

"I thought you really liked him, Tasha. It seemed like you did. You couldn't even talk about him without blushing.''

"I do like him,'' she answered quietly. "I like him a lot. But . . . but this is more important. This is family.''

"Is it?'' he asked boldly. "Because we've been standing here for nearly fifteen minutes, and I haven't heard you mention anything except money. You haven't even said you like the lady.''

Tatiana's eyes fluttered wide. "Well, I don't know her very well yet.''

"Yeah, that's what happens when someone abandons you for eighteen years.'' His face was tough and bold. "I'll tell you what, Tasha. You can say what you want about how poor people don't like girls. But don't forget, it was a rich family that had you sent away and a poor family that raised you and treated you right.''

Tatiana averted her eyes a moment. "I'd hoped you would be happy for me.''

"Yeah, well, maybe Markov will be.''

She turned back to Lev, looking at his sarcastic smirk with eyes that boiled. Why did he make it sound as though she were dealing Erich some terrible hand? She wouldn't forget about him. She wouldn't stop seeing him. This would be a blessing for them both, really, for she would be out of his hair, and he wouldn't have to worry about her being on the streets. Why couldn't Lev be happy for her? And why, she wondered miserably as she turned her toes toward home, did she have the sinking suspicion that Erich wouldn't be either?

She found him lying in bed, alone in the dark, his hands behind his head. She stood in the doorway, fully dressed, gazing down at his beautiful rippled body. He knew she had come in, but he did not look at her. He gazed placidly out the window, into the beautiful starry night. It was the window he had always kept closed before she came. He said nothing. And she said nothing. Neither of them moved for a long time. She thought about saying hello, she thought about apologizing for running out in such a hurry and then returning so late. But she did not. She found herself breathless. Her heart was pounding. Her knees were buckling. And she could bear to tell him nothing except what plagued her most of all. "I'm moving in with Anna Kratchaya," she whispered shakily.

He still did not turn his head. His voice was deep like the night. "I know."

She undressed awkwardly without the lantern light. She crawled into bed, as far from Erich as she could manage. Her eyes were wide, her pupils enormous. Her breath was loud enough to be heard. Neither of them closed their eyes even once that night, nor did they speak, nor did they reach out to touch each oother. They stared through the same window and let the same breeze soothe their faces. And when the sun began to rise, they both watched. Silently, they observed the beauty of the orange light emerging where there had been only darkness for hours. But they were not amazed, and they were not in awe. For the power of a sunrise to transform the sky was nothing compared to the power of chance to transform their lives.

Chapter 25

"I can't let her go!" Erich stormed back and forth across the parlor as Senta watched from the comfort of the chair.

"Why not?" she asked lightly. "You said you can trust her not to tell our secret. And since I owe you one, I'm taking your word. So what's the problem?"

"The problem," he shouted, "is that I love her! I've never loved anyone before, and I'm not going to let her leave just like that."

This was a very bad day to be talking to Senta about love. Actually, there was no good time to confide in her on such matters, since she was hardly a sentimental sort. But today the subject was especially touchy. She was having problems of her own related to that very topic. She had spent all night in the arms of Tomasz, not making love, as she was employed to do, but being held. That's all he had wanted, to lie there and hold her. The guilt was unbearable. It was one thing to play trickery upon a man who was using her. It was quite another to deceive a man who claimed actually to love her. Her patriotism was overshadowed by her sense of personal honor. She felt that what she was doing with Tomasz had become wrong.

Worse yet, Senta was beginning to return his feelings. As far as she knew, no man had ever loved her before. Not a lover, not even her father had truly cared for her. For that reason she was completely unguarded against this deep affection Tomasz showed her. She had built many walls to ward off treachery and violence but not one to protect her from this tenderness, this unforeseen enemy. She had tried to tell herself that he loved Irina, not her. But the more time she spent with him, the more she felt certain that he knew her deepest heart. He did not know her thoughts. He did not know her secrets. But he knew her heart and could feel the rhythm of its waves. She had never felt so happy or so torn. The task of keeping her mind on business grew harder and more tiresome. To do it, she had to shut down her feelings completely, especially all thoughts of love. And it was because she was working so hard to be cold that she answered Erich's plea in such a heartless way.

"You're in love?" she scoffed. "Is that what you call it?"

Erich looked at her with surprise. He did not understand her meaning.

"That's funny," she said, sauntering toward him dramatically. "Because I had gotten the impression that you were a decent man, a man of morals and integrity."

"What?" He squinted, confused. "What are you talking about?"

Senta's smile was evil. "It's not like you, Erich. You're usually so sharp about people. I'm surprised you can't see better into your own self."

Erich responded only with a bizarre and questioning look.

"You know what I'm talking about," she said cruelly. "If you look in your heart, you know what's going on here."

"I do?" He looked almost amused by her strangeness.

"Mmm-hmm." She nodded. "Don't tell me you've never

thought about it. Come on, Erich. You buy her clothes, you order her about, you even sent her to bed without her supper the first night. What's that all about? You tell me.''

Erich stiffened. ''I had to buy her clothes,'' he answered uncomfortably. ''She had nothing to wear. And she was a captive—I had to exercise control. And I don't order her around anymore! At least, I try not to.''

''Erich,'' she said patronizingly, as though she understood. ''Why don't you just admit it? She's girlish and innocent, and that's what you like about her. There's nothing wrong with that, but it's not love.''

''What . . . what?''

''Think about it,'' she said dryly. ''I know we're both pretty isolated here in this godforsaken city, but that's no reason to start thinking we love people we don't!'' She lowered her voice when she realized she'd become impassioned. ''Erich,'' she began again, ''it isn't love. It's some kind of a . . . a sickness you have.''

''What the hell are you talking about?'' His eyes were narrow with uncertain rage.

''You don't want a lover!'' she blurted out. ''You want a daughter!'' She whispered hoarsely into the silence that followed. ''And with Tatiana, I guess you've found both.''

Erich was so stunned, he looked at Senta as though she were some sort of demon. If she had been a man, he was sure he would have punched her. Since she was not, he didn't know what to do.

''Oh, it's not so bad,'' she consoled him. ''Believe me, I know what it's like to lose your senses on this mission. But you've got to let her go. She's distracting you. You've got to let her go just like I—it just isn't love, all right? I know it isn't love.''

Erich was shaking his head, trying to ward off the darkness Senta had summoned. He was perspiring. ''It's not like that,'' he croaked. ''It's not true. I—I just love her.''

"You don't want to be her father?" Senta challenged.

"No, no, of course not."

"Then, tell me this," she ordered, stepping even closer to him. "How old are you, Erich?"

He looked weak. As huge as he was, he suddenly looked too feeble to hold himself up. "That's not fair," he whispered quakingly. "That's not fair. I lost my youth to this job. You know that. The time I spent in prison—it doesn't count."

"It doesn't count?" she asked brutally. "Or does it count twice, Erich? Did it age you not at all? Or did it age you even more rapidly?"

Erich swallowed, his throat swelling and thinning violently.

"How old are you?" she asked.

"Thirty-two."

"Thirty-two," she repeated as though she could not imagine a higher number. "That's a lot of years, Erich. And how old do you suppose your little Tatiana is?"

He muttered something incoherent.

"What?"

"I don't know!" he shouted, then lowered his voice again. "I never asked her."

"Well, then, guess."

"I—I don't know."

"Do you think she's even twenty yet?"

Erich bowed his head.

"Well?" she demanded.

"Probably not," he admitted.

Senta's nod was triumphant. "I see." She placed a hand on his broad shoulder, but he shook it off. "Fine," she relented, lifting her palm to the air. "I won't touch you. But I suggest you don't let that little girl touch you anymore either." She waited for Erich's retort, but none came. Finally, she said, "Look. She has her whole life ahead of her. Let her go to her mommy, Erich. Finish your job, and let the little girl go to her mommy."

Erich regained his strength but not his determination. He knew that Senta was right. He knew that he was too old and jaded for love, and especially for a lively young girl like Tatiana. He knew that he would only be holding her back from a life of promise. And worst of all, he knew that he loved her youth and vigor, just as Senta had said. And that his feelings were at times . . . fatherly.

"You'll thank me someday," Senta assured him.

His eyes held bite. In fact, they were so startlingly hostile, Senta fell away from them. "I shall never thank you," he assured her. "And I shall never really like you. You have taken from me the only thing I've ever wanted for myself and not for my country. Your words persuade me, but your cruelty does not evade me. I shall never think you have done this for my benefit." He stormed upstairs to help Tatiana pack.

Chapter 26

The farewell was not a tearful one for Tatiana. After all, she was quite certain that she and Erich would see each other again soon. And besides, she was too excited to be forlorn. This day had been like a dream.

Erich let her keep all the clothes he'd bought her, including the golden ball gown. She chose her white, ruffly dress for the carriage ride. With a bounce in her step and white feathers in her hat, she watched anxiously as Erich loaded her trunk into the buggy. "Don't drop it!" she cried nervously.

Erich shot her a look that showed he was insulted, then proceeded to lift her luggage effortlessly. He kissed her cheek good-bye and did not let her see his pain. He wanted this to be nothing less than the happiest day of her life, and so it was. Her new parents had sent this carriage, and it was a fine one. It was sleek and black on the outside, red and soft on the inside. The horses were black, lean, and majestic. Tatiana kept wringing her hands, looking outside the window as though she had never seen St. Petersburg before. It was a bright, sunny day despite the cool temperature, and Tatiana felt certain that the morning was welcoming her to a new life. Her smile was fed by the joy deep within. She couldn't have stopped grinning if she'd wanted to.

When the buggy pulled up to her mother's yellow house, Tatiana could have sworn it looked more beautiful and welcoming than it had before. The tall windows seemed to glitter in the sunlight, and the many flower boxes on the sills and porch made the place look homey despite its enormity. She was surprised when General Kratchy himself raced to help unload her trunks. "You must be Tatiana!" he cried jovially, forcing an embrace upon the girl.

Tatiana liked the look of him. He was tall and stout but not at all menacing. His rosy cheeks were fat and cheerful. His hair was a marvelous silver, as was his outrageously long mustache. It curled upward at both ends, giving it something of a comical look. Only a dot of hair served as a beard. "I'm pleased to meet you," she said, curtsying as best she could.

"Oh, no need for such formality," he chuckled. "You're family now. And did Anna tell you how much I've just been itching to have a little girl?"

"I'm not a little girl." Tatiana frowned. "I'm eighteen years old."

"Oh, I beg your pardon," he said, twisting his mustache. "All I meant was, well, that it'll be nice to have a young woman around the house. And you're such a handsome one too," he added.

Tatiana gulped. "Really? Do you think so? I've never been called handsome before. I always suspected my neck wasn't long enough for handsomeness. Don't handsome women have to have long necks? And oval faces? Mine is round, you know."

General Kratchy laughed with delight. "Oh, Tatiana. You're just as your mother said you were. Welcome to the family." His blue eyes sparkled with friendliness.

Tatiana felt overjoyed. General Kratchy was a nice man, she

decided. And he accepted her fully even though she was fathered by another man. Living with the Kratchys, she believed, would be a delight. There was nothing more to fear now. She had met them both, had seen their home, and everything was in order. It seemed there would be no obstacles to her newfound happiness. She followed eagerly behind as the general carried her luggage. The inside of the house was even fancier than she'd remembered. How long had it taken to collect so many useless and beautiful antiques? Oh, how she wished Lev were here so he could see she had told the truth about her new mother's home. Oh, how she wished the whole world could see her now!

Her bedroom was positively luxurious. She loved it instantly. It was on the third floor and had a beautiful view of a park. Standing in the window, she could look down and, way below her, see children running and playing as well-dressed couples walked arm in arm through the grass and trees. Her bed was wonderfully soft and puffy. It was a white canopy bed splattered with patterns of spring flowers of pastel pink, green, blue, lavender, and yellow. When she playfully spread herself across the mattress, she felt clean, surrounded by so much white and softness. This room had a white rug. It was soft and shaggy and made Tatiana feel as though she were walking through snow. The numerous ornate dressers were so crammed against the walls that Tatiana did not think she could ever have enough belongings to fill them. But it didn't matter, she supposed. For their shining reddish presence added elegance to the otherwise girlish room. Yes, she felt she would easily find herself at home in this little hideaway on the third floor.

All in all, her first day passed smoothly. There was a little tension after she had finished settling in and now she had to find some way to fill the afternoon. The general was in his study and was not to be disturbed. Anna was busily crocheting, a hobby to which Tatiana had no previous exposure. "What should I do?'' she asked Anna, expecting somehow that there should be a very obvious answer.

The woman lifted her pale gold eyes from her task. ''Well, I don't know. What are your hobbies?'' she asked.

Tatiana shrugged. Robbing people? Drinking vodka? Driving Erich mad? She wasn't sure what to say.

''Well, why don't you read a book,'' her mother suggested kindly.

''Can't read.''

Tatiana had said this without shame or hesitation, but Anna was shocked. ''My word, child! You can't—'' Her mouth kept moving, but no sound emerged. Finally, she got hold of herself and suggested, ''Well, why don't you draw a picture, then. We have smocks and paints in the art room.''

This sounded like fun. Tatiana, of course, had never painted a picture before, but how hard could it be? ''What should I paint a picture of?''

''Why, whatever you like.'' Anna smiled.

''Can I paint a picture of something I don't like?''

''Why, yes. I suppose so.''

''Does it have to be a person? Are paintings always of people?''

''No, not always. Many of Russia's finest painters have specialized in scenery, or even the portrayal of simple objects.''

''Why do they draw scenery when people can just look out their window and see it?''

Anna had to cock her head to think about this one. ''Well, I suppose,'' she reasoned, ''that an artist tries to show beauty in the things he paints. Beauty beyond what is obvious to the naked eye.''

That settled it for Tatiana. ''I think I'll paint a chair.''

''A chair?''

''Yes.''

''Why on earth would you choose a chair of all things?''

''Well, everyone knows that flowers are pretty, and sunsets

and birds. Why should I tell them something they already know? Shouldn't I try to show the beauty in something they think is too ordinary to be lovely?''

Anna was grinning. ''I suppose you have a point there.''

''Of course I do.''

''Good, then, go paint.''

''A chair?''

''Yes, yes, fine. Go on.'' Anna shook her head as she returned to her crocheting. ''Paint a marvelous chair. Just be done before supper.''

Tatiana was delighted when she found the art room. It was a hidden room, tucked in the back of the house, facing a little fence over which Tatiana could not see. One wall was made entirely of glass. From the canvas, she could look into the little rear flower garden, imagining that there was nothing beyond that yellow fence. This room, though filled with light, may have been the most private room she'd ever seen. She eagerly tied a paint-splattered smock around her waist, fearful of spilling anything on her white gown. It took some rummaging through unfinished pottery and abandoned drawings to find the paints, but when she found them, she was delighted. So many colors! Oh, this painting thing would be a delight. There was even a rugged little unfinished chair in the corner of the room that beckoned to be this artist's first subject. Tatiana began her project with a sigh of delight.

Then she ran into trouble. It was quite plain to her that the chair had four legs of equal length, yet somehow, when she drew them that way, they looked all wrong. She had to erase it. But how does one erase paint? She tried to rub it off with her smock, but that didn't work at all. In fact, the smear looked far worse than the funny legs had. Then she had another idea. The white paint. She would use it to cover her mistake. Of course! Unfortunately, adding white to her brown only made a horrible shade of beige and did not erase her drawing one bit. She decided she must continue, skipping over that section of the chair until she came up with a solution. She would draw the seat. Hmm. This led to problems as well. The seat was perfectly square in real life, yet, in her drawing the square seat looked as though it were standing upright! This was disastrous. She hated painting.

Angrily, she kept striking at her canvas with the brush, hoping that if she kept moving her hand, eventually, something would look like ... well, like something! She struggled with the wretched artwork for hours, but it was no use. She was making a big mess, and her "painting" was getting uglier and uglier by the second. Flustered, she made a fist and knocked the canvas to the ground. Now she had paint all over her fist. She rubbed it anxiously against her smock, but it would not come clean. That infuriated her. That stupid painting was not only ugly, it had ruined her hand—perhaps forever! Oh, no. That was a horrible thought. What if paint could not be removed? What if she would always have a streak of red across her knuckles? Angrier than ever, she kicked what was left of her hopeless painting, screaming when she realized she had now soiled her boot.

"Tatiana?" called Anna. "Is everything all right in there?"

Tatiana panicked. She tore off her smock and threw it to the ground, covering the broken, wet canvas that was now sticking to the floor. "Everything's fine!" she called. Oh, no. Oh, no.

"How is your painting?"

"It's—" She bit her nail. "It needs work."

"Well, wash up, dear. It's almost time for supper."

"W-wash up?" She looked at her brightly colored fist.

"Yes! The paint remover is by the basin."

Tatiana thought she would collapse in relief. It took her another half hour to scrub herself, the floor, and the walls with paint thinner. But at last, with her hair loose from its knot in several awkward places, she arrived at the dinner table.

She was stunned by the beauty of it. The dining room was a dark, romantic place encased in wood paneling. Grand French doors were opened wide, welcoming in the crisp night air. Tatiana could see a small iron patio just on the other side of them. And beyond that, moist grass glimmered in the moonlight. Above her head was not one but two crystal chandeliers ringing in the breeze. And then there was the room's centerpiece. A real tablecloth was draped over a heavy, thick oak table. The cloth was of red lace and hung in round swoops over the edge like curtains. On the center of the table were long white candles whose flames struggled to stay alive in the wind. And each place was set with what looked like genuine silver.

The general sat on one side, his wife on the other. Tatiana was urged to take her place between them, facing the open French doors. There was a graceful moment when the general bowed his head in blessing. It was a good blessing, a traditional Orthodox blessing like the ones Tatiana's father used to give— or the man she'd thought was her father. When the general's words ended, he smiled and urged the ladies to begin eating. Tatiana immediately reached for her fork, proud of herself for remembering not to use her hands. Then a servant brought in the food, the likes of which Tatiana had never known.

In fact, Erich's culinary skills may have been superior to those of the Kratchys' chef. His food had a nicer taste about it. But it was never presented so elegantly, nor was it made from such expensive ingredients. Six kinds of caviar were spooned onto Tatiana's plate. Steaming rye bread was accompanied by three different styles of mustard. Marinated smoked fish, spicy tomatoes, pickled cucumbers, and heavily salted, roasted fowl were all piled onto her plate at command. Tatiana hoped the Kratchys did not think she was eating too much, but when she looked up from her plate worriedly, she saw that they were only smiling. Apparently, they were taking delight in her enjoyment of the meal. "Is there any vodka?" she asked, disappointed to find plain water in her cup.

Anna gasped. "Tatiana, ladies do not drink vodka!"

Now it was Tatiana who gasped. "They don't?"

"Of course not!"

The general broke in with a jolly smile and peacemaking words. "Why, Tatiana, haven't you ever heard of Peter the Great?"

"Sure." She shrugged.

"Well, then, surely you know what he said about women."

"Uh . . . no."

He chuckled good-heartedly. "He said that women are the great civilizers of men. Without their decency and respectable behavior, men would be nothing but barbarians. In fact, that was the case before Peter insisted that women be allowed to attend all social functions. Before that, social functions were ugly, brutal, unappetizing events. But when women arrived on the public scene, they civilized us men. Taught us that there's more to fun than drinking and brawling."

Tatiana felt she ought to feign understanding, but she did not comprehend one bit. After a moment of silence had passed, she said, "So . . . I guess that's why you won't give me a drink?"

"Precisely."

She jerked her head in confusion but decided the matter was better let alone. After all, she could break into their liquor cabinet later on. There was no sense in arguing.

"So, my dear," the general continued, "I understand you've become an artist today."

Tatiana took a big bite of fowl, then, with her mouth full, replied, "No, I've decided that painting is very difficult."

The general laughed. "It's not easy the first time, is it? Why, I believe I've taken up that peculiar hobby over a dozen times but never had the gumption to stick with it."

Tatiana was too busy eating to reply.

"Well," Anna offered courteously, "soon, she won't have time for such hobbies anyway. She'll be far too occupied with all her new beaus."

Tatiana looked up from her plate. "I will?"

"Why, yes," Anna cried. "In fact, I have the suspicion that a very eligible young man from the Chekov family is going to pay you a visit tomorrow."

"Why?"

Anna laughed beautifully. "Oh, silly. Because he wants to meet the new young lady in our home, of course. He wants to court you!"

Tatiana wrinkled her forehead. "But he's never even seen me."

"He doesn't have to see you, darling! He knows all about you. I've been bragging about you."

"Wait a minute, wait a minute. He's never even seen me but he wants to court me?"

"That's right."

"Just because I'm your daughter?"

"We're a respectable family, you know."

A huge grin overwhelmed Tatiana's face. "I like it!"

The couple laughed delightedly. "I think we're going to have to keep an eye on her," the general teased. "She might be just a little too fond of the boys, I think."

"See to it you're at least a little bit choosy," Anna advised.

"Choosy?" Tatiana asked. "You mean there will be more boys courting me? Not just one?"

"Dozens, I should think."

"Ah, don't be so modest." The general grinned to his wife. "Once they get a look at her, they'll be swarming in by the hundreds."

"Oh, I don't think so," Tatiana protested, shrinking into a blush.

The general's eyes twinkled with fatherly pride. "Don't you underestimate yourself, my dear. All you need is a man with a good eye. A man with a good eye would pick you from a crowd of a thousand."

"A thousand *men,* maybe."

Both the general and his wife burst into laughter at that. But

Tatiana smiled dreamily throughout the rest of the meal. Would the men really find her pretty? Would they really come to call on her? She hoped they would be handsome. What would she do if they weren't? Oh, well. There'd be time enough for rehearsing rejections later. Right then she needed to get her beauty sleep! That's what Anna had called it, and Tatiana hoped it would work.

She lay in her soft white bed, gazing out her window into the empty park. It had grown cold, but Tatiana would not close the window. She wasn't afraid of the elements. She never had been. In the countryside, she had learned to face the weather and, no matter how threatening it was, to hold her chin high. There was no hiding from cold when you are poor. She was glad for those lessons she had learned as a girl. For while others bundled up as though the slightest chill would carry their death, she had faced this enemy, this cold. And she had made her peace with it, would never be afraid of it again. Like Erich.

She was frightened by the silence all around her. The Kratchys slept on the second floor, while she slept on the third. She could hear nothing. No creaking, no whispers, nothing. It was as though the world would be dead until morning. Tatiana froze in that thought. Then her heart gave way, and the tears began to fall. She had not thought of Erich once all day. Not once. But now, in the silence, her heart fell. It tickled as it dropped; it bent her in half. Gripping her stomach, she wailed out her cries of longing, a feeling she had not known was there. Within seconds, her entire face was a wet sponge, her mouth could not close, and her body convulsed. "Where are you?" she thought. "Oh, come get me. Please. I miss you so badly. Why aren't you here? Please." She had never seen this coming. She had never known that she loved him so much. But tonight, she thought her body would break if it could not be wrapped in his embrace.

* * *

"Poor girl," Anna said, from a distant room below. "She seems like such a sweet thing."

"I'll agree with that," her husband said, nestled snugly between a pair of satin sheets.

"She really is such a delight," Anna continued as she brushed her long hair. "I almost hate to trick her like this."

"I know what you mean, my love. I've been feeling that same guilt. But we must do what we must."

"I know," Anna sighed. "But won't she be disappointed when she learns the truth?"

"Who says she has to learn it?"

Anna was startled. "You mean—"

"We'll see," he replied sleepily. "We'll see how she works out."

Chapter 27

Erich did not weep or pine away for Tatiana. He thought of her at every moment of every hour, but only in the far reaches of his mind. If he had learned anything over the course of his career, it was how to tuck away his pain and move forward. He was frozen again, just as he had been before Tatiana came into his life. He did not enjoy his food, he did not sleep, and he looked forward to nothing. But at least he was productive. He was making great strides in his relationship with the Will of the People. He was helping them purchase the explosives and weapons necessary for their dastardly work. He was earning their trust, learning more specifics regarding their plans. It would not be long before he could go home.

Tatiana had been gone only a day when he received a strange pounding at his front door. Eyebrows raised, he answered it but did not recognize the furious man on the other side. "Can I help you?"

"Yes, you swine!" the handsome youth cried. "You can keep your filthy hands off my fiancée!"

Erich acquired a look of something between amusement and astonishment, his blue-green eyes twinkling wide as his mouth curved. "Gladly. Who is your fiancée?"

"You know damned well who she is! Irina!"

Erich suddenly recognized this lad. He looked different with his long hair hanging loosely about his shoulders, but he was the man who'd escorted Senta to the ball. He was Tomasz Muronov. "Oh, Tomasz. It's good to see you." Erich smiled disrespectfully, proving that he was not affected by the young man's threats. "I haven't seen you since the Winter Palace. Things are going well with Irina, I take it."

"They were until you came along!" The man was at an age at which he took himself very seriously. He was using all his might to stay angry in the eyes.

"I see," Erich replied curiously. "It seems we should discuss this somewhere else. My maid has taken ill today, and the house is not presentable. Shall we walk?"

Tomasz brushed back his hair, wondering whether it would be virile enough of him to agree to this. "Fine," he said at last. "But you have some explaining to do."

"It sounds that way." Erich toyed with him. "One moment, I'll fetch my coat."

Erich reappeared in his usual black uniform, the long coat flowing behind him in the breeze. He kept his hands in their pockets for warmth but did not touch his gun. He was not afraid of lovestruck boys. "Listen, you," Tomasz began, trying to recover his anger. "I want to know what Irina was doing here last night. Or, rather, I don't want to know, but I want it to stop! Look, I know what she used to do for a living, but all of that is over now. She's my fiancée, and she's off limits! Do you understand me?"

Erich wrinkled his brow. "What brings you to believe she visited me last night?"

"I saw her! I followed her here!"

"Oh, I see. That's very, uh—" he searched for the word. "Disturbed?"

"Damn you!" Tomasz cried, his face reddening from anger and frustration. "Can't you see? I love her, and I don't want anyone else to touch her! I woke up last night. She thought I was sleeping. But I saw her leave, and I had a suspicion that she was still seeing . . . well, customers. So I followed her and saw you answer the door."

"Ahhh." Erich started to feel pity for the boy. The poor thing really was suffering over this illusion. "I suppose you wouldn't believe me if I told you I didn't touch her."

Tomasz looked as though he wanted very much to believe just that. But he needed a reason for his faith. "Why would she be visiting so late at night if . . . well, if . . ."

"Because she owed me money, and I'd threatened that if I did not receive it by midnight of last night, I would come for her to collect it." Erich had always been good at making up excuses on the spot.

"Why did she owe you money?" Tomasz asked suspiciously.

"Do you really want to know?"

He nodded.

"Very well, then. I did hire Irina many weeks ago, long before she met you. Before she left that night, she told me a pitiful story about needing food for her children, whom I later learned did not exist. I can only imagine where she spent those rubles." He tried to look frustrated and cheated. "But I don't know any man who can listen to a woman sobbing without doing whatever it takes to appease her. So I gave her the money but told her it was only a loan. She avoided me for weeks, but when I happened upon her yesterday, I told her in no uncertain terms that I was to be paid by midnight. I don't know where she got the money," he mused. "You might want to check your pockets. But the important thing is, I have been repaid and will not have to carry out a threat against a woman, a task I did not relish.''

Tomasz was visually relieved by this elaborate though smoothly presented lie. ''Well,'' he sighed, ''the next time Irina owes you money, you just come to me. She's my responsibility now.''

Erich did his best to nod humbly.

Tomasz started walking again, this time at a more leisurely pace. Erich followed, allowing a long silence to travel with them, until it seemed the right time to bring up the very obvious next topic of conversation. ''So . . . when exactly did you become engaged?''

''Last night,'' Tomasz boasted. ''I asked her to marry me, and I couldn't believe it. She actually said yes.''

Erich supposed he shouldn't ask any of the questions that were crossing his mind, like ''Are you sure she heard you?'' ''Was she awake?'' ''Was she sober?'' Senta had not mentioned this startling news when she'd come over to update Erich on her progress. But even if he'd not seen her at all, he'd have known this news was false. Senta would never marry.

''I know what you're thinking,'' Tomasz said.

''You do?'' That seemed unlikely.

''Yes. You're thinking she's too old for me.''

Erich stopped walking and burst into a fit of laughter. He tried to muffle it with his sleeve, but it just kept coming.

''What is it?'' Tomasz demanded. ''Is it so amusing that I should love an older woman?''

Erich couldn't believe that he wasn't able to stop laughing. But when he managed to get a breath of air, he asked, ''How much older is she?''

Tomasz swallowed hard, then answered uncomfortably. ''Eight years.''

The laughter returned to Erich, and it was another minute before he could put his arm about Tomasz's shoulder to apologize. "I'm sorry, comrade," he said at last. "I'm sorry. My laughter has nothing to do with you. Please, tell me more."

Tomasz felt uneasy but nonetheless continued. "Well, I don't see why just because I'm twenty-one and she's twenty-nine, we can't have a perfectly happy life together. I rose quickly in my career. I was at the top of all my classes at the university and was selected immediately to work directly beside the tsar. I think that should say something about my ability to take care of a wife."

"Unquestionably."

"And most important," he concluded, "I love Irina." His eyes were sober, his face filled with longing. "I can see her. I can see her heart as though it were sprung from my own. Oh, I know she puts on airs, pretending to be so frivolous all the time. But deep inside she's hurting. And I can feel it. When she suffers, I do as well. And that's why I know that I must devote myself to her. I must marry her. I must see to it that she never weeps again. Not even on the inside."

Erich had spent much of his life studying people and their lies. He knew without a doubt that this boy was no liar and meant every word he said. He knew that Senta had stumbled into something much bigger than she had anticipated.

He waited for her, a cup of hot coffee in his hand. Part of him looked mischievously forward to teasing her about this lovestruck boy who was following her around. But part of him felt so desperately sorry for the boy that he wanted to scold Senta for leading him on. Humor won over in the end. "Hello," he said sarcastically, helping her out of her cloak.

"Ah! What a day I'm having," she complained.

"I understand congratulations are in order."

She looked at his patronizing expression and returned it with her own. "Why, Erich. I believe that's the first time you've made a joke since Tatiana left."

He winced inwardly at the sound of Tatiana's name. But his body remained stoic. "What makes you think I'm joking?"

Senta put both hands on her hips. "Erich Reitz, you know perfectly well that I am not engaged. Where did you hear about that?"

"From a young man who came over here ready to beat me senseless because he thought I was taking advantage of you."

"He thought what?"

"Thought we were having an affair, or actually something less decent than that. But don't worry, I straightened him out." He poured some Prussian wine into a glass. "When's the wedding?"

Senta rolled her eyes as she accepted the drink. "There won't be a wedding," she snapped. "It was probably the sixth time he'd brought up marriage. I was afraid if I didn't say yes this time, he might cut off relations with me, and I can't afford that. He's about to get the tsar's schedule for next year's trips to St. Petersburg. We must have it."

"You mean to say you're going to break that poor boy's heart?" Erich asked, leaning against the wall with his arms crossed.

"Not yet, I'm not."

Erich raised an eyebrow. "You aren't even a little drawn to him?"

"Of course not. He's Russian."

"But he's handsome."

"I don't think so," she lied. "I never find foreigners handsome. I like my own kind." She tried not to look at Erich when she said that, for she did not want to remind him that he was a perfect specimen of "her own kind."

"Oh, what's so bad about Russians?" he asked.

She flicked her eyelashes upward, then returned to her drink. "They're our enemy."

"Not yet," he reminded her. "They were on our side against France."

"Last time, they were. But you know perfectly well that their loyalties are shifting. We won't be able to count on them again."

Erich consented to that. But he added, "Still, I wonder whether that's the real reason for your aversion to young Tomasz."

Senta met his eyes challengingly. "Oh?"

"Well," he said, trying hard to repress a smile, "there is the other obvious problem between you."

"And what would that be?"

"Being the moral woman you are, I'm sure you can see the error in seducing such a vulnerable child as himself. Especially," he added with absolute devilishness, "at your great age."

Senta's eyes narrowed. "What great age? I'll have you know I am only twenty—five."

"That's not what I heard."

Senta was fuming, her teeth grinding, her eyes smoldering. "I would not betray my country by falling in love with a . . . with a half Slav!"

"Watch it," he warned her, and she retreated. She was coming too close to insulting Tatiana, and Erich's eyes showed he would not tolerate it.

"But if I wanted to," she continued quietly, "I'm sure I could marry any young man in this filthy country, or ours, for that matter. I am not too old!"

"I see," Erich said, letting her wallow in her own hypocrisy.

After a few awkward moments, she asked, "Is this about Tatiana? Because if it is—"

"No," he interrupted, turning to face the window. "No, this is not about her. You were right that I should let her go. It wasn't fair of me to drag her into my cold world, to expose her to my bitterness. I have no doubts about that now." His words were hollow, expressionless, and unconvincing. "I wish only that I had realized it sooner."

"Why?" Senta asked, becoming suddenly concerned. "You mean, before you bedded her?"

Erich was silent, and something in his stillness gave him away.

"Erich," she gasped. "You didn't ... you didn't ... you didn't take her virginity, did you? Surely, a girl like that had been around, right?"

Erich crossed his arms and sighed heavily. There was nothing he could say, no way to undo what he had done. He hoped only that somewhere, in a lovely room across the city, Tatiana was happy and oblivious of the magnitude of what he had taken from her. Perhaps she would find a husband who did not mind, a husband who would make her forget her dark days of captivity.

Chapter 28

Tatiana came to the breakfast room late in the morning, for there had been no one to awaken her. The Kratchys were a bit annoyed by her unhurried arrival, but they did not scold her. Anna only looked up from her morning soup and said, "I hope you don't mind we started without you, Tatiana."

"Not at all," she replied, failing to catch the underlying complaint. She settled herself into the beckoning seat but looked at the fare with some disinterest. She had eventually fallen asleep last night, after a good deal of crying. But she had not awakened refreshed but with a heavy stone in her heart. She sighed sluggishly. "Is this *ukhah?*" she asked of the soup.

Anna nodded while blowing on a spoonful of her own.

Tatiana ladled some into her bowl, but her eyes were drowsy, and her hands did not move quickly.

"Is something troubling you?" the general asked, a lift in his rosy cheeks. "I wouldn't think you'd be so sullen on the day Gleb Chekov is coming to court you."

"His name is Gleb?" she asked miserably.

"Why, yes, he's the sixth Chekov with that name in only seven generations."

"Yuck. I hate that name."

"Tatiana!" Anna scolded her. But the general let out a chuckle.

"Oh, don't be so serious, Anna. I think I'd have to agree with the girl. It's a terrible name." He and Tatiana shared a moment of laughter, eyes locked in shared delight.

"Well, a name doesn't make a man," Anna interrupted. "The important thing is he is well bred and very well suited to her."

"Is he handsome?" Tatiana asked eagerly.

"I think so," Anna replied.

Tatiana turned to the general. "Do you think so?"

"I'm afraid I'm no good at predicting the fancy of a young girl, but if I had to place a bet, I would say you'll be pleasantly surprised." He winked reassuringly.

This improved Tatiana's mood somewhat, as she thought it would be very nice to be courted by a handsome man. Still, her movements were sorrowful as she ate.

"What is the matter?" the general asked again.

"Oh, it's nothing." She moped. "I was just wondering whether you're expecting anyone else to visit today besides Gleb."

"Should we be?"

She shrugged defeatedly. "I guess not. I'd just hoped my friend Markov would visit. But you haven't heard from him?"

Anna clutched her napkin frantically beneath the table, but her face remained serene. The general was the one to offer a reply. "I'm afraid we haven't. Who is this friend of yours again?"

"Oh, you know, dear." Anna smiled, blinking rapidly. "He's the one who helped me find my beloved Tatiana again, the one who escorted her to the Winter Palace."

"Ah, I do remember now. A blond fellow, isn't he? A rather impressive stature?" He made a tall gesture with his hands.

"Yes, that's the one," Anna said. "The poor man was so lonely, he had our Tatiana here pretending to be his fiancée just so he wouldn't have to go to the ball alone. Isn't that right, Tatiana?"

Tatiana nodded but said no more. Talking about him, she found, was even worse than thinking about him. She missed him so much, and it had been only a day since they parted.

When the Kratchys realized that the conversation had reached a halt, they worked hard to start it again. "Come to think of it," Anna ventured, "that was a strange thing for him to do. Tell us, Tatiana, how is it that such a striking bachelor would need to lie about having a fiancée?"

Erich had drilled her thoroughly on how to answer questions such as these. Tatiana did not even have to think before replying. "He wanted to make an old lady friend jealous, so he came to the ball pretending to have a fiancée and instructed me to seem wildly happy. After the ball, we had to keep up the lie a little to save face."

The general's question was more clever. "But do I sense a little regret?" he asked, his eyes twinkling over his teacup. "Is it possible that you would have liked to be more than only his pretend fiancée?"

Tatiana's back stiffened. "I didn't say that." Not only the Kratchys, but even the servant could see that her defensiveness gave her true feelings away. "I just ... I just would like to see him again. That's all."

"Well, it was so kind of him," Anna agreed, "to rescue you from poverty and let you stay with him. We really should all be grateful."

"I trust he was a gentleman?" the general asked.

Tatiana looked away worriedly. She was such a poor actress that her thoughts were easy to read, and the Kratchys realized with horror that this Markov Evanov fellow had been no gentleman at all. One look at her face told them that he had rescued her from the streets but only for the most selfish of purposes.

"Well, you'll like Mr. Chekov," Anna said. "He may not be quite as handsome as Mr. Evanov, but he's surely of a more respectable nature."

"A real Russian too," the general said. "I never cared much for those Nordic-looking Russians. They're all descended from Vikings, you know. I prefer the more traditional good looks."

Tatiana giggled. "You think Eri—Markov is descended from Vikings?"

"Well, mixed with a little German, I'd say, with those sharp features. Say, what is it you almost called him?"

Tatiana froze. "Nothing," she lied badly. "What do you mean?" Her eyes were wide, and she was shifting uncomfortably.

The general smiled warmly, unthreateningly. "A moment ago you said 'Air' and then you changed it to Markov. Do you remember?"

Tatiana's breathing became more rapid. "I was thinking of another friend for a moment."

"Oh?" he asked gently. "And what's his name?"

"Who?"

"Your other friend. What's his name?"

"Erich." She could not think of another name that began with "air."

"Interesting. That's not a Russian name. What is your friend's nationality?"

"I don't know, I never asked him."

"How long have you been friends?"

"Not long," Tatiana said, embracing the opportunity to change the subject. "In fact, we're not friends at all anymore. I won a bet with him, and he never paid me. That's the kind of thing I just can't put up with. Don't you agree?"

Anna and the general exchanged looks of satisfaction, then finished their meal in silence.

* * *

Tatiana chose her dusty-rose lace for meeting Gleb. It was a wonderful color against her smooth skin, and the lace front dropped low, showing off her breasts just as an ornate frame shows off a painting. She piled her chestnut hair high on her head, lengthening her neck, slimming her face. Though she didn't know it, she looked scrumptious. Her big eyes were so moist and engaging, and the rosy hue of her cheeks were brought out so nicely by the pink gown. Her skin was always so soft, warm, and flawless that the more she showed of it, the better. And this dress showed a great deal.

She had thought Gleb would take her out somewhere exciting, perhaps to a dance or at least a walk in the park. But to her disappointment, she learned that he was merely to be entertained by her in the parlor. One of the servants had prepared some cakes for Tatiana to bring him, as well as a pot of tea. This seemed so terribly dull, as she had not left the house all day and had hoped her new suitor would provide her with an escape from the dreariness of indoors. But Tatiana was gaining the impression that proper ladies did not leave home very often. Anna, it seemed, never went anywhere unless there was some special event. It appeared she was going to have to get used to a life indoors.

She was sitting in the cluttered parlor, gazing longingly at the sun outside, when there was a knock at the door. The servant answered it, but Tatiana rose to her feet just as quickly. Her heart was suddenly racing, and a hand leapt to her hair, feeling carefully for any sign of disarray. When she heard an unfamiliar male voice in the distance, she looked upward to say a quick prayer. She did not want to make a fool of herself. Hurriedly, she practiced several different poses. She wanted to look just right when he walked in the door. She tried leaning dramatically against the windowsill, sitting casually on the love seat, pretending to examine an interesting painting. None of them worked, and she was running out of time. Footsteps were drawing near.

"Miss Kratchaya," the lady servant said. "May I present Mr. Chekov."

At first, Tatiana turned her head to see whether Anna had entered the room, but she had not. She had never been called Miss Kratchaya before, and it took a moment to realize that was her new name. Or was it? She wasn't sure how she felt about that all of a sudden. Wouldn't she always be Tatiana Siskova? The young man stepped forward, interrupting her thoughts. "It is my honor to meet you."

As the general had promised, Gleb was a nice-looking man, but not nearly so handsome as Erich. He had brown hair slicked back closely to his head. His eyes were a rich shade of hazel but held no mystery or intensity. They were plain almond-shaped eyes that revealed his every simple thought and stored no secrets. His chin was a bit long, as were his legs and fingers. He was slim and fit but narrow from bottom to top. Tatiana's first thought was "Oh, drat. Erich could squash him like a grape."

"Hello," she said. The smiling servant made a quick exit. Tatiana didn't like that smile. It had looked as though the woman thought she was leaving two love birds behind, and that was embarrassing. Tatiana held out a tray of cakes. "Would you like one?"

"Oh, how lovely," he said kindly. "Don't mind if I do."

Tatiana was pleased to see him smile. He had a very friendly grin, so unlike certain other men, who never smiled at all. "Is it good?" she asked, watching eagerly as he took his first bite.

"Splendid," he replied, thinking it rather amusing that she should ask. "Should I, uh, ..." He looked around awkwardly. "Should I sit somewhere?"

Tatiana hit her own forehead. "Oh, yes!" she cried miserably. "I forgot to offer you a seat. I'm so sorry, I completely forgot. I mean, in a room with this many chairs, it just seemed so obvious that you could sit, I just—"

"It's quite all right," he assured her, settling himself on a beautiful but rather hard and uncomfortable couch.

Tatiana sat across from him, looking longingly at the tray of cakes. She had a suspicion she wasn't supposed to take one, though they looked delicious. Perhaps she could have one after he left. There was an awkward pause. What on earth were they supposed to talk about?

"This is a lovely parlor," he said. "The windows certainly let in a lot of light."

"Thank you," she replied. "That is, I agree with you. I mean, I probably shouldn't thank you for saying the room is nice, since I didn't build it or anything. I certainly had nothing to do with the windows, but—"

"That is a lovely gown," he interrupted suavely.

She touched it, then met his eyes with cheerfulness. "Thank you." She paused, then added, "Of course, that's really the same sort of problem, isn't it? I mean, I didn't sew the gown. I didn't even buy it, really. I just—"

"But it is you who makes the gown lovely," he broke in.

Tatiana froze in mid-speech. She thought it a good thing she was sitting, else her legs might have given way at that very moment. "Do you . . . do you really think so?"

"Absolutely," he replied, thinking her quite an easy target for flattery. He had no doubt that this fish would be his should he decide to yank the line. And that was a pleasant, powerful feeling, though he had not yet decided whether he wanted this particular catch. Her body was deliciously curved, and her face was adorable. But she seemed to lack grace. He had been assured that she'd spent her entire life at a distant boarding school for girls, so he was surprised to find her so clumsy. He had always thought those places emphasized rigid propriety. "What are your hobbies?" he asked at last.

"I'm a painter," she answered, but then confessed, "Well, I'm learning."

"Wonderful," he exclaimed. "I would like very much to see some of your work."

Tatiana shook her head vigorously. "It's not ready to be seen yet! I—I—what are your hobbies?"

He stretched his legs out more comfortably before him, preparing for a lengthy discussion of his favorite topic, himself. "Well, I am a big fan of the ballet, of course."

"The ballet!" she cried, raising her hands to her plush lips. "Oh, I would love to see the ballet sometime."

"You mean you haven't been? Oh, we must remedy that."

"Oh! You don't mean it, do you? You're going to take me to the ballet?"

"Perhaps," he replied casually.

Tatiana scowled. What did he mean by that? Was he taking her or wasn't he? It didn't seem very nice to toy with her feelings that way. "Well, what else do you like to do?" she asked, trying to keep from pouting.

He chuckled. "Well, naturally, I don't have a great deal of spare time, you understand. I'm headed for a career in politics. In fact, your father, General Kratchy, is doing a great deal to help start my career."

Tatiana felt an uneasiness. Her mother had told this man that General Kratchy was her father? She supposed it was natural that Anna should be ashamed of the circumstances surrounding her birth, but something about this web of lies was beginning to disturb her. An image flashed into her mind. It was her father standing at the whipping post, meeting her young eyes with courage and reassurance. Her mother, clutching her sister, shielding her eyes from the horrific injustice before her. She did not belong here. The thought came quickly and left quickly. But the feeling left by the image lingered on.

"Is something the matter?" Gleb asked, watching his hostess turn white, as though preparing to faint.

"No," she assured him blankly. "Not at all. Umm." She stroked the lace of her skirt as though trying to bring herself back into this time and place. "Umm, what do you hope to do in politics?"

"With the general's help, I hope to move up as high as I possibly can. Maybe even be a diplomat to a foreign land."

Tatiana became interested. "Really?" she asked, leaning toward him. "Do you think you will travel to a lot of different countries?"

"I hope to."

"How exciting!" she gasped. "And do you know what else you could do?"

"What's that?"

"Once you get there, you could infiltrate their government and try to find out what they're up to. Then, late at night, you could meet secretly with your network of comrades and send word back to Russia."

Gleb tried to decide whether she was being serious or whether he should laugh. "My dear," he said at last, "are you talking about espionage?"

"Yes!" She wrung her hands together with excitement.

"Well, I would never engage in such a thing," he replied indignantly. "It's too dangerous."

"So? What's wrong with a little danger?"

"Well, besides that, it's immoral."

"Oh, that," she replied, disappointed. "Yes, there is that, I suppose. But not if you're doing it for your country, right?" she asked with great hope.

Gleb chuckled disbelievingly. This conversation had become so inappropriate that it was now amusing. "I suppose not," he agreed. "But I'm afraid I could never be patriotic enough to risk my safety and freedom. No, I love my country, but I have limits."

Not Erich, she thought dazedly. His love has no limits. Would Gleb sacrifice his safety and freedom for anything at all? Probably not. She remembered the night she first sacrificed herself to Erich, the night he shed his own blood for her. Was there anything he would not risk for what he loved? No. He had given everything to his country, his lifelong mistress. And he would sacrifice anything for her too. Then why had he let her go? Why was she sitting here, talking to this stiff, dull man? Where was Erich? Why hadn't he stopped her?

"Oh, dear," Gleb said, looking at a grandfather clock with a start. "I must be going. I'm afraid I've enjoyed your company so much that I simply lost track of the time."

Tatiana found that unlikely, as he had stayed only a few minutes. But she rose to her feet and curtsied, thanking him for his visit. She did not want him to kiss her good-bye, yet strangely, it annoyed her that he didn't try. Worse, she suspected that if she asked for a kiss, he would be offended and complain to her mother that she had not been a lady. Erich never minded being asked for a kiss. If ever he said no, it was only because he feared the passions it would unleash. But Gleb, she could tell, would be more afraid of her passion than his own. She watched with disinterest as the servant led him to the door.

"Erich," she said in a whisper, "where are you? Why haven't you visited?" A horrific thought entered her mind. What if he were to meet someone else? What if, while she was cooped up in this house, he began courting someone new? It was an unbearable possibility that another woman might be in his bed just then. She had to stop thinking about it, else she would tear out her hair, scratch her own face, or run out in search of him. *Erich,* she thought, *you had better come, or, I swear, I will come to you instead.*

Chapter 29

Weeks passed without any sign from Erich. Tatiana realized her mistake. If she had made him promise to visit, he would have, for he never broke a promise. But she had merely assumed he would come, and for that she was paying. She managed to distract herself from his memory most of the time. During the day, she wandered about the many rooms of her new home, examining all the silver knicknacks, the old paintings, and the exquisitely carved furniture. There were so many beautiful things in this house, crammed in as though in storage, that she could spend literally hours in one room discovering new, hidden treasures. Occasionally, she would be interrupted by potential suitors, none of whom were any more interesting than Gleb had been. They never stayed long, and the conversations were tiresome. Worst of all, Anna had told her that the young men spent their days moving from one maiden's home to the next each afternoon on a sprint of courtship. This ruined Tatiana's image that they were all dressed up just to see her and made her feel that the tedious hostessing she was forced to perform was that much more senseless.

In the evening, she enjoyed her meals with the Kratchys. She loved the candlelit atmosphere they created each dinnertime, a nightly ritual of elegance. And she enjoyed telling the Kratchys all about her day, and the ridiculous suitors who had visited her. The general always laughed good-heartedly at the stories of their boring monologues and Tatiana's notion of their unappealing looks. Anna frowned over Tatiana's fussiness but did not speak out, for secretly, she enjoyed the stories just as much as the general did. Tatiana really liked her new family and her new home, though she wished she could go outside more often. Throughout most of her days, she felt rather cheerful. But at night, in her bed, everything was different.

Tatiana had always been a sound sleeper, but no more. Her nights were filled with an eerie hollowness. It was the silence that scared her so much, the sensation that she was surrounded by nothing. Had she heard ghosts or ghouls in the darkness, she would have been relieved, for at least then she would have felt some intrigue. But the thought that life could be completely still and empty scared her to death. She rolled to her left and then to her right, always wishing that there was a strong chest there for her to hold. To bury her face in Erich's clean-smelling skin would have been ecstasy, to feel his arm around her would have lulled her to sleep. And sometimes, when she had been awake far too long, she found her legs parting, beckoning an invisible man to come to her, to have his way with her. It was on those nights that she found no sleep at all.

The Kratchys had come to adore this new addition to their household, but Tatiana had a lot of learning to do, that was for certain. They arranged for her to receive lessons in reading and writing as well as in the French language. When her new tutor reported that she was the fastest learner he had ever encountered, the couple beamed with pride. Anna, who had always spent her days alone while her husband worked, now enjoyed the presence of such a bright young lady pattering about the house, asking questions about every heirloom she found. The two women enjoyed a ten o'clock teatime each morning, and Anna found herself looking forward to it immensely. The general loved having someone to call "his daughter" and could not have been more pleased with the one God had picked for him. She was so refreshingly honest and full of life that he looked forward to nothing so much as listening to her chatter over dinner each night.

There had been, of course, a few glitches. On one occasion, the general had not been able to open his desk drawer, for he had misplaced the key. Greatly flustered, he had stormed all over the house in search of it, only to find that Tatiana had opened the drawer without one. "Here you go," she had announced delightedly.

The general and Anna gave each other wary looks. "How did you do that?" Anna demanded.

Tatiana shrugged. "Picked the lock." She looked at their worried faces and asked, "Aren't you pleased?"

They were not. They knew she had suffered a hard life before arriving at their door but had hoped she had never known a life of crime. That little incident told them a great deal that they did not want to know. She was a thief.

"Do you think our valuables are safe?" Anna asked her husband late that night.

"Oh, don't be ridiculous," he scolded. "She opened that desk drawer only to help me. She likes us, Anna, she isn't going to steal from us."

"But who knows what she was doing when she was living on the streets after the Siskov family died of fever!"

"Who knows?" he asked. "I think we do, that's who. That we've learned she was a thief should only reassure us that she was not something worse."

"I suppose you're right," Anna agreed. "But I can't help

worrying. Just imagine! We have let a thief into our home, unsupervised much of the time."

"Anna," he scolded, "she is the same girl she was before we learned about this. We loved her before, there is no reason to stop now. She is a doll, and I for one am willing to trust her completely."

Anna broke into a hesitant smile. "I suppose you're right."

"Of course I am," he said, hugging her.

"Oh, she is the sweetest thing, isn't she?" Anna chuckled despite herself. "The way she talks when she gets nervous, as though the words just can't come out fast enough?" They both laughed. "Oh, Boris. We're not going to tell her the truth, are we? We're just going to let her stay here, aren't we?"

He studied his wife with concern. He had not seen her this happy in seven years. Seven long, miserable years. "You really want her?" he asked sternly.

"Oh, yes," she whispered, a strange and haunting light in her eyes. "Oh, Boris. It would mean the world to me if . . . if we could have a daughter again."

Boris stiffened. "You don't mean to say that you wish me to give up my plans."

She fell to her knees. "Please, Boris. Please." She buried her face in the hem of his robe. "You have had so much fullness in your life already. Can't you give up this one scheme and let me have something for once? When I look back on my life, there has been so little, so little to treasure."

General Boris Kratchy loved his wife, and he had grown to love the girl Tatiana as well. But even so, as he took his wife about the waist and swung her in his arms, whispering "Then we will keep her," he worried. He worried terribly . . . for Tatiana's safety.

Erich was at a meeting when he first became suspicious. There was much laughter at the close of this council. The men were gossiping and laughing in a way Erich thought would be more becoming to schoolgirls. At first, he paid little attention to their prattling as he gathered up his papers and mentally prepared for his meeting with the Will of the People that evening. But then something caught his ear.

"Of course, if Kratchy had his way, we'd all be arrested and brought in for questioning."

"What's that?" Erich asked.

The men were surprised at his interest. Erich had developed quite a reputation as a man who never spoke unless he had something of the utmost importance to say. "We were talking about General Kratchy," one explained. "You've probably never met him. He's a real character."

"How so?" Erich was getting a sinking feeling, not only because he sensed something was wrong, but also because this discussion was forcing him to think of Tatiana. To hear mention of anything remotely related to her brought him pain.

"Oh, he's just a really jovial old general who's on the brink of going senile. Don't misunderstand me, he's a very admirable man. He led an important mission during the Crimean War that helped us secure the entire Balkan region. But that was nearly twenty years ago now, and the man is degenerating into a suspicious old soldier with no enemy to fight."

"Suspicious?" Erich asked, giving away nothing of his deep concern, letting no worry escape his cold, eerie turquoise eyes.

"He thinks he's surrounded by spies," the man explained. "Thinks there are spies from all over the world infiltrating every aspect of the Russian government. That's what happens when a career soldier retires. Can't stand to be without an enemy, so he dreams one up."

Erich didn't like this at all. It was too great a coincidence that such a man would have become entwined in his own life. There was something terrible going on here, and he decided not to meet with the Will of the People that night. He would do nothing until he made sure that Tatiana was not in danger.

And there was only one way to find out. Nikolai Ruskravolin. Erich's photographic memory never failed him. That was the name Anna Kratchaya had given him, he had no doubt. Now all he need do was find the man.

Erich stormed into the Kratchy home less than three days later. He knocked but was unwilling to wait for the slow servant to answer. After counting to three, he marched in, uninvited and unapologetic. Anna rose from the dinner table. "What on earth!"

"Erich!" Tatiana cried with unbridled joy. "That is"—she slouched—"Markov."

He scowled at her, shaking his head scoldingly.

"Whoops, sorry."

"No matter," he grumbled. "I believe it matters no more, does it, General?" His eyes fixed on the heavily mustached man.

General Kratchy remained calm as he bravely met the gaze of his most unwelcome guest. "Tatiana," he asked gently, "might your mother and I have a moment alone with Mr. Evanov?"

But it was too late. She had thrown her arms around Erich and was all but weeping into his shoulder. "Erich," she whispered near his warm ear, "I've missed you so much, I—"

"It's all right." He hushed her, returning her hug with full force while still keeping his eye on the general. "It's all right. Let me speak to the Kratchys alone, as they've asked."

She shook her head wildly. "No, no. I want to talk to you, I want you to stay."

"I know," he whispered, "but let me talk to them first. Go on." He had to wrench her hands from him and point her toward the exit. "Go on," he repeated, nodding at the door. Tatiana could not bear to lose sight of him but realized that she was alone against the will of three and thus reluctantly made her departure.

As soon as she was gone, Erich tossed a folder on the dining table, not caring that it landed in the caviar. "This is a list of every professor employed by the University of Moscow for the past twenty years," he explained, pacing to the head of the table. "There is no Nikolai Ruskravolin in there. An administrative error? No." Still standing, he leaned into the table, holding himself up by the arms. "He is not listed because he does not exist. An imaginary man cannot be Tatiana's father, therefore, I can only presume that you, Madame Kratchaya, are not her mother."

The woman looked to her husband for guidance.

The general was strangely undisturbed, eerily calm. "Please sit down," he said to Erich.

Erich did not want to, for he was worked up, and an angry man cannot sit. But he saw that the general was prepared to speak frankly, so he forced his raging emotions to find stillness, at least long enough to allow him a more casual posture. He sat down.

"You are quite right," the general said, causing his wife to gasp. "No, no," he assured her, "it's all right, Anna. There is no sense in lying to the gentleman. He already knows, and our lies will only anger him."

Erich was impressed that the general did not take him for a fool. He crossed his leg over his knee, prepared to hear the old man out.

"You see," the general explained, "I know who you are." He paused, giving Erich time to argue or explain himself, but not a sound stirred from the man's lips. Erich did not even blink. "Very well," the general continued. "As you are not the one on trial at this moment, I respect your choice to remain silent. So allow me to be the one to fill in the details. I know that there are spies all over this crooked government," he stated, a hard glint in his eye. "You people don't fool me for one minute. Russia is the greatest empire in the world, and all of you want to destroy it. We have spies from England, Prussia, France. I wouldn't be surprised if the Americas had started sending their scouts by now! But the problem is, no one believes me. Every time I try to warn the officials about foreign infiltration into our government, they say, 'Oh, there's that senile old Kratchy again, ranting and raving.' That's the problem with growing old, Mr. Evanov. You'll learn about that someday."

Erich said nothing but only continued to stare in his icy, haunting way.

"Still," the general continued, "this old fool wasn't ready to be written off for dead just yet. I have done a great deal for my country, young man. And I was ready to do one thing more. I wanted to expose just one spy, to prove to my people that I was not insane. When I saw you at the ball, with your Germanic face and your stern reticence, I knew you were one of them. I just knew it. And when I found out you were a newcomer to St. Petersburg, transferred from Moscow, well! I knew that was a thin lie if ever I'd heard one. When I was told that your lady friend was also from Moscow, I assumed she was working with you. I investigated you both with all of my ability and connections. Naturally, I found nothing on yourself. Your tracks were covered well by your own government. All your papers were in order, and all your lies well documented. But the girl— she was all wrong. When I found out she was not a lady from Moscow but an orphan from a peasant family, I knew I had you!"

"Of course," he continued with a disappointed sigh, "I had no proof of espionage. That your fiancée was a dressed-up peasant would make excellent gossip for the babushkas but would provide me with absolutely no evidence in court. I knew I could get no confessions from you, for all you people are well trained to hold your tongues, even under torture. I know that. But would that be true of a peasant girl? I thought not. It was a wonderful coincidence that my wife bears some resemblance to the girl. The similarities aren't striking, but when you look for them, you can see they share some coloring in the eyes. So that, we decided, would be our plan. We knew the girl's history, so all we had to do was exploit the details in order to convince her and you both that she should come live with us. And in time, we knew she would talk. For what secrets does a young girl hold from her very own mother?''

''What about the lost sister?'' Erich demanded. ''The one Madame Kratchaya pretended to be. Who was she really?''

The general shrugged. ''Just a poor girl trying to escape serfdom, I presume. As I understand it, she was shot upon discovery, for it was quite illigal to escape from her family's debt. That is probably why the Siskovs never told their daughter much about the girl. They didn't want her to know her sister had been killed.''

Erich sighed heavily.

''But there is more,'' the general said.

''Oh?'' Erich touched his pocket, making certain his gun was in easy reach.

''Yes, you see, another interesting turn of events has taken place.''

''I'm listening.''

''It's a funny thing.'' the general chuckled uneasily. ''But God delivers in the most mysterious ways. You see, as it turns out, my wife and I have grown terribly fond of Miss Tatiana.''

Erich scowled.

''It's true,'' the general assured him. ''We had no intention of things winding up this way, but you see, we are . . . well, unable to have children of our own. My wife was not lying when she said I had longed for a daughter.'' He took his wife's trembling hand in his own. ''So, you see, Mr. Evanov, this puts a new twist on things. We don't want to let her go.''

''We love her,'' Anna chimed in.

Erich studied both their faces, trying to determine whether they were telling the truth. He felt uneasy knowing that Anna had been able to trick him before. That meant she was a great actress and could be acting then.

"I am willing to make you this proposal," the general offered, "and I believe you will find it an attractive one." He paused dramatically. "If you will not tell Tatiana what you have learned, if you will let her stay here with us as our daughter, then . . . then I will pursue you no more. You see"—he leaned forward, giving Erich a glimpse at the wisdom and honesty in his eyes—"I have given a great deal to my country already. I can live knowing that I passed up the opportunity to give them one little spy among hundreds. I am willing to accept my retirement and worry no more about the inevitable. But if you tell that darling girl out there that we are not her family, and that her only real family died of fever ten years ago, then we will lose her forever. And that, sir, I cannot live with."

Erich groaned audibly.

"Please be reasonable," Anna begged. "Where will she go if she finds out? She has no family, no home. And your life is too dangerous, Mr. Evanov! Surely you know that you cannot take care of a woman. Why, already she could be implicated for aiding you. Please listen to reason!"

Erich could see they were both very sincere in their love for Tatiana. And how could he blame them? He himself had fallen under her spell, had been swept away by her tender heart and her unsophisticated charms. It was a very easy thing to believe, that they had grown to adore the girl in such a short time. And, of course, what Anna had said was true. There was nothing for Tatiana to return to. It was this or the streets. He had told her once that he would make sure she had a suitable place to live before he went home, and this was it. What could be more suitable than a home with loving parents and tremendous wealth? It hurt him more than he could bear, but at last, he choked out the words. "Just let me say good-bye."

The husband and wife grabbed each other in a violent

embrace, the woman weeping for joy. It was over. They would have their daughter after all.

Erich made his way to the parlor, where Tatiana was waiting anxiously. He had intended to make this farewell a formal one, but when he saw her, knowing it would be the last time, he nearly broke down. He found himself clutching her, caressing her ear with lonely lips, reaching for her hair, freeing it from its pins. "Are they good to you?" he asked in a whisper. "Tatiana, they don't beat you, do they?"

She shook her head. "No, of course not. But, Erich, I miss you, I—" She felt his lips pin hers down, making them move at his command. He opened her, then closed her, pierced her with his tongue, then withdrew. She could not stand it. She had not felt anything like this since she'd left. She wanted him to take her. She wanted him to lift her and carry her to his dusty bedroom on the second floor. Then she wanted him to ravage her. But he pulled away.

"If they are good to you," he said shakily, "then I must bid my farewell. For my work here will be done shortly, and I must go."

He may as well have struck her. A thousand lashes with a belt would not have been as painful. "No!" she cried, grabbing his massive arm, trying to hold him still. "You can't mean that you won't ever visit me again!"

He was in as much pain as she was but knew he must not let it show. She would recover from this more easily if she thought he truly believed it was the right thing to do. Any doubt on his part would create doubt in her. "Your parents are nice people," he assured her. "They love you."

Tears were streaming down her cheeks, and her plush lips were quivering. "But I'll not stay here much longer," she said meekly. "They're trying to marry me off. Every week I have to entertain at least a dozen boring men who are trying to win favor with the general by courting me."

For a moment, Erich's jaw flexed. The thought of another

man trying to win Tatiana made him furious. But then he reminded himself to be reasonable. It was a good thing, he thought firmly, it was a good thing that Tatiana would find a husband. She should. She should find someone who would take care of her, someone to treat her well and provide for her children. "Well, I hope you'll come to love one of them," he said gallantly.

"Never," she wept, still clutching his arm. "Never. Nobody I meet compares to you, Erich. You're the only one I could ever—" She burst into a fit of tears that made Erich want to cry as well. His eyes were growing very narrow.

"Tatiana," he pleaded, "don't make this any harder than it needs to be. Please. Look, do you remember how excited you were when you first found out about your mother? When you first came here?"

She nodded miserably.

"Well, you've got to hold on to that. It's what you've always wanted, Tatiana. A real home, a real family. Lots of fancy parties," he added with a smile. "Men like me come a ruble a dozen, but a family is forever."

She sniffed back tears. "But I can't stop loving you," she said.

"You don't have to." He got down on bended knee and took her hand. "I know that I will never stop loving you." He looked up at her rosy face, moist with fresh tears. He met her golden eyes, worshiping them. "You can still love me, Tatiana. But you must love me from afar, the way you love . . . oh, say, the Siskovs. You still love them, don't you?"

She nodded.

"Love me like that," he urged her. "Send me your love every night before you rest your eyes, and I swear to you, I will receive it." She smiled down at him, the ludicrousness of his suggestion making her giggle, but she saw that he was not laughing. As always, he was completely serious. "I shall think of you every night, and wait for your love to reach me before

I fall into a dream. I don't know whether it will work, Tatiana, but we can try. And as time goes by,'' he ventured, ''you may meet someone who makes you forget to send that love each night. And I will understand. The night I do not receive it will be the night I sleep the most soundly, for then I will know you have found happiness.''

"Erich,'' she gasped with astonishment, ''I had no idea you were so romantic.''

He shrugged. ''I was saving it for a special occasion.''

That made her laugh, and soon they were both laughing. Erich rose to his feet and grabbed her. He swung her around, reminding her of their first dance together. Then slowly, he led her in the very movements they had rehearsed so long before in his parlor. Tatiana felt that she would collapse in his arms, she was so weak from crying. Erich felt that if her breasts brushed against him once more, he might lean down and kiss them despite himself. Soon they were dancing gracefully in the silence, feeling the light grow between them, feeling the warmth of union return to their aching bodies. It seemed they had been partners forever and would always be. But it was only an illusion. At last, Erich leaned forward and kissed the only part of her he dared, her forehead. ''Good-bye, my love.''

She watched in a daze as his majestic form turned away from her, and his black coat floated behind him in his departure. She could not believe he was really going forever. She could not believe it and did not believe it. She stood alone in the dark parlor for several minutes after he left. She stared at the door and thought of nothing. She felt nothing. She could not bear to. Erich, on the other hand, felt a great deal more than he wished to. He did something that evening that he very rarely did; he drank too much. And he would soon regret it.

Chapter 30

Lev had been at Yura's all day. He hardly ever went anywhere else anymore, for the Will of the People had become his family and their meeting place his home. Like the rest of the group, he was surprised that Erich hadn't shown up on time. The man was usually more reliable than the sunrise and more prompt than a bride at her own wedding. He was the sole member who had that leaning, of course. The only people less driven by time than university students were street dwellers. It was these two casual groups who comprised the leadership of this movement. So it was not at all unusual for Erich to arrive hours before the meeting began, waiting patiently for the others while flipping through the pages of a novel. But tonight the meeting had begun without him.

When he finally crashed through the door, he surprised the members even more by ignoring their gathering and taking a seat at the bar. Something about him was so frightening tonight that no one dared call him over. He was always a bit of an intimidating sort, with his dark clothes and that look in his eye, as though he knew something no one else did. But no one had ever seen him look angry before, and it was enough to give them all shivers. Lev set his gaze steadily on Erich and not just because the man looked so threatening. Lev was worried about something else, a potential disaster brewing in their midst. For though Erich did not realize it, he had just taken a seat beside Daveed Vinitsky, Tatiana's bitterest enemy. Lev knew that the two men did not know each other but feared that if they struck up a conversation, in the state of mind in which Erich appeared to be, a terrible fight would break out.

"Markov!" Lev called. When Erich gave him his reluctant notice, he nodded toward an empty chair. "Come, sit with us!"

"Later," Erich muttered, then ordered a double shot of vodka.

Daveed took interest in the sinister man at his side. He had seen Erich come and go from this place before and had always been interested in meeting him—as a businessman, that is. For Daveed got few customers who were as well-to-do as this one appeared to be. A few clients like this could bring a lot of money to someone in Daveed's line of work, and his ladies would likely thank him for the handsome find. "From around here?" Daveed asked.

"Leave me alone," Erich grumbled, not even bothering to glance in the direction of his aspiring acquaintance. He swallowed his shot in one gulp, then ordered another.

"What's the matter with you?" Daveed asked with a chuckle. "I don't bite, I just wanted to make your acquaintance. Is that so much to ask?"

"At the moment it is," Erich said dryly.

Daveed tried a new approach. "You seem like a man who's had a hard day. Do you want to talk about it?"

"No."

"Oh, come now, you might be surprised. I might be exactly the man you needed to bump into tonight."

Erich ordered another drink.

"Slow down," Daveed laughed. "You know, the cheaper the vodka, the higher you fly. And let me tell you, the stuff here is really cheap." When Erich still did not look at him, he muttered, "All right, well, I'm ... I'm sure you look like a man who can handle his liquor. But, you know, I have something even better than that. I have something that'll calm you down, lift you up, anything you want."

"What's that?" Erich asked.

"Women."

Erich looked at his unwelcome companion for the first time. His expression was incredulous. "What?"

"Women," Daveed repeated, thinking he had succeeded in piquing Erich's interest. "Any kind you want. Tall, short, blond, brunette. You look like a breast man to me. I'll bet you like them real thick in the top and bottom, eh?"

"Markov!" Lev called again. "Why don't you come join the meeting!"

"Not now!" he shouted, then turned to Daveed once more. "I don't need your desperate, poverty-stricken women in my bed. You make me sick." He was quite prepared to walk away, if only Daveed had not stopped him.

"Oh, come now," he said, "nobody's forcing these women to do anything."

"I'll bet," Erich growled with a look that would have made a smarter man tremble. But Daveed never knew when to quit.

"I swear it," he cried. "They come to me, not the other way around. All I do is help them. Now, tell the truth. Wouldn't you like a nice, soft woman tonight?"

"Yes," he said, "but that doesn't mean I'm going to rape my sister or bed one of your whores. Now, get out of my way."

"Markov!" Lev called again.

This time it was Daveed who replied. "Will you be quiet, Lev? We're having a conversation here." He turned his attention back to Erich and whispered, "I hate that fellow. He's friends with the tramp who broke my nose.'' He pointed to the oddly shaped feature.

A sickening thought darkened Erich's already troubled mind. ''Who broke your nose?'' He remembered that evening in the alley so long ago, when he held Tatiana and touched her swollen face. ''Don't worry,'' she'd said. ''I think I got the best of him. I think his nose is broken.'' Erich remembered the name. She had mentioned it only once, but his uncanny memory for detail never failed him. ''Are you Daveed Vinitsky?'' he asked.

Daveed grinned. ''You've heard of me, then?'' A fist landed on his face.

Never draw attention to yourself. It was one of the most important laws of espionage, and one Erich had taken seriously throughout his career. But at that moment, he was not a spy. He was a man. A man who had lost his only true love, a man who had no hope of finding another to replace her, a man who knew he had sentenced himself to a life without marriage or family. And he was facing an easy enemy, a slimy, unscrupulous twit who had once brutalized his angel. Fist after fist flew out from his shoulders. It was a short fight, an unfair fight. Erich had been trained in all the most effective forms of hand-to-hand combat, and though he fought rarely, he never lost.

He had barely worked up a sweat, when Daveed crumpled to the floor, begging for mercy like a child. ''How do you like it,'' Erich asked, ''when someone twice your size beats you up? Huh?''

Daveed was sobbing and pleading. ''You're crazy. Leave me alone.''

''Did you hit Tatiana Siskova?''

Daveed only then realized what this was about. ''You know Tasha? Yeah, I hit her, but she hit me first.''

Erich gave him a swift kick in the ribs. ''Do you hit your grandmother when she slaps your face for cursing?'' He leaned down and grabbed Daveed by the back of the hair. ''Now, you listen to me,'' he whispered menacingly. ''I come here often.

If I ever see you strike a woman or call her a tramp, I'll beat you senseless. Do you understand?''

Daveed nodded violently.

''Now, crawl out of here, and don't you ever mention Tatiana Siskova again. You aren't worthy to speak her name. Crawl!''

Daveed did as he was told, slithering toward the exit on his belly. When he reached the door, he rose to his feet and darted as though the devil himself were on his heels. He left a silent pub in his wake.

Erich returned to his barstool, pressing some money into Mr. Yuravin's palm. ''I'm sorry for the disturbance,'' he said with complete sincerity.

''Oh, don't worry about that,'' Yuravin said, pocketing the rubles. ''I hear nothing and see nothing. It's my job.''

Across the room, there were many wide eyes. No one had ever seen someone fight with such admirable technique. They were used to seeing brawls in this place, men throwing sloppy punches at one another until, at last, in frustration, the opponents would hug each other and wrestle the fight to its end. But no one had ever seen a man topple another by throwing only three or four perfectly aimed punches. It was disconcerting. ''Is anyone else getting the feeling that Markov isn't just some radical rich man?'' one member of the Will of the People asked.

''No matter,'' Pyotr, the leader, answered. His eyes were fixed admirably on the man in black. ''No matter who he is, we need him. We need someone who can do what he just did.'' Many muttered their agreement, but Pyotr was still gazing thoughtfully across the room. He was starting to suspect the truth. He didn't know why he had never thought of it before. All the money Markov was giving him, the access to explosive materials. How could an ordinary man, even a rich one, be able to arrange such things? It seemed so obvious now. By God, he didn't even look Russian. Some Russians were blond, but none had such fine cheekbones. ''I don't want anyone to ask about it,'' Pyotr said, to everyone's surprise. ''I don't want anyone to question Markov. Don't mention what you saw today to anyone, got that?''

Everyone nodded, though they did not know why Pyotr was saying such strange things. Pyotr now knew, for the first time, that he was betraying his own country. He had never seen it that way before. The movement of the Will of the People had been to improve his country, not to double-cross it. But he now knew that he was accepting the help of a foreign spy, a man who thought perhaps this revolution would weaken Russia. It bothered him. It ate at his conscience for nights afterward. But ultimately, he continued to accept Erich's help without question, for the cause must live on at all cost. Pyotr was no less true to his work than Erich was to his. Both men were willing to do what was wrong in order to achieve something so terribly right. And so their partnership grew stronger.

Chapter 31

Tatiana was growing horribly restless. Every day seemed the same. She would have loved to escape the house, take a stroll through the lovely park she so often watched from her bedroom window. But her mother would not let her leave without an escort, and she never had an escort. She loved the house, of course, and could devote hours to exploring one single room. But her skin was growing pale, and her eyes were growing weak from lack of sunlight. One night at dinner, she tried to sidestep Anna's authority by asking the general if she might go for a walk the next day.

He said, "You must listen to your mother. She knows more about how a young lady should behave than I do." And so, it was decided. Tatiana would have to sneak away.

She waited until the Kratchys were soundly asleep and surely thought her to be as well. She turned out her bedroom lantern but did not change into her sleeping gown. Instead, she worked diligently at tying her silk sheets into a long rope and adding her blanket where they fell short. She hated to soil the beautiful flowered fabric, but this was an emergency. She would go mad if she did not get some fresh night air. The mere thought of going to Yura's again, having a real drink for a change, and possibly even seeing her oldest and dearest friend, Lev, made her jittery with excitement.

She had little difficulty maneuvering the climb downward. It was three stories, but she was quite adept at making escapes and did not fear it. Once she reached the bottom of her rope, she darted in a fit of laughter, throwing her arms out to the sides, trying to catch the very wind in them. It was one of those nights in which the sky never fully blackened but remained a sharp navy blue, freckled with starlight. The faster she ran, the more she could breathe. She didn't care that her hair had fallen loose and was cascading behind her like the flowing tail of a running horse. She kept flying until she ran out of breath, and then she slowed down with her mouth open wide, welcoming in the raw, chilly air.

By the time she got to Yura's, she was moist from the trek, though the temperature was cool. She stared at the wooden door with joy as well as regret. She missed this old place. Perhaps she had not realized how much until that very moment. So much had changed since the days she'd slept beneath the stars, wrapped in blankets and snuggled beside Lev. She looked down at her soiled but still beautiful tangerine gown as evidence of how much had changed. But there was loss as well as gain in all transition. And just then, Tatiana felt a deep sense of loss, for she remembered clearly a time when this door to Yuravin's had provided her with sanctuary on each night of her life. Tonight, she made a rare appearance, and only as a refugee.

Lev could not believe his eyes. For a moment, he did not speak, but only squinted, as though making certain his vision did not deceive him. "Tasha!" he cried, rising from a stool to race for her. When he caught her, he picked her up as best he could and swung her around.

"Stop it," she laughed.

He gave her an indecent kiss on the lips, bending her backward in his efforts. From any other man, Tatiana would have seen this as an assault, but from Lev, she knew it was a joke. When he straightened her out once more, she kicked him playfully in the shin. "Ouch," he teased, "why is it that all the women kick me after I kiss them?"

"Maybe because you don't ask first," she laughed. "Now, come on. Buy me a drink. I don't have any money."

"You don't have any money?" he asked, incredulous, leering at her from head to toe. "What is that gown made from? Silk? Satin? Oh, you poor dear."

"I'm not kidding, Lev. Ladies don't get to carry around money of their own, you know."

"How convenient," he chided, reaching into his pocket. "Yuravin, get a drink for my friend?"

"Well," Mr. Yuravin replied jovially, "I haven't seen that pretty thing in here for a while. And just look at you! You're all dressed up!"

"Are you joking?" she asked, touching her tangled, fallen hair. "If my mother saw me, she'd have a fit. Mmm, thank you," she added upon receiving her shot glass.

Lev suggested they both take seats, then smiled at her endearingly. "Tasha, you look beautiful," he said. "You really do."

"Really?"

He nodded. "Your skin's gotten a lot milkier. Your hair looks . . . wow, it just looks shiny. I guess you've been brushing it and washing and all of that."

Tatiana wanted desperately to keep up the guise that she was incurably happy in her new home. Why, she wasn't sure. Perhaps in the process of convincing Lev how wonderful everything was, she would be able to remind herself. "Oh, yes," she said haughtily, "I have the most wonderful hairbrush, you wouldn't believe it. And here, smell me." She extended her arm. "Real perfume," she explained. "Smells like lilacs, doesn't it?"

Lev sniffed, then shook his head disinterestedly. "I wouldn't know. Never smelled a lilac."

"Well, of course not," she reasoned, "you've never been to the country. But doesn't it smell wonderful?"

Lev shrugged. "To tell you the truth, Tatiana, I like your natural smell better."

"What?" She threw back her shoulders defensively as she'd seen Anna do when she was offended. "What do you mean by that? I don't have a natural smell!"

"Sure you do," he said gently. "Everyone does."

"Well . . . well, what do I smell like?"

"Like skin. But it's your skin, not someone else's. Your skin has a certain sweetness to it. It's hard to explain."

"So"—she looked warily at her perfume-laced wrist— "you're saying I should take off the perfume?"

"I'm not telling you what to do," he said. "You just asked my opinion, and I gave it."

Tatiana felt strangely humbled, though she didn't know why. "Well, anyhow," she began again, "how have things been here since I left?"

Lev tilted back his chair, a relaxed grimace on his face. "Oh, it's been all right, I guess. I have a new housemate named Mikhail, and—"

"Someone else is living in our alley?" she asked.

"Yes, his name is Mikhail, and . . ."

Tatiana bowed her head. She could not imagine someone taking her place on that beloved pile of blankets beneath the stars. She did not want to imagine it. That alley belonged to her and Lev and had for years. No one else had even been allowed to know about it for fear they would try to move in. Nothing could have made her feel more detached from her life than learning she had been replaced. She hardly heard Lev's endless stories about Mikhail and how annoying he could be.

She did not listen to anything until Lev suddenly broke from his story and said, "Oh, and, Tasha! There was something you should have seen just the other night!"

"What's that?" she asked, leaning into her drink.

"A fight." He grinned. "You would've loved it. Markov started it, actually."

Tatiana stopped smiling. Lev had just mentioned something else she would never have again. This outing was turning into a rather painful one. "S-started a fight?" she asked. "With whom?"

"Guess." He grinned again, devilishly.

"I can't."

"Guess."

"I don't know, Lev. Tell me!"

"Daveed Vinitsky." He laughed loudly. "Tasha, you should have seen it. It was great. Daveed was trying to get him to be a customer, you know the way he does. And I could tell right away there was going to be trouble. I guess Markov has some kind of moral objection to prostitution. You would know better than I do. Is that right?"

Tatiana nodded sadly.

"Well, that makes sense, then, because he started arguing about how it was wrong and everything, and then he found out that Daveed's the one you got in a fight with that one time. Remember?"

Tatiana's eyes widened as she nodded again.

"So he beat the poor fellow senseless. It was great. You really should see him fight, Tasha. He's a marvel."

Tatiana touched her heart instinctively. "He did it for me?"

Lev thought about that for a moment. "Yes," he decided, "I guess it was for your honor and all of that. But I'm sure Daveed's slimy personality didn't help any." He chuckled and expected Tatiana to join him, but she was silent. She was still touching her chest.

"I can't believe he beat someone up for me," she remarked distantly. "Nobody's ever done that before."

"I would have," Lev objected. "Well, as long as you didn't ask me to beat up anyone too big," he added with a sly grin.

Tatiana was not listening. "That is so romantic," she said.

"Well, I try."

"Not you," she snapped. "I mean Eri—Markov. I can't believe he did that for me. Oh, darn it!" She pounded her fist on the table. "Why couldn't I have seen it? Was Daveed sorry?" she asked excitedly. "I mean, was he really sorry?"

"I'd say he probably was, especially when he had to crawl out of here on his belly."

She squealed with delight. "Oh, you're just saying that, aren't you? Do you mean it? Eri—Markov really got him that good?"

"Well, he's still walking, but, uh, I don't think he'll be forgetting about it anytime soon."

Tatiana bounced up and down in her chair.

Lev smiled at her knowingly. "Seems like you still think about him."

Tatiana stopped bouncing. "Yes."

"Well, then, come on, Tasha," he urged, reaching for her hand. "Why don't you just go tell him? Why don't you tell him you want . . . you know."

"What?" she asked.

He met her eyes with frankness. "That you want to marry him."

Her mouth flung wide. "I didn't say that! And besides," she sulked, "we've already said our good-byes. He doesn't want to see me anymore."

Lev was startled. He had seen the way Markov looked at Tatiana way back when they were first getting acquainted. It looked to him as though Markov was completely smitten, and as a man himself, Lev felt he knew that expression well. He didn't think it looked like the sort of fleeting fancy that would wear off with time. No, if Markov had changed his mind about Tatiana, they must have had an argument. "Why?" he asked uncomfortably.

Tatiana shrugged. It would be a hard thing to explain when there were so many details that must be left out. "I suppose his interest in me lasted only as long as I needed him," she suggested. "Now that I'm taken care of, he just wants to be left alone. He's planning to leave St. Petersburg, you see."

"Really? Well . . . why doesn't he take you with him?"

"Because he thinks I'll be happier where I am."

Lev narrowed his gray eyes. "Is he right? Are you happy, Tatiana?"

She shook her head miserably and felt that tears might come.

Lev suddenly looked much older than he ever had before. He squeezed both of Tatiana's hands so hard, it was as though he were trying to press through the skin. "Tasha," he said in a low, quiet voice, "I need you listen to me. Are you listening? I mean, really listening?"

She nodded in puzzlement.

"Good," he said, "I'm going to tell you something. Something you're not going to like." He lowered his voice even further. "I have agreed to do something very dangerous. Tasha, I don't know how many more times I will see you."

She gasped, "What—"

"Shhh." He shook his head sternly. The cynical yet jovial look he usually wore was gone. He had aged greatly since her departure, she could see that. He was not a lanky young man anymore but a budding warrior. "Tasha, I was the only logical choice for the job. I can't tell you what it is, but it's dangerous. All the other boys had families or homes, or at least an education. But I had nothing to lose, so I volunteered."

"For what?" she whispered shakily.

"I can't tell you," he repeated. "But I want you to listen, because we may not have many more chances to talk. I love you, Tasha. You're the only friend I've ever had. You're the only person who's ever cared what happened to me.''

She shook her head emotionally, wanting desperately to say something, but he interrupted her.

''There's no use trying to dissuade me. Our paths have gone different ways, and that's fine. I'm glad for you. But you've got to let me follow my course as well. Now, listen. I love you, and I like Markov. I really do. He's a . . . a strange sort, but a good, upstanding kind of a fellow. And, Tasha, I don't care what you say. I think you love him. I've thought it ever since the first night you stayed up thinking about him. I knew what was going on, and I still do. Now, I'm not going to tell you what to do, but I'm going to tell you what I wish.'' He swallowed back what might have been a sob. ''I wish you would stop playing dress-up and go get Markov.''

''But I—''

''Listen,'' he commanded in a tone much unlike the old Lev's. ''Do what you want, but I would feel a lot better knowing that you were with him, and that someone like that was taking care of you. That's all I have to say.''

Tatiana let a short silence follow before raising her objections once again. ''Lev, didn't you hear me? I told you he's the one who ended it, not me.''

He looked at her steadily. ''Just think about what I said. Promise?''

She was exasperated, but she nodded. ''Fine, I promise.''

They chatted for only a little while longer before Tatiana felt she had to go. She had to get at least some sleep before morning, else she would spend all of tomorrow feeling that her head was filled with sand. And she had two boring men to entertain. She hugged Lev, feeling that even his body had aged. He had always been so skinny for his height, but tonight her arms were squeezing some genuine muscle. When the embrace ended, Lev kissed her on both cheeks. His silver eyes sparkled with joy, a joy she had never known him to have. Even his spiky brown hair was growing long enough to be brushed. She touched it affectionately. "I've missed you, Lev. You'll always be my fondest playmate."

He smiled. "It's too bad we're not still children, isn't it?"

She nodded. "It was a rugged childhood but a fun one."

They hugged one last time; then Lev separated himself. "Go on," he said, "you'd better hurry."

She nodded and fled, not knowing that she would never speak to Lev again. Lev knew it, though, and watched her speed away. He stood on the sidewalk outside Yura's, arms crossed, a smile on his lips, watching her fade into the distance. "I'll see you in heaven," he whispered.

When Tatiana arrived home, she found that her rope was missing. She rummaged frantically through the bushes, hoping to find that her sheets had fallen harmlessly upon leaves, but there was no sign of them anywhere. She looked up at her third-floor window with dismay. How could she possibly climb all the way up without a ladder? She hated to pick the lock on the front door, for then she would be forced to creep up the main stairs and risk waking up the Kratchys. What on earth had happened to her rope?

Just then she heard the front door open. She jogged around the corner to see the face of Anna Kratchaya, illuminated by a single candle under her chin. The tiny flame made her face look skeletal and heavily shadowed. "Looking for something?"

Tatiana flushed in shame. "I—I'm sorry, I—"

Anna held up the rope of sheets. "I brought this inside," she said, her voice scratchy from lack of sleep.

Tatiana couldn't help letting out a nervous giggle. Arms crossed and hair blowing in the wind, she felt that being caught like this was at least a little humorous. "I'm sorry," she repeated, "I just wanted to go for a walk."

"I thought I'd made myself perfectly clear."

Something in Anna's perfectly round eyes was scaring Tatiana. The woman looked unfamiliar this evening, almost inhuman. "I'm sorry," she said once more, creeping past her through the entrance. "I'm sorry," she said one last time on her way up the stairs.

Anna said nothing and in fact did not move until Tatiana had returned to her bedroom. But the next day she ordered all the windows in the house nailed shut.

Chapter 32

Tatiana missed not being able to let fresh air into her bedroom. In fact, it really hurt her to have to look out at the children playing in the park and not be able to smell the breeze. Things had certainly gotten worse. If Tatiana had once missed the feeling of sun on her skin, she now missed outdoor fragrances just as much. When she complained to the general about her plight, he said only that she should not have tried to run away. But there was some regret in his voice, perhaps even some sympathy. "But I didn't run away!" Tatiana objected. "I came right back!"

"Your mother doesn't see it that way," he grumbled, looking uneasily at his wife. And that was the end of the discussion.

Morning tea, which had once been such a pleasurable ritual of Anna and Tatiana's, was now quite strained. They said hardly a word to each other save "pass the honey." On one occasion Tatiana tried desperately to reason with her mother. She said, "Mother, I know that you don't want me to wander around on my own, but couldn't you arrange for someone to escort me somewhere? Just so I could get out of this house?"

The older woman only scowled stonily, as one possessed by some joyless demon. "And what is wrong with this house?" she asked eerily. "It was good enough for you before."

"Nothing is wrong with it," Tatiana replied meekly. "I only long for some fresh air. Couldn't the general take me out some afternoon? Or one of the local boys?"

"You'll see no more boys," Anna snapped.

Tatiana was startled. "What? I thought you were pushing me to marry."

"I have changed my mind," she heartlessly informed the girl. "You are too undisciplined for marriage. You will stay here."

Tatiana couldn't believe she had heard correctly. "Stay here? For how long?"

"Until you are more cultured."

Tatiana got a queasy feeling, a feeling that something was terribly amiss. "How long will that take?" she asked, a pain welling in her throat.

"At the rate you're going"—Anna smiled evilly—"you will never be ready."

That was exactly the answer Tatiana had feared. "You mean," she said, swallowing breathlessly, "you mean, you might want me to stay in this house forever?"

"We'll see" was all the answer Anna would give.

Tatiana could not believe that all this had come about simply because she'd slipped out one night. Of course she had known that if she were caught Anna would be angry. Of course she expected yelling and worrying and perhaps even punishment. But not this. This was insanity. And she had no idea from where this new, malevolent side to Anna's personality had sprung.

Her first clue came some two weeks later. She was shuffling through antiques, as she so often did to pass the time, when she happened upon something fascinating. The moment she saw it, she knew instinctively that she had not been meant to discover it. She didn't know what gave her that feeling, but she found herself looking carefully over each shoulder to make certain she was not being observed. She looked down at the silver-framed portrait and blew off the dust. What she saw was shocking enough to make her heart leap. For had she not known better, she could have believed that her own face was staring back at her.

It was a picture of a girl about her own age. She had chestnut hair tied primly behind her head, so that from the front, it appeared short. Her face was full and rosy like Tatiana's own. Her lips were just as plush, and her eyes . . . her eyes were just like Anna's. In fact, the resemblance was so striking that Tatiana thought this might be a portrait of Anna in her youth. Hurriedly, she glanced at the inscription on the bottom. It read: TAMARA ANNOVNA KRATCHAYA 1873. Tamara? Who was that? Tatiana had seen pictures of all her cousins, and this was not one of them. But to be so young in 1873, only seven years ago, what could this girl be if not a cousin?

Even as the thought first entered her mind, she rejected it. It couldn't be, could it? Tamara's face seemed to laugh at Tatiana, mocking her from behind the portrait. She looked just like Anna. Tatiana's mind raced for another explanation, a more plausible one. But every time she thought she'd come upon a new answer, she met Tamara's eyes and saw the truth shining through them. It couldn't be. If Tamara were Anna's daughter, if Anna had once had a child and that child were about sixteen years old in 1873, then the story of becoming pregnant for the first time with Tatiana in 1861 had to be false. Not one piece of the story of Tatiana's birth, from being unwed and with child to being forced to the countryside with her infant, none of it would make sense. And if the story were false, then . . . oh, no.

Tatiana would not let herself jump to conclusions. She did

not know for certain who this Tamara was. No, she would calm herself. And she would wait for the general to come home, and then she would learn the truth. In the meantime, she returned the portrait to its hiding place in the dusty back room. She felt a queer excitement for the rest of the day. It was a mixture of anticipation, wanting to uncover a mystery, and absolute terror. For every time she passed the front parlor, where Anna was busily crocheting, she wondered whether she was at the mercy of a madwoman. Her hands were unusually trembly all day long.

When the general came home, Tatiana had to work up her courage. It was difficult to corner him at a moment when there was no one else around, and when she saw her opportunity, she had to push herself to grab it. For some reason, she was scared, and she heard her voice quiver when she asked, ''May I speak with you alone?''

The general grumbled as though this were a terrible interruption of his nightly ritual. He would so prefer just to wash up and enjoy his supper. Worst of all, he feared the girl wanted to discuss her captivity again. And he could not grant her the freedom she sought; only Anna could do that. But alas, he did have a weakness for this particular young lady, and so he grudgingly agreed to meet her in his study, where not even a servant would dare disturb them. ''What is it?'' he asked unwelcomingly. He sat in the room's tallest chair so that he might appear less approachable and might discourage Tatiana from quarreling over her indoor status.

Tatiana, sensing this meeting might be adjourned at any moment, wasted no time in getting to her point. ''Who is Tamara?'' she asked, not even bothering to sit down.

The general's eyes froze in their widest-open state. He had not seen this coming. For several moments it seemed he would not reply. It seemed he was too bewildered and taken off guard to reply. But at last, he said softly, ''Why don't you sit down, child.''

Tatiana obliged him. "Well?" she pressed anxiously.

He rose to his feet and began pacing the room. With shaking hands, he lit a cigar, hoping it might calm him. But it had no effect. "I had hoped this day would never come," he announced, his mysterious words making Tatiana stiffen. "But I suppose it was inevitable. And I suppose it is best to have this discussion sooner rather than later." He sighed heavily, his conscience cutting him deeper with each breath. "Tamara was our daughter," he said plainly, turning to face Tatiana with tearful eyes. "She was sixteen when she died from smallpox."

Tatiana's mind and heart were both racing. "But"—she spoke rapidly—"but if Anna already had a daughter, and was married, then she couldn't have—"

The general interrupted her with a sorrowful candid look. "Yes," he said with regret, "I fear you have already deciphered the truth. I'm sorry, child. You are not Anna's daughter by birth."

Tatiana began to gasp uncontrollably, touching her throat as though to make herself stop. This couldn't be happening. It just couldn't.

"But we love you just the same," the general tried to console her. "Tatiana, you must believe me. I have never seen Anna happy after the day Tamara passed away. But since you came into our lives, there has been light and laughter in the house. Anna loves you, and I love you too," he said, a proud, fatherly glow in his eye.

Tatiana only shook her head. "It's all a lie?" she gasped.

"Not all of it," he pleaded. "That's what I'm trying to tell you. It hasn't all been a lie. That we love you, that we want to keep you as our daughter, that part is not a lie."

"Anna doesn't act as though she loves me," Tatiana objected. "She acts angry and bitter."

"She'll get past it," he promised her. "You must understand. When Tamara died, Anna fell so ill, I thought she would die as well. And when you disappeared that night, and Anna awoke finding you had escaped, she thought it was happening all over again. She thought she was going to lose another daughter, and she couldn't stomach it. She loves you, Tatiana. She only fears that you will slip away, just as Tamara did.''

"How could you lie to me?" she cried, rising to her feet at last. She stomped her foot and nearly spat out the words.

"Please understand," he begged her. "I—I wanted my wife back. She had distanced herself from me over the course of these long years. She never left the house, she never sang, she never kissed me when I came home. She only wallowed in her misery and refused to speak the name of the child who had caused her such pain by slipping away. When you came into our lives, I heard her laugh again. She shared stories with me at night about things you had said and done. We were growing closer again, and it was all because of you. You dear, sweet girl.''

Tatiana would hear none of his flattery. "Then, you brought me here," she accused him, "just to keep your crazy wife company?''

"No," he replied gravely. "I'm afraid that was not at all my original intent. But let us not delve into that. All of that is behind us. What matters now is only that my wife loves you, and you have brought this household back together. I know you are disappointed to learn that you are not a Kratchy by birth, but surely you realize that you are fortunate to have made our acquaintance. Surely, you know that your future with us will be bright, that you will be well loved.''

"Bright?" she scoffed. "Anna won't even let me accept suitors anymore. She said I'm not to leave this house until she says so, even if that means never.''

The general bowed his head with regret. "I'm sorry about that," he said honestly. "But I'm sure she'll get over your little escapade if you just give her some time. I'm sure everything will be fine.''

"How can you say that?!" she cried, throwing out her arms. "I gave up my whole life for a lie!"

"What life?" he asked in complete frankness. "You had no life."

"I did!" she protested. "I did!"

"Please lower your voice," he urged her.

She paid him no heed. "It may not have seemed like much to you!" she shouted. "But I was happy! I had friends! I had freedom! And I had . . . love," she added in a whisper.

The general observed her with great skepticism. "I think you are glamorizing your past a bit. You were poor and illiterate. You had to run from the law, and frankly, I believe that your relationship with Mr. Evanov was not at all as you describe it. If I am to assume that you refer to him when you say you had love, then I am afraid you're in need of some education, young lady. When a man takes you into his home and ravages you without so much as suggesting marriage, that is not love. That is a vile and cruel exploitation of innocence."

Tatiana was not at all disturbed by his words. She knew what it had been. And Tatiana was no fool. If anyone had been exploiting her, it was the man twisting his mustache in her presence right now. "I want to leave," she announced. "You have been very kind to me, General Kratchy. I have truly enjoyed my stay. But Anna is being cruel to me, and I don't wish to spend any more time with her. I want to pack my things tonight and leave in the morning." Her head was bowed low, but she had no doubt about her decision.

The general frowned heavily. "Tatiana, be reasonable," he said with authority. "You'll be happy here, I promise. Anna will become easier to live with in time. We love you terribly, and besides"—his voice became even more threatening—"it would destroy Anna to lose you—to lose another daughter. I can't allow that."

Tatiana looked up with fear. "What do you mean, you can't allow it?"

"I mean," he replied heavily, "that I can't let you go. Please"—he tried to speak kindly—"please, just think about it awhile longer."

"There's nothing to think about," she snapped. "I want to leave!"

"But where would you go?" he laughed cruelly.

Tatiana did not have to think. The answer seemed so obvious, she didn't know why it had taken her so long to reach it. *Erich,* she thought. *I want to be with Erich.*

"I will return to Markov's house," she answered determinedly. "He has said good-bye to me, but that's only because he thinks Anna is my real mother and that this is my real home. When I tell him the truth, that she isn't who I thought and that she's being mean to me, he'll be glad to have me back. I'm sure of it."

The general's face darkened, for it was only at that moment he realized the girl's plan would work. If she ever got hold of this Markov fellow and told him that she was being held prisoner here, he would free her. And Anna would lose another daughter. And he himself would lose Anna. "I'm afraid I can't allow that," he said menacingly. "You see, Tatiana, I know who he is."

"What?" she gasped.

"That's right. I know all about him. And if you don't do as I say, I will turn him in. Do you know what they do to spies, Tatiana?"

She shook her head with round, terror-filled eyes.

"They execute them," he explained. "But not quickly. They do it slowly, painfully, and in public."

Tatiana caught his arm and begged, "No! No, you mustn't turn him in! Please!"

He smiled over his victory. "I won't as long as you stay here," he promised.

"I will," she breathed. "I will, I will. Just please don't turn him in!"

"Very well," he replied coldly. "Then, we have an agreement?"

She nodded, though bitter tears fell from her eyes.

"Good. Now let's get ready for supper. It may be growing cold."

Tatiana collapsed into a chair, curling into a ball and weeping. She had never felt so trapped in all her life. What evil fate had decided that on the evening she realized what she wanted most in life, to always be at Erich's side, she should also learn she could never have it. She had never missed him as much as she did at that moment, for she had never truly believed he was gone, even though he'd told her it was so. She had always believed their paths would cross again. But now . . . now, even if he came to her door, she would have to refuse him. She would have to turn him away lest he be killed.

She stood at her bedroom window that night, peering through the glass, wishing desperately she could open it and let in some night air. She had promised to send Erich her love across the stars. But instead, she sent him a plea. "Oh, please, Erich. Come rescue me from this horrible place." She collapsed into a fit of tears and later fell asleep against the windowsill. But he did not hear her cry, and he did not come.

Chapter 33

Tatiana would not accept her captivity. She knew she mustn't openly resist it lest she endanger Erich's life, but she would find her escape somehow. The general and his wife were cursed with the innocence of those who had known too much privilege. They did not understand the criminal mind and therefore did not grow suspicious of Tatiana's uncannily cheerful mood. They both assumed that she had come to accept her fate and perhaps even come to realize that her life with them would be a happy one. Neither of them suspected that she was merely trying to disarm them while she engineered her emancipation.

After several days, she had devised a plan. Her reasoning fell along these lines: The Kratchys obviously did not realize that Erich's stay in St. Petersburg would be a temporary one. They seemed to be under the impression that their threat to turn him over to the police would hold her indefinitely. She must not discourage them from thinking thus. However, she knew quite well that Erich would soon return to Prussia and that once he had done so, she could leave this place without endangering his life. Breaking through the locks would pose no problem, of course, for it was no easier to keep a thief in than to keep one out. Naturally, the general would try to find her, would do everything in his power to bring her home, but she could deal with that. She had learned well how to hide in shadows and disappear among the traffic of street rats. The only thing holding her there was the threat she would pose to Erich by leaving. She must wait for him to get out of harm's way before making her move.

The trouble was, of course, that she had no idea when Erich would leave. He had said "soon," and that was some weeks ago now. For all she knew, he had returned to Prussia already. But she must be certain. She could not make her escape until she knew that he was well out of the line of fire, and there was only one way to make sure he was gone. She would have to go to his house and see whether it was still occupied. It was a dangerous plan. If she were caught either leaving or returning from this place, Erich's life might be forfeit. But if he were already gone, she simply must find out. She would not stay in this prison one day longer than need be!

She selected Christmas Eve to execute her scheme. It had been more than a month now since Erich had told her he would soon depart. She felt her chances of finding him already gone were good. And most important, Christmas Eve had been a night of tremendous jubilance at the Kratchy household. Both the general and his wife had far too much to drink and would surely sleep soundly once their heads struck feathers. Tatiana did not burden herself with luggage. If she found that Erich's home was vacant, she would indeed move on and never return to this place. But she did not need the gowns or the hairpins or the shoes. She brought only two things: the gown she had worn to the Winter Palace and a good set of picklocks.

There were no tearful good-byes to her beautiful bedroom, for she'd been captive within its walls for long enough to hate it. Nor did she look back at the beautiful paintings or antiques she was leaving behind. All of this held only pain for her, and she would not miss an inch of it. The treasures she now sought were those of the breeze and the starlight, the sun and the sparkling River Neva. Never again would she dream of a life of luxury, for in the world outside there would be all the luxury she had ever really needed. The luxury of freedom.

She crept downstairs in her stealthiest mode. She did not dare smash one of the sealed windows lest she should wake the general, or at least a servant. She would have to sneak all the way to the front door, past the Kratchys' bedroom, without being heard. She did this, but it was not without great effort. Tatiana had always waited for homes to be empty before robbing them and had not gotten nearly enough practice with sneaking. When she reached the front door, she felt some relief but still had a dangerous task ahead of her. The front door had been locked with a key and could not be unlocked, even from the inside, without the same. She would have to pick it silently. Her anxiety made her fingers stiffer than usual, and she felt she was working clumsily. But at last, the lock sprung, and with her breath held, she silently opened the door, whose creak she had never noticed until that moment, and then closed it behind her.

She did not run immediately, for she feared it may have been her rapid footsteps that awoke Anna the last time she escaped. Instead, she continued to walk silently, as though still inside the house, until she could no longer see the yellow prison behind her. Then she sprinted forward in a fit of laughter and relief, letting the wind catch her long, thick mane of hair. She ran until she had no breath left in her and then merely smiled for the duration of the long walk to Erich's. *Strange,* she thought suddenly. *I don't know what I'm hoping to find there. If he is gone, I'm free. But then . . . but then he's gone.* This dampened her mood somewhat, but she still enjoyed the cold moonlight on her face.

At last, she arrived. The house looked different somehow, perhaps because she had not seen it in so long. Peering into the dusty parlor brought back such memories, she thought she might cry, not from pain but from joy. The joy of being blessed with such recollections. She saw the chair in there, the one they had squabbled over at each breakfast. She saw the heavy blue curtains swept to the sides. Why had his favorite color been blue? She never had gotten an answer. There was so much more she would have liked to know about that mysterious, beautiful man.

"What are you doing here?"

She spun around to find Erich, clad only in his underwear, standing on the lawn with his pistol drawn. His powerful, rippled chest was bare. His golden hair was disheveled from sleep. He looked like some beautiful, ancient statue come to life. "I asked you a question," he reminded her sternly.

"I—I just—" Tatiana bowed her head. She had thought of no excuse, had planned no explanation. Really, she had assumed he'd be gone. She felt a finger lift her chin, and then she was looking into his eyes. Those dangerous turquoise eyes that could be so callous. Tonight, they were fluid and unguarded, softened perhaps by the beginnings of sleep, and by her.

"I told you I didn't want to see you again," he whispered, then troubled her with a kiss. One brush with her plump lips was not enough, and he swept down for seconds.

Tatiana's head fell back, her lips parted in a muted request for more. The feel of his rough mouth, the sensation of being held upright by his massive arms—these were things she thought she would never experience again. And his smell! That clean scent that always rose from his soft skin! She had missed it desperately.

Erich smiled awkwardly when he noticed his gun was still in hand. He let her go for a moment and extended his arms sideways, looking for someplace to stow it. He thought about stuffing it in his underwear, but muttered "No, too scary" with a breathy laugh, then finally placed it carefully in the grass. To Tatiana's surprise, when he returned to her, he lifted her into his arms. Once he had her cradled, he planted a few rough kisses on her forehead, then carried her inside. She was not surprised to see that she was traveling upstairs. And she could not wait to get there.

He tossed her on the bed, smiling as the mattress bounced her. She smiled back even when he threateningly touched the top of his long underwear. "I thought you'd be angry with me," she confessed. "I thought you'd be upset that I came."

"I'm very angry," he replied gruffly, standing with his back to the moonlight. "Remind me to scold you as soon as I've had my way with you." He lowered the only piece of clothing he wore and stood hauntingly in the darkness. Every muscle was tight and glorious. With the night sky shining in the window behind him, he looked like a god just come to earth. He reached for Tatiana's ankles and used them to drag her to the foot of the bed. But she sat up and stopped him.

"No," she whispered before he could tackle her. "You're so handsome. Let me look." She clasped his buttocks with both hands, squeezing them though the intimacy made him nervous. Then she moved her face close to his member and let her fingers trickle down his belly, all the way to that most precious part of him.

When he could take no more, he forcibly removed her hands, ignoring the resistance he found there. He lowered her fighting wrists to her sides, then fell upon her with kisses. "Why can't I let you go?" he asked in an ethereal whisper. "Every time I try, you come back, or I come back, or . . ." He tickled her earlobe with his fluttering tongue. Her whole body shivered from it. "Why can't I stop thinking of you?" he asked, letting his kisses drop to her throat. He carefully tore away the cloth that stood between him and her delectable bosom. "I've missed these." He grinned naughtily, then plunged his head into their softness and sucked with all his strength.

His mouth felt so good fastened around her lonely breast that she did not mind the force with which he possessed her. Even if he bruised her tonight, she would feel the pain only as the most pleasurable of memories come morn. She lifted her chest so that he might consume more of her, and he accepted this offering with gluttony. Soon she was parting her legs, panting, and begging him to move on. "You should not have come back," he groaned, at last lifting his head.

Tatiana could only smile. "I don't know about that, Erich. I don't know about anything. Except maybe," she added, wrapping her arms about his neck, "that I'm looking forward to that scolding you promised."

Erich scowled playfully. "Don't say that," he whispered in half seriousness. "Senta already accused me of acting like I'm your father."

"That's because Senta is in love with you," she replied, a rare glow of wisdom seeping through her youthful gold eyes.

"Nonsense," he dismissed her. "Senta loves nothing but her job."

Tatiana shook her head, disbelieving that such a worldly man could be so blind.

Erich was steadily working his hand into the cushion of Tatiana's thigh. "Why did you come?" he asked, lifting one finger until it tickled her tenderest spot.

Tatiana nearly jumped. "I—I don't know," she lied. She could not tell him the truth, could not confess that she was being mistreated, that she was no more than a prisoner in that beautiful house.

"You're a terrible liar," he remarked from some distant place in his mind. "You've always been. I think that's why I first loved you."

Tatiana looked longingly into his magnificent yet puzzled eyes. "Lev said I should marry you," she blurted out, then laughed to cover her embarrassment. "Isn't that silly? He said you would take good care of me, he said you were ... a good man."

"He doesn't know me, does he?" Erich asked rhetorically, then slid his hand away from her womanhood to rest it on her hip. He gave her a firm squeeze there, looking frankly into her eyes. "Tatiana," he asked, "are you really happy?" A piece of him hoped so desperately that it was not so. For he could never take her away knowing that she had a good home here.

Tatiana nodded, but again Erich saw the lie.

He bent his head low, frustrated with himself more than anything else. Why couldn't he force himself to do the right thing and just leave it? Why did he keep making this so complicated? "Well, I hope that it is so," he said quickly. "Of course I hope that you are happy. But you know that if you weren't . . . that if, well, if they ever hurt you or, God forbid, beat you . . . well, you'd have a place to stay." It wasn't what he'd wanted to say. What he'd intended to be a genuine invitation had sounded like no more than a vague hypothetical offer. He waited tensely for her reply.

"Thank you," she murmured. "But I'm fine."

His head dropped. His passionate mood was broken. He had thought too much, and now he saw the error in his actions. "I mustn't do this," he remarked, removing his hands from every part of her.

"Wait," Tatiana cried, reaching for his hands, trying to put them back where they belonged. She found them immovable, like the rest of him. "But I want you to," she begged.

He shook his head with a frown. "No." Rising to his feet, he searched anxiously for his breeches or his stockings, or anything to cover his obscenely yearning body.

"But, Erich, I . . ." She propped herself on her elbows, her chestnut hair flowing enticingly behind her. She wanted to tell him that he had aroused her, and that it was cruel to leave her with need. But she did not have the words. She just punched the mattress in her frustration.

"I'm sorry," he said, yanking on some clothes. "I should never have started that. I could make you with child and ruin your entire life."

"I can live with that," she pleaded.

"Well, I can't," he replied, glancing at her still provocatively displayed body spread out across the bed. "Do you need help dressing?" he asked, eager to get her covered. Before she could reply, he was refastening the front of her gown and yanking her skirt as far down as it would go.

"I can dress myself," she insisted, lightly slapping away his hands. Her body felt rejected, unwanted, even though she knew in her mind that Erich was forcing great discipline upon himself to resist touching her. "Erich," she asked, sitting upright, fastening the last of the buttons at her breast. "Is there any way I could persuade you to come visit me? I have missed you."

"No, that's impossible," he replied coarsely in a tone that better resembled that of a commander denying his soldier shore leave than a man dismissing his lover.

"Why?" she asked weakly. He was draining her with his rejection, making her weary from fighting his discipline and common sense.

"Isn't this evidence enough of why not?" he asked, gesturing toward the bed. "I obviously don't have enough self-control to be with you." He sounded genuinely disgusted with himself. "And it isn't fair to you. I am leaving soon, and I mustn't leave you in a . . . compromised state."

"When is soon?" she asked.

"The end of March."

Three months away! How could she remain imprisoned for so long? Well, at least she had a date now. At least she knew for certain when she could make her final exit. "Erich," she suggested, her voice quivering from shyness. "Do you think I would like Prussia?"

He looked at her with shock. "It's out of the question," he announced loudly.

"Why?" she asked.

"Your life is better here."

"How do you know that?" she asked, rising to her feet.

"Because you said so."

She bowed her head but reached for his broad shoulders.

She could not tell him the truth. She feared it would send him into a fit of rage, causing him to face the general and fight for her freedom, thereby sealing his own dark fate. She could not allow that, but if she could only persuade him to take her with him when he left! "Erich," she pleaded, bending her head into his stiff chest. "I am eighteen. It is time for me to take a husband soon anyhow."

"And you're suggesting me as a candidate?" he scoffed, backing away from her cuddling advances. "You must be mad. I have a dangerous job, little money to fall back on should I quit, I am cold and bitter, and, Tatiana"—he met her eyes with a touch of shame—"I am . . . past thirty years."

"I don't care," she insisted.

"You should!" he barked. "There will be plenty of other men. Men with stable employment, men with good hearts, men who are your own kind! Russians, Tatiana."

Her lips held firm as her head shook wildly. "No," she said strongly, "you are my own kind, Erich. Russian or not."

Erich would not look at her. He was unfit for marriage and would make a terrible husband. Why must she torture him with such talk! He had long ago promised himself to another love, his country. And though his enthusiasm for that courtship had dwindled so much earlier, the union could not so easily be undone. Even if he abandoned his loyalty today, Tatiana would be receiving soiled goods, just as surely as if he were leaving a wife. A wife with whom he had squabbled and suffered for fifteen years. "Let me walk you home," he said gruffly.

Tatiana wanted to scream her frustration. Battling him was like yelling at a statue. No matter what she said, he remained unchanged. "Fine!" she cried, reaching for her cloak. "But you'll have to leave me about a block from home. I'm not supposed to be out, and I'll have to sneak in."

"Tatiana," he scolded mildly, "don't anger your new parents. Young girls aren't supposed to be out at night by themselves. Don't you know that?"

"Oh, believe me," she moaned, "I know."

He helped her with her cloak, then slid on his own. He wanted to give his arm as a gentleman ought but decided against it. It was safer to keep his hands stuffed in his pockets. "Do you always keep a gun in there?" Tatiana asked, pointing to his long black coat.

"Usually," he muttered, opening the front door for her.

"Why?" she asked. "How can you live in such constant fear for your life?"

They stepped out into the freezing cold night, finding that a few snowflakes had begun to glitter on the cobblestone road. "Oh, look!" she cried, forgetting about her question. "It's snowing! It's Christmas Eve and it's snowing! How wonderful!" She threw her arms up into the air and spun around, catching a few snowflakes on her tongue. "Isn't it beautiful?" she asked excitedly.

Erich couldn't help smiling. When he'd seen the snow, he had been annoyed that he would have to walk in it. But now he could see it through Tatiana's eyes, all glittering and peaceful, falling from a pale night sky. "It is," he replied, but he was not really talking about the snow. Tatiana's brown hair had caught some silvery specks of ice and was shimmering around her rosy cheeks, so moist and full of life.

"Oh, look at the Christmas candles!" she cried, pointing at the windowsills along the road. "So many of them! Oh, Erich! Why don't you have any at your house?"

He would have if Tatiana lived there with him. Of that he was certain. "I don't know," he mumbled. "I guess I've never celebrated Christmas."

"You what?" She sounded as though he'd told her he'd never seen snow. "Why not? I thought Protestants were Christians too. Isn't that what you said?"

"Yes." He shrugged. "But I guess I've just never done anything much about holidays. I suppose not having a father, and my mother always . . . working.'' He winced. ''We never fussed about it much. Then I joined the army so young.''

Tatiana frowned sympathetically. ''Well, that's no reason not to celebrate it now.''

His reply came after a long pause. ''I don't . . . I don't have anyone to . . . I guess I'll be alone tomorrow.''

Tatiana thought that was terribly sad. Why, even when she'd lived on the streets, she and Lev had always done something special for Christmas. Just having someone say ''Merry Christmas'' was so much better than nothing. ''What about Senta?'' she asked. ''Might she come over?''

He shook his head fiercely. ''No. I doubt she even remembers it's Christmas.''

''Well, perhaps you could remind her.''

''No, I don't think I'll do that.'' He burst into a short, awkward chuckle. ''To be honest, I don't really like her that much.''

Why that relieved her, Tatiana wasn't sure. But she was moved to ask, ''Erich?''

He turned his head. ''Yes?''

''Don't you ever get lonely?''

''Oh, no,'' he assured her with humor. ''I'm not allowed to. It says so in the description of my job.''

''I don't believe that,'' she remarked sternly.

''What? That it says that? Do you want to look?''

''Not that,'' she laughed, socking him good-heartedly. ''I don't believe that you never get lonely.''

''Well, I guess it makes no difference now,'' he replied, for they had reached their destination. They were exactly a block away from her house. Leave it to Erich to be precise, she thought.

''So this is . . . the end?'' she asked sadly.

''Probably not.'' He frowned. ''Every time I say good-bye to you, I wind up seeing you again. So let's not even bother this time. Let's just . . . let's just say good night.'' He trusted himself to give her one seemingly innocent kiss on the lips. Though he longed to plunge into a more intimate seduction, he refrained, and kept his warm mouth closed. "Good night, Tatiana."

She looked up at him with great hope. "Might I sneak away and visit you again?"

"If you do, I'll not let you in," he threatened icily. "I'm not bluffing, Tatiana. I want you to stay here and move on with your life."

"But who are you to say where my destiny lies?"

Erich shook his head. "It's too late to argue. Please, let's just part here."

Tatiana walked away slowly, almost in a huff. When she heard him turn around as well, she stopped. "Erich!" she called.

He turned and raised an eyebrow. "Yes?"

She smiled a bright grin. "Merry Christmas."

He returned her cheer. "Same to you."

He walked away, picturing her opening gifts in the morning. Surely, the yellow house would be heavily decorated in brilliant holiday cheer. He imagined her wearing a dress of red velvet, her hair tied primly in a braid. Course after course of fine fare would be set before her on trays of silver. Smiles, laughter, and song would ring throughout the house until dusk. And she would rest her head and dream of all the wonderful silks and hair ribbons she had received. Then he thought about himself, alone in his shadowy house, eating his usual breakfast. Yes, he decided, he was doing the right thing. Tatiana's life would be so bright now that she was without him.

Tatiana made it safely into the house without being discovered. There were Christmas decorations everywhere, but she did not see them. Without freedom, she could know no joy. And without Erich, no holiday would be bright. She would rather have spent the entire day walking with him through a park, basking in the beauty of the snow in the trees, or lying naked in his bed, loving his touch, letting him keep her warm and safe from the outdoor chill. All the brightly wrapped packages in the world could not bring her that sort of happiness.

Chapter 34

As the weeks passed, not a rippled appeared in the stale waters of Tatiana's life. It seemed that the river of her youth had brought her to this wretched place and left her. It was a dead end from which nothing ever flowed. Her energy had dwindled, and that was, in its own way, a blessing. For now her inactive mornings, lazy afternoons, and lonely nights did not seem so intolerable. There were times, in fact, when she wondered whether she might abandon all plans to escape. In April she could perhaps gain her freedom, but in April she would also have lost her most important reason to be free. Maybe, she thought on occasion, looking out at the piles of snow that had taken over the world outside her windows, maybe this is not such a bad place to be. She was, after all, safe from the cold in winter even if she were also kept away from the brilliance of spring.

Erich was enjoying himself no more than she. The Russian winter was difficult to bear. He did not like wasting firewood, as he had always thought using too much heat was a sign of weakness, a sign that one was too fragile to withstand the elements. But nonetheless, he found himself reluctantly throwing log after log into his fireplace. His hands and feet would grow numb if he left the parlor even for a moment. There were days when he would dare to look ahead at the future. After all, his mission would be complete come March. He would be returning home and perhaps be offered retirement after all he had done. But his brief, daring speculations into the years to come were painful. He had no friends. His mother was gone. He would be leaving his solitude only to return to a new one.

There were afternoons when memories of holding Tatiana in his arms were so vivid that it hurt. There were mornings when his eyes turned inadvertently to the left, where he hoped in vain to find Tatiana resting soundly at his side. There were nights when he put his gun away more slowly than usual, placing it thoughtfully in his dresser drawer, examining its barrel with steady, hopeless eyes. Could the pistol, which he'd learned to fire at far too young an age, which had followed him from nation to nation, the very symbol of his deepest violent nature, could this pistol offer him sanctuary from a lifetime of emptiness? He felt too frozen to do it, too ambivalent. He could have died for Tatiana, but for himself he would not bother. He did not have enough compassion for himself to pull the trigger.

The only person who seemed to be enjoying the richness of life right now was, incredibly enough, Senta. For though she would not admit it to herself, her evenings with Tomasz had become a source of constant joy. She anticipated them throughout every long day as she waited eagerly for the dim winter sun to set. She found herself grinning like a schoolgirl every time she knocked on his door. And this grin was not that of the bubbly Irina, but of Senta herself, filled with an excitement she had not known since childhood. "Surprise!" she greeted him on February 2, shoving a wrapped package into his expectant arms. She had shocked even herself by remembering that today was a Russian holiday, Candlemas. Why, she rarely celebrated her own holidays, much less those of the enemy. But she had so desperately wanted to give Tomasz a gift that she had looked actively for an excuse to do so.

"Thank you," he said without even looking at the package. "I'm absolutely stunned. I—I fear I didn't get you—"

"Never mind that," she interrupted cheerfully. "Open it."

As Senta tore off her cloak and knelt by the fire to warm herself, Tomasz opened the wrapping with great care. There was a piece of him that did not want to look at the gift, for the very fact that she had given it was more delightful than anything he might find inside. "A watch!" he cried in astonishment. "It's beautiful! Irina, it has rubies, and the chain is magnificent silver. How did you—"

"That isn't a polite question," she interrupted again. "Don't ask that. I'm just glad you like it." She stood up to her full height, which was less than that of his shoulders, and offered him a sensational hug.

Tomasz had an uneasy feeling about the watch. It was too expensive, too extravagant a gift from a woman who had so little. He couldn't help fearing that she had stolen it but did not want to suggest as much. "Irina," he said, settling his arms around her slim waist. "Once you are my wife, you will not want for money." He looked warily at the watch in his hand. "I just want you to know that."

Senta stood on her toes to kiss him. "Let us not discuss that."

He pushed her away with force. "You never want to discuss it," he barked, wandering aimlessly away from her. "Why not?" He dared himself to look at her for just an instant before turning away again. "Why may we never discuss our marriage? We are still betrothed, aren't we?" It was a frightening question alluding to a dangerous demand. He was requiring her to answer his proposal again. It was a risk he had never before wanted to take. For months they had said nothing about their wedding, their marriage, or their future. Every time Tomasz had broached the subject, she had evaded it. Not until then did he dare reopen the door to rejection.

"Oh, must we be so serious?" she asked seductively. "Can't we just enjoy ourselves now and make plans later?" She slinked up behind him, capturing him in a light, silky embrace.

"This is later," he remarked miserably. "If this is not later, then later will never come. Answer my question."

It may have seemed wise to force Senta into a commitment, but in fact it was the worst thing he could have done. Senta was falling in love with him, was relishing the joy of having a beau. If he had allowed her to continue the lie, to pretend that she was loving him only in the line of duty, her heart might someday have conquered her prejudice. But because he forced her to answer now, while the idea of love was too new to defeat her conscience in a head-on battle, he received the reply that would break his heart. "Very well," she said breathily, dropping her arms to her sides. "Then my answer is no."

"Why?" he cried, his face red from a sudden outbreak of perspiration.

Her face was as cold as a spy's ought to be. "Because," she remarked indifferently, "I do not love you."

"That's a lie!" he shouted. "I know it is!"

She laughed as though destroying his hopes had been the easiest thing she'd done all day. "How do you know that?"

"Because," he replied passionately, "I have seen love in you. I have seen something in you that you never wanted me to see, a little girl who wanted more from life than this, a vivacious child who wanted to make everyone like her, a lonely woman who liked it when I held her through the night."

His words did not leave Senta unfazed. There was a muffled voice crying out from the depths of her mind to run into his arms and tell him everything, to abandon her father's plans for her and grab one last chance at happiness. But that voice had not been given time to develop. It was still so much quieter than the voice of her father telling her she must return home in glory, a successful spy, and not a weak-hearted woman. "I'm afraid you're quite wrong," she informed him, collecting her cloak.

"Don't leave here," he warned her. "Don't you leave me, Irina, or you shall regret it."

"Is that a threat?" she asked indignantly.

"No," he whispered. "It is an observation. There is no happiness in the future for someone who rejects it now."

"What makes you think I'd be happy with you?" she blurted out callously, then started for the door.

"Because I'm happy with you," he insisted. "And I would not have been if I were alone in my joy."

"Nonsense!" she cried, though she did not hurry to the door as she had planned. She moved sluggishly, as though hoping he would block her way.

"I love you, Irina." He spoke the words not as a plea but as a means to haunt her. Whatever she might think when she looked back upon their days together, she must never believe that his love had not been sincere.

Senta thrust her chin into the air. A thousand times she had called Erich a man of ice, but never had he been so cold as she was then. "I'm sorry to hear that," she announced, and left the devastated man in her wake as she pushed herself through the front door.

It surprised her to find herself collapsed into a heap of sobs on the other side. Never had she expected to find her cheeks so red or her chest so convulsed over something so trivial as a man. But Tomasz knew that she would weep the moment she left him. He could feel her crying on the other side of his wall. He had known more about her than she was willing to believe. In fact, he knew her so well, he did not follow her.

He knew that she was lost forever and that, unlike himself, she would never again find true love. If she had refused it this once, she would refuse it always. Once again the disease of self-control had conquered its host and robbed the world of another lover.

Chapter 35

It was to be a glorious day. After nearly four months of captivity, Tatiana would be taken on an outing. Tsar Alexander II would be traveling through St. Petersburg in an open carriage, and everyone would gather along the roads to watch him pass. Tatiana had not been this excited since the ball at the Winter Palace. Not only would she breathe fresh air on this day, she would lay eyes upon the tsar himself. She was allowed to wear her most elegant dress. It was of wine-colored velvet and clung to her snugly. With a charming, gay bow in the back, and layers of black lace petticoats beneath, it made her look like a lady of the highest degree. In fact, looking at Tatiana on this day, with her cinnamon-gold eyes shining so brightly, her thick hair so healthy and adorned with dark red ribbons, her lush figure pulled tightly with velvet, it would have been impossible to guess that she had once been a mere peasant girl.

Anna held her hand as the family took their carriage to town. She held it as though fearing Tatiana would bolt the moment she was released. But Tatiana did not mind this, for nothing could spoil the splendor of the afternoon. It was March, and though snow still threatened to ruin the ladies' boots, there was a promising sun overhead. Tatiana tried to lean her face from the carriage to let the golden heat fall upon her skin, but she was reprimanded repeatedly for her efforts. No matter. She was determined to bask in the glory of this outing. The tsar had just signed an agreement that would allow peasants to run their own villages. Zemstvos, they would be called. No more would aristocrats make laws for workers whom they did not understand. Instead, villagers could elect their own local officials. Tatiana was delighted and had never wanted to see the tsar as badly as she did that day. For he was not only her king now, but her hero.

The Kratchys insisted on remaining some distance from the crowds. It was humiliating, they thought, to stand in a mob. Tatiana was terribly disappointed, for she would not be able to see as well from this faraway spot, but she did not argue. If she had learned anything over these past several months, it was to choose her battles wisely and not to engage in trivial contests of will. She stood with her "parents" and smiled, determined to enjoy the excitement of the day. But something was wrong.

First, she spotted Lev. Naturally, she wanted to call out to him but decided she should not. She settled for trying desperately to make eye contact with him, a difficult feat in a crowd so large. Miraculously, he looked in her direction, but then he looked away. She was certain he saw her, certain he recognized her. Yet, he made absolutely no acknowledgment, not even a smile. Then she saw Erich. He was not avoiding her gaze but was staring right at her, monitoring her, looking after her. Something was wrong. She heard the wheels of the tsar's carriage venture down the road. She heard crowds cheering, saw handkerchiefs waving their praise. Naturally, she was curious about the fine lean horses clopping toward her, but her concern was interfering with her excitement.

Then it happened. A loud noise and a small explosion. Tatiana saw one of the beautiful horses fall to its belly. In one moment, it had been walking toward her, proud of its fitness and of the precious cargo it hauled. The next, it fell. The tsar rushed from his carriage to see what had happened, why he had stopped moving forth. And that is when she saw Lev raise his arm. "No!" someone beside him cried, but it was too late. He had thrown the fatal explosive, and the tsar looked out at his people with one last twinkle of life. His expression was one of love, one of hope, and one of very deep regret. Then he was no more.

Anna fainted into the ready arms of her husband. Tatiana felt frozen until the police ran for Lev. He had a strange look on his face, a peaceful look, the expression of one who had come to accept his fate even before he had sealed it. As the police pulled him from the crowd, Tatiana found herself pushing forward. "No," she cried until she was quite hoarse. But an arm prevented her from gaining any distance toward Lev.

"Let him go," Erich ordered in a voice so soft, it was nearly a whisper.

She struggled desperately, as though if not for Erich's restraint, she would be able to save Lev from certain execution.

"He knew what he was doing," Erich assured her. "It's what he wanted."

"Let go of me!" she cried, tears fogging her vision. "Lev!" He would not look at her.

"Stop it," Erich snapped in a whisper. "You'll be arrested too if you don't stop," he warned. When she continued to yell, he decided he must wrestle her from the crowd. He did so with ease, forcing her to join him in the solace of a nearby grove. The general was too busy fanning his wife to notice. "Be quiet," Erich urged her, wrapping his arms around her warm, sobbing body. "You mustn't let anyone know you're acquainted with him. That's why he won't look at you. He doesn't want you to be implicated."

Tatiana shook her head wildly, her face so wet it shone. "They can't take him," she wept. "Erich, don't let them take him."

The only consolation he could offer was the one he kept repeating. "He knew what he was doing, Tatiana. He knew the consequences."

"But why?" she cried. "Why would he do such a dreadful thing?"

To this Erich replied with a steady look. "You knew him better than anyone else. Why do you think he did it?"

This stopped Tatiana's weeping momentarily. But before she could gather her thoughts, he grabbed her arm roughly and led her toward the crowd. "Come," he said. "We must return before we are noticed."

"But, Erich—"

"No buts," he ordered. "Lev would never forgive me if I let you get in trouble."

She followed his lead, weeping into the lifted hem of her gown. "He wanted us to marry," she rambled, stumbling into the crowd. "It was his last wish." But when she looked up, she saw no one. Erich had disappeared, leaving her within inches of the family she did not want.

Anna had recovered from her dizzy spell and was now fanning herself with fury. "Those damned peasants!" she rasped. "They should all be shot! All of them!"

The general dabbed a few tears from the corner of his eye. "The tsar tried to help them," he mused. "And they were too daft to appreciate it."

"I hope they torture that boy who did it," Anna sneered. "No punishment would be harsh enough for him."

"I would have to agree," the general said, leading his family away from the crime scene. "He is the most unconscionable criminal this nation has ever known."

* * *

What should have been a day of celebration had instantly become a festival of mourning. The Kratchys fasted on this evening in reverence of their fallen tsar. This did not trouble Tatiana, for she was suffering from a grief all her own. For among the tens of thousands who mourned the death of their tsar, she may well have been the only person who mourned the fate of the man who'd killed him. When had Lev become a man? When had her childhood playmate, the gray-eyed prankster with the lanky arms and devilish wit, become a cold-blooded killer? Had it happened on one night as he lay in the alley, his arm wrapped around Tatiana, gazing up at the distant stars? Or had it happened gradually, drink after drink, meeting after meeting, lost hope after lost hope?

Oh, what difference did it make? she decided as the hour for sleep drew near. What use was it to judge him when his fate was not in her hands? She may have been the only person who had ever loved him and, as such, she had an obligation. An obligation to keep on loving him. She must not let him die without a tear shed on his behalf. She must remember the friendship he had given her and return it now and forever with all her might. She turned out her lantern and lit a single white candle. She placed it on the sill of her locked bedroom window and knelt before it.

"God," she said aloud, "I know I'm not exactly your favorite person in the world, but I wonder if you would tell my friend Lev that I love him and that I'm thinking of him, and that he always had a family, even though it was just me. I hope you'll forgive him for what he did, even though it was really bad. And I hope you won't let them torture him, even though I guess they'll have to kill him. And I hope, well . . . maybe that you and I will get to know each other better someday. I've always believed in you. I just never . . . well, I never really thought you liked me that much. Hope you change your mind. Hope you tell Lev that you're real, because I don't think he believes in you. Not that he's a bad person, but he never had any parents, so they couldn't tell him about you. It's not his fault. So, anyway, I guess that's about it. Good night. Or, um, amen.'' She rose to her feet with care, feeling somehow that she'd forgotten something. "Oh, yes!" she remembered suddenly as she fell back to her knees. "And please send Erich to come rescue me. Thanks!"

Chapter 36

"Success!" Senta cried, storming into Erich's parlor. "We are finished! The new tsar has already ordered the execution of all leading members of the Will of the People. He has vetoed his father's plan to allow zemstvos. He swears to punish the peasants for their ungratefulness. And against this, even the peasants who once hated the Will of the People are now becoming avid supporters. Oh, Erich! Russia will disintegrate into civil war, and it is all thanks to our help!"

"And you're happy about this?" he grumbled, tossing some shirts into a trunk.

"Of course!" she cried. "Aren't you?"

"No," he answered flatly, though he continued to pack. "I am never happy to see an empire fall."

"Not even an enemy empire?" she asked indignantly. "Erich, you have worked just as hard for this as I have. Surely, you're pleased with our success."

"I did my job," he replied coldly. "It was only a job, and I took no pleasure in it."

"Hmph. I certainly hope my next partner is more jovial, at least in victory."

Erich looked up from his trunk and raised an eyebrow. "You're going to continue this line of work, then?"

"Well, of course!" she cried, her green eyes alight with excitement. "My first mission went well! I'm sure they'll offer me another job. Why, aren't you going to go on another mission?"

He grunted as he shook his head. "Never. I'm finished. The chancellor has offered me retirement, and I'm going to take it."

Hearing this changed the expression on Senta's face dramatically. For though she could do without Erich's frigid company, she did have tremendous admiration for the man. He was perhaps the most able spy Prussia had ever known, and he was a man of dignity and honor. She felt blessed to have worked with him, especially knowing that he would now retire and surely become legendary among his peers. She would be one of the very few people who could claim to have been his partner. "It is Prussia's loss," she told him, a proud but sad emotion catching in her throat.

Erich bowed gracefully at the compliment. "Thank you, fraulein. It has been a pleasure working with you."

Senta blushed furiously. "Has it really?" she asked, her voice weak with hope.

He nodded in all sincerity. "You have a bright future, Senta. You are an excellent spy."

"Will you—" she started to ask, then bowed her head in shame. She could not force herself to make such a bold request.

"Yes," he replied, guessing her meaning. "I will give you my highest recommendation to the chancellor."

She clasped both her cheeks in her hands. "Erich! Really?"

"Yes."

There seemed to be nothing more to say. Senta was so overjoyed and flustered that she did not want to break the spell by uttering a word. She decided to help him pack instead. They worked side by side for some time, folding clothes and examining knicknacks to decide whether they were worth taking. Then, at last, Senta said, "Oh, Erich, aren't you just a little excited to be going home?"

"No," he answered miserably. "And I'm a bit surprised that you don't have some mixed feelings yourself."

"Why?" she asked, thoroughly confused by the suggestion.

He looked at her with stern and knowing eyes. "I'd rather thought your heart had been stolen by a certain young Russian."

"Tomasz?" she asked, trying to maintain the illusion of surprise. "Oh, that was a bunch of nonsense. I broke things off with him weeks ago."

"Nonsense?" he asked skeptically. "That's a strange thing to say, for I had really thought you were in love."

"That's what I mean by nonsense," she muttered.

At this, Erich stepped back from the trunk. "You think love is nonsense?"

"Of course it is," she snapped. "What does it bring? It does not help to gain Prussia its rightful place as ruler of Europe. It does not bring wealth, at least not in this case. It doesn't accomplish anything really."

"What about happiness?"

She shrugged. "I'm happy enough. Aren't you?"

His head shook involuntarily.

"Oh, well," she continued. "In any case, I don't believe a Prussian has any business marrying a Russian. I mean, honestly, they are an inferior race."

"Bite your tongue," he interrupted breathlessly. "The Russians are a beautiful people. Robust, rosy-cheeked, and healthy." He formed a perfect image of Tatiana in his mind. Her luscious, dark hair falling to her waist in waving glory. Her sweet eyes, so full of tenderness. The smile that so often touched those plush, naturally blushed lips. Her full, squeezable body, so innocent of a man's yearnings.

"Well, even without that," she insisted, "he was too young for me."

"But it didn't bother him," he pointed out. "If it didn't bother him, why should it bother you?"

"I don't know," she confessed. "But there were other problems."

"What other problems?" he demanded, a certain anxiousness permeating his voice. "Tell me what other problems."

"Well"—she paused—"there was also the matter of my career. How could I continue it if I were saddled to a man?"

Erich need not reply to that one, for he was about to retire. "Go on," he urged her.

"Well, he's probably better off without me," she said at last.

"Has he said that?"

"No."

"Well, if he says that isn't so, then how do you know what's best for him? How do you know he is happier without you? Shouldn't he decide that? Not you?"

She scoffed at his romanticism. "I suppose, but what difference does it make? I've already rejected him, I've already told him no, and he probably wouldn't take me back even if I wanted him to. It's too late."

"Not for me."

"What?" She turned around just in time to see him yank on his coat. "Erich, where are you going?"

"Tatiana gave me her answer, but I was too stubborn to hear it. She isn't happy. She wants what I want, and it is not my place to question why."

"What are you babbling about?"

He slammed his trunk closed and lifted it easily by its leather handle. "Good-bye, Senta. I wish you only the brightest of futures in Prussia. I will not be going with you."

"What? Oh, no! Don't tell me! You're going to marry that peasant?"

"One more word and I'll strike you," he warned. "You're to speak of her only with the utmost respect."

"What?" she gasped. "Erich, this is madness. You can't stay here in Russia."

"I don't intend to."

"But you can't bring a Russian peasant, uh . . . lady, back to Prussia with you! Everyone there hates Russians."

"I know. That's why I'm not going there either."

"Then, where—"

"Switzerland." He grinned. "I think Switzerland would have to be the place for us."

"Do you think the chancellor would give you the false documents to get there?"

"Absolutely."

"But . . . but your family!"

"I don't have one. And neither does she."

"But your country!"

"My country is too ambitious. Not a safe place to raise children if you don't want them to become soldiers, which I don't."

"But . . . but this is madness!"

He was now on his way out the door. He turned to face her one last time. "I will not make the same mistake you have," he told her bluntly. "This is my last chance."

"But my recommendation!"

"The chancellor will receive it along with my request for false papers. I wish you well."

"But how do you know she will say yes?"

He smiled distantly as he thought about that. "I think I'll skip the asking just to be safe. She told me once she would marry me, and I think I'll hold her to it."

Chapter 37

A young servant was nearly toppled over by the intruder at the front door. "Where is Tatiana?" the agitated man in black asked.

"Why, she is in her room," the flustered girl stammered. "But you can't just barge in here and—wait!"

He was already climbing the stairs, four and five at a time.

"General!" she cried. "General, where are you? There is a man here who—oh, dear." She hurried through the maze of rooms in search of her unsuspecting employer.

Erich flung open every door on the second floor, and then every door on the third. When at last he intruded upon his golden-eyed beauty, midway through the act of dressing, he wrapped the startled girl in his arms. "You're coming with me," he said fiercely. "You're going to share my bed, you're going to bear my children, and you're going to be my bride." He lifted her from the floor into the cradle of his chest, bouncing her once just to prove that her luscious figure was not too heavy for his arms. Roughly, he kissed her precious lips, bruising them as though to mark them forever his.

Tatiana's eyes had been gaping from the start, but now her grin joined them in their openness. "I thought you'd never come," she laughed, her eyes squinting in their joy.

"I almost didn't," he confessed, brushing his lips against her silken cheek. "What a fool I was."

"Shouldn't I pack?" she asked as he threatened to carry her into the hallway.

"No. From now on everything you have will be given to you by me. I want you to own nothing else."

"Well, what about my golden dress? Can't I at least have that?"

"You already do. You left it at my house the last time you were there."

"Oh!" she cried excitedly, squeezing his chest with all her might. "This is so exciting! I can't believe you're kidnapping me. Should I resist?"

"That would be romantic of you."

"Oh, help," she cried softly, a big grin on her face. "Someone rescue me from this madman."

"Give up," he teased gruffly, carrying her to the staircase. "You will be my bride whether you like it or not."

"Someone, help!"

"Just wait until you see what I do to you tonight," he threatened.

This actually did give her a little nervous tickle. But she played along, saying, "I swear you'll not get away with it, you rogue."

"And who's going to stop me?" he asked boldly.

"My Prince Charming, that's who!"

"Ah, he'll never make it before I ravage you." He lifted her high enough to kiss her breast.

They were stopped at the bottom of the stairs by the general and his wife. Erich's face lost all humor and became as cold and threatening as that of the villain he'd pretended to be. "Out of my way," he warned sternly. "I'm marrying your daughter."

"You are mad!" Anna cried. "Boris, do something!" She tugged frantically at her husband's sleeve.

The general had brought his pistol when he'd heard about the intruder. It was secured safely in the depths of his pocket, but he did not draw it. Instead, he wore a look of confusion, a look of one whose heart was blocking his better senses.

"Boris!" Anna cried again, but she received no response. She looked angrily at Erich, her eyes steaming from a fire in her belly. "Listen, you criminal, you spy! We have already talked about this. You were to get out of our lives or face the consequences!"

"I'm afraid that threat has expired," he informed her sternly. "I will be gone before you can effectively carry it out."

"Boris, do something!" she cried.

And then the dazed general said something no one had expected to hear. He looked Tatiana steadily in the eye and asked, "Is this what you want, child?"

Erich lowered her to her feet so she could answer with more dignity. It took her a moment to straighten her skirt, but then she replied, "Yes, very much so."

The general was torn. To keep the girl against her will when she had nowhere else to go was one thing. To keep her when she had an offer of marriage was quite another. He did adore the girl, after all. And he could see the playful light glistening in her eye as she looked up at this handsome intruder. "Don't you want to think about it some more?" he asked hopefully.

Tatiana shook her head. "I want to go with him." She grabbed Erich's elbow and looked adoringly at him.

Anna would hear no more. "Boris, you must stop them! I'll send a servant to fetch the police."

"You will do no such thing," he objected, causing her jaw to fall open. He looked Erich in the eye, man to man. He was impressed by the strong, steady gaze he found there. Erich had integrity and courage, he could see that quite plainly. "Do you love Tatiana?" he asked.

Erich's reply was instantaneous. "I do."

The general nodded his satisfaction. "Then be good to her."

"I swear it."

Anna screamed. "Boris! What are you doing?" Her face was hot with unabashed fury.

"Anna," he said gently, "there are orphanages overflowing with children who need our love. Let us go find one this afternoon."

"What?"

"Tatiana is not ours," he reminded her. "We deceived her in order to secure her angelic presence in our home. I do not regret it, for she has shown us that our money and our lavish lives are worthless without someone with whom to share them. But I would regret it if we held her back from happiness. Somewhere out there"—he gently took her hand—"is a girl who needs us more than Tatiana ever has, and we will need no lies to bring her here."

Anna bowed her head, the closest she could come to consenting. The general held his arms out to the girl who had been his daughter for a mere five months. "Come," he said, "let me give you my blessing." He embraced the girl as though he were a child squeezing a teddy bear. "I love you," he whispered in her ear. Tatiana lifted her head and saw in his sparkling eyes that it was so. He really had loved her, even though their acquaintance had been so brief. "If this brute should mistreat you, you'll always have a place to come." He winked at Erich to show that he did not truly think him a brute.

"Thank you." Tatiana grinned, her round face beaming with joy. Anna was still too forlorn to say a word, but Tatiana believed that someday she would realize this had been for the best. Someday she would look back on Tatiana and hope she was happy.

"Are you ready?" Erich asked, taking his lady by the hand.

Her flushed cheeks and bright eyes should have said enough, but still, she nodded. "Yes, let's go."

When they had made it past the barrier of the front door, Tatiana burst into a yelling run. "I'm free!" she called, laughing and letting the wind blow through her teeth. She twirled around under the sunlight, her hair falling from its bindings. "Can you believe it? Can you believe it?" she asked Erich, jumping up and down as though skipping a rope.

Erich bent down and lifted her into the carriage, asking, "You think you're free, do you? Far from it. You're mine now."

She waited for him to sit beside her, then snuggled her head against his strong shoulder. "That's all right," she sighed peacefully, holding on to his waist. Erich let her do this even though it distracted him from driving the carriage. A year ago he would have been annoyed by an interruption of any task, no matter how trivial, but he had grown. Now he would never dream of asking his precious bundle of warmth to move away. He allowed himself to drive carelessly with one hand while the other stroked her long curls, glimmering in the sunlight.

Days of adventure have a different feel from days of routine. They are less heavy, less thoughtful. While they give one more to think about, they tend, by their very nature, to discourage thought. It's for this reason that Tatiana had not yet fully absorbed the importance of what had happened to her that day. All the misery she had experienced during her lengthy isolation had been cured in but a few brief moments. Yet, she had not stilled her mind long enough to realize that her life had been completely transformed. Though she was suddenly on her way to being a wife and perhaps someday a mother, with a bright future in a foreign land, it would be a very long time before she would see herself as anything other than a peasant girl on another quick adventure.

It was by boat that the Prussians had arranged Erich's escape. And it was beneath the green waves, in a secluded cabin, that Erich parted his lover's thighs. "Are you afraid?" he asked her, his voice dark and soothing.

"No," she replied, though she sounded meek. "I trust you completely." She wrapped her worried hands on his shoulders.

The ocean waves lapped against the boat, but the ride was still smooth. Tatiana closed her eyes and imagined the clear night sky overhead, black as oil and sparkling with magic. She could remember the icy breeze on her face as the boat pulled away from shore. And now Erich's breath took its place. "I'll take you gently," he promised. "As I should have all along. As you would have made me do had you known enough to ask. I'm sorry." He kissed her. "I'm sorry I never showed you the tenderness a man should."

"But you did," she whispered.

"No, I was rough with you," he confessed. "But not this time. This time I'll give you what a woman needs."

She watched him lower his breeches, the green glow of the water shining behind him from the porthole. The gentle rocking of the boat, the constant sound of the ocean waves, and the beauty of the strong man standing over her caused her eyes to close. When she opened them again, she thought she had come face-to-face with the water outside, but in fact she was looking into Erich's magnificent eyes. A strand of golden hair fell over his forehead just before he kissed her. With a gentle push he laid her on her back, covering her with his hot skin, moistening her thighs with soft caresses. "I love you," he whispered.

Tatiana reached for her own bodice and untied all the laces. "Take me," she said, lifting one breast and then the other from her gown. "Suckle me, Erich."

With an irrepressible grin, he looked at the fruits laid before him. They were so fleshy, so ripe. What had he ever done to deserve a maiden so luscious, and so giving of herself? He lowered his lips in the darkness to her hardened tips and kissed them as gently as he could. Even as he allowed her silky flesh to fall into his mouth, he tried not to suck, for he did not want to hurt her this time.

"Harder," she begged, "I want to feel your passion."

And that was all the provocation he needed. He widened his mouth, consuming as much spongy breast as he dared. He sucked as though receiving from her bosom some vital nutrient without which he could not live. Tatiana's hips lifted off the mattress, her hands rubbed his silky hair, her mouth flew open as though she, too, were needing this. And finally her legs parted and wrapped around his flexing buttocks. "Do it," she begged. "Go inside. Please."

He wanted to take his time, wanted to put her at ease. He had gone too quickly with her before, had taken her virginity as though he'd had something to prove. She didn't seem to realize it, but that was only because she had been so innocent. She'd not known it could be done soothingly. This time he swore to himself he would be tender. He rested his hardness against her but did not breach her entrance. "Tell me if anything hurts," he requested, noticing miserably that he had bruised her tender bosom.

"It hurts!" she cried. "It hurts!"

"What hurts?" he asked with a startle.

"The waiting," she moaned, pulling him toward her with all her might.

Though her tugs did nothing to move him closer, for he had more or less the weight and sturdiness of a small mountain, he did smile at her effort. And gradually, of his own accord, he pushed into her. "Oh, that feels so good," she gasped, throwing her head back. "Deeper."

He pushed until she felt completely violated in the most wonderful way possible. He was sliding in and out of her as though he held a slick knife that could miraculously slice her wide open, cut deeply into her gut, and then leave her unharmed. She was in awe of his powers, as though he were the only man in the world who could do this. Gradually, his movements became more fluid, and Tatiana's eyes opened. She looked at his finely carved face with a curious and sincere gaze. It suddenly felt as though they were dancing again, as they had done so many times before. The golden light that had formed between them as he'd swept her across the floor of the Winter Palace was growing again, though their movements now were so much more subtle and so much more intimate. She glided her fingers along his bare shoulders and neck, as though trying to convince herself that this was real, that he really belonged to her now, that she could do this with him anytime she wanted.

"You're so soft," he whispered, looking down at her with a kindness that did not match his forceful thrusts. "Do you know you're as soft inside as you are outside?"

She shook her head and nearly giggled, so strong was the embarrassment he'd caused her.

"It's true." He smiled lovingly. "I love it."

Tatiana felt her knees begin to tremble. She knew what was happening, for this wave had overtaken her once before. Her legs opened wider and wider, her hips pushed deeper against Erich's thrusts, her fingers dug into his raw back. It was this that pushed Erich over the edge, for he loved being scratched by a woman's wild hands. In fact, the paradox of feeling the sting of her nails at the same moment that he was about to find his greatest pleasure was so delicious to him that he urged her to dig deeper. And then he lost control, shaking her body with rough, merciless pushes into her very depths. His expression was fierce as he jerked her forward and back with his final thrusts. Just before he flowed into her, he saw her own lips part. A yearning had been building in her flesh, and the feel of his forceful, almost angry need of her as he slapped against her body mercilessly had driven her to bursting. They moaned simultaneously, whispering words of love and need in each other's ears. And then they collapsed into a bundle of cuddling companionship.

"Oh, no," Erich said, brushing the hair from his moist forehead. "I did it again. I took you too hard." He cradled her fiercely against his chest, as though in repentance.

"That's just how you are," Tatiana assured him, nestling into his comforting chest hair. "You don't want to admit it, but you're a passionate man. And I don't mind. I love you."

He kissed the top of her sweet-smelling hair. "Well, I'm sorry," he said, rubbing her backside affectionately. "I should be more gentle."

She breathed in his clean scent and made herself comfortable for a pleasant sleep, using his body as a unique combination of pillow and mattress. "Oh," she sighed, "just listen to the ocean. Isn't it beautiful?"

His clear eyes looked out at the black water, barely illuminated by the moon. "Yes," he whispered, "it's beautiful."

"Beautiful, violent, and complex," she continued. "And it never apologizes."

He squeezed her with a fierceness that showed no fear of breaking her. "I love you, Tatiana. What heaven sent you to me?"

She smiled mysteriously. "Heaven? Oh, that reminds me. When we get to Prussia, I'll have to start going to church."

"Why?"

Her smile brightened. "I have an enormous debt to repay." Before he could ask anything more, she kissed him, loving his lips and then his neck, and then his collarbone. "Will you hold me all night?" she asked, settling back into his chest.

"I couldn't sleep otherwise," he answered truthfully, giving her one last thankful squeeze good night.

Chapter 38

Tatiana was delighted by her first glimpses at Prussia. The ocean was an unusual shade of sapphire the day their boat pulled into a safe harbor. She had never been to a foreign country, nor had she any hope of doing so, as traveling abroad was quite illegal for peasants. Her first day was filled with wonders. She and Erich stayed in a boardinghouse by the ocean and had an enormous room with an expansive view. Like most of the other houses here, it was lifted by stilts to protect it from flooding. This she found enormously funny, though she loved the brown wooden criss-crosses that adorned the walls and roofs, making the houses look like toys.

"Oh, Erich!" she cried delightedly as they walked hand in hand along the shore. "I really like it here."

"Well, don't get overly accustomed to it," he warned, bright sunlight catching in his flaxen hair, making it shimmer with hints of silver. "As soon as our paperwork comes through, we'll be headed for Switzerland."

"Well, I'm sure I'll like Switzerland too!" she promised,

kicking the wet sand with her bare feet. Erich didn't mind that she let her hair hang freely down her back, even though it was no more the custom here than in Russia. Nor did he ask her to keep her skin away from the sun. When she'd suggested she should carry a parasol and had looked at him as though hoping he might stop her, he had done just that. He told her that a golden glow suits her better than an artificial fairness of complexion. He encouraged her to wear only her most comfortable gowns. "What was that bread we had at breakfast this morning?" she asked excitedly. "That dark kind?"

"Pumpernickel," he said.

"And what about that yellow stuff that you said I wouldn't like. What is that?"

"Sauerkraut, and you wouldn't."

"I like the *kartoffa*—oh, I don't know, but I liked it."

"*Kartoffelsalat.*" He chuckled, then pointed to the mountains ahead. "Look there. Do you see those cliffs?"

"Yes," she gasped. "They are so beautiful!"

"Well, those are nothing compared to what we will see in Switzerland. The mountains there are the largest in all of Europe."

"Really?" She smiled enthusiastically. "Oh! Will we be able to see them from where we'll live?"

"We're going to live right in them."

"No!" she cried, shaking him by the waist. "You don't mean it!"

"I do," he promised. "And wait until you see our house. For all my complaints, I have to say that the government is finally thanking me for my hard work. I'd never dreamed they would take care of us so well. The house is made of stone and sits near the top of a cliff with a beautiful view of the mountain ranges."

"Oh, I can't wait to see it!" she cried, jumping excitedly with her fists clenched. "Have you been to Switzerland before?"

"Yes, briefly. I think you will like it. But I'll have you know

I'm very particular about a clean home. I expect that house to be kept spotless.''

''Whew, it's a good thing you're retiring, then. How else would you have time to scrub all those floors?''

He grabbed her from behind and tickled her mercilessly, then released her just as quickly. ''I can see I'll have to run my home with a strong hand,'' he chided her.

''Why don't you just hire servants?''

''I don't like having so much company. The house will be for you and me only. Well, and our children,'' he added, patting her belly suggestively.

''Well, if I have to have the children,'' she pouted, ''then I'm certainly not going to clean the house.''

''Fine,'' he agreed much to her surprise. ''We'll work something out.'' He had never been a man to compromise, but then, he had never had such incentive to make another person feel comfortable.

''Can I have a horse?'' she asked. ''I mean, one that's just for riding.''

''Certainly.''

''What about a dog? Oh! Do you know what kind I like? Those little curly ones. Poodles, I think they're called.''

''French poodles?'' He winced. ''Out of the question. We'll get a German shepherd. Now, that's a real dog.''

''All right. Oh, Erich! Do people in Switzerland speak German too?''

''Where we're going they do.''

''Well, what am I going to do?'' she asked nervously. ''I hate not being able to understand anything people say.''

''You're smart,'' he assured her. ''You'll learn quickly.''

''Do you think so?''

''Yes, but I don't want you to learn Swiss German. I want you to speak properly, and I'll see to it by teaching you myself.''

''Oh, I still don't see why we can't just stay here,'' she remarked, looking about at the bright blue ocean whooshing against sandy beaches beneath jagged cliffs. "Your country is so beautiful. And I'm getting used to shaking hands. I did as you said and stopped kissing people's cheeks. Did you notice?"

"Yes, thank you."

"And I never drink until the hostess says 'prosit,' right?"

"Correct."

"And though you people tend to wake up a little on the early side, I think I could get used to it. Oh, Erich, I like it here! Why couldn't we just stay?"

He stopped walking and made her face him. "Tatiana, I love my country, don't ever think it otherwise. But it has had too many victories and grows bold. By the time our sons reach my age, our land will be in a state of war. I'm sure of it. And I would not have my children make the same mistake I nearly did." A gentle hand touched the silken rose of Tatiana's cheek. "I would not have them sacrifice themselves to a mistress they cannot see or touch or cherish."

Tatiana nearly swooned over the feel of his sturdy hand on her face. Her hair blowing behind her in luscious, brightly colored waves, she parted her lips, inviting him to enter. When he did not accept the challenge, her eyes flung open wide. "What's the matter?"

"Nothing," he whispered, brushing her lips with his thumb. "I was just thinking."

"Well, who asked you to do that?"

He broke into a smile. "Don't you even want to know what I was thinking about?"

"No," she answered dreamily, grabbing hold of his strong hand. "Because I already know what you were thinking."

"Oh?" he asked skeptically.

"Yes," she replied, swinging his hand as they walked on. "You were thinking how easy it would be for us never to have met. Why, if I had chosen a different house to rob, or you had not been home . . ."

"I'm uncomfortable with coincidence," he admitted. "It

makes me feel vulnerable to the elements. But how did you know what I was thinking?''

''Because I was thinking the same thing. That, and the other thing you had on your mind.''

''And what is that?''

She stopped walking and faced him. ''That I love you.''

''That's a good thing,'' he grumbled, fiercely drawing her into his arms, ''because you're stuck with me now.''

''Just so long as you don't nail the windows shut.''

''What?''

''Never mind. I'll tell you about it another time. Kiss me, you brute.''

He did so, and continued doing so until the sun set over the sea. The magnificent wild ocean whose bottom would remain always a mystery broke in waves of beauty all night long. And no matter how cold the world around it grew, it never could freeze, but only grow bitterly chilled. Only the bravest and most youthful would venture into its icy waters once it had seen the harshness of winter. But those who could would find its motions soothing, its power arousing, and its depths a source of limitless fascination.